RED
MOON

RED
MOON

MICHAEL CASSUTT

A TOM DOHERTY ASSOCIATES BOOK / NEWYORK

RED MOON

Copyright © 2001 by St. Croix Productions, Inc.

A Forge Book
Published by Tom Doherty Associates, LLC
175 Fifth Avenue
New York, NY 10010

Design by Heidi J. B. Eriksen

www.tor.com

Forge® is a registered trademark of Tom Doherty Associates, LLC.

Library of Congress Cataloging-in-Publication Data

Cassutt, Michael.
        Red moon / Michael Cassutt.—1st ed.
            p. cm.
        "A Tom Doherty Associates Book."
        ISBN 0-312-87440-5 (acid-free paper)
            1. Space flight—Fiction.   2. Soviet Union—Fiction.
        3. Astronauts—Fiction.   4. Space race—Fiction.   I. Title.

    PS3553.A812 R4   2001
    813'.54—dc21
                                                    00-048449

First Edition: February 2001

Printed in the United States of America

0 9 8 7 6 5 4 3 2 1

For Russ Jensen

RED
MOON

PROLOGUE

Autumn, Last Year

In Russia these days, nothing is easy.

I'm sure you could make the argument that nothing there has *ever* been easy, but the old order changeth, and now pensioners find themselves selling apples on the street while mafiyosa cuddle in restaurant doorways with six-foot-tall blondes all the while yelling into cell phones. You can walk into an office and see computers running Windows 3.0, but won't find a toilet with a seat. Homemade garages sprout like mushrooms at the base of Khrushchev-era worker storage units while cars choke the inadequate streets. A McDonald's gets built in two days as Red Square is swept by men with straw brooms.

My contact was an hour late. Had that happened to me at home in California, I'd have been thirty minutes gone. But in Korolev, formerly Kaliningrad, a grim industrial suburb an hour's drive north of the Kremlin, an hour's tardiness was expected, forgiven, hardly noticed.

Besides, the steady deliveries of German beer, ordered from the wary staff of the Rendezvous restaurant by universal semaphore, encouraged me to be charitable.

Then again, there was nothing else I wanted to be doing. I had come to Moscow to report on the delicate situation between Russia and NASA concerning the International Space Station. This $25-billion project was starting to kick into high gear, except for the fact that a key Russian component called the service module was falling behind schedule, threatening the whole program with delays and higher costs. A U.S.

congressman and his staff who had come to Moscow to, as they said, "draw a line in the sand," had done no such thing. The Russian spacecraft builders had conceded the problem—no money—and blamed the government for failing to deliver the promised cash. I could see that the next week's activities would consist of various parties commiserating over that unfortunate situation, a bit of hand-wringing here, some posturing there, without changing the basic facts.

During a break in one of these meetings at the Russian Space Agency, I found myself sitting in a hallway with Dennis Gulyayev, who recognized my name from a book I had written on the Apollo-Soyuz docking some years back. "You know a lot about our space program," he said, adding, before I could preen, "for a Westerner."

"It's always been a hobby," I told him. "I grew up watching American astronauts doing spacewalks and going to the Moon. But I always wondered about *your* side. You guys were first, after all. Sputnik, Gagarin, the spacewalk."

Dennis got a faraway look in his eyes. "We could have been first to the Moon, too."

I had heard a bit about the abortive Russian man-on-the-Moon program. "Come on, Dennis. You were nowhere close to beating *Apollo 11.*"

Now he got amused. "That's what the histories say." He stubbed out his cigarette. "The histories are wrong."

"Well, I guess I'll just have to take your word for it."

"If you're interested, I could introduce you to a friend of mine. He knows the real story. He might tell you."

I got suspicious. Russians were always trying to sell things to Westerners these days. "For a price?" I said.

Dennis shrugged. He knew exactly what I meant. "No, he'll tell you because you wrote that Apollo-Soyuz book. I've seen it in his flat. He reads and speaks English."

Several people passed us, the congressman among them, along with one of the deputy directors of the Russian Space Agency. We smiled and held our places.

"He's getting old. He'd like to tell the story. But nobody in Russia will publish it."

"There aren't many in America who will publish it, either."

"I think he would like to tell the story to someone, even if it only gets printed after his death. He's a friend of my father's. They worked together."

I was bored, I thought it couldn't hurt. "What's his name?"

"Ribko. Yuri Nikolayevich Ribko."

"Never heard of him."

"You wouldn't have. But he was everywhere—at Korolev's bureau, at Star Town, at Baikonur. He saw more of the story than most."

What the heck: I might get a good anecdote about the pioneering days of the Russian space program that would help my ISS piece. I told Dennis to arrange a meeting at the Rendezvous, a restaurant that happened to be located within walking distance of my hotel in Korolev.

Not that the hotel was anything special: It was a former center for the reeducation of Party cadres or something like that, much like a school dorm at a hick American junior college. It had been chosen for easy access to the heart of the Russian space program, since the flight control center, the gigantic Energiya Corporation headquarters, and the Central Research Institute of Machine-Building (don't try to say that too quickly) were all nearby. I could walk to the Rendezvous, saving myself the challenges of getting around Korolev, or Moscow, at night without an escort.

So I nursed my third beer and watched a young and prosperous-looking Russian couple finish their dinner. The only other customers that night were four Scandinavians—carton manufacturers from Oslo, as I recall.

Shortly after eight, Ribko entered.

He was, I judged, in his late fifties. Short, red-faced, with a full head of silver-black hair, he was slim, as Russians go. Blue eyes behind thick glasses. A quick smile that showed some literal steel, but handsome. We shook hands and I thanked him for coming. "Dennis insisted," he said, shrugging.

"It seems that Dennis wanted us to meet."

I ordered him a beer and asked if he minded my taping.

"No, I've been taped many times before." He gave that quick smile again. "This, however, will be the first time my permission was asked."

To warm up, I asked Ribko what he was doing these days. It was risky, if you don't like awkward replies: I know of one former space official who survives by making Venetian blinds; another is a dispatcher in a factory. "I'm a consultant, you would say, to the Air Force Academy in Monino. I teach . . . earth studies." He pointed a finger at the ceiling, then at the table.

"Space observation?" He nodded. "And you used to work in the Moon program."

"Program L-1/L-3, yes."

"Which almost beat the U.S. to the Moon."

"We could have. We came very close."

I sat back, assuming a posture of friendly skepticism. At least that's what my editor calls it. "You really think so? I know you were close to a manned lunar orbit. But a *landing*?"

Ribko continued to smile, but his eyes narrowed ever so slightly as he leaned toward me. "I know the stories that are being told. They only have part of the truth, because the tellers don't know, or can't face it."

"But you do. Because you were—"

"At the heart of it. For three years, I was at the very heart of Program L-1/L-3."

"I wonder," I said at that point, as much for myself as for Ribko, "if anyone cares."

He wagged a finger at me. "The world would be different now if we had won. The same things that stopped us are stopping you, on ISS."

"Well, then," I said, substantially more intrigued. "Tell me."

NOTE ON USAGE

Since Yuri Ribko spoke to me in English, I have retained his usage regarding Russian names for people, places, and things. Some, such as Red Square, are given their English equivalents, especially if these have become familiar to Western readers. Others, such as Chkalov air base or the Soyuz spacecraft, are given in transliterated Russian.

To ease the burden on American readers, however, I have eliminated Russian case endings for these names (*Chkalov* instead of *Chkalovskaya*, and have dispensed with the Russian patronymic, the father's name that is often added to a first name in conversation (*Yuri Nikolayevich*).

SCORPION 1

A STATE OF
CONSTANT ALERT

1 THE KREMLIN HOSPITAL

I was present at the beginning of the end.

The winter of 1965–66 was my final one as a student at the Bauman Higher Technical School, a huge wreck of a place situated on the west bank of the Moscow River. Founded in 1830 as the Tsar's Vocational School, Bauman was later honored with the name of an obscure Bolshevik who had never attended it, and could not, in fact, have passed the entrance exams.

The name, like those of so many Soviet institutions, was deliberately misleading, suggesting a small college with a student body specializing in, perhaps, auto mechanics. But Bauman was actually the equivalent of your California Institute of Technology. It was an engineering university with twenty thousand students, the elite of Soviet secondary schools, who were trained for jobs in the missile and aircraft industries, and in the intelligence community.

The basic course lasted six years; over half the students flunked out or transferred to less-demanding schools. If you survived to the fifth year, your main challenge was to convince the placement committee to give you the job you wanted, meaning *any* job as long as it was in Moscow.

My father, a deputy Air Force commander in the Moscow military district, could have arranged such a job for me with a single phone call. But, with that flair for bullheadedness that I share, he refused. Fortunately, I had good luck in the assignment of a thesis adviser.

Vasily Filin was a senior engineer and deputy director of the Experimental Design Bureau Number 1, the organization that created and built my country's first intercontinental ballistic missile, that launched Sputnik, that made Gagarin the first human in space. Filin was a tall, nervous, long-faced man, quite old to me at the time: He was fifty-nine. He oversaw my work, and that of half a dozen other fifth-year students, with precision and decency, unlike some I could name. But we had no personal interaction until one day in October 1965, when he suddenly raised his head from the papers on his desk, looked at me as if seeing me for the first time, and said, "Ribko, what are your plans?"

He didn't need to specify, of course. He meant career plans. "The Rocket Force, I think," I said without much enthusiasm. I had done my summer military service north of Moscow in godforsaken Orevo, at a camp for future missileers. Unless one of the civilian design bureaus in the giant defense industry requested me, I was going to be commissioned as a senior-engineer lieutenant the coming June. It was one of the many ironies of the Soviet system that only a major effort by my father—a career military officer and Hero of the Soviet Union—could keep me a civilian.

I wasn't upset at the idea; far from it. I looked forward to fulfilling whatever task the Party chose for me.

"You'll be wasted in uniform," Filin said, sniffing with unconcealed derision. He folded his hands on the desk, examining them for defects. "What about my organization?"

"I'd love to work at the bureau, but I heard that your quota was filled."

I think I embarrassed Filin. "Well, yes," he said quietly. "There are many important people with nephews this year."

When the silence grew awkward, I rose to gather up my papers. Filin put his hand flat on them. "How are your secretarial skills?" he asked suddenly.

"Well, I can type," I said. My late mother, Zhanna, had given me a typewriter for my thirteenth birthday, hoping I might become a poet rather than a soldier.

"Now we're getting somewhere!" What Filin proposed was that I, a graduate of the Bauman School, should join his organization, the Korolev bureau, as his *clerk*. "The important thing is to avoid wearing green."

As I said, I would have been happy to wear a uniform, but other factors made military service less attractive than Filin's offer. For one, my father had warned me that if I went into the Rocket Force, I was likely to be stationed north of the Arctic Circle. "We're expanding the missile base up there," he said, "and they're hungry for young, unmarried engineers." Such an assignment would likely last five years, and I found Moscow cold enough already.

More important, I was desperately in love with a fellow student, Marina Torchillova, and dreamed of marrying her. There would be no wedding if I moved to Murmansk.

Proving that, like so many of the fellow students I had criticized all my life, I could also put my selfish needs above those of the Party, I began spending one or two days a week out in the suburb of Kaliningrad, typing letters for Filin, serving as his courier, and sometimes—once he discovered that I was licensed—as his driver.

And continued to pine after Marina, who, strangely, still resisted my charms.

On the leaden, snowy afternoon of Thursday, January 13, 1966, I arrived at the Kremlin Hospital with a stack of documents for Filin to review. I had learned, in three months of part-time work, that he was prone to ill health, especially in times of crisis. And there was often a crisis. The upper levels of the Korolev bureau, which included Filin, were routinely criticized by their masters on the Council of Ministers for continued failures at putting an unmanned probe on the Moon. The more complaints the ministers had, the more Filin's head ached, and so he was off to the Kremlin Hospital, not far from the Bauman campus.

The location wasn't remotely convenient for me. I still had to rise before dawn to catch the metro to Yaroslavl Station, then the train out to Kaliningrad, where I would collect Filin's daily load of documents and be assigned a car, which I would then drive *back* into Moscow. The trip never took less than three hours.

During my several visits that week, I had decided that the Kremlin Hospital was a pleasant refuge. Aside from the doctors themselves, said to be the best in the country, there were the nurses, who, whatever their medical skills, had obviously been selected for their good looks. No wonder Filin ran here whenever he could.

I found him sitting at the desk in his room, talking to Boris Artemov, one of the other deputy directors at the bureau. Filin was wearing slacks and a white shirt rather than a hospital gown. He accepted his documents and I turned to wait outside. "I should have you take these down the hall when I'm finished," Filin said. The look on my face must have showed my confusion at this statement.

Artemov, a handsome, bald Ukrainian even older than Filin, cleared his throat and spoke: "The chief is here today."

"Korolev?" I said.

Filin nodded. Sergei Korolev was the genius who had designed and built our country's first missile. I had only glimpses of him so far, this small, thickset man with a short neck, always moving somewhere in a hurry, never alone. He was our von Braun, though nobody outside Russia knew: It was forbidden for his name to be published.

"Is he sick?"

Filin waved a hand dismissively. "Some routine procedure. He sprang it on us last week."

Artemov nodded toward the door. "He was taken into surgery not too long ago."

"I hope it goes well," I said, knocking on the wooden table near Filin's chair.

"I wouldn't want to be the doctors if anything happened to Korolev. People don't disappear quite the way they used to, but an exception would be made, believe me."

Filin and Artemov turned to their papers; dismissed, I went out to the hallway, where I sat down on a bench and took a book out of my coat pocket. I was noting the filthy linoleum floor, the peeling paint on the walls, the dim lighting, when I was startled by the sound, not far off, of a man *screaming*, then quickly silenced. Before I could truly react, I heard a familiar voice: "Yuri! What are you doing here?"

I looked up to find my father, Nikolai, approaching. "Papa?"

He was wearing his green uniform, of course, with the three stars of a colonel-general, and his red Hero of the Soviet Union medal. I had not seen him in two weeks. In fact, in those days I rarely saw him more than once a month. He was often traveling on business for the Air Force's general staff, where he had worked for the past few years. Even when my mother was alive and we all lived together, he was often absent.

To my surprise, he hugged and kissed me. This demonstration from the unusually reserved, severe Colonel-General Nikolai Ribko made me stammer as I explained about Filin, not mentioning Korolev. My father nodded. "I hope you're not here as a patient," I said to him.

He smiled as he always did whenever I used phrases that weren't strictly functional. "I'm in excellent health. I'm visiting Vladimir."

Vladimir was my uncle, my mother's brother, an official of State Security. "Is he all right?" That Uncle Vladimir could be hospitalized without my knowing it was no surprise: I was only in his company two or three times a year, and his activities were completely secret.

My father tilted his head to one side and shrugged. "He's heavy, you know." This was true: Uncle Vladimir was taller than my father and me, a trait that must have served him well as a young Bolshevik thug, but in late middle age he had grown hugely fat.

My father didn't look well himself. Normally very confident, even swaggering, he seemed lost, older than his fifty-five years. "Let me get you some tea," I said.

"What I need is vodka." That, like the kiss, was also strange: My father only drank vodka when forced to, never by choice.

Nevertheless, he followed me to a table where a pretty nurse tended a pot. "How long is Vladimir supposed to stay here?"

"They're running more tests. If they don't find anything new, he will go home tonight." He practically gulped the tea and slammed down the cup. "I'll tell him you said hello." He did not offer to take me to him.

At that moment a pair of younger officers, a colonel and major, both in their thirties, appeared. "Good morning, General!" one of them addressed my father, though with nothing like the deference one would expect from a relatively junior officer. Then I realized why: The young colonel was Yuri Gagarin, our country's first man in space, a bright-eyed, handsome man whose most notable trait was his small stature. He barely came up to my chin, and I am not tall.

Introductions were made, and I learned that the taller, dark-haired, hawk-nosed and almost aristocratic major was named Ivan Saditsky.

It was a brief encounter. Gagarin and Saditsky were on their way out of the hospital. In moments they were gone, and so, with another hug, was my father.

He had barely disappeared around the corner when Filin emerged from his room, papers in hand. Artemov was not with him.

"I'm sorry," I said. "I didn't realize you were finished."

"I'm not." He waved the papers. "There's so much noise here today."

"And important visitors." I told him about my brief encounter with the famous Gagarin.

"Here to check on Korolev, no doubt."

"Is there any word on his condition?"

He grunted. "No. By my count, he's been in surgery for five hours."

Five hours seemed like a long time for a routine procedure. "What's wrong with him?"

"He told me last week it was a polyp. He's lucky if that's all it is, since he's been working himself to death. He spent time in the camps, too, you know."

Before I could say more, the door to the operating chamber opened. A man in a bloody surgeon's gown came out. "Dr. Cherbakov," Filin said, turning toward him.

Cherbakov ignored him, speaking instead to the pretty nurse who had been serving tea. "Call Katayev again. I need him." The nurse reached for the telephone and began to dial.

"Why is this is taking so long?" Filin asked Cherbakov, who was lighting a cigarette with trembling hands.

"There are some complications."

"What kind?"

"A tumor. Where is he?" Cherbakov was more interested in the nurse than in Filin.

The nurse said, "There's no answer."

"Damnit, I've got a man on the table!"

"He had to drive in from his cottage—"

As Cherbakov turned away, Filin grabbed his arm. "What's going on?"

"I'm calling in a specialist." He tugged his arm free and headed to the theater door.

"I'm not through talking to you!"

"Talk to *him*." Cherbakov nodded at a man in a gray suit, the hospital administrator, who had suddenly appeared and was now urgently conferring with the nurse.

Before Filin could say anything, the administrator approached him. "You're Comrade Korolev's associate? You should know that the original operation was a success. The polyp was removed."

"Then what is the problem?"

The administrator was sweating. "A tumor was discovered. The size—" He turned to the nurse, who held up both fists. "—Well, very large. That was successfully removed by Dr. Cherbakov and the patient is stabilized."

"So far, I've heard nothing but good news."

"Unfortunately, the patient continues to hemorrhage."

"How badly?"

The administrator hesitated a moment too long. Filin got red in the face. "You're telling me Korolev is in there bleeding, and we're waiting an *hour* for this specialist?"

"The government always wants us to call in a specialist in these cases. I can show you the document."

"Fuck your document. That won't save you."

"Katayev is the deputy minister of health. He's Brezhnev's personal surgeon."

"If he's that good, he should have been doing the operation in the first place!"

With the administrator warned, and the potential accusation stated, an agitated Filin returned to where I was standing, helpless. "Remember what you've seen and heard," he told me. "You are my witness."

The telephone rang at the nurse's station. The nurse answered it, handed the phone to the administrator, who then ran to the door of the operating theater. A moment later he emerged with Cherbakov, just as a very polished man of fifty, wearing gold-rimmed glasses and a French suit, arrived from down the hallway.

Filin rose and joined the three men. "Are you Katayev?" he asked.

"Yes," the new man answered, handing his overcoat to the administrator. From that point on, he completely ignored Filin. "Where are the X rays?"

"Inside," Cherbakov said.

"I'll scrub." He slapped Cherbakov on the back. "Don't worry, children," Katayev said. "Your savior is here."

Filin followed them into the theater, leaving me alone with the administrator and the nurse. Both of them looked at me with a mixture of fear and anger: Until a few moments ago, I was just another worker. Now they had to worry about what I might say.

Minutes later, looking paler than he had when he went in, Filin burst out of the operating theater. The door flew open far and long enough for me to see, inside, a mass of bloody linens and discarded plasma bags piled to overflow in one corner. The floor was slippery with blood.

The patient, of course, was in the glass-walled chamber beyond, hidden by sheets, assistants, and support gear.

I realized that Filin had walked completely past me, completely past the worried administrator and nurse. A moment later Cherbakov emerged, immediately lighting a cigarette. His hands shook even more.

Finally Katayev glided out, shaking his head and snapping his fingers to the administrator. "My coat."

"Where are you going?"

"Back to my cottage."

"What about your patient?" the administrator pleaded, with a sidelong glance at me. "Aren't you going to operate?"

"I don't operate on dead men."

Then he plucked the cigarette from Cherbakov's shaking hands, and walked away.

2   STATE SECURITY

After the disturbing scene with the doctors concerning the fate of Sergei Korolev, I moved around Filin's hospital room, bundling up his papers. "Should I take these back to the office?"

"Yes," he said, numbly, like a man who had been struck.

"Would you like me to call a doctor for you?"

"Those butchers! No!" For a moment he looked lost. "Yuri, what are we going to do without him?"

"Is he really dead?" It was a stupid thing to say, but that's what came out of my mouth.

"You heard the big specialist." Filin lowered himself to his bed, making himself even smaller. "And he wasn't even sixty!"

"Who will tell the people at the bureau?"

"Not me," he said, swinging his legs up on the bed and lying flat on his back, arms over his face. "His family is around somewhere. It will be up to them, and the Central Committee." Every facet of Korolev's life and work was a State secret. "Fifty-nine years old!"

"You're sure you'll be all right? Is your family coming to visit you?" I knew Filin had a wife and son, though I had never met them.

"They'll be coming to get me out of this place tonight, if I have anything to say about it!" Suddenly he reached out, took my hand, and looked into my eyes. "You were my witness, Yuri."

"Yes, I was right there—"

"There are going to be a lot of questions. I'll have to answer them, and you have to stand by me."

I had no idea of what he was talking about. "Yes."

It wasn't until I drove away from the hospital that I realized the significance of Filin's obsession with Korolev's age. He, too, was fifty-nine.

Back in Kaliningrad, after a miserably slow drive, I returned the car and carried Filin's papers upstairs. It was getting dark—on those short winter days the sun would set at four in the afternoon. The main administration building seemed deserted, a disappointment: I was hoping to see what Korolev's death would mean. But the news had not spread, and I certainly wasn't going to be its messenger.

I returned to Bauman via the train and the metro, and a cold walk in the dark to what would be a lonely weekend, since Marina had gone off to visit her parents in Orel.

I shared a flat on October Street with three other students. One of my roommates, a dark, good-looking Georgian named Lev Tselauri, and I went out to a movie on Saturday night, a film about the Great Patriotic War—not that we cared: It was just a way to get out of the two-room flat. The rest of the weekend we studied, since we both had an exam on Monday morning.

There was no mention of Korolev's death—or existence, for that matter—on Saturday, not in the papers or on the radio.

Sunday morning, however, the headlines in *Pravda* and *Izvestiva* proclaimed the death of the great hero. Not on the front page, but inside, filling pages three and four. It was Lev who showed me. "Is this where you're working? At Korolev's bureau?" he said.

Technically, my place of work was a secret, identified only by a mailbox number. But Lev knew that my particular mailbox dealt with manned spacecraft and interplanetary probes. It was pointless to deny it, and I didn't.

"That means we're rivals." Lev had told me weeks ago of his assignment to a different design bureau, this one known only as Number 52 and concentrating on, I assumed, missiles or aircraft. This was the first I'd heard that my country had a *second* bureau for spacecraft.

Rivals.

On Monday, Lev and I caught a bus on Spartak Street, hoping to connect with one moving north and west on the Ring Road to Leningrad Prospect. Our exams would take place at the Ilyushin aircraft bureau. The bus was a better choice than the metro, given the time we would have to spend walking between stations. And even during the October 1964 coup, when Khrushchev was forcibly retired and tanks could be seen at most downtown intersections, the buses still ran on time.

Today, however, with the temperatures below freezing and half a meter of snow on the ground, the bus simply stopped in front of the Dynamo Stadium on Leningrad Prospect.

I was jammed in the back, standing next to Lev, when we heard someone up front say, "Christ, what's wrong now?"

"Roadblock," the driver said.

Lev shouted, "Get your fat ass out there and tell them to open it!" He grinned with the knowledge that the driver would never know who had said this.

I looked out the window and immediately saw the reason for the delay. A stream of military trucks was flowing out of the old Central Airport and turning south onto Leningrad Prospect, presumably headed for Red Square, less than three kilometers away. First built when the Tsar was in power and now surrounded by military design bureaus, airplane factories like Ilyushin and Sukhoi, as well as the sprawling Moscow Aviation Institute, Central was all but useless as an airport now. Its proximity to Red Square made it a good place to land troops for parades, however.

"Has there been another coup?" Lev said.

I finally realized the cause of the traffic jam. "It's Korolev's funeral. We could be stuck here all morning." Polished green trucks rolled past, with parade troops huddled in their open backs. An occasional Zil or Mercedes limousine roared down the VIP lane in the center of the prospect. I was beginning to see how important Korolev had been.

"Oh, yes, your great genius is dead. You should transfer to my organization right now if you want to put the first man on the Moon."

"Your organization."

Lev gave me a sly look, then touched a finger to the tip of his nose. "Number 52. Ask around."

Suddenly the bus lurched back to life, to scattered, sarcastic applause.

With the delay, however, we were late for our exams. Strangely, our proctor was more frantic than we were. "Ribko, what are you trying to do to me?"

I didn't know what he was talking about. "A man was just here looking for you. State Security." Typically for a Russian, the proctor made it seem as though I was doubly at fault, not only for the tardy bus, but because I had kept a security official from handing out some no doubt well-deserved punishment.

"Do I take the test or not?"

"Yes. He said he'd be back, so don't mess around." He actually slapped the papers down in front of me. Lev gave me a sympathetic look, and took a seat as far away from me as he could.

I was too shaken—State Security, for me?—to concentrate on my test at first. But my five years of training at Bauman paid off. Pretty soon I was solving equations faster than I could write the answers.

I returned the test before the time was up. The proctor accepted it, then nodded me toward a door where a tall State Security type in glasses and black overcoat waited. "Your Uncle Vladimir wants to see you."

My father had told me once that Uncle Vladimir did not work out of the dreaded Lubiyanka but from the fourth floor of the building behind the Belorussia Station. That is where my escort delivered me.

There is a saying that fat men are graceful; if so, Uncle Vladimir was an exception. He wasn't hugely fat like Nero or some mountainous caesar—just round, like a pink, hairless bear, and about as coordinated. If there was a glass of water on a desk, he was sure to knock it over. His office had to have been the despair of the housekeeping staff. God, not they, only knew how many important files had been ruined, or lay cemented together, on Uncle Vladimir's desk.

Not that he was untidy; far from it. He dressed better than any Russian I knew, and was obsessively neat about his person. I would almost say he was fastidious, as much as any man in his business could be. In that he was a Nefedov, like my mother.

As I arrived, he closed a red-colored file that was open in front of him and removed his glasses. I think it hurt his face to smile, but he tried. He did not rise: Though he and my father had little in common, both were more reserved than the average Russian man. "How was your test?"

"I passed it."

"You don't have many more to go before you get your degree."

"Half a dozen, I think." He nodded, as if processing the data, so I asked, thinking of his recent hospital stay, "How are you feeling?"

Uncle Vladimir seemed surprised by the question. "As good as I ever do this time of year." He changed the subject without protest from me. "How do you like your job in Korolev's organization?"

"Well, I'm not doing the work I was trained for. But I hope to get a position in the spring."

He tapped on the red folder. "You can have one now."

"There are no vacancies."

When Uncle Vladimir managed a smile, it was only with his eyes. "Korolev is gone: That's one vacancy."

I didn't know how to react to a statement like that. I liked Uncle Vladimir and felt comfortable with him. I had even tried to model myself on him, to be as cultured, well-read, informed, interested in the world. I felt I could be irreverent with him on our infrequent family occasions, but not here. So I said nothing, and he went on, more seriously: "Korolev's death has upset many of our leaders, notably Ustinov. This doctor, Cherbakov, turns out to be a regular butcher. What he was doing operating on the chief designer no one understands. Who hired him? What really killed Korolev?"

"I assume someone will do an autopsy."

"They cremated him. Hard to do an autopsy on a pile of ashes." Uncle Vladimir consulted another file. "It seems his death couldn't have come at a worse time. The Americans just made a two-week-long spaceflight. Apparently they put one of their Geminis together with the other—"

"They made a rendezvous. Not a docking."

Uncle Vladimir nodded. "Good, you follow these things. Ustinov and the others are afraid that because Korolev is dead, the Americans will beat us to the Moon."

"I thought we were far ahead of them."

"Not by much, and not for long. Yuri, our leaders are worried. 'He who controls the high ground of space controls the world.' Do you know who said that?"

"Lenin?"

"Lyndon Johnson. The same ruthless bastard who killed Kennedy so he could become President. Imagine what he would do to us if he could put his missiles on the Moon."

Even then I knew that Mr. Johnson already had quite a few missiles much closer to Moscow than the Moon, but, again, I kept my mouth shut.

Uncle Vladimir folded his fat hands on that red folder. "I've been asked to find a volunteer for a special mission inside the space program. Specifically, inside Korolev's organization."

I had trouble understanding what he wanted. My confusion must have been obvious. "Yuri, I want you to start looking around at Korolev's bureau. Keep notes. Report to me."

"Become a spy?"

"Think of it as being a criminal investigator."

"Why me? I'm an engineer, not an investigator."

Uncle Vladimir tapped the folder. "Because of your technical training. And because *I* can trust you." Only then did I realize that the red folder on his desk was my personal State Security file.

"All right." I saw nothing wrong with helping a criminal investigation into Korolev's death. Filin would approve. "When do I start?"

"As soon as you go back to Kaliningrad. Your boss, Dr. Filin, will be informed that you are to be promoted to engineer in his section. Try to act surprised."

"I'll do my best. How do I make reports?"

"To me, personally. It means we'll be seeing more of each other." He hauled himself to his feet and extended his hand to me. I shook it. Then Uncle Vladimir caught me staring at the red folder.

"Something on your mind, Yuri?"

"What else does it say in there?"

Uncle Vladimir laughed. "Go home."

3

EXPERIMENTAL DESIGN
BUREAU NUMBER 1

The next morning, as ordered, I presented myself at Filin's office. However, for the first time in the weeks I had worked for Filin, I was forced
to wait in the outer office with Nadiya, Filin's birdlike secretary. The
many phones on her desk rang constantly, preventing us from having
any conversation about the death of Korolev, the future of the bureau
and Filin himself, and—most importantly for me—whether the bureau's
personnel department had left any messages regarding a promotion for
administrative assistant Ribko.

Presently the door to Filin's office opened, and half a dozen men,
both civilians and military, emerged. The civilians had the look of engineers—white shirts, glasses, and, since Korolev never wore one, no
ties. The military guys, some of the dozens of representatives of the
Ministry of Defense at the bureau, had glasses, too, but wore ties with
their green uniforms. Filin waved me in.

His desk, at one end of the office, was actually the top of a T whose
leg was a long conference table lined with chairs. He motioned me to
one side of the table, and sat down.

He was looking much better than he had in the hospital last week.
Years younger, in fact. I said so. "I've always been able to respond to a
crisis," he said, with quiet pride. Well, any man who had risen to this
level in the armaments business had survived many crises. Filin had told
me once, during one of my early errands, how during the Great Patriotic

War he had narrowly escaped death at the hands of military officers just like those he had ushered out of his office.

His job, in the dark days when Nazi armies were plundering European Russia, had been to supervise the acceptance of Katie bombardment rockets by the artillery forces. The Katies were some of the most effective firepower our army had at that time, but a whole batch of them, already accepted on Filin's signature, had just failed, flying far off target or exploding in their launchers. And in Stalin's time, any hint of sabotage or "wrecking" was punishable by instant execution without trial.

Filin got a tip from a friendly State Security officer—if that's not a contradiction in terms—that he was going to be blamed for the last series of failures.

Thus warned, Filin stayed awake the entire night preparing a defense. He knew, for example, that the faulty rockets had conformed to the standards. So some other factor was involved.

The next morning he was summoned to his commander and told officially of the charges against him. Thanks to his research, he was able to point out that the solid fuel used in the Katies was susceptible to extremes of temperature. They were being used in brutally cold winter weather for the first time, and this factor, so Filin said, was changing their centers of gravity, making it impossible for them to fly to their targets.

The commander glared at Filin, then summoned one of the scientific staff into the meeting, making Filin repeat the story. "Is this possible?" the commander asked the scientist.

The scientist thought for a moment, then said: "Yes. In fact, it's obvious. We should have thought of it ourselves."

So the commander exploded at the scientist, and Filin took that opportunity to escape from the office. As he did, he passed five men with rifles—the execution squad, who had been calmly waiting for the order to shoot him.

"What's going to happen here, without Korolev?" I asked.

"That's what everyone is trying to decide. Who will run the bureau?"

"One of Korolev's deputies, I assume." That group included Filin himself.

"That's logical, but the ministry is trying to ram one of its people down our throat." He nodded at the closed door, indicating the group of people who had just departed. "We were just discussing ways to . . ." He smiled, choosing the word carefully: ". . . deflect that."

He cleared his throat, then reached for a paper on the table. "Speaking of personnel changes, I have just been told that, in spite of restrictions on the size of my section, I am authorized to hire a junior engineer for it." He waited for my reaction.

"May I apply?" It was all I could think to say.

"The job is yours, Yuri. It pays two hundred fifty rubles per month." I couldn't tell whether I had failed, or passed, some test. "I think you'll find the work interesting."

"Is it working on spacecraft?"

"Oh, yes. Manned spacecraft," he said. "Manned spacecraft to the Moon." Now he had surprised me, though I can't explain why. I knew my country had a space program, but even then, the business of putting a man on the Moon still seemed to me a fantasy, like the socialist paradise we all hoped to inherit. Only at that moment, when someone in authority openly proclaimed it, did I finally believe. "You will finish your studies at school, of course. As your adviser, I could hardly encourage you to leave now.

"But you can divide your time between here and school. You will report to Stepan Triyanov in Building 11 tomorrow at eight A.M."

So ended my career as an errand boy. I made the long trip back to Bauman, to attend another class, then hurried home just as it was getting dark.

The five-block hike to my building was more difficult than usual because I was carrying a bag of groceries. I had stood in line at a kiosk for an hour just to buy half a dozen oranges. It would be a little celebration for Marina, who was supposed to return from Orel tonight. My roommates had promised to stay away until ten P.M.

As I approached the building, I noticed a black, official-looking Zil limousine idling near the entrance. Near the entrance was all right. You had to worry when it was parked in the back, near some stairway. That meant some poor soul was about to be hauled out of his flat, dragged downstairs, and driven off to an interrogation cell.

Or, at least, it had in the old days. Growing up in and around Moscow most of my life, I had played "Knock" with my friends. One boy would be the agent of State Security. He would suddenly point at another . . . who then had to run to home base for safety before the rest of us could catch him. If we did, we took him out and "shot" him. It was a pretty good game, far more interesting than hide-and-seek, but we had to stop after Yegor Sinchik's grandmother caught us and beat the hell out of us. I didn't expect the "knock" to come for me these days—especially given my current assignment for Party and country. But it was still a reminder.

My father had made himself right at home. He was sitting at the table reading a book and drinking from a tiny shot glass, which he kept filling from a vodka bottle.

"Where did you get this piss?" Those were his first words to me as I opened the door.

"The booze or the book?" I squeezed past him to set the groceries on the counter.

"The booze. The book's okay."

I saw that the book was a romance I had received as a gift when I was eleven, Herbert Wells's *Time Machine*. The book represented another attempt by my mother to steer me away from a military-industrial career and into the arts. "What's wrong with the booze? You brought it."

"When?"

"May, I think. We drank a toast to your Order of Kutuzov's beard or whatever."

"It was the Red Star and that means this swill has been *open* for seven months! Don't you ever drink?"

"Not enough, apparently. And when did you get so interested in vodka?"

Slightly chastened, the general got up to his full height of five-feet-three-inches and kissed me, awkwardly. "It's my work." He sighed. "I may be a bad father, but I'm the only one you've got."

"What brings you across the river on a cold night?"

The general moved to the living area, peering out the frosty window. "I had a call from Vladimir, something about a possible new job for you."

"Yes. He wants me to keep my eyes open at the bureau. And report to him."

My father seemed to slump. "I asked him not to involve you."

"In what? His work? It's Party business, isn't it?"

"Yuri, there is a big difference between Party business and Vladimir's dirty work."

I had unloaded some of my groceries, putting out some black bread and herring. I scrounged a chunk of sausage and put that on the table, too. "Did you want me to say no?"

"What I want is for him to stay *out* of your life."

I had never seen my father like this, at least not on the subject of Uncle Vladimir. He was actually red-faced, uncomfortable. "Did you tell him that you were at the hospital the other day?"

"No. Did you?"

"No. And you shouldn't."

"Why not?"

He was already making that familiar gesture with open hands, the one that said, *don't ask*, before taking a healthy bite of the sausage and grunting with satisfaction.

"What's this all about?"

"Can't I be concerned about your welfare?" he said, mouth full, crumbs flying. "I'm a military officer. I understand honor and truth. You won't find that in State Security. You'll have to lie to everyone from now on."

"That's ridiculous!" I was annoyed. I had been enjoying the secret thrill of being an agent of State Security, especially since it had gotten me the bureau job I wanted. And here my father was, ruining my fun.

There was a knock at the door. My father almost jumped. "Are you expecting someone?"

"Yes," I said, rather sharply. I opened the door to Marina.

She looked lovely, though somewhat hidden, in her fur hat and heavy coat, carrying a bag much like the one I had carried. Her dark hair, her green eyes, her smile, her voice—all conspired to excite me. We held each other until my father said, "Well, come in and close the door."

Marina set her bag on the table. "It's nice to see you again, General."

He barely grunted as he buttoned his tunic, prelude to a quick departure. Marina smiled at both of us and moved into the kitchen.

"What will you tell her?" the general asked me quietly.

"What do you care? You didn't even say hello to her!"

"I told you, she is the wrong woman."

"So that allows you to be rude?" To be honest, I rarely spoke to my father like this. But I was angry at him before Marina's arrival, and thanks to my new job and association with Uncle Vladimir, feeling more independent.

I must have reached him. "Tell her I'm sorry."

"You tell her."

He shook his head. "If only her father . . ."

"What about her father?"

"That's just it: No one seems to know. But everyone seems to think it was bad."

"Let me handle it, Papa."

"He's not good with women."

We were cleaning up dinner, not that there was much left. I carefully unwrapped the oranges and presented them to Marina. "For you."

"Are you sure?"

Instead of answering, I kissed her. She slipped away. "I taste like salt—"

"I like salt."

"You're a sex maniac. It's very bourgeois."

"Hey, I'm the guy in the Komsomol. By definition, I'm not only authorized to define bourgeois, I'm also allowed to be a sex maniac." I got my arm around her, began rubbing her hip. We kissed again.

She broke away. "Let's finish cleaning up." Her voice had suddenly grown husky. "When are Lev and the twins back?" My other two roommates, Mark and Sasha, were as dissimilar as two men could be: Mark was tall, brooding, thin, a bit stupid. Sasha was short, happy, fat, and brilliant. Sasha was even four years older than Mark. Nevertheless, because both of them happened to be from Omsk, Marina dubbed them twins.

"At ten."

It was almost nine. "We'll have to hurry," Marina said, unbuttoning her sweater.

Early on in our relationship, Marina had decided she would be the responsible one, watching what little money either of us had (not much, given our student allowances), cleaning up the leftovers, and, most specially, worrying about appearances. Some of my roommates might blithely fornicate with their girlfriends while I was sleeping in the same room: That was a fact of life in the student apartments. To my relief, Marina insisted on privacy.

This personal dignity was one of the things I loved about her, especially since I felt I had none. I consoled myself with the knowledge that Marina was three years older, and in the fashion of women everywhere, much more mature.

We had met during my fourth year at Bauman, when Marina became my tutor in English—a subject in which, you will not be surprised, I showed great and sudden improvement. There was an undeniable instant attraction between us which, naturally, neither of us acted upon for months. I knew that she had recently ended a marriage that seemed to have been State-ordained, possibly for some diplomatic assignment in Europe. Marina was understandably very reluctant to talk about it, and I knew better than to keep asking. Her age was another early obstacle. My father, hearing later that Marina and I were getting serious, wondered how we would ever have children!

But, slowly and awkwardly, we had found each other.

Within minutes the flat was clean. I unfolded the bed as Marina drew the blinds and, magically, continued her dance of the seven veils—sweater off first, then bracelet, watch and earrings, then shoes and stockings. Only when I turned out the light did she remove her blouse and let me unzip her skirt, which I carefully folded. I took her in my arms.

In spite of the fact that she was older and had been in a marriage, Marina was much less experienced in bed than I, quite a trick given my own relative innocence when we met. Her ex-husband, she said, simply demanded sex every three days, like a clock, caring nothing for her pleasure or state of mind.

Naturally, I did my best to be nothing like this former brute. From Marina's pleased reactions, I believe that I succeeded.

When we had satisfied ourselves, Marina rose to wash her face. From the kitchen—a few feet away—she asked me how my job with Filin was going.

"Fine." She emerged from the kitchen, looking pink and pretty, and started gathering her clothes. As I helped her, I said, "They're making me a junior engineer."

Her eyes widened with pleasure and surprise. "That's wonderful! I was worried that you wouldn't be accepted there!" *And would have to leave Moscow* was the unfinished threat. "You said it was going to be impossible."

"Something changed. I start real engineering tomorrow. When I finish my degree in a couple of months, I'll be full-time."

"You should have told me earlier."

I laughed. "Why? Would you have done something different?"

She arched an eyebrow. "I guess you'll never know." While I was considering those possibilities, she said, "Are they going to find you an apartment in Kaliningrad?"

I hadn't thought of that. I couldn't stay in the Bauman student housing past spring, certainly. A good apartment was very difficult to find in the Moscow area. Marina read the confusion on my face. "You stick to the engineering, darling. When it's time, I will deal with the apartment."

She kissed me again, then reached for her coat.

"Do you have to go?"

"Yes."

"It's the middle of the night. And it's below zero." I got off the bed, feeling that we had unfinished business. "I'll walk you."

She put her hand on my chest. "I've done this a hundred times. And your roommates will be here any minute." We kissed at the door. "In spite of *extreme* provocation, I still love you."

"I love you, too," I said. Then she left.

From the window, I saw her slip on the frozen street under the yellow light, then disappear around the corner.

Only then did I realize that something had changed in our relationship. I had not told her about being present at the death of the now-famous Korolev, about my other new job with Uncle Vladimir, about the fact that my new job at Experimental Design Bureau Number 1 was courtesy of Uncle Vladimir.

My father always warned me that there was a black mark against Marina. I told myself it would be better for her if she didn't know.

But I couldn't forget my father's words. On my first day with State Security, I had started lying to Marina.

4 DEPARTMENT 90

The next morning, it took me two hours to change my status from part-time assistant to Vasily Filin to junior engineer in Department 90. Once I received my pass, I left the overheated personnel office and returned, as ordered, to Filin's. "All set? Good. I hoped to introduce you to Triyanov personally, but now I have a meeting. Hurry over to Building 11 and you might be able to catch him."

"Will Triyanov be in the meeting, too?"

"Yes. It's all about our next manned space launch."

With minimally useful directions from Nadiya the bird woman, I headed out the back of the main building, entering an area that looked like a village square, and probably served that purpose. In front of me was a huge portrait of Korolev himself, bordered in black. At the base of the portrait were heaps of flowers. As I walked toward Building 11, I wondered where the mourners had gotten so many flowers in the middle of winter.

Experimental Design Bureau Number 1 was located on the site of a former Tsarist arsenal in what used to be the village of Podlipki. Podlipki—except for its train station—had since been renamed in honor of the late arms minister Kalinin, and was, in fact, no longer a village, but merely a suburb of Moscow, just outside the planned Ring Road.

Given the size of the bureau, and my lonely mission, I suddenly felt lost, like a stranger in a foreign city.

Building 11 was a four-story pile of gray with dim corridors painted a dark green. Endless rows of office doors, with no signs to indicate what lay behind them.

Eventually I found Department 90, and Stepan Triyanov, who turned out to be a wiry, wizened man in his mid-fifties. I would later learn that he had been a glider pilot back in the thirties—just like the late Korolev; it was where they met and became friends, who wound up commanding partisan units during the war. Triyanov had won a Hero of the Soviet Union medal in combat, then gone into test flying, doing some of the first service tests on the MiG-15.

Triyanov glanced at my papers for perhaps a millisecond. "Filin telephoned me," he said, which obviously explained everything. "So, Yuri," he continued, "whose nephew are you?"

That was an embarrassing, if all-too-typical Russian question. Before I could stammer my way through some inadequate answer, Triyanov said, "Any relation to General Nikolai Ribko?"

"My father."

"We worked together briefly after the war on rocket assists for jet planes. I would have thought he'd put you in the aircraft business."

"He didn't put me here. I came from Bauman."

Triyanov ignored this. "I haven't seen him for years, though I hear of him from time to time. Your mother?"

"She died six years ago."

"Life," Triyanov said. He turned and gestured around him. Department 90 was a large office crammed with desks. "This is the kindergarten, where we keep all the college students," Triyanov said. Half a dozen men about my age looked up from their work. "Here's a new victim," Triyanov announced. "Equipment-tester third class Yuri Ribko. Make his life miserable." Then he called, over his shoulder, "We're going to the meeting," and led me out.

It was a cold day, and I was still freezing in my heavy overcoat, but Triyanov wore only a military flying jacket. He seemed not to feel the cold. Or to care who might hear him. "You'll like it in Department 90," he said. "It's where the real fun is. We have access to our own fleet of planes and helicopters by ministerial decree—the Air Force can scream, but they can't do anything about it. One of those boys with the slide rules comes up with something, we find out if it'll work. It's very hands-on. By the way, do you fly?"

"No," I told him, as I struggled to keep up.

"You can learn here, if you want. You should. We may be forming our own cosmonaut team."

That was a surprise. "I thought the cosmonauts were all in Star Town." Star Town was a military village farther down the Yaroslavl Highway.

"That's just the Air Force detachment. Gagarin and Bykovsky, those guys. Even Tereshkova." He made the name of the famous woman cosmonaut sound like a disease. "Do you know Feoktistov?"

I remembered Konstantin Feoktistov as the scientist in the crew of *Voskhod 1*, the first spacecraft to carry more than a single pilot, launched fifteen months earlier. I said so.

"Scientist!" Triyanov laughed. "Feoktistov is one of this bureau's most important engineers! He *designed* Voskhod, in fact, which was why Korolev wanted him to fly on it. The Air Force wouldn't let him. They said they needed three pilots, which was a pile of shit—a rabbit could fly Voskhod.

"They lost that argument, so they said Feoktistov wasn't healthy enough. He had a back injury and couldn't do parachute training.

"The Vostok cosmonauts needed to be parachutists, because that's how they landed. But the Voskhod crew was going to come down right inside the spacecraft! Nobody was going to be ejecting!

"So then they got political and said Feoktistov had never joined the Party. He was unreliable.

"But he'd been a partisan in the war. He had been put before a Nazi firing squad along with his friends and gotten machine-gunned! The bullets missed and he crawled out from under his dead buddies after dark! Don't tell me he's unreliable!"

We had returned to the main administration building, where there was an auditorium on the ground floor. Several men and women—all of them quite young—were hanging around the lobby, some in conference, some having bitter arguments. None of them paid me or Triyanov the slightest attention as we opened the door to the auditorium proper, Triyanov still talking: "Eventually the Air Force had to give in. But only on Feoktistov! No more civilian cosmonauts, they said.

"Well, as they say, 'Once the first pickle's out of the jar.' We're just waiting for the new ship, Soyuz, to start flying, and we're going to make sure that someone from this bureau is in every crew."

We waited for a moment. There were perhaps fifty people in the room, about a dozen of them at a head table covered with green felt, with the rest in the audience. I spotted Filin himself at the head table. "There's Feoktistov."

The scientist-engineer-cosmonaut was seated one over from Filin, and turned out to be a mild-looking, silver-haired professor around forty years old. He even wore glasses. "He's not what I expected," I blurted.

Triyanov laughed. "That's just the thing. Before Gagarin's flight, the damn doctors figured you had to be some kind of superman to fly in space. Well, it turns out to be a lot less stressful than flying a jet. Anybody can do it, unless you've got a bad heart or something." Triyanov smiled. "*I'm* going to do it."

I couldn't hide the astonishment on my face. "That's right: fifty-five years old. Korolev would have cleared *himself* to fly, if he could have. He was only four years older than me." Triyanov suddenly became reflective. "He just ran out of time."

I became aware that the man sitting between Filin and Feoktistov—none other than bullet-headed Boris Artemov—was speaking: "I'm against putting another ruble into any more Voskhod flights. We should cut our losses and move on."

"That's Artemov," Triyanov whispered to me. "He was Korolev's number-one deputy."

"Is he going to take over the bureau?"

"He'd like to, but he's not Russian. And he has a lot of enemies." Triyanov grinned. "Sounds as though he's making more today."

Filin had pushed back his chair and was looking at Artemov with astonishment. "Sergei Korolev hasn't even been in the ground a day and we're already spitting on the grave! The chief had a plan for four more missions, and we should stick to that plan!"

Artemov was already shaking his head. "Look at those plans in light of what's happened."

"Now, your boss Filin has suddenly become the dark horse," Triyanov went on. "As long as Korolev was alive, he was stuck where he was, below Artemov and others. But now anything can happen."

Artemov went on: "The next mission is supposed to prove that two men can live in space for two weeks. A month ago we needed to know that, but now we don't. Two men named Borman and Lovell just lived in space for two weeks, or don't any of you read the papers?"

Someone in the audience spoke up. "How do we know what kind of condition they were in?"

"We saw them walking on the aircraft carrier. They looked fine. There's been nothing in the press about medical problems."

"What makes you think the Americans would tell us if there were?" That from a man in an Air Force uniform off to one side. I had seen him coming out of Filin's office the day before.

"Think about it," Artemov snapped. "They showed the recovery live on television . . . something we don't have the guts to do. Have they postponed any flights? No, they're going to launch another Gemini in March!"

"There's still the test of the spacesuit," Filin said.

"Test it on Soyuz! My point is that four more Voskhod flights are a diversion of time and energy away from our real goal, which is beating the Americans to the Moon!"

That brought forth a murmur of agreement. Artemov pressed on. "Look, we all realize that Voskhod existed because the chief wanted to keep Khrushchev happy. The Americans are going to put two men in space? Fine, we'll put three. They're going to walk in space? We'll beat them.

"We've managed to forget how risky the system is. Maybe I should ask Dr. Feoktistov here—" Artemov nodded to the engineer-cosmonaut "—how confident he was riding the booster with no launch-escape system."

No one in the West knew it at the time—and very few in my country, even within the space community—that the vaunted "multiman" Voskhod was nothing more than a Vostok shell with the safety equipment (pressure suit, ejection seat) removed to make room for three men without spacesuits.

Voskhod also lacked *any* means of escape in case of booster failure during the first minutes of flight—much like your Space Shuttle to this day.

Worst of all, the system that allowed Voskhod to thump down on land was a second retro-rocket attached to the lines of the main recovery chute. A sensor on the Voskhod itself triggered this reserve rocket when the shell was just a few feet off the ground, slowing it to a gentle landing.

"The boosters worked well in both cases," Feoktistov said, looking like a man wanting to avoid an argument.

"Lucky for you. Of course, Belyayev and Leonov wound up spending a night with the wolves because of another little malfunction." Artemov spread his hands. "The evidence is staring us in the face. We have a pointless program that is only likely to kill someone. I say we drop it."

There was a moment of silence. Finally Filin said, "Remind me, Boris, not to have you speak at my memorial service." There was laughter, except from Artemov, who stared at the table and shook his head. Filin continued smoothly, "We are a collective right now. We've heard from both sides. Is there a move to make this radical change? Hands?" Artemov's shot up. His was the only one at the head table. "Well, it seems we should all continue working as before. Including those of you working on the third Voskhod. Thank you."

Some of those in the meeting still wanted to talk, but Artemov was already leaving the stage. Before he disappeared, Triyanov had me on my feet. "Well," he said, "that was a good example of what it's going to be like around here."

"Chaos?"

"Korolev's meetings were like that, too. People shouting at each other, calling each other idiots. Of course then the chief would make a decision, and that would be the end of it. Artemov doesn't have that power. As for Filin, we'll just have to see. . . ."

I was still fairly reeling from the experience. "Did Filin and Korolev get along?"

"Who knows? They fought like dogs. When the chief went into the hospital, they hadn't spoken for three weeks."

Triyanov seemed lost in thought for a moment. I waited as long as I thought polite, then said, "Where should I start work?"

He turned toward me, his old self after that momentary lapse. "I need an assistant for a test I'm conducting tomorrow. Ever been weightless?"

"Never."

Triyanov smiled. "Perfect. Be in the department tomorrow at six A.M. We'll drive to the airfield from there."

Seeing someone he knew, he excused himself, leaving me to think about what Uncle Vladimir had said, that I would find suspects wherever I looked.

I realized that the least likely—and therefore most likely—suspect had been in front of me from the very beginning.

Filin himself.

5 THE TEST FLIGHT

Chkalov air base, named for a test pilot as famous in Russia as your Chuck Yeager is in the U.S., lay no more than twenty kilometers to the east of the bureau, yet the trip took an hour and a half. This on top of my train ride and hike through darkness to the bureau itself. I met up with a cheerful, tireless Triyanov and several of my new coworkers, then boarded a bus that rattled off to the highway. We passed through cottages, then into a mixture of open fields, white with snow, and birch trees.

Triyanov told me that this bus carried workers from the bureau to the cosmonaut training center at Star Town every day, though we got off before that.

By eight I sat in the ready room dressed in a track suit, going over my notes on the Voskhod life-support systems. Triyanov had made me read a stack of documentation before leaving the night before. Naturally the documents were too sacred to be permitted off the bureau grounds, so I had had to take notes . . . I even made sketches. Here were the oxygen bottles, here was the nitrogen tank. Here was water. These were the switches that controlled the system. These were the dials telling you how much of anything was left.

It might as well have been written in Chinese.

"All set?" Triyanov said, startling me. He, too, wore a track suit, in addition to a leather flight jacket and a stocking cap.

"Will it do any good if I say no?"

Triyanov laughed. "Not a bit, but I like your spirit." He looked at the notes. "Don't worry about that shit. It's all been flown before. Maybe I'll let you try it out yourself."

"With all the vast amount of training I've had?"

"Look, you've got about as much training as one of the crewmen is going to have. He's some scientist that Korolev wanted to fly, Keldysh's nephew. He's not a pilot, either." (You know, of course, that the scientist was not literally nephew to Keldysh, the head of the Academy of Sciences, but a protégé.) "Besides," Triyanov added, "we find out most about a system when it's used for the first time by an absolute novice. If anything can go wrong, it will. Triyanov's law."

I picked up my jacket and, lamb to a slaughter, followed Triyanov out to the plane.

Even at eight in the morning I couldn't tell if the sun was up. The leaden, cloudy sky was gray rather than black, so I was willing to believe a rumor to that effect. I just wished it would go ahead and snow . . . preferably before I had to board the aircraft.

I had ridden in a Tupolev-104 three times in my life. The twin-engine jet was the standard liner of the Air Fleet. But this one had been modified—or, looking at it another way, ruined. Most of the seats had been removed from the passenger compartment. Those that remained were more military in style—made of uncomfortable-looking metal—and crammed forward.

The rest of the compartment was taken up by a mess of cables, consoles, and a shiny metal ball about two meters across.

As Triyanov helped me up the ladder, I blurted, "What the hell is that?"

"That is the Voskhod spacecraft," Triyanov said. "Don't tell me you've never seen one before."

"Sorry." In my months as Filin's assistant, I had only seen a schematic of the Luna landing probe, which looked much like a basketball, but nothing of Vostok, Voskhod, or Soyuz.

"What did you expect it to look like?"

"I don't know. A cone, maybe. Like the American ships."

"Soyuz and Sever are our cone-shaped vehicles. We are just getting ready to fly Soyuz unmanned."

"We've got four different kinds of manned spaceships?"

"Actually, there are about six . . . if you believe all the rumors from other bureaus." Triyanov patted the rusted metal surface of the Voskhod. "This ball was in space a few years ago, can you believe that? One of the unmanned flights before Gagarin. No place in a museum, however. Right back to work."

"Efficient use of Party resources. I think that was one of the slogans from the last congress."

"Well, we want to be in line with the correct thinking." I got the clear impression Triyanov cared little for Party slogans. "Voskhod is actually the same shape as Gagarin's Vostok. Only that earlier version was built for one pilot. This carries two or three seats—"

"—With no escape system. That much I do know."

"Don't say that too loudly," Triyanov said, jerking his head toward the forward compartment. "Some people around here are sensitive about that."

I saw why when the door to the cockpit opened, and out came a familiar-looking young pilot, puffing on a cigarette.

Triyanov started to introduce us, but the pilot surprised me by smiling and holding up his hand. "I know Yuri. Nikolai Ribko's son. We met at the Kremlin Hospital." Now I recognized him: Ivan Saditsky, the young major who was traveling with Gagarin the day Korolev died.

Saditsky snuffed out his cigarette and crawled inside the Voskhod mockup. "Is he flying the mission?" I asked Triyanov.

"He's been the leading candidate for the past few weeks, but Kamanin keeps changing his mind." Kamanin was another general, this one in charge of manned spaceflight and the military cosmonaut team.

Saditsky immediately began complaining loudly about a set of switches on the control panel being out of reach. Triyanov gently explained that the mockup was not configured as a flight simulator, but merely to test life-support systems.

"How do I know you've got them in the right place when everything else is cockeyed?" Saditsky snapped, pulling himself through the circular hatch. "I've trained on a different system for six months. Sitting inside that piece of crap will set me back."

Triyanov glanced sideways at me. "What do you want me to do?"

Saditsky smiled at me. "Are you the bureau's test engineer, Yuri?"

I glanced at Triyanov, who answered, "He certainly is!"

Saditsky slapped me on the back. "Then *you* can test your bureau's system!"

"Where are you going?" Triyanov asked, as Saditsky headed for the hatchway.

"Back to the center," he snapped. "I'll be looking for your report."

And he was gone. "What a prick," one of the other bureau engineers muttered, but only when Saditsky was safely out of range.

"Speaking of pricks," Triyanov said, pointing at me, "we'll need yours."

"Excuse me?"

"The *test*, Yuri. It's part of the life-support system. How does man piss in weightlessness?"

"I thought they'd have mastered that by now."

"The Vostok cosmonauts couldn't get out of their spacesuits, so they just peed into a hose, like pilots. Even Tereshkova . . . they rigged some kind of catheter for her.

"Feoktistov and his two pals on the first Voskhod were the only ones to fly without suits, so far. We had them wearing hoses and bottles, too, which was tolerable only for a day. The next flight is two weeks long. Who wants to be putting on and taking off a condom the whole time?"

"None of us, I'm sure."

"Step inside. Shoes off." Triyanov moved aside as I bent down to unlace my sneakers. Then I grabbed the access bar mounted above the circular hatch, as I had seen Saditsky do, and slid in, feetfirst.

There was only one seat, on the far wall of the sphere, and it was mounted at right angles to the hatch. On the "floor," which was a collection of tubes, wires, and netting, someone had thoughtfully placed several wooden blocks—steps. I used those to reach the seat, careful not to bump anything.

There was light from the hatch, and a single lamp just above my head. Otherwise the sphere was dark. I was reclined, almost on my back. The seat was covered with a blue cushion and felt surprisingly comfortable. In front of me was an instrument panel like that of a small airplane. At my right hand was a pistol-grip controller. I found I could reach the panel and the controller without even extending my arms.

"Cozy, isn't it?" Triyanov said.

"I could take a nap."

"That's about the only thing these guys will be able to do for two weeks."

"I think I could stand it for maybe a day."

"Well, they say that in weightlessness it all seems so much bigger."

"All right," I said, "two days." Triyanov laughed, then I continued: "Now, what about this pissing tube?"

"That's the genius of these guys at the medical institute. They want to do away with the tube completely. For one thing, it would save space inside the cabin. The tube also means that a lot of the precious body fluid is lost. It evaporates, it never gets where it's supposed to go."

"So what?"

Triyanov was taking extreme delight in this. "Some of them have the idea that if we can *save* that piss, we can purify and filter it, and turn it back into drinking water." He must have seen the look on my face. "Don't worry, we're not testing the recycling system. Though you've drunk worse if you've ever turned on the tap in downtown Moscow. . . ." Triyanov jerked a thumb toward a receptacle in the cabin wall below my feet. "There."

"There?" The instrument looked more like a saddle than a toilet seat. Instead of being flat, the rear and forward areas were raised.

"You apply yourself to the 'fountain,' close it down." Triyanov showed that the front section pivoted open and shut. "Then do your Party business."

"Sitting on the wall?"

"It won't make any difference in weightlessness."

"We're not weightless."

"We will be soon."

I climbed out of the spacecraft as the last test crewman came aboard, tugging the airplane hatch closed. I could feel rather than hear the jets starting up.

"We can simulate weightlessness by first diving the whole plane, then pulling up into a climb. As we go over the top of the arc, we float. Just like cosmonauts."

"For how long?"

"About forty seconds." He winked. "Long enough." He handed me a plastic bottle. "Drink up!"

Fifteen minutes after takeoff, we had reached an altitude of ten thousand meters, orbiting above the clouds east of Moscow and headed toward Noginsk, when Triyanov told me to get inside the spacecraft. Other crewmen loaded film into cameras aimed through the porthole.

"All you have to do is unstrap, float over, sit down, and launch."

"It might take me a couple of tries."

"Don't worry about that. We're supposed to fly twenty arcs." I edged into the seat. Triyanov reached inside and helped me close the restraints, then slid out to find his own seat.

The aircraft seemed to topple forward, and I felt myself flung toward the ceiling of the Voskhod as we dove toward the ground. Once my father took me to an amusement park in the Crimea. The big attraction there was a roller coaster, and I badgered him until he allowed me a ride. He also insisted on coming along. I found the ride terrifying and wonderful. The merited test pilot of the Soviet Union threw up. Strapped into this little cabin, being shoved toward its ceiling, I felt like my father had felt, queasy and disoriented.

Pulling out of the dive was a bit better—for me, as I sank into the comfortable blue cushion. For a few seconds I felt a bit like a cosmonaut during launch. The others in the compartment, who were having the blood in their bodies pushed toward their feet, were turning various shades of white and green.

Then the plane began to climb, so sharply that I now felt as though I were standing on my head. Only the straps saved me from tumbling in a reverse somersault.

The angle of climb changed slightly . . . and the loose ends of my straps began to float. I had meant to get a head start on the test by slipping off my pants. Too late. I unbuckled, wondering how many seconds I had lost, and immediately turned the wrong way. I braced myself against the cabin roof and pushed backward.

"That's the way!" Triyanov was floating outside the hatch. "Farther back . . . and lower."

"How much time left?" I felt as though I'd been floating for five minutes already.

"Don't worry about that. Get in the saddle."

I finally managed to brace myself to where I could begin to think about my duties. I was sweating like a boxer now.

A claxon sounded.

"Okay, try it next time," Triyanov said, swimming back to his seat. "Leave your pants off."

I hadn't quite managed to get myself back in the seat when the plane began to dive again. My shoulder and side ached, but I twisted into position, and clapped on the chest restraint.

Over the roller coaster again.

On the second arc, I started out by turning the right way, and had myself braced, pants down, when the claxon sounded.

On the third, I got my bare bottom into the saddle.

On the fourth, I closed the pivot and managed a trickle.

As the fifth arc began, some of what little urine there was began floating inside the cabin.

"Piece of shit," Triyanov said, meaning the device, not me.

Then *he* threw up.

During the next three arcs, I made further attempts, none of them entirely or even remotely successful. "The tank is empty," I finally told Triyanov, and I didn't mean Voskhod's.

Green and miserable, he waved me out of the spacecraft. "You've done enough."

I strapped myself into one of the metal chairs and rode out the next few arcs as a passenger. I realized that the other test work—incomprehensible to me—had largely stopped, as the other test-crew members strapped themselves down like Triyanov, heads lolling, useless. In fact, I soon realized I was the only man still standing. "How long does this go on?" I asked.

"We ordered twenty arcs, twenty arcs is what we'll get, even if we're all dead." Well, with the aircraft diving and climbing, it was impossible to imagine walking to the cockpit door to tell the pilots otherwise.

From the look on Triyanov's face, the remaining eleven arcs were an agonizing eternity. I felt bad that I didn't feel worse . . . allowing myself to unstrap and float freely during the thirty seconds of freefall for each arc.

It was like being on that roller coaster again, with Triyanov in place of my father.

Eventually we leveled out, and people began to recover. "Well," Triyanov asked, once he had regained his proper color, "what shall we say about our space toilet?"

"It didn't seem well-designed."

"Good. That's exactly what we will report." He smiled wanly. "Be sure your name goes ahead of mine."

"If you say so."

"The organization's first response will be to blame the tester. You will probably have to repeat your space pissing."

"If that's what they want."

"I can see that these flights don't bother you, Yuri. Maybe I should get you into our cosmonaut team."

It was a joking comment, but it hit me like a fist. And I thought, I had become a spy without even trying. *Why not a cosmonaut, too?*

6 OSTANKINO TOWER

I spent the rest of that week in more mundane tasks at the bureau, charting the data from the tests and learning just how little I knew. The idea that I could somehow compete with the senior engineers around me in any bureau business—much less that of becoming a *cosmonaut*—soon struck me as foolish.

Returning exhausted to my building on Friday evening, I found a message from Uncle Vladimir waiting for me with the key lady. This was necessary because we didn't have telephones in our student flats.

The key lady's name was Liliya, and, like most middle-aged or elderly Russian women, she was round and potatolike. She had lovely blue eyes, however, and a ready smile, so some of the guys flirted with her, which caused her to blush and look quite pretty. Perhaps this sort of maneuver softened her up, or maybe she was just a romantic, but you could sneak girls past her at will. If she caught you, she might wag her finger—but always with a smile.

This day, Liliya seemed unusually concerned when she handed me the message, which simply said for me to meet Uncle Vladimir at the restaurant in the Ostankino Tower tomorrow at noon.

Noting Liliya's frown, I asked her if there was a problem. "The man who brought it was an *officer*," she said, referring to an officer of State Security, which in her world only meant bad news. Explaining my relationship with State Security was not, of course, an immediate option. "He said you would be here in five minutes," she added, which did chill me: I had stopped for bread at one kiosk on my walk from the metro station, then even lingered at another kiosk, which happened to be offering shoes—all of which turned out to be the same size, too big. But no one could have predicted *correctly* when I would arrive home.

Was Uncle Vladimir having me followed?

I knew the Ostankino Station and environs quite well. It was a fairgrounds devoted to the Exhibit on Scientific and Technical Achievements, dominated by a gigantic sweeping spaceship monument, a tribute to Gagarin. There you also found the new thirty-story television tower and its revolving restaurant.

Gagarin's anonymous engineers, such as the newly deceased Korolev; my boss, Filin; and his rival, Artemov, lived in a series of handsome flats—almost like the individual condominiums you see in Scandinavian countries—literally in the shadow of the monument. Consequently I had come through the station here twice a day for weeks, but had never been motivated, or rich enough, to enter the tower itself . . . the top of which, on this wintry Saturday, was shrouded in mist.

When I showed my documents to the guard, I was separated from the line and sent into the elevator. No one grumbled: They would have done the same and never looked back.

When I emerged on the thirtieth floor, there was no Uncle Vladimir, nor any sign of him, and none of his helpful State Security associates. The restaurant itself was largely empty—whether it wasn't open at this hour, or just not open to the general public, I didn't know. I had never actually eaten in a restaurant at that time in my life . . . cafés, yes. But this place was in a different class. It had a name—the Stakhanov—emblazoned on the wall in gold script, and was equipped with many expensive-looking furnishings, silver spoons, white tablecloths.

I glimpsed a waiter and a waitress, and possibly even a cook, but all three were seriously busy not working. To them, I was a thin young hooligan in a cheap overcoat, not a customer.

I stood there looking out the window, hoping for a view of Moscow sliding by slowly beneath me, but saw only clouds. Finally, as we made a complete revolution back to the elevators, Uncle Vladimir appeared, alone, his great bulk almost filling the cage.

"This way," he said, nodding to one of the empty tables, passing several (I thought) perfectly good tables on the way.

We had barely settled into the overstuffed red chairs when the staff, recognizing a dignitary, descended on us likes flies on a pile of shit. Words I had never heard in my life tumbled out of their mouths—appetizers, entrées—all accompanied by a lot of head-bobbing. Suddenly they were peasants and we were lords. I was torn between disgust at the display and the disturbing feeling that I could easily get used to such service.

They brought us vodka and smoked salmon, to take the chill out of our bones, and cleared off to prepare the lunch, which, to my relief, Uncle Vladimir ordered. I couldn't help saying, "They certainly live up to the name." Stakhanov had been a legendarily tireless, much-cited, heavily rewarded—and if not fictitious, then grotesquely exaggerated—hero–coal miner of the 1930s.

Uncle Vladimir allowed himself the briefest of smiles. "A restaurant doesn't have a State quota, Yuri. It either has good food or it doesn't. Which this place does. Korolev thought so." He glanced out the window in the general direction of the bureau's residences. "He used to bring his girlfriend here. Then kept coming after they were married, always sitting at this same table."

"I knew there had to be a reason we were here."

"We have to meet someplace other than the office; why not somewhere pleasant . . . and historically relevant?"

We tossed back our second shots of vodka and salmon. My hands betrayed my nervousness . . . I spilled some of the vodka as I refilled Uncle Vladimir's glass.

I apologized, but all he did was shrug, and dip a piece of the salmon into the puddle on the table. For all his sophistication, he was a true Russian: He wouldn't even let a milliliter of vodka go to waste. "How are you and your girl getting along?"

Marina was off in Kaluga baby-sitting a group of European tourists, and I had not seen her in several days. "Fine."

"Marriage plans?"

Marriage to Marina was an idea I had only fantasized about. I had never actually proposed it to her. "Not so far."

"A wife can be an impediment at your age. Besides," and here he managed a painful smile, "why buy the cow when the milk is free?" He laughed, too, a frightening sound.

There was an interruption as cabbage soup arrived. Only when the waitress had withdrawn did Uncle Vladimir turn to business. "What do you think of the bureau?"

Grateful for the change in subject, I quickly laid out my impressions of the open tension between Filin and Artemov, and threw in some of Triyanov's comments as well. The time I had spent chained to a desk in Department 90 had convinced me that while Korolev had been widely loved, he had also been feared.

As I made my report, Uncle Vladimir consumed everything on his plate, wiping up whatever was left with a piece of bread. When I was finished, he nodded, rested his left elbow on the table and pointed directly at my nose. (I don't think I realized until that moment that Uncle Vladimir was left-handed.) "By the power of the Party and the Central Committee, I am appointing you deputy prosecutor. Who do you charge with Korolev's death?"

"Aside from the doctors and officials of the hospital?"

"Should the death turn out to be something more than plain negligence, yes."

"My first choice *would* have been Artemov . . ." I paused dramatically. It is embarrassing to think of how smug I felt that day. ". . . But now I would place Filin at the top of the list."

"Your own boss."

"He was present in the hospital the day Korolev died."

"So was Artemov."

"Yes. But not in Korolev's room."

"As far as you know."

"As far as I know." I plunged ahead. "But Filin was under great stress for some mysterious reason—"

"Like someone from a Pushkin story, perhaps?"

Now I was starting to hear my own words as I spoke them—a sure sign that I was floundering. All I could do was finish weakly. "He tried to cancel some of Korolev's projects the moment the man was dead."

Uncle Vladimir smiled with real warmth. He was enjoying himself. "All right, let's examine the case of brother Filin, then. He and Korolev first worked together twenty years ago, in Germany. They were on our team that rummaged through the rubble in search of Nazi secrets. Of course, in those days Filin was the chief and Korolev was the deputy."

"So there's even more cause for resentment."

"Oh, yes. I agree completely that Filin would be a good candidate."

He settled back. "Now look at brother Artemov. On the surface, the perfect deputy to Korolev. In private, however, they disagreed about everything up to and including the time of day. Artemov was either at Korolev's throat or at his feet.

"Better yet, *their* association went back thirty years, to GIRD." I had heard something of GIRD, the Society for Rocket Research—starry-eyed students who managed to convince General Tukachevsky to give them a pittance to fund a few early rocket flights, until Tukachevsky was arrested and shot in Stalin's big purge. The same fate befell the heads of the GIRD; some of the junior members, such as Korolev, were merely arrested and shipped off to the Gulag. "The letter denouncing Korolev was written by Artemov to save his own ass."

That was a stunning revelation to me. "Then how could Korolev stand to have Artemov around?"

"People will say or write anything once they find themselves in the basement." He meant, of course, the basement of the Lubiyanka Prison. "Korolev himself had to denounce some of his colleagues. And, perhaps he felt guilty that he had stolen Artemov's wife."

It was clear that I was completely out of my depth. "It's a good thing I'm not a state prosecutor."

Uncle Vladimir acknowledged the joke, then said something that I remembered years later: "You would be surprised how little attention was paid to evidence in those days." He went on. "But you see the complications, Yuri. These people . . . they fight, they argue, they plot, but still they have this special bond. They want to go to the Moon. Yes, they will build armaments for our country—but the armaments they like best are the ones that fulfill *their* dreams, not the needs of the Soviet people. Their arguments are about the best way to accomplish this. Like rabbis arguing about God."

It was clear he was disgusted with the whole bunch. From my brief encounters with Uncle Vladimir in a family setting, I knew he disdained believers in God, especially Jewish believers in God. "There is even another party, another potential killer. Korolev's true rival, Chelomei."

"I don't know that name."

"He is even more secret than Korolev was, because all his work so far has been for the military. I want you to be alert for any information about him, too."

I misunderstood. "But I just started working at Korolev's bureau!"

I said, protesting as strongly as I dared. People didn't change jobs in those days the way they do now, believe me. I expected to work at the bureau long after my spying for Uncle Vladimir was finished.

Uncle Vladimir was already huffing with effort as he hauled himself out of the chair. "You will stay right where you are, Yuri. I want you to exploit your existing connection to Chelomei."

"Who?"

"Your roommate." Another piece of the puzzle. Lev Tselauri had mentioned his mysterious boss, and the "rivalry" with the late Korolev. So his secret "post-office" bureau was headed by this Chelomei! "Of course, all of this may add up to nothing. Remember that you do not carry the whole weight of the investigation on your young shoulders. Others are also working."

I stood then, too, and when Uncle Vladimir reached over and snatched a piece of cold veal off my plate, I realized I had been so busy showing off I had not eaten more than a few bites of my first restaurant meal. "You have a natural talent for this work," he said. "As time goes by, I see a growing need for young people with technical and mathematical skills inside State Security. This could be a great opportunity for you."

"Thank you."

"I wish your father would." For a brief moment Vladimir Nefedov changed from a mysterious figure from the dark world of State Security back to a fat uncle chewing my food. "When do you see him next?"

"Tomorrow."

Uncle Vladimir gave me no message; he only nodded. "We will leave separately. I go first." And thus I was back again in the world of State Prosecutors, the basement of Lubiyanka, the knock on the door. I had to be very careful. I was furious with myself for even entertaining that brief fantasy about becoming a cosmonaut.

I had gone to lunch in hopes I might be reaching the end of my association with State Security. When I left, it was clear I had barely begun.

7 THE EMBANKMENT

Sunday dawned clear and cold. At noon I was supposed to take the metro over to the Frunze Embankment, to my father's flat, so I could have slept late. But my lunch with Uncle Vladimir haunted my dreams, and I awoke early, just as the sun rose in the southeast, shining through the shadowy buildings onto the frozen Yauza River.

Years of practice had taught me how to keep quiet while moving around the flat, just as years of practice had no doubt taught the Omsk Twins and Lev to sleep through anything short of a nuclear attack. I made a cup of tea and had a roll for breakfast, then sat on the couch going over the last of my school papers. Triyanov had told me that my report on the Voskhod toilet would serve as the basis of a senior thesis on habitability systems for manned spacecraft. Without making any conscious choice, I was being shunted onto a specific career track that had nothing to do with my interests in mathematics or trajectories. I suppose I should not have been surprised. After all, I was rapidly being turned into an investigator for State Security, too.

"Breakfast reading?" Lev appeared out of the other room suddenly, surprising me as he picked up the typist's latest draft of my report.

"That's secret," I told him.

"It should be," he said, making a face. "It's years behind the ones we're designing."

I hadn't planned to quiz Lev so early; had wondered, in fact, just how I would ever begin to probe for Chelomei's secrets. But here it was.

"I must have missed the flights of Chelomei's spacecraft," I said. "Which ones were they?"

"I see someone has been talking. Your father?" Fortunately, Lev took my embarrassed silence at the accidental mention of Chelomei's name as confirmation of my father's supposed talkativeness. "Fine. The general staff loves my boss, because he works for them.

"As for our spacecraft, you'll see soon enough," he said, rising to the challenge. He began ticking them off on his fingers. "First, there's our space station, which was just approved by the Council of Ministers. Then there's our lunar orbiter—your dead boss Korolev was trying to take that away from us, but now he's gone."

"The new heads of my bureau have allies, too."

Lev spread his hands at the insanity of it all. "They have to use our launcher! The only way a Korolev bureau spacecraft is going to the Moon is on top of a Chelomei rocket! They don't even fit together . . . it doesn't make sense."

"You make Chelomei sound like some kind of genius."

"He is. He's a passionate man . . . very cultured. I was in his office just this week, in fact. You should see it, Yuri. He's like one of those people in an American movie, with a dark suit and a bright tie. He's surrounded by polished wood, hundreds of books. Poetry and novels, too, not just engineering texts."

I had never seen Korolev's office, but I had seen Korolev's style, which was strictly functional.

"He has a vision, too. It would be very easy for him to sit back and do whatever the generals want. Build bigger missiles. Shoot down American spy satellites. Collect his State prizes. He does all this, but he still *believes*, Yuri. He wants to see man—a Russian man—walking on the Moon. On Mars. And you know what?" Lev needed no encouragement to keep speaking. "He wants his people to fly his spacecraft. Yes, he'll let the military cosmonauts fly the military vehicles, but not the lunar spacecraft. He's very close to creating his own group using new people."

"New people like you?" I debated telling Lev that the Korolev bureau was way ahead of him already.

"Why not? I'm fit. My eyes are good. I'm learning to be a pilot." I hadn't known that. "Besides, I would much rather explore space than fight a war."

Then, perhaps feeling that he had revealed too much, he stopped.

He pointed to the Voskhod papers on my desk. "I'm sorry . . . it's really not that bad."

"No, I tested it myself: It *is* a terrible design."

"That's because Voskhod is small. Chelomei's space station is so large it has sleeping quarters as well as a bathroom."

There was a knock at the door, loud enough to wake the Omsk Twins in the other room. I answered it; Liliya, the key lady, had a telephone message for me. "Your lady friend is coming back early," she announced, handing me a slip of paper. "She says she will be home at noon."

The moment she was gone, Lev laughed. "Why does she bother writing it down when she's going to scream it all over the building?"

The Omsk Twins stumbled in then, effectively ending my interrogation of Lev. While it was now easier for me to picture this mysterious Chelomei, all I had learned was that he was a kindred spirit to Korolev, Artemov, and Filin. (Lev seemed to be one of them, too.) Not a murderer.

And what, exactly, was I?

Marina lived in another block of student flats not far from my own, but on the eastern side of the Yauza. I had hoped she would be alone—not an unusual expectation on a Sunday, with roommates who could be off studying in the library. Not only was she not alone, but one of her roommates was screwing her boyfriend in the next room.

Marina's hug and kiss were hurried. "Let's go, please." She grabbed her coat as I tried not to hear the creaking of ancient bedsprings.

Once we had exited the building, our boots crunching on the January snow, Marina relaxed, became playful, taking my arm, letting me stop her for a kiss. Kaluga had been cold; the trip had been shortened because pipes burst inside the big Tsiolkovsky Museum. One of her tourist charges had flirted with her. "He was a rich Western journalist, very handsome, too," she said.

"With a wife and four children back in Paris. Not to mention another set in London."

"He swore that he was unmarried."

"If you're trying to make me jealous, don't bother," I said. "Take the best offer you can get."

Then, disappointed that I didn't want to play her game, she pouted, but not for long. It was only when I told her that I was on my way to visit my father that she showed real annoyance.

"Yuri, he *hates* me."

"He likes you better than he likes me these days." I was trying to be encouraging, but failed.

After much pleading, she agreed to come with me, on the condition that we would leave after a few hours.

We emerged from the Frunze Station into another world. Handsome buildings rose all around us. The cars that zipped down the wide street were shiny and black, in spite of the snow and slush. Marina noticed this as I did. "It pays to be a general," she said. It was true: This part of Moscow belonged to general officers working at the Ministry of Defense headquarters, or at the many, many military academies and institutes around the city. Even the kiosks looked more prosperous.

It was a five-block march from the station to my father's building. I hurried Marina as much as I dared, knowing that my father had expected me to arrive at least two hours earlier. I must have been too intent on the task, because Marina suddenly stopped. "What's wrong?"

"What are you talking about?"

"You haven't said a word since we left the station. We hardly talked all the way over here."

She had that ability—common enough in women, I have learned—to read a man's state from body language and things not said.

"Nothing's wrong."

"Something has changed with you in the past week or so. I wasn't sure before I went to Kaluga, but now I can see it."

"Well, I have a job now. It's very difficult. Maybe that's it." That wasn't it, of course—what was different was my secret job with State Security.

Only then did I ask myself . . . why not tell her? Marina had her own associations with that world. A simple statement that I did, too, should end all the questions with hugs of understanding. No more hiding.

The words were forming in my mouth when Marina said, "Oh, God, look at that man!"

A man in the green greatcoat of an Air Force general was standing ten meters away, urinating against the wall of a building. As we watched, he clumsily zipped up, then stumbled away.

Staggering drunks were hardly an uncommon sight in Moscow in those days, though it was shocking to see one on a Sunday, and here on the Frunze Embankment, home to generals. "Go home!" Marina shouted, causing the man to turn, bleary-eyed.

There were more shocks to come. The drunken pisser was my father.

"Oh shit," was all I could say. Marina recognized him at the same time I did. We looked at each other in horror.

"Go," she said. "Go to him." And she turned away.

"What about you?"

"I'll be at home."

Hoping for, or perhaps needing, a good-bye kiss, I reached for her hand as, behind me, I heard a slurred version of my name. This from my father, who prided himself on *not* being a typical Russian drunkard. Pissing in the street in the middle of the afternoon!

Marina jerked her hand away. "Don't call me," she said.

I had so little experience with drunks that I did not know what to expect from my father's condition. Generally one is either sloppy and sentimental, or violently angry. Given General Ribko's normally testy disposition, I was relieved to find that he was weeping.

"Where's Marina?" He had seen her.

"She had to leave." I got him headed toward his building, which was across the street.

"You love her?"

Strange to hear my father, who never spoke of emotions of any kind, use that word. "I think so." Into the elevator.

"I loved your mother."

Now I knew my father, the grim, hardened hero of two hundred combat missions and a dozen military-political intrigues, was truly wounded. In the six years since my mother's death, he had never mentioned her. The only sign she had ever shared his life was a portrait of her in a place of honor in the main room of his flat.

There was no time for me to probe at this opening; just as I got him safely inside his flat, he vomited. The rest of the evening is best left to the imagination.

Only when I was sure he was in bed, safely asleep, did I turn down the lights and go out into the cold winter night.

8 CLANS

Early the next week, with the weather still frigid, Moscow locked in winter's cold fist, I was called to Filin's office. I bundled up, but still froze as I hurried across the facility.

Filin's bird-woman secretary looked even more fragile than ever . . . perhaps it was the heat in the building, which was almost suffocating. "He wants to talk about your schoolwork," she told me, I guess to make sure I didn't bring up any bureau business. "He needs to leave for the airfield in half an hour."

Filin was smoking and signing his way through a stack of documents when I entered. He ignored me until I had found a chair. Then, last paper signed, he pushed back the papers. "There. It's all shit, but nicely wrapped." Like a swimmer coming up for air, he blinked and focused on me. "Good morning." He grabbed a draft of my report off the cabinet behind him.

Mindful of the bird-woman's warning, I launched into a brief description of my work on the Voskhod crew equipment, just as I had briefed him on more mundane subjects in the past. Filin listened only long enough to light a new cigarette, then waved me to silence, the trail of fresh smoke describing a Z in the air. "You don't think much of the habitability systems on our Voskhod."

I was the most junior of the junior engineers and my experience with these habitability systems was limited to that unpleasant ride on the Tu-104 and some additional research for my report. I really had no business writing a critical report.

Yet, I had learned that one of the reasons *Voskhod 3* had not been launched in the fall of 1965 was due to serious shortcomings in life support. The oxygen-generation system was underperforming in tests, a serious problem. On a simpler, but more baffling level, Voskhod lacked a way to measure water consumption by the cosmonauts—it hadn't been necessary with single cosmonauts flying for a few days, because the spacecraft carried more than enough water. Two men in orbit for twenty days was much more challenging, yet all the big brains in Department 90 had come up with was a plan to have the cosmonauts *count the number of mouthfuls they used!* The temperature controls were tricky and unreliable, and the foam covering for the walls turned out to be flammable, and gave off particles that could easily irritate eyes and lungs. And so on.

So I felt confident in maintaining my negative position. Filin seemed to surrender. "Well, we hope to fly a pair of dogs next month. Hopefully we can fix some of the problems then." He handed the report back to me. "Triyanov thinks you have promise. Listen to him. He's a good man."

I didn't know what else to say, offering only a lame, "How is your health?"

He threw open his hands. "There are days when I feel like a college boy. But today I feel like a dead man." He stood up, heading for the window, gesturing vaguely toward the east with his cigarette. "I don't like flying to the launch site. Five hours sitting on a metal bench, bouncing all over the sky."

"Is that where you're headed today?"

"Yes. Another Luna launches next week. We got so close last time." *Luna 8* had been in its final descent to the surface of the Moon near the crater Galileo when its braking engine switched on . . . seconds too late. The little lander couldn't slow down enough, and smashed into the lunar dust. Filin, Artemov, and even Korolev, had been summoned to the Kremlin to be "beaten by the hammer," the hammer in this case being Comrade Sergei Afanasyev, the head of the ministry, a giant of a man with a volcanic temper, whose intimidating physical manner justified that charming nickname. "The Hammer is threatening to cancel the whole program if we screw up one more time."

"How can he do that unless he cancels the manned missions as well?" The Luna probes were designed to gather data about the surface so a manned lander could be designed. Otherwise there wasn't much point in them.

"I mean, he will cancel the *bureau*'s part of the program and give it all to other organizations."

"Like Chelomei's?"

I uttered that name without really thinking, and was surprised at Filin's reaction. He slowly turned to face me. "Not many people know about Chelomei," he said.

I mumbled something about having heard him mentioned at Bauman, which seemed to satisfy Filin. "He is one smug, political bastard. He went out and hired Khrushchev's son and made him one of his deputies! The Hammer loves him, too. They party together down in the Crimea.

"This is a very difficult time for our organization, Yuri. With Korolev gone, we could tear ourselves apart. The Hammer is always saying we do too much . . . we build missiles and launchers and spy satellites and communications satellites and space probes and manned spacecraft. He already got Korolev to start selling off the pieces before he died, and maybe that's right. Maybe we try too much.

"But not the Moon program. You can't spread that all over a bunch of different organizations. Look at the Americans: Everything is NASA. They used military rockets only when they had to. Now they're building their own big Saturns and Apollos, and they don't have to fight with the generals.

"If I thought that giving Chelomei the lunar program would beat America, I might feel better. But he's a terrible engineer, very dictatorial, in love with his own ideas even when they make no sense. He doesn't realize that you can't change the laws of physics by wishing. His greatest skill is theft." Theft meaning the copying of Western designs, a rich tradition in my country in those days.

Filin paused then, to catch his breath before spewing further, I thought. But the silence stretched, so I offered a comment: "We'll use his Proton, won't we? For our own lunar spacecraft?" Once again, I had blundered, mentioning the secret Proton.

But Filin was so intent on his tirade that he didn't notice my lapse. "We *may* use his Proton, assuming he can get the damned thing to fly properly." He described two successful launches of the big booster the previous spring, but though both had delivered large payloads to orbit, the violence of the ride had made them useless, and would have seriously injured a cosmonaut crew. "That's another thing: Chelomei will give the generals any damn thing they ask for, whether they need it or not. The Proton was designed to carry a fifty-megaton nuclear warhead. Who needs a big cigar to blow a deeper hole in the ground?"

He flopped down behind his desk again, stacking and restacking papers. "Chelomei is supposed to use his Proton to send a cosmonaut around the Moon in his own little spacecraft," he said, much more quietly now. "The Central Committee gave him that job when Khrushchev was still in power. Just before he died, Korolev got them to think about giving it back to us. He showed them how ridiculous it was to use Chelomei's spacecraft, which had no proven propulsion, guidance, recovery, or environmental systems, when we here at our bureau have done all these things over and over again.

"It's still up in the air, though. It all depends on my new Luna." I could see the point: It would validate the Korolev team's guidance, propulsion, and deep space communications, for starters. "The bonus is, if it works, we also beat the Americans. Their Surveyor won't be ready for months yet."

Nadiya the bird-woman was in the doorway. "They're here for you," she said, her face a mask of annoyance at me, at Filin, and for all I know, at her lot in life.

Filin actually started at this rebuke. Then, as if catching himself, he smiled. "A minute." Nadiya glared at me before withdrawing, at which point Filin burst into laughter. "For the tiniest moment, I thought she meant the black van was finally here for me!" The black vans, of course, were favored by State Security in rounding up enemies of the people not so very many years before. "I was sure something had happened to the spacecraft!"

He was clearly manic, a man under extreme pressure. As if I needed any further proof, when I excused myself, he suddenly seized me and kissed me like a son. "Yuri, you have stood by me. Keep up the good work, and God willing, you will take the next trip at my side."

Wondering what Filin meant, I got out of there.

The office was practically deserted when I returned. Some of my colleagues had gone off to the cosmodrome with Filin, while others were no doubt at lunch.

Triyanov saw me sneaking back in and asked where I'd been. Filin's office, I told him.

"How was he?" Triyanov seemed genuinely concerned.

I tried to describe Filin's mood swings without going into the substance of our conversation. Triyanov heard me out, then nodded. "I'm not surprised. There is tremendous pressure on him to make this flight. None of us have Korolev around to frighten the ministry or go to Ustinov."

"I thought the ministry and Ustinov were the same."

Triyanov showed me his steel teeth, shaking his head like a grandfather tolerating a child's question. "In a socialist paradise, Yuri, every worker has the same goal. Since we have not yet achieved that paradise, emotions and alliances affect every decision.

"Ustinov has been the master of the arms industry for twenty-five years. Korolev, Korolev's bureau, and Artemov have been loyal supporters, producing many triumphs for him. So he protects us and listens to our complaints.

"But Ustinov is not God. He was never part of Khrushchev's clan, so there were always checks on his power. His rival is a general named Grechko, whose creature the Hammer is."

"And the Hammer supports Chelomei. Who hired Khrushchev's son."

Triyanov nodded. "Exactly. Now, when Khrushchev was kicked out, his whole clan suffered. Ustinov has an excellent relationship with Brezhnev and Kosygin, the new leaders, so we have been insulated against punishment for our failures.

"But the war goes on. The Hammer wants to put his deputy, General Tyulin, in charge of the bureau. Tyulin is a part of Ustinov's clan . . . but the Hammer trusts him much more than he will ever trust Artemov or Filin. It's also a great way to get Tyulin out of his office."

"Would that be so bad? Having a deputy minister come in and take over?"

"Not at all. Tyulin is an old rocketeer; he worked for GIRD when he was a college student, before the Army got hold of him. He's very wise in the ways of the world. You'll meet him.

"But whatever his virtues, he has not grown up here. So all the pretenders to Korolev's throne will join forces against him."

It was bad enough trying to deal with the hard work of engineering, with facts and figures. How could I possibly be expected to keep straight all these personalities, these clans? "It sounds medieval," I said.

Triyanov laughed and shook my hand. "Nothing less!" Then his tone changed. "Speaking of matters medieval, there is a meeting of the bureau's Party members tomorrow evening in the main auditorium." Triyanov obviously knew that I was, like any ambitious student at Bauman, a member of the Party's youth organization, the Komsomol. I had joined as a Young Pioneer at the age of twelve, much as an American male would join the Boy Scouts. I had managed to progress through the ranks without distinguishing myself. No one had ever asked me to become secretary of a Pioneer or Komsomol group, for example.

And though I would laugh at other people's jibes—such as those I'd heard from Triyanov on our test flight—and might even make a cautious one myself, I was not anti-Party by any means; and I put in more than my share of time on Saturday potato-picking and other Party work. Even as I realized that my country, my government, my Party had committed errors, I believed they rose out of pure motives, to create a better world. I did not approve of the West, with its money-grubbing and imperialist wars, such as the one in Vietnam.

Yet, in my last year at Bauman I had grown wary of the petty jealousy that infected Party activities, having seen promising students denounced anonymously, so I had not been especially active. Which was to be expected and, in fact, was tolerated in last-year students. Besides, I was an engineer; engineers were allowed certain eccentricities, as long as their work was directed toward the betterment of the worker's paradise. And there was no profession more glorious than aviation engineering.

I thanked Triyanov for the notice. "Will I see you there?"

He laughed so hard he got red in the face. "I never joined the Party. Otherwise I'd be wearing two stars and sitting in some office over at Chkalov. I went to meetings, of course, when I was younger than you, primarily to meet girls. But their fathers and mothers and relatives kept disappearing, and it made me think there were dangers involved in being a Bolshevik. Then the war came along, and nobody cared whether you had a Party card or not. They wanted to know if you could kill Germans."

I didn't know what to say to him. The situation didn't require sympathy. But, as a good Party member—or potential member, since I was still only in the Komsomol—I could hardly be enthusiastic.

Triyanov noted my discomfort, standing and taking me by the arm.

"You go, Yuri. Keep in mind, however, that five percent of the population of our Soviet Socialist Republic are Party members. But one hundred percent of our cosmonauts."

The cosmonaut business again.

It was only much later, as I took the train back to Moscow, that I did the math: Triyanov was fifty-five years old, since he had recently left active duty in the Air Force. He would have been about twenty-seven, close to my age, when the awful purges began, when Stalin massacred thousands of old Bolsheviks and a lot of young ones, in addition to God knows how many others.

What must Party meetings have been like in those days? With the Terror loose in the land? When any innocent statement could be twisted into a slander against the Soviet State?

I shuddered, and not from the cold.

9

"THE MOON SPEAKS RUSSIAN!"

At 9:44 Moscow Time, on the evening of Thursday, February 3, 1966, a vehicle once known in the bureau as the thirteenth in the E-6 series, officially *Luna 9*, a two-meter-tall collection of cylinders topped by an onion-shaped covering much like a church dome, began firing its single retro-rocket as it dropped toward the dark-gray surface of the Moon. Locally it was just after sunrise on the Ocean of Storms, near the lunar equator.

For forty-five seconds the motor fired, slowing Luna's rate of descent to twenty-five kilometers an hour. Then the onion dome blew open and an object the size and shape of a basketball sprang free one second before the cylinder and its rocket crunched into the lunar soil. The basketball landed softly some distance away, bouncing once, twice, into a crater perhaps twenty-five meters across, rolling to a stop on the dusty upslope.

Four minutes passed as the top of the basketball opened like the petals of a flower, sprouting four whip-wire antennas and a small panoramic television camera. The basketball had been deliberately made bottom-heavy, so the top of the basketball wound up on top. The petals themselves served as antennas for receiving commands from Earth.

Then a message was beamed across three-hundred thousand kilometers to the giant receiving antenna at our deep-space tracking site in Simferopol, Crimea. It took a second and a half for the radio signal to travel that distance. *I'm here! I made it! Luna 9* said.

The control room, filled with tired men in civilian clothes and in the green uniforms of the Central Space Office, erupted in cheers. After five years of failure, the USSR had soft-landed a spacecraft on the Moon, beating the Americans by months. Now we—not the Americans—would discover just what the surface of the Moon was really like. Was it covered in dust that would swallow a heavy spacecraft and a cosmonaut? Or was it solid ground like some Earthly desert?

At 4:50 the next morning, the first pictures began to arrive at Simferopol. Over the next two hours, half a dozen photos would be transmitted, showing a panoramic view of ordinary rocks casting their long shadows, the rim of the crater, the black sky of a lunar day, and even one of *Luna*'s own antennae.

Some of the pictures were broadcast live over Moscow television as they were received, which is where I first saw them on the morning of the fourth, in the common room of my apartment building just after breakfast. Given the nature of our Soviet-built television, the pictures were little more than black-and-white blurs accompanied by what sounded like a rush of static interrupted by occasional beeps and blips— telemetry from the probe.

Yet, this was a tremendous achievement. The Americans had managed to crash a Ranger probe into the Moon, but they were nowhere near ready to land one softly as we had. (That day's *Izvestiya* was headlined, "The Moon Speaks Russian!") It was obvious that the lunar landing rattled our American and European rivals, since the Jodrell Bank Observatory in England pirated the *Luna 9* photos and published them without permission.

I'm ashamed to say that *Luna 9*'s victory also served to show the superiority of our bureau's systems to those of Chelomei, as I reminded Lev, who joined me in the common room to view the pictures. "If your boss needs directions to the Moon," I teased, "we can help."

"Comrade Chelomei would merely thank your bosses for lighting the way for his glorious and much larger Proton rocket and our spacecraft—which will be successful long before its *ninth* try." Lev was as sarcastic as ever, but in his eyes I saw conflict. He was pleased that our country had accomplished the landing, but also knew that the Korolev bureau would get the acclaim. In the battle over which organization would make the lunar flight, every weapon counted.

———

Filin and his team returned to Kaliningrad the middle of the next week, the day after the heroic *Luna 9*'s batteries expired and the pictures stopped coming. The weather was so awful—clear skies with a vicious wind—that the triumphal reception was moved inside.

I was lucky to squeeze in, and then only because Grechko, one of the future bureau cosmonauts, worked on Filin's team and was able to get a pass for me.

The welcome was a big deal. A lectern had been set up at the front of the hall next to a long table covered in green baize. The various masters of space were there, in strict order of rank—from the Hammer himself, Afanasyev, who really did loom over the others like a monolith. Next to him was the mysterious Tyulin, the bureau's master-in-waiting; then Artemov, looking flushed and possibly drunk; and several unfamiliar faces, all of whom were soon identified as Barmin, Ryazansky, Pilyugin, Babakin—heads of other enterprises that had contributed to the success of *Luna 9*.

At the very end was Filin himself, surprisingly subdued with this talk of space victories and State prizes. I said as much to Triyanov, catching up to him on the walk back to Building 11. "It's probably just exhaustion," he said. "Even before Korolev died, Filin bore the brunt of all the failures. I think he took them personally, even though most of them were caused by exploding rockets." Here he smiled wickedly. "Artemov's rockets."

I recalled Filin's habit of taking to his bed when things were especially bad; certain personalities would have the same reaction when things were going especially well for them, as if intense emotion of any kind caused a collapse. "Well, this must be a happy day for the whole bureau."

"Yes and no. Right now the Hammer is over in the main building telling Artemov that he wants this bureau to take over the program to send a cosmonaut around the Moon." Triyanov did not mention the name "Chelomei," nor did I offer it up. I was learning.

"I thought that had already been decided. We were to build all the manned lunar vehicles."

"We were given the manned lunar *landing* back in 1964, but another organization was given the manned lunar *orbit*. Can you imagine anything so stupid? You build one set of vehicles, a launcher, and a manned craft, to go ninety-nine percent of the way to the Moon, and turn around and build a whole different set to cover the last twenty kilometers!" He shook his head. "Well, that was the Khrushchev style.

"Before he died, Korolev had managed to shoot a lot of holes in this arrangement. He showed how we could send a simplified version of our own Soyuz spacecraft on the lunar orbit, and had lined up Ustinov and others behind it. It helped that the competition was shooting itself at the same time.

"But no one, not even Ustinov, was going to risk a war with the Hammer and the others as long as we were still crashing Lunas. Now, though . . ." He paused as we flashed our passes to the guard and entered our building. "Filin is probably the only one who realizes how much work has landed on their shoulders. And how pitiless the Hammer will be about our deadlines."

We went up four flights of stairs—I don't ever recall seeing Triyanov take an elevator—and down the hall to the flight-test office. As he was about to open the door, Triyanov paused. "Take a good look at your colleagues, Yuri. Grechko, Makarov, Yeliseyev." These were some of the members of the kindergarten. "One of them is going to be on that first flight around the Moon. If Artemov and I have anything to say about it, one of them might take the first step on the surface."

Naturally, when I entered the office I found none of the future Moon orbiters or walkers present. Grechko and Makarov were almost certainly busy with Artemov and Filin. But I looked at their desks—not so very different from mine—with a greater sense of wonder.

Riding the train back to Moscow that night, I got an idea: Knowing how devoted Lev was to the whole idea of manned spaceflight, how perfect he would be for the flight-test department, and how shattered he would be when Chelomei lost the lunar mission, why not introduce him to Filin? Transfers between bureaus were rare, but not impossible, especially with Lev, like me, in the prediploma stage.

I was feeling quite good about my generosity when I walked up the steps to my building to have Liliya, the giant key lady, practically fly out of her kiosk with another message in her hand. "Yuri, it's your father. He's in the hospital."

The message directed me to the Aviation Hospital, which was in So-kolniki, northeast of central Moscow and, as these things go, fairly close to Bauman. I hurried back to the metro and retraced my path to the Kursk station, then around the Ring to Komsomol Station, changing to the blue line, exiting two stops away.

The Aviation Hospital sat surrounded by the huge Sokolniki Park just a few blocks from the metro stop. It was dark, of course, as I reached the entrance, and it took half an hour to get past the various guards and key ladies and find my father.

I was worried about him, naturally. Beyond that, I felt sorry for him, knowing his feelings about the Aviation Hospital. "A bunch of optometrists" is what he called them. The staff of the facility was famous for its precision in judging pilots' eyesight, and not much else. Of course, like all Soviet military medical establishments, it was blatantly politicized: If somebody higher up wanted a particular person medically disqualified, *some* disorder would always be found.

There was a young Air Force officer sitting outside his room who told me that my father had had an "accident" while returning from a visit to some research facility out in Shchelkovo, a town a few kilometers out from Sokolniki close to Chkalov air base and the cosmonaut training center. "What kind of accident?" I asked. "How is he?"

The officer would only tell me that my father seemed to be resting comfortably. He insisted on getting a doctor to answer any other questions. I allowed myself to be relieved that my father had not, at least, been found frozen to death in some snowbank.

The doctor was even younger than the officer; he couldn't have been much older than me, in fact. And instead of answers, he had questions. "Has your father been under stress lately?"

"No more stress than usual," I said. We went back and forth like this for a few moments before I learned the story:

My father had visited an institute in Shchelkovo for some celebration, having been driven there. As expected, the vodka flowed freely, and my father had climbed into the car and driven off. The doctor was not about to claim that my father was drunk, but to me it was obvious: Father had been an ace pilot in his day, but, to my knowledge, had never qualified for a driver's license.

"He headed back to Moscow, but missed a turn and ran off the road in Lukino. He was lucky he was close to a militia station, because two of them noticed the tracks going off into the snow when they came off work, and decided to investigate.

"Your father suffered a broken collarbone and was suffering from exposure when they found him."

"May I see him?" The doctor led me into the room—a private one for a general and Hero of the Soviet Union, of course, on a floor filled with private rooms.

My father was sleeping, but could not have been very comfortable. His left arm and shoulder were wrapped in a giant elevated cast. There was a nasty cut, now stitched and bandaged, and a bruise on that side of his face. All I could think to say was, "How long will he have to wear the cast?"

"Eight weeks."

At that moment a nurse appeared in the doorway. "Yes?" the doctor said.

"There's someone here to see *him*," the nurse said, indicating me. "Her name is Marina."

"When did you decide to forgive me?"

Those were my first words to her, as we broke what seemed like a desperate hug.

"What makes you think I have?" Before I could respond to that, she said, "How is your father?"

I explained, adding, "He's asleep now, so you don't have to worry about him."

"Well, I *am* starting to worry about him." His drinking, she meant.

"Me, too."

She took my hand. "I'm sorry I was such a bitch. I love you so much, and I was afraid your father was going to take you from me." She told me how she had decided to surprise me at the flat, and had learned from Liliya about my father's accident.

"I wouldn't let him do that."

She kissed me again. I could not let her go. Shocking as it may sound, within moments we—my shy, private Marina and I—were making love, passionately, frantically, in one of the empty rooms, as my father slept off the effects of his accident and a disapproving nurse shook her head in dismay.

10 THE STATE COMMISSION

The first two weeks of February 1966 were a blur of schoolwork, bureau tasks, and Marina. She had schoolwork, too, of course, but spent more and more time at my room. If the Omsk Twins cared—or noticed—they said nothing.

Lev, busy with his own burden of school finals and diploma work, had taken to spending nights with a friend out in Reutov, home of the Chelomei bureau.

My father was discharged from the Aviation Hospital on the ninth, little more than a week after his accident. We had not discussed the accident in any detail. Perhaps you find this strange; looking back, I do, too. But our conversations had never been long or deep, except on those rare occasions, when I was younger, that I was able to get him talking about flying combat missions in the Great Patriotic War, or testing Sukhoi and MiG fighters. The week after the accident, his only comment was that he had been "a damned fool."

Even when I telephoned him from my office at the bureau the night before, to tell him I would try to be present when he left, he had been blunt. "They're sending me to Foros," he said, naming the resort on the Black Sea often used by the Air Force.

"Then I want to see you before you go."

With great difficulty, I managed to get to Sokolniki at eight in the morning, his scheduled time of discharge, only to find that I was too late. The nurse on his floor—the same nurse who had witnessed my disreputable lovemaking with Marina—happily informed me that General Ribko had been driven away only minutes before!

Confused and angry, I sat down on a bench inside the main entrance, gathering my strength before submitting to the cold, the metro, the train to Kaliningrad. It was another gray, nasty day, like most of them that month. "So you didn't listen to your father," a voice said, startling me.

Uncle Vladimir stood there, slipping on his gloves, accompanied by two obvious State Security types.

We embraced. "He didn't tell me to stay away."

"Not in so many words, I'm sure. But I'll bet he didn't encourage you to come all the way over here to see him in his agony."

"His agony?"

"His helplessness." He gestured awkwardly with his left arm. "He can't even dress himself with any ease. Fortunately, he won't be tempted to drive, either."

With a nod of his head at his two companions, and me, he headed outside. I chose to follow, and was glad I had when he said, "Let me drive you to your bureau."

Uncle Vladimir's car was a black Zil, newer than bureau Zils I had driven during my time as Filin's errand boy, and much better maintained, its engine running smoothly, which was a relief. In my experience, at least one motor trip in five from Moscow to Kaliningrad would involve a breakdown of some kind.

I settled in the back as the two goons got in the front. No sooner had we pulled onto Korolenko Street headed for Preobrazhensky than Uncle Vladimir said, "Korolev was murdered."

I said nothing. "We not only reviewed all the medical data with specialists from different organizations—" here he smiled "—but questioned everybody who was in contact with Korolev that day.

"He had come through his surgery in surprisingly good shape, for a man of his age and health. He was most probably smothered."

All I could do was nod. Until that time, my own probings and speculations had felt like a more grown-up version of hide-and-seek, dress-up, or pretend. If Korolev had been murdered, then one of those who saw him that afternoon was a killer.

"We will be watching Chelomei, Artemov, and the others very carefully," Uncle Vladimir said. "But I am depending on you for information on Filin."

"I understand."

We drove in silence for a while, turning off crowded Preobrazhensky onto the Ring Road, heading north and west back toward Kaliningrad. At one rutted, potholed stretch we almost collided with a truck. As our car swerved to safety, the driver, speaking for the first time, said, with satisfaction, "I got that son of a bitch's number."

"Relax," Uncle Vladimir said. "This road is like a minefield."

It was true. In spite of the luxurious accommodations, I was getting motion-sick from the sudden swerves and bumps—I, survivor of the vomit-inducing flight in the Tu-104!

"Nikolai has started drinking," Uncle Vladimir said, a statement of fact that did not invite contradiction.

"I think so."

"He only has a year left on active duty." That could have explained his depression: My father's entire life was the Air Force, and he faced a mandatory transfer to the "reserve" at age fifty-five, a forced retirement that, for him, would be a living death. Theoretically, his three-star rank could have kept him employed for five years longer, but, thanks to his freely offered opinions, he had been passed over for all the jobs that would have made that possible. "Even if the high command wanted to keep him on, they won't now." After the accident, he meant.

"Can't he join one of the aircraft bureaus?" Many retired Air Force generals took jobs at aircraft-design bureaus such as Tupolev or MiG.

"The aircraft business is dying," Uncle Vladimir said, a hint of sarcasm in his voice. "Our State resources are going toward building the missile shield, and landing men on the Moon. Now, if your father had moved to the Rocket Force . . ."

We both knew how silly that idea was; my father despised the Rocket Force, whose leadership had come from artillery: "Those who crawl will never fly," he was fond of saying.

"None of this matters until he regains his health, I suppose."

It was all I could offer, but Uncle Vladimir seized my hand as if I had just won a Lenin prize. "That's what we want."

In order not to arouse suspicion, he dropped me where the Yaroslavl Highway crosses the Ring Road, within walking distance of the bureau's main gate. The precaution was unnecessary: When I entered through the main gate, I saw half a dozen black Zils lined up, making their entrance. Some meeting of bigshots on one of the bureau's many projects, I assumed.

Uncle Vladimir's reluctance to be seen close to the gate did make me wonder, briefly, about the Korolev bureau's own First Department, the State Security representatives attached to every significant Soviet enterprise. I could not then have identified the head of the First Department—he would not have been secret, but the bureau had thirty thousand employees at that time, with dozens of "deputy directors" such as Artemov and Filin—but assumed he had approved my hiring. Had my papers come to him with the endorsement of State Security? Or just a clean bill of health?

Did anyone else in the bureau know that I served two masters?

Back in Department 90, I had barely resumed work when Triyanov loomed over my desk. "Back early? Good. How was your father?" I muttered something noncommittal. "Good. We have emergency visitors who want to talk about Voskhod. Come along."

Triyanov marched six of us to the main building, where we joined a presentation to the State Commission for Manned Spaceflight. The chair was none other than Georgy Tyulin, the Hammer's deputy.

Actually, it was about half the actual commission, normally about two dozen representatives from the ministry, the bureau, the Central Space Office, and others. Since the agenda of the meeting was the upcoming launch of two dogs aboard a Voskhod—by my thinking, half a spaceflight—the number of commissioners seemed about right.

There was a group of military officers present, sitting together down near the front. I recognized Gagarin and Saditsky, and thought again of Korolev's murder: Had these two seen him during their visit to his hospital? More suspects!

The subjects of these meetings were predictable: status of communications, tracking- and flight-control systems, booster, recovery forces, and so on. The plan was to fire two dogs into space aboard Spacecraft Number 5 in two weeks' time, around February 23. The poor animals were originally supposed to stay aloft for thirty days, but before the gang from Department 90 even found chairs, we could hear the commissioners deciding to cut that to twenty. For one thing, there was apparently some pressure to get the *manned* Voskhod launched and in orbit before the big Party Congress on March 29. Even assuming that everything went well with the dog flight, they would be landing around March 22, and there would be no time to analyze the data and make changes before a manned launch that same week.

It was also apparent that the life-support systems would not keep the pups alive for a month. At this point in the proceedings, Tyulin looked up from his spectacles and asked, "Wasn't there a critical report on crew systems from Department 90?"

As one, my half-dozen colleagues and Triyanov turned to me. I blushed, waiting with horror to be told to stand up and give an accounting of myself. Fortunately, Artemov himself took the microphone and said, "There are a number of open issues on life support and all departments are looking at them carefully. They do not affect the launch of Number 5, however."

The commission moved on to the next point. I couldn't help glancing over at the cosmonauts, where I caught Saditsky smiling at me. He gave me a formal salute, whether applauding my criticisms or mocking me, I couldn't tell. It was strange to think that he was just a few weeks away from rocketing into space history.

I wanted to speak with Saditsky, but as the meeting ended, the cosmonaut contingent left with Tyulin and several other uniformed types. I returned to the kindergarten with Triyanov and the others, only to be met by my roommate Lev Tselauri, furiously arguing with the guard to Building 11.

I immediately remembered that I had arranged for him to come and meet Filin—the pass had been good enough to get him through the gate, but insufficient to get him into any of the buildings. The problem was that I had not confirmed the meeting today with Nadiya, Filin's assistant, and with members of the State Commission wandering around loose, it was unlikely that Filin could take any time for Lev.

I felt terrible: He had traveled all the way from Reutov and even done a Stakhanovite job of shaving and wrestling himself into a tie. But I tried not to show my confusion, explaining about the emergency meeting, and reversing course back toward Filin's office.

Filin's woman lived for moments like this, where she had the power and I was a crawling serf. "As you can imagine," she said, with immense satisfaction, "his whole morning was taken up with this meeting, and I'm sure he won't have any time for student interviews." She made "student interviews" sound like "colonic surgery."

I was trying to think of how I could make this mistake up to Lev when Filin entered, looking surprisingly happy. "Yuri! You dodged a bullet in that meeting today."

"I was afraid of that."

"Several members of the commission, including Tyulin, would love to kill the Voskhod flights. But others want them to go ahead. You don't want to be in the middle of that war, my friend. Keep yourself out of the line of fire when you get to the cosmodrome."

Filin had, in passing, mentioned a possible trip for me to Baikonur, but I had assumed it was months in the future, and said as much. "No, we're leaving tonight! Didn't you hear the commission set a launch date?" He became aware of the bird-woman twitching at his side. "What *is* it, Nadiya?"

Both of us explained the matter of Lev's interview as Filin nodded with amusement. "Where is he now?"

"Out in the hall."

"Well, since he traveled all the way out here . . . bring him in." I tried not to show any sign of triumph as I brought Lev in, but I'm not sure I completely succeeded.

As Filin held the door for Lev to enter, he turned to me one final time: "What are you waiting for? Go and get packed!"

11 STATE SCIENTIFIC TEST RANGE NUMBER 5

My country's giant launch center, known to Western powers as Baikonur Cosmodrome, held as many outright lies as secrets, beginning with its name: Baikonur was actually the name of a town some two hundred kilometers to the northeast, the direction the early Sputniks, Lunas, and Vostoks were launched. Our Party leaders knew that American spy systems would be able to detect any launches, but hoped to conceal their source for as long as possible by pretending the site was farther along the trajectory than it really was.

This ruse was thought necessary because until 1960 the cosmodrome had the only pads capable of launching long-range missiles against America. Of course, on May Day 1960, an American U-2 spy plane was shot down over central Russia, after having flown directly over "Baikonur" with its cameras clicking away, and not for the first time.

Nevertheless, the facility known in bureau paperwork as State Scientific Test Range Number 5—to its growing number of residents as Tyuratam, Kazakh Soviet Socialist Republic, and to any friends and relatives who might try to write them as Post Office Box 500, Tashkent—*still* bore the entirely fictitious name of Baikonur Cosmodrome.

The facility had been dug out of trackless desert beginning in 1955, when our missiles began to outgrow State Test Range Number 4 near Volgograd. A commission had weighed sites in Perm (north) and Stavropol (south) before settling on the third choice of an open pit mine a few kilometers north of the railhead at Tyuratam on the Syr Darya River.

It allowed Sergei Korolev and the other early missile designers to fire their R-5s, R-11s, and R-7s over vast emptiness toward Kamchatka in the Far East, where warhead reentries could be tracked.

The construction was a miserable business: Winters in this desert could be brutal, and following a brief spring when tulips bloomed on the steppe, the crushing heat of summer followed, with temperatures easily climbing into the thirties and hot sand blowing. Have I mentioned the flies? The utter lack of trees?

Nevertheless, the labor battalions did their job, and the first launch-pad grew on the edge of an old quarry. Others began to sprout to the east and west—what the locals called the "left flank" and "right flank" as opposed to the "center."

Baikonur's growing pains were years in the past when our plane arrived late on the wintry afternoon of February 12 at the Outskirts Airfield at Leninsk, the name for the new military city surrounding old-town Tyuratam. To give you some idea of the scale of the place, we were still forty kilometers south of Baikonur's center and its Voskhod launch-pad. There wasn't a single structure to indicate that we were near the world's first spaceport.

We lived in a hotel in Leninsk, from which we were bused to the center every morning at seven A.M. The less said about the hotel, the better. What I remember most is that the bathroom in the room I shared with another bureau engineer was so foul (and the weather too cold to allow us to open the windows for fresh air) that we quit using it, preferring to use a common one on the floor below.

The drive took the better part of an hour, though halfway there we passed the first signs of the space complex itself, the huge tracking antennas of Area 21, situated on the only hill for kilometers around.

Area 2, the heart of the center, was dominated by the giant slab-sided assembly building. It was here that segments of the bureau's launch vehicles, brought by rail from the manufacturing plant in Samara (the launch vehicle itself) or from Kaliningrad (the upper stages), were assembled on a kind of giant rotisserie; the core of the launch vehicle would be rotated a quarter turn so that its four strap-on boosters could be attached. This was the genius of the Korolev team: In 1954 they had been ordered by the Kremlin to build a rocket strong enough to carry our heavy atomic bombs. But no country possessed a single-rocket engine capable of lifting the things, so Korolev's team clustered four simple, reliable engines in a central stage, then surrounded that element with four tapering strap-ons, each with four clustered engines of its own.

Shorn of its upper stages, the vehicle (in its basic form known as the R-7) looked more like a cone than a slim, needle-nosed rocket ship. Certainly it bore little resemblance to its distant parent, the Nazi V-2. Looks didn't matter; the Seven did its job admirably well. And in my first days at Baikonur, learning of this for the first time (because the configuration of the Seven was still secret from everyone in the world except American intelligence services), I was struck by its size, ruggedness, and reliability.

I spent a week inside the assembly building, climbing in and out of Spacecraft Number 5 in my stocking feet from dawn to after dark. I had many supervisors, each with a set of alligator clips or leads that needed to be plugged into various systems inside the spacecraft.

Even though a Voskhod had held three cosmonauts (admittedly, not in comfort), there was damned little room for me; unlike the test vehicle used on the aircraft tests, this was configured to hold two dogs. Naturally, the hounds couldn't be expected to sit in couches, so a spacecraft-within-a-spacecraft had been built, with two side-by-side harnesses that would hold the canine cosmonauts, who would be hooked up to an amazing number of wires, hoses, and so on.

Nevertheless, I did my best to follow the orders of engineers from our bureau as well as researchers from the medical institute, and a couple of scientists as well.

In my few spare moments I marveled at the lack of sterile conditions. I had by then seen pictures of American space vehicles being prepared for launch inside chambers that resembled hospital operating rooms by technicians in surgical masks, with the air pressure higher inside than outside, to keep dust particles from penetrating.

We all wore white smocks, but that was as far as the comparison went. People wandered in and out, smoking cigarettes. There were times when one or more of the doors stood open to the weather.

"Doesn't that contaminate the spacecraft?" I said to Yastrebov, one of my bureau colleagues, a testy man of forty who had no college education of any sort, but a thorough practical knowledge of space vehicles.

"Our electronics are so rugged that a little dust won't hurt them," he said, proudly. "Remember—in a few days this whole thing will have a bomb set off underneath it!"

I accepted the statement at the time, but then remembered how many puzzling failures had occurred with our spacecraft—such as eleven Lunas in a row—and wondered if a more controlled environment might have helped.

In any case, one exhausting week after my arrival at Baikonur, I stood shivering outside, mouth open in wonder at the rollout of the giant launcher with Spacecraft Number 5 safely tucked inside its shroud, when I felt an elbow in my ribs. "Need a warm-up?" A battered flask appeared in my hand, and I took a swig. The single shot of vodka—assuming it was vodka—spread warmth through my frozen bones, as if I'd just backed up to a fire.

My benefactor was a tall, scrawny sergeant I had seen wandering in and out of the assembly building running errands several times during the week. We had not actually spoken until now, when I thanked him. "If it's good enough for the Seven," he said, showing a mouth half-filled with steel teeth, "it's good enough for us."

For a moment I was afraid I had just taken a swig of honest-to-God rocket fuel—not an unusual occurrence, I was to learn later, since the Seven burned a mixture of liquid oxygen and good old alcohol. But I wasn't struck blind, and the sergeant seemed in good spirits, so I quit worrying.

The sergeant's name was Oleg Pokrovsky, and he had come to Baikonur with the first labor battalions almost eleven years ago. I couldn't guess his age—anywhere from a hard thirty to possibly fifty. "How many launches have you seen?" I asked.

He shrugged. "Two hundred, maybe. Here, there—" He nodded over his shoulder toward the right flank, where the even more gigantic pads for Chelomei's Proton stood on the horizon. "Out east, too." He pointed with his flask to the left flank. "Where we had the accident." I had heard rumors back in Kaliningrad, then seen a monument flash by on one of the bus rides, that some years back a missile had exploded on a launchpad while workers and various officials, including Marshal Nedelin, head of the Rocket Force, were present in the open. Something like a hundred of the poor souls, including Nedelin himself, had been vaporized in the thousand-degree flame. "How about yourself?" he said.

"This will be my first."

"Ah, a virgin." Pokrovsky laughed and offered me another swig, which I was happy to take, the sweet warmth of the first having faded away. "Now, follow me."

I had no chance to protest, since he was already turning away from the crowd watching the rollout.

Not far from the assembly were a few small cottages left over from the early 1950s, when several miners and their families lived here in a tiny settlement known as Zarya. Korolev himself lived here for weeks at a time during the first tests of the Seven as an intercontinental ballistic missile, as well as the launches of the first Sputniks, Lunas, and Vostoks.

The cosmonauts traditionally spent the night before their launches in one of the cottages, too. I thought of my friend Saditsky and his copilot, trying to go to sleep some cold, dark night a few weeks from now, knowing they were to be fired one hundred fifty kilometers up. Like being shot at sunrise!

Pokrovsky told me all this as he led me across the frozen ground, toward what, I didn't know. But then he stopped. "There they are."

Inside a fenced compound, a pair of husky mutts were at play. They seemed cheerful, their hot breath visible in the cold air. "Breezy and Blackie," Pokrovsky said. "Your cosmonauts."

It was my turn to laugh. I had been hearing about the "dog" flight for weeks and had spent days crawling in and out of a spacecraft designed to accommodate two pups in harness, but had never seen the animals themselves. And here they were. "They're going to take a ride few people will ever take," I said.

"Or would want to," Pokrovsky said with a grunt, helping himself to another swig. "I've seen two hundred launches, and I'll bet I've seen fifty of them go wrong."

True, of course. Rockets were notoriously unreliable. This might be one of the last times these dogs would romp at sunset in their short lives.

Even if things went as planned, was it fair to punish these dogs? What sins had they committed to deserve to be trapped in a sphere for three weeks and flung around the world three hundred fifty times?

Sergeant Oleg pulled a piece of greasy sausage out of a pocket, tore it in half and tossed it to the dogs, who happily devoured it.

"The doctors might not like that," I said.

"Are you going to report me?"

I had three shots of Sergeant Oleg's rocket fuel under my belt. It made me daring. "Of course not." At that moment I was called away by one of my coworkers, since our bus was leaving.

Behind me, the Voskhod launcher trudged toward its black gantry.

At Baikonur I saw Filin only from a distance, his white smock one of many moving in and out of the assembly building, or in passing at the hotel. But chance put us together on the bus back to Leninsk.

"I liked your friend, Lev," Filin announced.

"Can you find a place for him?"

Filin spread his hands. "It's too early. We have been trying to steal the lunar orbit mission from Chelomei, but we have no real plans. If I had a dozen like your Lev right now, to tell me just what Chelomei has learned, then we could make progress, but . . ."

Another engineer interrupted us at that point, ending our brief encounter. I realized I had done almost no spying during my week in Baikonur—had not even seen Artemov, for example. Would Uncle Vladimir feel I was failing?

I began to wonder how Marina was doing. And my father. I had not been in contact with either of them for a week at that point.

As for the launch of Breezy and Blackie aboard Spacecraft Number 5, I got no closer than the television screen in the support room of the launch control center. Right on time, the twenty engines in the launch vehicle's first stage lit up. As the rocket rose, the ingeniously designed tulips of the launch structure—four counterweighted arms—fell open. We could feel the roar even inside our protected building.

The newspapers called it a Cosmos satellite, the 110th in a series. But to me, it would always be Spacecraft Number 5, Breezy and Blackie's ship.

12 THE COMMAND AND CONTROL CENTER

Later the day of the launch, our whole team packed up and got back on the plane. But we did not return to Moscow. Our first stop was the Crimea, the city of Yevpatoriya, where the military had built a satellite tracking-and-control center that our bureau was beginning to use for manned flights. (A dozen kilometers away, there was a deep-space tracking site; we were forced to cluster them in the Crimea because it was one of the southernmost parts of Soviet territory.)

By the time we arrived, after dark, we knew that *Cosmos 110* had been placed in its initial orbit and that the upper stage had fired again to raise that orbit's high point to nine hundred kilometers. This would cause Breezy and Blackie to pass through the Van Allen radiation belts on each trip around the world, as part of another questionable scientific experiment. (Was it really a mystery, twenty years after Hiroshima, that radiation was likely to be harmful?)

The dogs were in a sleep period—induced by sedatives delivered to them by one of the many intravenous tubes I had helped install and test—timed to coincide with the eight hours out of every twenty-four in which we had no ability to track and control our manned spacecraft. In those days there were sixteen sites spread across the middle of the USSR, from Latvia in the west to Yelizovo on the far eastern Kamchatka Peninsula. All of the stations were farther north than desired, but that could be said of Baikonur and the rest of the USSR. We also had a pair of specially designed tracking ships on station in the Atlantic Ocean.

Even so, we could only communicate with our spacecraft two-thirds of each day.

Veterans of the trip from cosmodrome to tracking station had thought to buy food for themselves before leaving. As a first-timer, I was unaware of the total lack of facilities at Yevpatoriya, which was much smaller than Leninsk. We were to bunk in a military barracks near the airfield, and though I saw a couple of kiosks, they weren't open. And while we had escaped the snows of Moscow and Baikonur, it was still cold and rainy, not a night to be out.

Fortunately, one of my colleagues saw my empty hands and took pity on me, offering me half a loaf of bread and a pickle.

It was still raining in the morning, and the Crimea, my former sunny homeland, looked pretty dismal in the gray, cold light. I was able to get a proper breakfast at the officers' canteen next to the barracks, and went off to the tracking station on the bus.

The Yevpatoriya tracking site—Command and Control Center Number 16, according to the documents—was dominated by a huge dish, with another one being built right beside it. A long building about three stories tall held the primary control room, and it was here that I found myself stationed for an entire shift.

Along with a group of medical people, I was put in the last of four rows of tables. Many of the other tables had control panels on them; one or two even had television screens of some sort that displayed data from *Cosmos 110*. My "display" consisted of three thick notebooks. Presumably I was to leaf through them if so ordered.

Things were going well so far with *Cosmos 110*, at least as far as life-support systems went, so I had nothing to do but watch the various specialists, most of them military officers in their green uniforms, joking with each other and occasionally remarking on the progress of the spacecraft as its position was displayed on a giant display much like a movie screen. It was very crude. The big dog that represented *Cosmos 110* moved jerkily as the human operator manually placed it, much as you moved slides on an overhead projector. The data, which had to be radioed from other tracking sites, was often minutes out of date. I remember thinking that it was a miracle we had been able to put an object on the surface of the Moon with this technology.

During a dead zone in the flight, I was excused to get a drink of water, and saw cosmonaut Saditsky, who greeted me like an old friend. He was not wearing his uniform, and, in fact, looked tan, as if he had spent a week on vacation, which turned out to be true, in a way. "They sent us here from Moscow last week," he said, "and we had a few sunny days before the rain started." Apparently a Voskhod simulator of sorts had been set up in one of the other rooms in the building to allow Saditsky and his copilot, Kostin, to rehearse their mission time lines. "You get some idea of just how alone you are up there when you do that."

"So it's been valuable."

Now he shrugged. "Two days of it were valuable. They wanted to keep us here to do some work with the dogs. We have a hand controller that will allow us to turn their spacecraft up, down, and around." I didn't see a problem with that, so Saditsky slapped me on the back. "The damn high-rate antenna on the spacecraft didn't deploy. We can get medical readings from the dogs and send commands to the ship, but only if they're very basic, the equivalent of a few words." Low-rate commands were transmitted like Morse code. These were insufficient for steering the vehicle.

"That's too bad."

"At least I got some sun," he said, heading off.

"Good luck with the flight," I called after him.

"Don't hold your breath," was all he said.

This was the second time I had heard Saditsky make a negative comment about *Voskhod 3*. I was still trying to figure out why—fear?— when I returned to the control room in time to take part in my first crisis.

When *Cosmos 110* had come into radio contact again, the telemetry showed that the temperature inside the spacecraft was rising. It wasn't dangerous yet, but it had crept up and up over the past hour.

I had been excused by Yastrebov, the bureau's shift flight leader, but when I walked back in, you'd have thought I had allowed an assassin to take a shot at Brezhnev. "Have a nice walk?" Artemov snapped at me. He was surrounded by other bureau bigshots as well as a uniform or two. I could smell the liquor on his breath. "Why is the spacecraft over-heating?"

"I don't know," I said, reaching for the documents on my desk.

I saw Yastrebov close his eyes, like a cow waiting for the butcher's blow, as Artemov exploded. "Don't *know?* Then what the fuck are you doing in my control room?"

My father had a temper and I had been on the receiving end of some tirades in my life, but nothing quite like this. My face burned with shame, but I kept calm. I think I sensed that the others were embarrassed—certainly Filin, who could be seen over Artemov's shoulder, raised his eyes to heaven. "Maybe it's a stuck thermostat," I said.

"Maybe the dogs have built a campfire!"

I tried to keep calm, turning to Yastrebov. "No one has reported an anomaly in the life-support electrical system. . . ."

"Correct." Had it been a thermostat, there would have been some sign that power wasn't being used properly.

"Then it can't be one of these systems."

"You're sure of that?" Artemov was rocking back and forth on his feet, as if girding himself to launch an assault on me.

Filin spoke up then. "There could a dozen reasons, Boris. The communications problem could be affecting thruster firings."

As Artemov weighed this, one of the other officials tugged on his arm, leading him off. The mass of officials moved with those two, like a cellular organism searching for material to be absorbed.

I was shaking as I sat down. My heart was pounding so hard I could practically hear it as I continued looking through the documents.

Filin returned then, patting me on the shoulder. "He's drunk," he said quietly. "He saw you come in late, and went for you. It could have been anyone. God knows there are enough things going wrong." All I could do was swallow. "Why don't you take a couple of days off—go down to Simferopol," he said, taking out a pad and a crayon. "I'll write you a pass to the hotel there."

A hotel in Simferopol sounded attractive. Then I remembered that my father was "recovering" just over the mountains.

"Thank you very much," I said, "but could you write me a pass for Foros?"

13) THE RESORT

I don't wish to discuss the tribulations of my journey from Yevpatoriya to Foros, a distance of perhaps sixty kilometers. Remember that much of the Crimea, in those days, was mountainous and undeveloped, while the beach communities were restricted zones, either for exotic installations such as Command and Control Center Number 16, or for resorts and sanitaria catering to Party and military officials. There were few decent roads; there was almost no regularly scheduled bus service.

Nevertheless, armed with my important-looking pass from Filin that had been countersigned by the commander of the tracking facility, I was able to hitch a ride on a military truck up into the Koshka Mountains to Simferopol, where I simply flagged down a series of personal vehicles or farm trucks, offering the drivers rubles for a ride to the other coast.

It worked well enough, though the trip took six hours. Fortunately the rain had stopped; the sky sharpened to that lovely Crimean blue I remembered, and coming down the eastern side into Foros, I was stunned by the beauty of the vineyards and the sea beyond. This took my mind off the terror of the ride on a switchbacked roadway in the front seat of a very old truck with its very young driver. Time has mercifully robbed me of his name, though not the image of him hunched over the wheel, knuckles white, swerving dangerously close to death.

After a stop at a crossroads kiosk, I reported to the first militia station I came to—never a bad idea in any case—where the presentation of a bottle of vodka won me the likely location of the sanitorium catering to generals of the Air Force.

So it was evening when I arrived at the gate leading to the sanitorium itself. The guards there were not remotely impressed with my pass, and I had no money for further gifts of vodka, but they were willing to escort me as far as the lobby, where other guards watched me with skepticism as a message was relayed to Colonel-General Ribko.

It was a long wait, which I filled by eating my dinner, purchased at that earlier crossroads, and realizing that a number of unusual personal transactions were going on around me.

I could not have made this comparison in 1966, but the lobby of the sanitarium was like a resort in the West. Its tile floors, shaded lamps, and couches all faced a desk where keys could be got and messages left. It seemed busy when I arrived—pleasantly busy in a way that Russian public places are not, filled with groups of men in relaxed clothing, smiles on their faces. Also women. Many women, most of them my age or younger, all too willing to cling to the arms of these men.

I was seeing my first prostitutes.

I was not so naive that I thought prostitution to be a capitalist curse, though that's what they taught us in Komsomol. I had just never seen one, that I knew of. Certainly not a whole flock, with their tinkling bracelets, low laughter, floral perfume, high heels—

"Satisfied?"

I turned, and here was my father, standing there with his left arm out to one side in its cast, a look of distaste on his face. His color was better than it had been in the Aviation Hospital, though that could have been caused by annoyance rather than improved health.

"Don't get angry with me. I'm not running your resort." My encounter with Artemov, not to mention an aggravating day of Soviet-style travel, had stiffened my spine.

My father sensed this and hugged me. "You're right. I'm the one who should be ashamed."

"You're a single man. You're allowed to have girlfriends." Now I was teasing.

"Not like this. These girls are all married women, can you believe that? The director thinks that it cuts down on disease." Now he was shaking his head. "What kind of a wife or mother would do this? What kind of a husband would *let* her?"

I followed him out of this den of iniquity to his room. What immediately struck me was the light in the hallways—there *was* light. Even in Command and Control Center Number 16, half the lightbulbs were stolen and taken home by staffers. This impressed me as much as the cadre of married socialist sex laborers. Or nearly as much.

My father's room was also nice, certainly the equal of his apartment on Frunze Embankment. There was a big bed, nice curtains, several chairs and a couch, and the biggest color television I had ever seen outside of a space-launch control room.

And food. One of the side tables groaned with caviar, good white bread, and meat. There were a couple of wine bottles, too, unopened, I noted with relief. Cards wishing General Ribko a "speedy recovery," signed by officers at the headquarters of the Moscow Military District.

I was speechless with admiration, and hunger. "Go ahead," my father said, waving at the sideboard. "I can't eat all that stuff."

As I dug in, he turned off the TV, then sank into a chair with a big sigh. "Now, what the hell are you doing down here?"

I explained the launch of the dogs and my job at the command and control center. Before I had finished, he was already nodding. "I remember these control centers. They're trying to build a big one out in Bolshevo," he said, naming yet another town in the forest northeast of Moscow. "I don't see why they have to build their own cities."

"Come on, Papa, you know the ministry won't let them use the existing bases." I had heard stories on my visit to Yevpatoriya, how the Air Defense Force in particular, who had their own radar dishes all over the place, had protested bitterly at these interlopers from the Central Space Office, complaining that the tracking and communications stations interfered with their very important radar and aircraft beacons. As if allowing another dish at some site in the Ukraine would open the doors to American nuclear bombers!

It was all a matter of resources. You have no idea of how poor my country was in those days, twenty years after the end of the Great Patriotic War, in which an ungodly number of people had died—over twenty million, certainly, and possibly closer to thirty. The Nazis occupied the best of our lands for several years, stealing whatever they could carry and destroying the rest.

We had emerged from the rubble—"victorious!"—determined to have a level playing field with rich, far-off America under its "gentleman shopkeeper," Mr. Truman, and had devoted most of our resources to the development of nuclear weapons, tanks, aircraft, and missiles. Even our schools, such as Bauman, were essentially military academies, training "soldiers" for this work.

This was why the hallways at Command and Control Center Number 16 were often dark. Why I had to hitchhike across the spine of the Crimea. Why the Air Defense Force guarded its bases, which is to say its allotted apartments and food supplies, so tenaciously.

And why I felt a growing outrage at the luxuries I was seeing here in this sanitorium in Foros, building on the unease I had begun to feel when dining at the Stakhanov with Uncle Vladimir.

Maybe I was still a good, pure little Communist. I didn't mind being poor, as long as everyone was poor and we were working toward the same goal. "I see that whoever runs this resort doesn't have to worry about resources." It bothered me that my father, a notorious straight arrow throughout his career, often openly critical of Party and military "fat cats," was resting his broken arm in this decadent spa.

"Yes, well, I don't know how they do it." He cleared his throat, clearly casting about for a change of subject. "How is your spaceflight coming?" Had we been anywhere other than the private room of a Hero of the Soviet Union, a three-star general, I would have taken my father's reluctance to talk as a sign we were being monitored.

"The flight is going fine," I said, and changed the subject right back. "I didn't realize Foros was so nice. Is this where you and your buddies would always run off to?" Active-duty Air Force officers were required to take five weeks of leave every year. "Did Mama ever come here?"

That was a low blow, a sure sign that I had lost control of my mouth. My father's eyes narrowed. "*I* never came here until ordered last week," he snapped.

That, at least, sounded like my father. But I had had to goad him into being himself! Something was wrong with him, something beyond a broken arm. His spirit had been shattered. By what? "Sorry," I said. "How long before they remove the cast?"

"Six or eight weeks."

"Just in time for spring." He was not amused. I decided to risk another opening. "At least you won't be wearing it at your retirement party."

Now I had truly angered him. "Who said I was going to *retire?*"

Uncle Vladimir, for one. It didn't seem like a good time to mention the brother-in-law from State Security, however. "Well, you are approaching the age—"

"—The age where I could go to the reserve if I wanted to. I still have lots of work to do, like keeping you rocket boys from bankrupting the country!"

I accepted the criticism. "Fine. Five years from now, when you do finally retire, what would you like to be doing?"

"I'll never retire." Awkwardly, still trying to learn to shift his weight with a heavy cast throwing him off balance, he got to his feet and turned the television back on. We were just in time for *Vremya*, the evening newscast. And in case I didn't get the point, he turned to me and said, "I don't want to talk about this anymore."

That was the highlight of my visit. I slept that night on the floor, dreaming of a dark-eyed Foros whore climbing into my lap. I woke up early, while my father was still sleeping, and began hitching back to Simferopol and Yevpatoriya.

I was saddened by my father's condition. He had always been a presence in my life, but now I could see the day when, like my mother, he would no longer.

Cosmos 110 continued to circle the earth, sixteen sunrises and sunsets every day, with Blackie and Breezy trapped in their special couches, eating and drinking from tubes. I imagined Saditsky and his copilot, Kostin, doing the same thing a month or two months from now. At least they could tell each other war stories, if they hadn't used them all up in training.

By March 15, the twenty-first day of the flight, there were signs that systems were starting to fail. Because of the mysterious overheating, the atmosphere inside the vehicle was getting foul as fumes and particles were baked out of the equipment.

Presented with this data, the State Commission chose to end the mission at the first opportunity, on the twenty-second day. I was at my console in mission control when the command was given to fire *Cosmos 110*'s retro-rockets, thinking, poor dogs! Liftoff had been a terrible shock to them. What did they think of *this*, after three weeks of weightlessness?

The equipment section of the spacecraft separated, to our collective relief. On several occasions, including Gagarin's flight, the separation had not taken place as planned, at great risk to the mission. A spherical spacecraft like *Cosmos 110* could not safely go through the fires of reentry with the conical equipment section still attached. It would start to tumble like a baton, heating unevenly and ruining its trajectory.

As *Cosmos 110* dived into the atmosphere, it created its own cloud of ionized gases, which prevented further radio communication. Now we had to wait for the recovery forces to report.

America's manned spacecraft splashed down in the ocean because America had a vast navy to deploy for quick recoveries. We did not. Our vehicles had to come down on land.

Gagarin and the other Vostok pilots had ejected from their vehicles, landing by personal parachute while the sphere, slowed by its own 'chute, hit rather harder. This method could not be used for a multi-manned vehicle—Voskhod-Cosmos had no ejection seats. Nor was it possible to build and safely deploy a parachute large enough to slow the five-ton ball sufficiently to prevent, as Korolev put it, "a week in the hospital" for the crew.

The bureau's geniuses had attached a second, smaller retro-rocket to the shrouds of the recovery parachute itself! As the spacecraft got close to the ground, a wirelike probe would spring out, hit the earth and trigger the rocket, which would fire for a second, enough to cushion the landing so that it felt like an elevator coming to ground.

We got word from the recovery forces that *Cosmos 110* had been sighted, that the parachute had deployed. The spacecraft's trajectory had been shallower than planned, and it had come down sixty kilometers short of the aiming point, southeast of the city of Saratov, at 5:15 P.M. The landing zone was fogged in, and the parachute rescue team didn't reach it until almost seven. The weather kept the recovery helicopters from landing until the next morning, but Blackie and Breezy were reported to be fine. A bit unsteady on their four legs, but healthy. They had survived their hundreds of visits to the Van Allen belt.

And cleared the way for Saditsky and Kostin to fly *Voskhod 3*. As we left Yevpatoriya under the light of a crescent Moon, a Moon where brave little *Luna 9* rested, we all felt we were about to catch up with the Americans, and then pass them for good.

14 PROGRAM L-1

I returned to Moscow on the afternoon of Wednesday, March 16. Triyanov, meeting our plane at Chkalov, told me to take a day off, a gift I appreciated, since I was technically still a student and there remained papers to write and exams to take. As a newly energized member of the Komsomol, there were also meetings of the school's Party committee to attend. I could even bore Marina with tales of my adventures at Baikonur and the Crimea.

I would have liked to bore Lev with them as well, but some job for the Chelomei organization was keeping him especially busy out in Reutov. Only the Omsk Twins were around, and all they wanted to hear about was the Crimean prostitutes.

Back at my desk in Department 90 that Friday, my first job was to write a report on all the decisions I made as a member of the flight support team during the dog flight. "Should I mention being chewed out by Artemov for no reason?" I asked Triyanov, who had already heard about the affair.

"If he had as much to drink as they say, he probably doesn't remember it. I wouldn't remind him." He had called me into his office to remind me to hurry up, since the manned follow-up to the dog flight was still looming.

"Oh, he was definitely drunk," I said. "In front of the generals and everyone."

"Artemov is a noted specialist in rocket fuels," Triyanov said, smiling faintly. "Besides, if you were sixty years old and staring into the open grave of your career, you'd drink, too."

"Would it be so bad for Artemov if Filin became the chief?" From Filin's jolly mood on the flight back, and the sudden deference shown him by other bureau employees and military space people, it was clear he was about to take over. The double success of *Luna 9*, which was Filin's alone, and of the dog mission, which he had championed over Artemov's objections, made him Korolev's true heir, a good engineer who was aggressive and—what Russians loved most—*lucky*.

And a murderer? That, too, was a Russian tradition.

"Not at first," Triyanov was saying. "You would have the usual congratulations all around, speeches about how Artemov will be his right-hand man. Then one day Artemov will be packed off to another institute, or to a university. He won't be happy taking orders from Filin, because he's not Korolev. And Filin will be unhappy that Artemov is unhappy."

"When will it happen?"

Triyanov shrugged. "There's still one big battle to be fought, about the lunar orbit program."

"I can't believe the ministry will let Chelomei keep it."

"Me, neither." He stood up, indicating that my time there was ended. "But I couldn't believe they gave it to that idiot in the first place."

I laughed at this, and was halfway out the door when Triyanov stopped me. "Yuri—have you had your tonsils out?"

"Yes." I wanted to ask why, but Triyanov intimidated me. More confused than ever, I left his office and returned to the kindergarten, where my senior colleagues were busy discussing the latest American space adventure.

On March 17, the Americans had launched another Gemini spacecraft, Number 8, piloted by astronauts Armstrong and Scott.

The two-man Gemini program had accomplished most of its original goals—to show that a manned spacecraft could change its orbit and rendezvous with another vehicle, to allow an astronaut to work in open space, and to keep a crew healthy and productive for four days, then eight, then fourteen.

The only remaining goal, and it was a terribly difficult one, was to link two spacecraft. If the Americans couldn't do this, their whole Apollo lunar landing program would be doomed, since it depended on making rendezvous and docking in lunar orbit.

Armstrong and Scott succeeded in docking their Gemini to an unmanned Agena vehicle within a few hours of launch, an impressive achievement that made me jealous.

Then disaster struck: A thruster on the Gemini started firing on its own, spinning the combined vehicles like a bullet. Mistakenly assuming that the problem was caused by the Agena's thrusters, the crew separated, and found themselves spinning faster now, with the added danger of a collision with the Agena.

Armstrong finally stopped the spinning, but to do so, he tapped into the fuel intended to steer Gemini through reentry. He and Scott were ordered to return at first opportunity, and they found themselves floating in the Pacific Ocean less than eight hours after their glorious launch from Florida.

It was the first time any manned spaceflight had been cut short by such an emergency—two of ours, by cosmonauts Popovich and Bykovsky, had been shortened by a day or two for less critical reasons, though no one knew this at the time—and the astronauts' escape from death overshadowed the triumph of the first docking in space. Our newspapers were very critical of the Americans for being so backward that they had to land their astronauts in the ocean, where they could easily drown. I guess this was considered more dangerous than almost being eaten by wolves in the Urals, like cosmonauts Belyayev or Leonov, or practically freezing to death in the wilderness outside of Saratov, like Blackie and Breezy.

The talk quickly turned to *Voskhod 3*. "It's too bad we have to let those dumbshit jet jockeys fly the thing," Yastrebov said. "They're only better than dogs because they can complain."

"How does that make them better?" another guy said, to much laughter.

I found this all disappointing—the contempt my fellow "test engineers" had for the military cosmonauts and Saditsky's clear reluctance to fly Voskhod. It all still looked like fun to me—dangerous fun, yes. Why couldn't everybody feel that way?

I got home late, and Lev came in even later, looking awful, as if he had slept in his clothes. More precisely, as if he'd been wearing them for days while not sleeping at all. "Let me make you some tea," I said, not that I was his mother.

"It's the least you can do," he said, collapsing into a chair in the kitchen nook. "Since your bosses have beaten us."

I knew he could only mean the lunar orbit program. "What happened?"

"The Hammer drove out to see Chelomei on Tuesday." That was the day *Cosmos 110* landed. "He told him the Military-Industrial Council was worried about our ability to deliver a manned spacecraft on schedule, and that we were going to have to let the Korolev bureau build it. Launching it on *our* Proton, of course.

"Chelomei practically tied him up and refused to let him leave the office until he promised to give us two more days to show him our progress." He yawned and let his head hang down. "Which is where I've been for the last forty-eight hours—wiring a test article so it looked like it could fly."

Lev didn't seem willing to admit that the council had been right. Chelomei *didn't* have a vehicle ready to fly, and wouldn't any time soon.

"The Hammer came back with a bunch of people from the council and they barely looked at it. So it's over. The first ship to fly around the Moon will be Korolev's."

"If it's not Apollo."

"The Americans are so busy fishing their astronauts out of the ocean that we can still beat them." That was Lev, competitive to the end.

I told him I was sorry, lying only slightly, then said: "Look, at least you got to meet Filin. He liked you, and he's probably going to take over the bureau. You can come there and build your Moon ship."

"Yes. And look like a traitor to all the friends I leave behind."

"Come on! You're still a student! People do get reassigned, don't they?"

He got to his feet, a bit unsteadily, as if he'd been drinking. "I'm going to sleep. Then I'll think about it."

Lev slept most of the weekend. The Omsk Twins went out of town, so Marina spent the night, which was something entirely new and pleasant. I returned to the bureau the next week and buried myself in work with new energy, ready to get *Voskhod 3* flying in spite of all its critics, anxious to storm the Moon.

By Monday, March 28, I had even done more work on my dissertation, and wanted Filin to see it, so I contrived a visit to his office. Naturally, I also hoped to eavesdrop on activities that were none of my business.

I could tell immediately that something was wrong. There were voices coming from inside Filin's office. Many voices. And Filin's bird-woman was so subdued I assumed she had suffered a death in her family. "He'll see you when they leave," she said, in a voice so pathetic I almost wanted her to be brusque and territorial.

After twenty minutes, Filin's door opened and eight or nine people came out, mostly bureau engineers and the usual brace of military officers. And one unexpected person—Artemov himself, who seemed momentarily surprised at my presence. Our eyes met for the slightest moment; he blinked, as if a stray shaft of sunlight had pierced his retina, then turned away and continued his conversation.

Afraid of what I'd find, I didn't want to go into Filin's office. It was almost as bad as I'd feared: Filin, normally lanky, was bent at his desk like a question mark.

"Hello, Yuri." He smiled sardonically. "Did you see the big parade?" Out of his office, he meant.

"It was hard to miss."

I closed the door. The office smelled like cigarette smoke and stale sweat. I handed Filin my papers, which he accepted numbly. Then he seemed to unwind, stretching, as if awaking from a bad dream. "It's very bad," he said, sighing with finality.

"I don't understand," I said, and I truly didn't. Filin should have been like a conquering general returning to Rome in triumph.

He waved toward the departed Artemov and company. "The medical institute had a disaster over the weekend. The Voskhod oxygen system had a failure on the nineteenth day of a simulated flight. So no one thinks we can fly that long."

"Eighteen days is still almost two weeks longer than we've flown so far."

"But only four days longer than the Americans have flown. And that's assuming we get even that far. Can you imagine what the Military-Industrial Council will be saying if we have to bring the cosmonauts back after ten days? Or a week? We'll look like failures."

"That's ridiculous."

"That's the business we're in, Yuri. Worst of all, this morning there was an accident at Baikonur, too." Having just visited the cosmodrome, I felt an irrational sense of alarm, as if I had a personal investment in what happened there. Well, perhaps I did. "A rocket failed."

"That happens frequently."

"It was the same sort of rocket we use to launch Voskhod. Had there been a crew aboard, they would have been killed. If the telemetry is right, we have a generic problem that will require weeks to fix."

"*Voskhod 3* won't be hurt by a few delays. It will give us time to fix the oxygen system."

Filin smiled at me as if I were a child, or worse, an idiot. "Every delay takes that flight one day closer to cancellation."

"Why do they want to cancel it? Haven't they already paid for the spacecraft?"

"It's the *risk*, Yuri. Not only the real risk of a disaster, but the risk of losing face by not breaking an American record. And there is money to be saved on recovery forces and salaries for tracking personnel, not to mention a whole rocket, which could all be used for another program." He cleared his throat. "Artemov says we need the money for our new lunar program, the one we stole from Chelomei. Program L-1."

"Won't the ministry give us the money they were going to give Chelomei?"

Now Filin laughed out loud. I guess the question was so ridiculous, he couldn't begin to answer it. He rose, indicating that my time was up, squeezed my shoulder again, and headed me toward the door. "You may be asked to do some unusual things in the next few weeks, Yuri."

"What kind of things?"

"Tasks. Tests. Do them. It will all turn out to your benefit, I think."

I had no idea of what Filin was talking about for several days. When I did get an inkling, it was too late to ask him. . . .

Filin had checked himself into the Kremlin Hospital.

15 | THE MEDICAL INSTITUTE

Department 90 of the Korolev bureau had been formed in the spring of 1964, specifically to train civilian engineers and doctors as flight-crew members. Colonel Stepan Triyanov, a test pilot at the military institute at Chkalov then in the process of being "transferred to the reserve," had been hired to run it.

In his first few months, Triyanov successfully prepared Feoktistov, one of the bureau's best engineers, as well as a civilian scientist and a doctor from the medical institute, to serve as benign spacecraft passengers, if nothing else. Feoktistov and the doctor, whose name was Yegorov, wound up making that first Voskhod flight along with Vladimir Komarov, one of the best cosmonauts from the military's team.

Naturally, the younger engineers of the bureau thought this was the dawning of a new day, when healthy, well-educated technicians would push aside the short, hard-drinking, relatively uneducated jet jockeys—not to mention the thoroughly uneducated female parachutist—who had piloted the Vostoks.

Five hundred employees of the bureau swamped Korolev and Triyanov with applications to be included in the next space crew. This turned out to be 497 too many. Forced to be ruthless by the realities of flight opportunities, Triyanov simply excluded those who a) had not been with the bureau for at least five years or b) had no higher education. The bureau's State Security department was allowed to reject applicants for lack of Communist Party or Komsomol work. These strictures eliminated a couple of hundred right there.

What really separated the true cosmonaut candidates from the pretenders was the centrifuge. Triyanov took a few busloads of applicants over to Star Town to witness a test run on one of the military guys. It was bad enough to see someone whirled round and round at the end of that big arm to the point of obvious distress, but the regime also called for the cupola containing the subject to be *tumbled*. The number of candidates melted like snow in spring—just from the *thought* of the centrifuge, not the test itself.

Eventually Triyanov found a hardcore bunch of about thirty who were qualified and willing, and in 1965 he shipped them into Moscow to the Institute for Medical and Biological Problems, the civilian center for space medicine. A dozen passed the tests.

There was no age limit, because Triyanov considered himself a cosmonaut candidate. He managed to squeak through the IMBP tests, too, though I don't know how: I had heard he was actually blind in one eye. Perhaps the doctors were intimidated by him.

These thirteen were told that they were going to be transferred to the Department 90 team "any moment now," but nothing happened for months.

Well, what happened was that General Kamanin, the military chief of cosmonaut training, who had accepted Feoktistov and Yegorov on the Voskhod crew only at gunpoint, found out about Korolev's plans for a civilian cosmonaut team, and screamed all the way to the Military-Industrial Council.

He was able to wave in their faces a 1960 Politburo decree giving the Air Force the sole right to select and train crew members for Soviet manned spaceflights.

He even went so far as to show that the Air Force was opening the cosmonaut team to other areas of Soviet society: He planned to train engineers and scientists at Star Town right alongside his pilots. All during 1965, Kamanin had been running his own set of medical examinations—through the Aviation Hospital, which, conveniently, reported to *him* through the Air Force chain of command—with the idea of selecting forty new cosmonauts.

But then it became clear that there was no room for forty new cosmonauts at Star Town—there weren't enough apartments, instructors, or equipment. Nor, since there were already thirty cosmonauts at the center, was there likely to be a *need* for that many crew members for years.

So Kamanin cut the number in half, and what do you know? The ones who got selected were mostly young Air Force jet jockeys! Yes, there were several engineers—all military. And a physician—military. No scientists. No civilians.

This, then, was the situation in the spring of 1966, as *Voskhod 3* waited and waited, as Program L-1 took its first steps, as the "advanced" spacecraft Soyuz took shape: Kamanin's center had fifty military cosmonauts, ranging from the famous Gagarin and Titov to the more obscure Saditsky, to a score of anonymous candidates still in their early training.

Korolev's bureau had a dozen engineers, and Triyanov, assigned to Department 90, but not called "cosmonauts" for fear of provoking Kamanin.

It was at this time that Triyanov asked me if I would go to the IMBP for medical tests, to see whether I would qualify as a full-fledged member of the department.

When I broke the news to Marina the Sunday before I started, she was completely against the idea. Not of flying in space, since that was only a fantasy at this time.

She didn't want me to turn myself over to the doctors at the IMBP at all. "Why not?" I demanded. "These are the best medical specialists in the country!"

"Then I pity our country," she snapped. She had traveled in the West and seen their clinics and hospitals. Ours, she said, were medieval by comparison. Given what I knew of Russian hospitals from Korolev's death, and my mother's long illness, I should have agreed. But I was too excited about my new adventure to think straight.

Ultimately Marina relented, and kissed me for good luck.

Thinking of hospitals and the fate of Korolev reminded me of my "other" responsibilities. I had no way of knowing just how closely Uncle Vladimir's people tracked my movements—other than having me followed when he wanted to meet me—and, in fact, had no official way of contacting him.

So I went down to the key lady's desk and begged the grandmother on station that Sunday night to let me use the telephone, calling Uncle

Vladimir at the only home number I knew, that of his dacha. To my amazement, he answered with a single word: "Yes."

I identified myself, and immediately noticed a change in his manner. He became jolly Uncle Vladimir talking to his nephew, not some mysterious force in the organs of State Security. "Yuri! Nice of you to call. What's going on? Is your father back yet?" And more of that kind of thing.

I took this as a signal to avoid any overt mention of my work for him. "I didn't know whether you'd heard or not, but I'm going to be at a medical institute for the next week undergoing some tests."

He hadn't heard—or so he let me think. "You're not ill, are you?"

"No. It's just part of my work."

We did more family chitchat, and I hung up. His last words to me were, "Call me when you get out."

There were five other bureau engineers who showed up at the IMBP on Khoroshev Lane in northwest Moscow, on the southern edge of the Central Airfield, the following Monday. Among them was Yastrebov, who had worked on the *Cosmos 110* support team with me. I ran into him at the Begoyva metro station and walked with him to the hole-in-the-wall entrance to IMBP, which had more barbed wire and grim-faced guards than Baikonur itself. (I learned years later that the institute was bordered on three sides by the headquarters of the military intelligence directorate.)

Both of us carried small bags containing toiletries and a change of clothes. We had been told to prepare for five days of examinations, though we were also warned that tests could be extended into the following week.

Inside the compound we were directed to a side building that looked much like a pre-Revolution family residence. The house had actually been a kindergarten building until the creation of the IMBP. On the first floor was a classroom of sorts, where we were greeted by a Dr. Vasilyev, a man in his thirties, with dark, slick-backed hair and glasses, who told us that we were not patients at the IMBP, but "test subjects," since the data collected from our examinations would be used in medical research papers. "There is a small bonus for this work, which will be paid to you at the end of your tests."

"If I like it here, can I come back again?" Yastrebov said, jokingly.

Even Vasilyev smiled. "First see how you like it."

There were forms to fill out—not only medical histories, but releases, security pledges, and soon. After a couple hours of that, we were shown our rooms on the second floor, where we got rid of our clothes, trading them for track suits. For the next week, everyone we saw either wore white lab coats or these track suits. Then we were split up to various rooms for the expected tests: heart rate, blood pressure, eyesight, urine samples. We were also measured, not just our height and weight, but in several other parameters, such as the distance from shoulders to hips; we had to be able to fit into the acceleration couches of a Soyuz, and into pressure suits.

After a lunch of porridge, which left us wanting more to eat, there were X rays and chest-thumpings and reflex tests—tedious, yes, but nothing unusual. During a break I happened to meet Yastrebov in the hallway. "This is nothing," I said.

"You idiot. They haven't even *started* on us. All this does is help them to identify your remains."

That chilled me. Obviously Yastrebov, who worked with men who had already gone through the IMBP, knew more than I did. But what could they really do? There was no room in the little kindergarten house for large torture equipment—not unless they had their own Lubiyanka-style basement.

Sure enough, my next test was the vestibular apparatus—imagine a dentist's chair equipped with a complete set of chest straps and restraints. I was belted into this thing, which then began to rotate to my left for a minute, all the while having to answer moronic questions from the examiner. ("What is twelve times eleven?") Fine. But then the chair suddenly reversed direction for another minute, with more questions to be answered. So far, so good. When it stopped, I was unstrapped and ordered to bend down and touch the floor, then straighten up.

I almost passed out. As I felt the room swirl and my stomach turn over, I noticed the examiner writing down my reactions.

Before the end of the day, I was locked into a soundproof room and told to describe what sounds I heard, if any.

One of the bureau candidates was dismissed that first day. I remember seeing him pack up, a wistful look on his face. His dream of space-flight was over.

Over the next few days we survivors would be stretched on a tilt table for over an hour, with the angle of tilt being changed according to some diabolical pattern, and our reactions to various angles duly noted. We would be encased in a kind of barrel from the waist down with the air pressure being bled out of the barrel. (Another one of us passed out after this test, and went home that evening.) We put on masks to measure our exhalations, then pumped away on a special bicycle. After every test, we would repeat the blood-pressure and heart-rate checks. The goal, we realized, wasn't just to test us to destruction, but to evaluate our organism's response to all these stresses.

There were also several sessions with psychologists of one kind or another, being quizzed about everything from what we saw in ink blots to what we thought of each other and the doctors examining us. One psychologist was deliberately insulting, hoping to judge our quickness to anger.

On Thursday the four of us were bused out to the cosmonaut training center for a ride on the centrifuge. After my experience with the bureau's "weightless" airplane, I was worried less about this test than any of the others, though I confess I had a bad moment once I was locked into the very tiny cupola and waiting to be swung on the end of the arm, the unfortunately named "dead-man switch" that would stop the test clutched in my hand. But it all started slowly, with the G loads building gradually, as they would on a Voskhod or Soyuz launch, peaking at five Gs, when the first stage would be low on fuel while the twenty engines were still blasting away. Then there was a drop-off, simulating the burnout of the first stage and its separation, followed by an immediate multi-G jolt as the supposed second-stage engine blasted to life.

It was the longest six minutes I spent in a week of many stretched, unpleasant minutes. I unbuckled myself and climbed out of the cupola with new sympathies for Blackie and Breezy. At least *I* had known what was happening to me.

The centrifuge test disqualified a third member of our shrinking team. The tests on Friday took us to one of the big, gray buildings in the IMBP compound, where we walked past a chamber under construction; it was intended to take three different "test subjects" on a simulated space mission lasting one year.

That afternoon the three "survivors" were gathered back in the classroom, as Dr. Vasilyev presented two of us—including me—with documents stating that we had passed the first stage of the medical commission.

Yastrebov hadn't flunked, but he was going to have to repeat some tests in the next week. He didn't look happy about it.

I rode home to Bauman with the evening crowds, feeling light and relaxed, as if I'd crawled out of a pool after a long swim.

On Monday I walked into Triyanov's office and proudly presented him with my IMBP documents. He barely looked at them as he announced, "*Voskhod 3* has been canceled. Artemov is the new head of the bureau."

16 THE SUCCESSION

I couldn't hide my surprise, my shock. "Why?"

"Why Artemov, or why no Voskhod?" Triyanov was inhumanly calm, a gift, I was sure, from his days as a test pilot. At that moment I could never hope to emulate him.

"Either! Both!"

"Well, they're the same thing. A month ago the big bosses had decided that the bureau was going to be run by Tyulin. Everybody was in agreement that no one man could replace Korolev, especially since even he had suffered a string of failures. Tyulin would break up the bureau into smaller units while the core—including this department—would concentrate on manned flights to the Moon, especially with Chelomei's lunar orbit mission given to us."

"That's what I don't understand: The ministers thought the bureau was being mismanaged, but still they wanted us to take over the Moon program."

"Clans. Chelomei's bureau is just as badly mismanaged, and he has the added burden of being hated by Ustinov, who felt that with an old pro like Tyulin as boss, our bureau—with some radical restructuring— could still do the job, which is to beat the Americans. Never forget that *that* is the goal.

"Our good friend Filin screwed everything up by succeeding with *Luna 9*, and with the dogs. Suddenly the bureau didn't look so mismanaged."

"But, shouldn't that have worked to Filin's advantage? Artemov was opposed to the dog flight, but it worked great!"

"In a perfect socialist paradise, it would have all been to the glory of Filin. But Filin's Jewish mother has always kept him from making the kind of friends Artemov makes, such as the Hammer himself."

I guess I had been blind. Filin's Jewish heritage never seemed relevant. Certainly he gave no outward sign of any suspicious religious activity, unlike my father and even Uncle Vladimir, who were always saying, "Thank God," "God be praised," like old Orthodox peasants.

"So Filin's good luck all landed on Artemov."

Triyanov smiled, like a teacher hearing a student recite a multiplication table. "Now you're getting it. It will still take weeks for things to play out . . . the Hammer has to wait for the Party Congress to distract Ustinov before Artemov can be officially crowned the new king." (This was a little pun on Korolev's name, which translated as "king.") "But you will see him everywhere now. And, much as I like Filin, it's good news for our little department here."

"How?"

"Korolev wanted to create his own cosmonaut team, but chose not to challenge the Air Force directly. Tyulin wouldn't, either, since he's still a military man at heart. Filin really doesn't care.

"But having pulled off this coup, Artemov is going to look for another battle, and he has always despised the military. He'll try to kick their pilots off the crews completely, you watch."

All these politics and machinations were too much for me. I wanted to be back at my desk worrying about numbers. Better yet, I suddenly wished I could go back to a classroom at Bauman, preferably about my second year, when I was happiest.

"Now, what is this?" Only then did Triyanov look at the certificate from IMBP I had placed on his desk. "You passed. Congratulations. How did you like it?"

"I learned a lot."

Triyanov laughed. "Very diplomatic." He slid the certificate back at me. "Well, when they picked the first military cosmonauts, no one had any idea what they would face, so they got perfect physical specimens and didn't worry about intelligence.

"Pretty soon they discovered that intelligence was as important as physical fitness, which is how Feoktistov managed to sneak in. You're lucky, Yuri: You have both, with the added bonus of youth. You could be making trips into space to the end of the century. You could walk on Mars."

I remembered that Triyanov himself wanted to fly in space, at the age of fifty-five.

"There are lots of people around here with more experience," I said, thinking of Yeliseyev, Kubasov, Grechko, some of my senior colleagues.

"Yes. They will get the first chances. They'll become Heroes of the Soviet Union. But you will have more fun, I think."

I stood to leave, then realized that Triyanov was still looking at me. "Is there something else?"

"I was a little worried about you, Yuri. You came out of nowhere, like someone's favored son. I handed you the shit jobs just to see if you'd do them, and you have. I don't care who your uncle is—" For a moment I thought he meant Uncle Vladimir, but he was speaking generally. "—take my advice and follow your better instincts. Over time, it is the only way."

Was he warning me? Embarrassed and confused, I walked back to the kindergarten, where several other engineers were hard at work in groups, on the telephone, moving in and out with great purpose. Something I, at that moment, did not have. Or, rather, I had too many purposes. To better myself. To satisfy Uncle Vladimir. To make Marina happier with me. To make my father happier with me.

That night as I left the bureau and joined the legions marching to the Podlipki Station, I felt the first warmth of spring in the air. Places on the broken sidewalks and muddy streets were suddenly bare. Steam rose from heating pipes and chimneys, covering everything in a light fog, the way I always imagined London to look in the stories of Sherlock Holmes. I wished for Mr. Holmes's brilliance that night, but felt only a mental fog.

I had not seen Marina since being released from the IMBP; impulsively, hoping to clear my mind or, at least, change my luck, I stopped at her building across the river.

Since she had resisted the idea of my medical tests, relenting only at the last minute, I had telephoned her first thing Saturday to tell her the good news of my hard-won certificate. Hearing that I had passed them did not ease her worries—it seemed to have the opposite effect. Suddenly she was "busy" that day. And Sunday.

And as she came down the stairs, she was already dressed to go out, and looked quite severe. If the appearance hadn't been warning enough, she actually turned her face away when I tried to kiss her. "So now they're going to shoot you into space."

"No. The real reason for the medical testing was so that I could do my work in the department. Many things would have to happen before I could become a cosmonaut. I'm still not even a full-time employee at the bureau." As I said all this, I could tell she wasn't listening. "Is something else wrong?"

She shook her head forcefully, but unconvincingly. "I'm just worried about everything." Then she did kiss me, which was enough to quell my growing anger. Maybe I was being selfish: Marina had troubles that had nothing to do with me. Her schoolwork. Her job.

"Where are you going?"

"Alla and I were going to a Party meeting." Alla was a rabid young Communist friend from Marina's hometown.

"Since when did I become less important than cookies and punch with the Komsomol?"

"I promised her I would go. I've made excuses the last couple of times."

"Well, let me walk you."

I felt our whole relationship hanging on her answer. "Please don't," she said, after a painful moment. She busied herself with her scarf and gloves. Then, with another kiss, she went out into the dark spring evening.

I thought about following her, then rejected the idea as juvenile. She clearly didn't want to see me right now. Without saying so, she was giving me an ultimatum: Give up the bureau, especially the idea of being a cosmonaut, and she would come back to me.

But giving up that idea not only meant betraying my soul, it also carried a very real risk. . . .

It also meant going against Uncle Vladimir.

INTERLUDE

Winter

My first sessions with Yuri Ribko took five long evenings at the Rendezvous in Korolev. It was somewhere around the end of the first discussion that I decided he had a story worth listening to, and I began to record the tale. I went back to the U.S., and contact between us ceased.

Then, unexpectedly, less than two months later, I found myself flying back to Russia. I telephoned Ribko, who agreed to meet again. Soon a pattern was established: Ribko would arrive late, grudgingly accept a beer, then insist on complaining about some new American slander against Russia on the International Space Station project, which had stalled because of the failure of the Russians to live up to an agreement to build certain components to an agreed-on schedule.

One night in our second session I got fed up. "If anyone should be complaining, it's America. Your government hasn't put a goddamn dime into the service module and right now it's going to delay the whole project by a year or more."

His face flushed and he reached for the bottle. "First of all, you expect us to give up our space station—" Good old Mir was still in orbit that winter, nine years beyond its design life and eighteen months after everyone on the planet thought it was finished. "—and surrender to yours." He smiled. "I'm not saying this is my personal view. But it is a view which would be shared in this neighborhood." The Rendezvous was on Tsiolkovsky Street, a few blocks north and east of Russia's Mir flight control center, which itself was just across the street from the gigantic facilities of the Energiya Corporation, what used to be Experimental Design Bureau Number 1, aka the Korolev Bureau. "And we hear that your Boeing company is as far behind on *its* module as we are on ours. But everyone prefers to blame the Russians."

With that, he clinked his beer glass against mine. "Through adversity to the stars," he said. After that, things went more quickly, though I had to miss a night because my editor wanted me to visit some nightclub on Kutuzov Prospect, which had the tallest, thinnest, most dangerous-looking women I've ever seen.

So there was a break in Yuri's narrative, ending in April 1966, with the cancellation of *Voskhod 3*, with Artemov as the new leader of the Korolev bureau, with new problems on the home front.

He wanted to pick up the story early the following year. "What happened in between?" I said. "It must have been important."

"What happened was one success after another for America, and one hidden failure after another for us."

Well, from my knowledge of space history, I knew that after the quasisuccessful docking flight of Armstrong and Scott on *Gemini 8*, NASA had flown four Gemini missions, each one aimed at improving techniques for rendezvous and docking, and for EVA.

Not that these missions were routine. Stafford and Cernan on *Gemini 9* had seen their Agena docking target fail to reach orbit—and an inert replacement failed to shed its aerodynamic shroud, so the crew could only rendezvous and not dock. Cernan's EVA had turned out to be pretty madcap, too. He was supposed to strap himself into a rocket-powered backpack and fly around. To protect Cernan's fabric pressure suit from the hot gases of the backpack's rockets, engineers had added a layer of wire mesh to his legs! Fortunately, Cernan's suit overheated and, blinded by sweat, he was unable to don the backpack at all, probably saving himself from an ugly and fatal accident.

Later missions—*Gemini 10, 11* and *12*, crewed by Young and Collins, Conrad and Gordon, Lovell and Aldrin—went progressively better.

At the same time, the U.S. matched the accomplishment of the bureau's *Luna 9* by soft-landing *Surveyor 1* on the Moon on June 2, 1966, and even improved on it: Surveyor landed under its own rocket power, like a future manned spacecraft, where *Luna 9* had bounced on the surface like a basketball. The U.S. did the Russians one better by scouting Apollo landing sites from above with two wildly successful lunar orbiter missions.

The first Apollo launcher and spacecraft were tested in 1966, too, though without astronauts aboard. The next steps were manned Apollo flights, scheduled to begin in February 1967, and the test of the giant Saturn 5 launcher.

As for the Russians—

They tried their own lunar orbiters, modifications of the E-6. The first, called *Luna 10*, was a success in April–May 1966, though it didn't carry cameras. *Luna 10* did manage to serenade the delegates of the 23rd Party Congress with a rendition of the "Internationale" played from lunar orbit, however.

The next orbiter crashed into Kamchatka. The third got safely on its way to the Moon, but suffered a systems failure en route. Failure. A fourth, *Luna 12*, finally carried Soviet cameras into lunar orbit.

A follow-up to *Luna 9*, *Luna 13*, bounced onto the Moon's surface near the crater Seleucus on Christmas Eve.

Work proceeded on unmanned tests of the L-1 and its Earth orbital precursor, called Soyuz.

Chelomei's Proton launcher, following two initial successes, failed in late March, grounding it for several months.

And at Baikonur, the assembly building and launchpads for Russia's giant Moon launch vehicle, the Carrier, took shape.

As the new leader of the Korolev bureau, which was given the clunky new name of the Central Experimental Design Bureau of Machine-Building, Boris Artemov plowed ahead with Soyuz, with L-1, with the Carrier rocket. He also defied General Kamanin and the Soviet Air Force by creating his own cosmonaut team under Stepan Triyanov. As part of the bureau's reorganization, it became known as Department 731.

Meanwhile, Yuri Nikolayevich Ribko graduated from the Bauman Higher Technical School and in June 1966 became a full-fledged member of Department 731.

SCORPION 2

ENEMY ACTIVITY REPORTED

17 THE LAUNCH

Baikonur had changed noticeably since my first trip there, not eight months in the past. Great strides had been made in construction of the Carrier rocket facilities: The giant assembly building, just a skeleton of girders in February, was now enclosed, solid, a monolith on the horizon.

Beyond that, the superstructures and lightning towers of the twin Carrier launchpads rose like church spires. I couldn't help but be impressed. I had no idea of what the Carrier itself looked like, but if the assembly building and towers gave any clue, it was two or even three times taller than the Soyuz launch vehicle—which seemed gigantic enough to me as I watched it roll out to the pad at Area 1.

Other than the incessant construction, the endless stream of trucks coughing their way past the facilities at Area 1, Baikonur felt the same. I had first come there in March, now I was here in December, with snow on the ground, leaden-gray skies overhead, a cold wind sweeping across the steppe.

The cold wind matched my personal life. Marina and I had barely seen each other in six months. We had met three or four times after our argument about my cosmonaut medical tests, but with my graduation and the end of her studies for the year, she went home to Orel for several weeks, while I plunged into full-time work as a flight tester for the new Soyuz spacecraft. Marina had not returned to Bauman immediately; her "translating" skills had required her to go abroad on a long-term assignment in Germany. She had sent me several letters and postcards care of the bureau's new "postbox"—Number V-2572—so I still had hope.

As I had with my father. He had shed his cast in time for my graduation, and seemed more fit and happier than I had seen him in many years—certainly since the death of my mother. I realize it was because he had lost weight and added some color during his forced rehabilitation. But when we saw each other during that summer—not often—he was not drinking. He didn't speak about his work, even to the extent he had, so I had no idea of what was going to become of him. Retirement still loomed.

Then there was Uncle Vladimir. I never expected to see him again, after my pathetic career as an investigator for State Security had obviously fingered the wrong man—Filin—as Korolev's murderer.

But I underestimated Uncle Vladimir's compassion, and tenacity. Shortly after my graduation, on one of the most beautiful summer days I can ever remember seeing in Moscow, he asked me to meet him in Izmailov Park, where half of the population of the city was busy shopping at the flea market.

Picture this: a bulky man in an expensive suit picking his way among the stalls, bartering with farmers offering cucumbers, lettuce, strawberries, stuffing his prizes into his bag. Meanwhile, two obvious agents of State Security follow at an indiscreet distance. What were the farmers thinking? That Uncle Vladimir was some provocateur from the Central Committee, testing the limits of "free market"? Or perhaps some important un-person, like former Premier Khrushchev, being let out for some air?

I immediately apologized for sending his investigation down the wrong road. He shrugged it off. "In the old days there would have been a rush to judgment. Someone would have been punished instantly— whether he was guilty or not. This way takes longer, but it's better."

There was a conversational detour while he engaged a farmer from Davidovo about some kind of peppercorn, I believe. "Aren't you going to buy anything?" he said suddenly. Before I could explain why not—I had not known we were coming here; was spending all my time out in Kaliningrad, eating at the bureau canteen—he went on: "You've piled up a tidy sum of money working for us, you know. Sasha!" He turned to one of his assistants.

I had not known I was getting paid as an informant for State Security. It only made me feel worse, especially when Uncle Vladimir pressed fifty rubles into my hand. "Get yourself some decent vegetables." So I shopped, too, under Uncle Vladimir's supervision. "I hope you'll have the chance to spend more time with Artemov. He has many powerful friends, and it's made him arrogant. Possibly even dangerous."

That had become quite obvious, after his coup against Filin, the Hammer, and poor Chelomei. "But he's head of the whole bureau!"

"Oh, Yuri," he said, patting me on the shoulder. "You're now a member of his pet department. You'll see a lot of Artemov as time goes by."

There was something in the casual way he said this that triggered a small epiphany for me: Uncle Vladimir's reach into the bureau or the ministry had not only gotten me hired, he had gotten me tested at the medical institute and thus qualified for Artemov's little cosmonaut team! I was even more impressed with his power that day, and more in doubt of my own skills than ever before: Had Uncle Vladimir *arranged* for me to pass the medical exams? Maybe I was really unhealthy, unqualified, in over my head?

I had come to Baikonur this time as a crew equipment specialist for Soyuz, in spite of the fact that there would be no crew aboard this mission. There should have been. Back in the spring, once the succession wars had ended, the ministry had forced Artemov to agree to dock a pair of unmanned Soyuz vehicles in October, and to fly two manned missions together in December.

Well, ministers can order, but machines will do what they want. The first Soyuz was not launched until November, and quickly demonstrated that there was room for improvement in its design. Within a few hours of launch, as the team at Baikonur was getting ready to roll out the second Soyuz to its pad, it became clear that a thruster on the orbiting vehicle had become stuck—just like the American *Gemini 8*!—and had not only used up all its fuel, but had left the spacecraft tumbling end-over-end.

Obviously there could be no docking. Not only that, but there was no easy way to return Soyuz safely to Earth—an important milestone in the testing of any manned spacecraft. Projections showed that Soyuz would dive into the atmosphere on its own around the 39th orbit, destroying itself somewhere over a foreign land, or over the ocean.

Some genius in the guidance area came up with the idea of firing the Soyuz's main retro-rocket in short bursts, which allowed the orientation system for reentry—not the same system that had spent all its fuel—to operate for brief periods, too. In this way the spacecraft could be gradually brought under some control, and commanded to reentry over the USSR.

Forty-eight hours after launch, on the 32nd orbit, a final burn was made. That, alas, was the last anyone saw of the first Soyuz. It was tracked as far as the city of Orsk, on the standard reentry path, then disappeared, very likely to automatic self-destruction.

It was a pretty thorough disaster of a test flight, but Artemov rallied the troops and convinced the State Commission—headed by none other than Tyulin—that the problems with the attitude-control system could be corrected, and that a single Soyuz could be launched in December to test the fixes, and prove out the landing system before the twin manned flights in late January.

After helping with the final checkout of crew equipment inside the vehicle, I became a spectator, watching the proceedings from the roof of the assembly building perhaps seven hundred meters from the pad itself. It was a cold afternoon, December 14, the sun already setting behind us.

The little group included some of the military cosmonauts training to fly Soyuz, including Saditsky. As the countdown reached zero, the twenty main engines of the Soyuz launcher roared to life, superhot steam spewing around the base of the vehicle.

Then stopped, as if someone had shut off a garden hose.

We all looked at each other. "That's not right," Saditsky said. We waited longer, stamping our feet nervously, but there was still no launch, no further activity out on Pad 31 except for whisps of steam blowing around the base of the gantry.

Liquid-fueled rockets like Soyuz could be shut down safely, of course, though it was hardly routine. An American Gemini launch had suffered the same fate almost exactly a year prior to this.

But the memory of the Nedelin disaster was still strong in the minds of the Baikonur launch teams, so their approach to the loaded rocket was cautious. It took almost half an hour before any cars and trucks headed toward the pad. The group included Artemov, bundled up in a black coat, wearing a black hat, as he hurried out of the building that housed the control center.

Once we saw the trucks, we knew there would be no further launch attempt that day, so we all went back inside. I glanced at Saditsky and his friends, who seemed very calm: Maybe they were telling themselves that this proved the reliability of the Soyuz safety systems.

Then we heard a muffled thump behind us, from the direction of the launchpad. As one, we turned and saw the escape rocket hauling the Soyuz into the air and downrange!

You must picture the entire Soyuz vehicle, the huge conical base (the four strap-on boosters clustered around the core) tapering to a narrow cylinder, which was the two upper stages. Atop them was a wider cylinder, the Soyuz itself—propulsion module, bell-shaped crew module and spherical orbital module, the latter two encased in a protective shroud. At the very tip was a long, mushroom-headed escape rocket intended to rescue a crew from disaster at zero altitude on up to an altitude of twenty thousand meters, where the first stage burned out.

The whole structure looked like an Arabian minaret, the difference being that a building couldn't explode with the strength of an atomic bomb.

"Well, that wouldn't have happened with Voskhod," Saditsky joked, knowing full well that Voskhod had no such escape rocket: A disaster on the pad would have meant death to its crew.

"Grachev wants his bonus," said another pilot. Grachev was the designer of the escape rocket. His bureau would get a financial bonus for a "flight test."

We saw the successful parachute deployment, and began to relax when General Kamanin and one of his aides suddenly appeared in the room. "Into the hallway, now!"

"What's the problem?" someone asked.

"Look for yourself." Kamanin pointed to the pad.

We had been so busy watching the escape rocket and the parachute that we forgot about the vehicle itself. The escape rocket *had ignited the fuel* in the Soyuz propulsion module and upper stages. Flames were shooting into the sky, and more ominously, flowing down the length of the vehicle to the very large amounts of explosive fuel in the first stage.

No one needed further encouragement as we pushed out of that room with its big glass windows and into a narrow corridor. The door was not even closed when we saw a flash of light, followed three seconds later by a *whump*! Then another and another. I lost count of the not-so-distant explosions, which knocked plaster off the walls and tiles off the ceiling, making the lightbulbs jerk. We almost choked on the dust.

Then there was nothing.

When I was a child, living with my mother in the Crimea, where my father was stationed, we went through an earthquake. This felt very much like that—short, violent shaking, then nothing. But you feel afraid to look. Has it stopped?

Some brave soul pushed open the door to the room where we had all been standing. I don't know which sight was more frightening—the shattered spire of the Soyuz rocket, now spewing black smoke hundreds of meters into the air, the twisted girders of the gantry (how many people had just been killed, I wondered? Artemov?), or the room itself, with the windows blown out, furniture upended, shards of glass embedded in the walls. We would have been riddled.

It turned out that only one officer was killed, a specialist who had tried to take cover behind a concrete wall when he saw the coming explosion. Several other members of the launch team were injured. Artemov was safe.

That was the end of 1966, a year of one failure after another.

18

THE OPENING

The commission investigating the latest Soyuz mishap quickly determined the cause—which was so odd and unexpected that Triyanov insisted on reading the final conclusion out loud to his pupils in the kindergarten, a group that included not only me and Yastrebov, but also Yeliseyev and Kubasov, the first members of Department 731 to be included in Soyuz flight crews.

"First, the cause of the shutdown was a broken fuel line in one of the first-stage strap-on boosters. Those responsible have been punished.

"Now, the question remained: What triggered the escape rocket? It was designed to fire if gryoscopes in the core stage noted a deviation in the planned trajectory, or if one of the strap-ons separated prematurely—" By this time I had seen film of just this amazing event, from early R-7 failures. "—Or if the boosters underperformed so badly that the vehicle would not reach orbit. *None* of those conditions applied."

"And those responsible have been punished," Yastrebov said, to growing amusement.

"To continue . . . another possible cause was a signal from the control center, which was not sent. Yet another was the possibility that moving the gantries back into place somehow jarred the rocket, but the gantries did not even touch the rocket. Yet, all of those responsible have been punished." Now there was open laughter, from Triyanov, too. He closed up the report.

"That's it?" Yastrebov said. "Where's the conclusion?"

Triyanov smiled. "I'll give you a hint. The gyroscopes were powered down, but not completely off. Anyone?"

No one seemed willing to venture a guess, so I raised my hand. "The Earth moved."

Triyanov bowed his head. "Correct. The gyroscopes sensed the rotation of the Earth and judged that the whole vehicle was off course, igniting the escape rocket. Junior engineer Ribko escapes punishment."

I wish I could say that my "brilliant" answer was the result of logical thinking and detailed knowledge of Soyuz guidance systems, but it was an intuitive guess: When I heard the word gyroscope, I immediately saw a spinning ball, which became the Earth itself.

I became aware that several of my colleagues were staring at me. I chose to believe some of them were simply noticing me for the first time, rather than hating me on sight.

So repairs were made to the Soyuz launcher and spacecraft, and another vehicle was targeted for launch no earlier than February 7, 1967—less than two weeks from that date. The manned twin launches would take place in April. We had to hurry: Having completed its Gemini program, America was even now getting ready to launch three astronauts into Earth orbit aboard the first manned Apollo. Their launch was scheduled for February 16. As I had been doing several days every week for the past three months, I got on the bureau's bus heading for the Chkalov air base.

At this time my work in the department involved pressure suits and equipment for extra-vehicular activity, since the bureau's plans for a manned lunar landing called for the pilot-cosmonaut to transfer from the Soyuz to the L-3 lunar lander using this method—an insane, impractical one I thought even then, but the construction of an internal transfer tunnel between the two vehicles was not possible because of the arrangement of the modules, and for reasons of weight.

As of January 1967, the Americans had performed ten hours of tests in open space, with results varying from the positive to the near disastrous. We had allowed Leonov to float at the end of his tether (in more ways than one) from the second Voskhod for less than ten minutes, and he had almost lost his life trying to reenter the spacecraft. His suit ballooned to rigidity, preventing him from bending enough to get back inside. He had actually let air out of his suit to make it more flexible, risking the bends as he did.

For the docking of the first two manned Soyuz craft, we had to send two men in pressure suits from one craft to the other. One cosmonaut would be launched first, alone, in the active ship, while a crew of three followed a day later in the target vehicle.

Why two and not one, as would be the case in the real lunar mission? During our very first tests with a cosmonaut wearing his bulky pressure suit and backpack, we saw that it was impossible for him to get through the exit hatch in the Soyuz orbital module. It was just too small. I know, because I was one of the bureau engineers who tried on several occasions to get through that hatch, both on the ground and, in one very unpleasant test, in our Tu-104 weightless laboratory.

How could that have happened? Well, some State decree two years back had specified that the pressure suit and backpack would be smaller than they actually turned out to be, and the hatch of the spacecraft had been designed to those outdated measurements. (Those responsible, of course, have been punished.)

Artemov and the other chiefs at the bureau had done their share of screaming at Severin, head of the organization that designed the pressure suit, but he pointed out—quite rightly—that the suit and backpack were new technology, that changes had had to be made based on lessons from Leonov's close call, and why couldn't the hatch be made a little wider?

Well, later models of Soyuz *would* have a bigger hatch, but it was too late to change the existing spacecraft. So accommodations had to be made. First the backpack was to be replaced, for these early transfers only, with a legpack. That is, the life-support package was put into a container that the pressure-suited cosmonaut would wear strapped to the front of his thighs. After all, it was not as though he would need to be able to walk: Legs were useless appendages in that environment.

The second change was to add an additional EVA crew member to help his partner with suiting and egress. It was much safer that way, and should have been standard procedure from the very beginning. (It was later for Apollo, Shuttle, and Mir missions.)

Of course, the addition of a second set of heavy EVA equipment forced us to make other trade-offs: We had to lose over a hundred kilograms of food, supplies, and machinery from a spacecraft that was already designed to a minimum.

These were the issues I dealt with at the bureau and at Chkalov during the cold, depressing winter of 1966–67. Four crew members, two from the military team and two from the bureau, were being trained as EVA crew members. Those of us on the support team had to fly with them, train them, observe their actions, make corrections in procedures and equipment, then try them out all over again.

Time was short and we began to work weekends. On Saturday morning, January 28, 1967, we had a particularly difficult session aboard the Tu-104. We wanted to have a film-and-television record of the EVA to help with future equipment design, and for cosmonaut training, not to mention propaganda reasons, but where to put the camera in order to get a good picture of the proceedings?

Someone had proposed having the lead EVA crewman, military cosmonaut Khrunov, hold the camera in his hands and float away from the docked spacecraft to a distance of ten meters. (I suspect this was the same someone who designed the Soyuz hatch to that minimum figure.)

On this Saturday, as we coasted into perhaps the fourth of thirty planned zero-G arcs, with one of the cosmonauts already green and ready to vomit, the very hard-working and intelligent Khrunov, inside his pressure suit with "backpack" strapped to his legs, struggled mightily to hook up a safety tether, take the camera into his hands, and somehow push himself off into space—or, in this case, the interior of the Tu-104. He pushed with one hand and immediately started tumbling. Grabbing the tether with his one free hand only made things worse.

And, just like that, he was out of time. No more free fall.

It reminded me all too much of my first flights testing the Voskhod toilet. Every time poor Khrunov pushed off, he turned over, then had to be supported through the crushing weight of another descent and climb by the aircraft.

A military doctor from the training center called a halt to the whole business, which started an argument that lasted through two more zero-G arcs, and then the pilot of the plane signaled us that weather was getting bad and we would be heading back to Chkalov earlier than planned.

Khrunov was dripping wet when we got him out of the suit. He said he thought he could master the maneuver, given time.

"You don't have time," I said. The other cosmonauts reluctantly agreed.

One of them suggested simply mounting the camera on a telescoping pole, allowing Khrunov to essentially film himself. That seemed more promising, though we would have embraced just about any alternative. But this camera-pole also represented a design challenge, and more training for the crew, and we landed feeling we had taken two giant steps backward.

Another aircraft landed just before we did, an An-124 transport. Planes like this were always going in and out of Chkalov, of course, but what caught my eye here was the presence of several official-looking cars and some familiar faces gathered around the aircraft. One of them was Artemov.

Mindful of my surveillance duties, which I had not performed in weeks, I wandered over to the transport.

Not only was Artemov here, but also Filin, still looking subdued after his defeat and hospitalization. He greeted me, and asked me how my flight had gone.

Within reason, I tried to be honest with Filin. "Not very well," I said, then sketched out some of our problems.

"Everything is going wrong," he said. "Look at this." "This" was the Antonov's cargo, a huge rocket engine, still covered in a clear plastic wrapper.

"What is it?"

"It's one of Kuznetsov's engines for the Carrier rocket, on its way to Zagorsk for testing. There will be thirty of these monsters in the first stage." At that time I still had not seen a sketch or model of the monster Moon rocket, but with each fragment of the puzzle, the beast grew in my mind. Thirty engines!

"Not Glushko's?" Glushko was one of the pioneers of the Soviet space program—if you didn't believe that, all you had to do was ask him—who had designed and built the engines for most of our missiles and space launchers by that time.

"He and Korolev disagreed about the fuels," Filin said, the remembered horror of that battle still plain on his face. "Glushko wanted to use devil's venom to get more power." Devil's venom was bureau shorthand for exotic fuels like fluorine or hydrazine that had been one of the causes of the famous Nedelin disaster. "Korolev wanted to stick with fuels he knew. He also didn't trust Glushko's schedule." Rocket engines were notorious for taking much longer to build than predicted. Even at that time, America was still struggling with its big F-1 engines for the Saturn 5. "So we're stuck using a big pile of engines built by a company that makes jet airplane motors."

"You don't sound optimistic."

"It's been a long few months. I have to fly to Baikonur tomorrow for the Soyuz flight, and I don't know that we've fixed the problems. The first L-1 is supposed to fly soon, too." He was clearly overwhelmed with the enormity of his obligations, and who could blame him? I was thirty years younger and staggering under the weight of my own more modest load.

"Are they really that far ahead?"

"They got started in nineteen sixty-one, while our Central Committee wouldn't even listen to talk about a man on the Moon until three years after that. Even if you assume that we are spending the same money they are, and we aren't, they have a three-year head start. Oh, yes, the Americans are about to take a great leap forward—"

"Vasily!" Artemov was calling to Filin as he approached. When I had looked his way, I had seen another man moving like a sleepwalker, a tortured soul. Now, just moments later, he seemed reborn. I wondered if he had taken a couple of shots of his own personal devil's venom.

Even Filin noticed this. "I'm not interested in any more of your 'good news,' Boris." He was quite curt for a man talking to his boss.

But Artemov was in a genuinely good mood. "You'll like this news, believe me. Last night the Americans had an accident at their cosmodrome. A fire in the Apollo."

I couldn't quite see how this was good news. Neither did Filin, glancing at me. "Was anyone hurt?"

"Oh, yes," Artemov went on, gleefully. "The whole crew, Grissom, White, and Chaffee, were killed. Burned to a crisp, their spacecraft destroyed right on the pad!" He was practically dancing.

"Have they said how long they're going to be grounded?" Filin asked. In spite of a clear effort to be sympathetic, the color was returning to his face, the life to his voice.

"If it were us, we'd say six months, knowing it was going to be a year. At least that much."

No American triumphs for a year! We could fly Soyuz, fly L-1 around the Moon, who knew what else, in that amount of time!

I was just as elated as Artemov and Filin. Bad as things had been, we had been given a second chance.

19 SABOTAGE

"It's not so much a matter of murder," Uncle Vladimir said, pausing as he split a log with an ax, cleanly, smoothly. "Now it's sabotage."

He handed the pieces to me; I was collecting them for a fire at his dacha here on the west side of Moscow, near Petrovo-Dalniye.

I had telephoned him upon returning to my one-room flat in Kaliningrad, in a new building about halfway between the main entrance to the bureau and the train station at Podlipki. (Yes, I had my own telephone by that point.) On the bus ride back from Chkalov, I had realized, yet again, that as a spy for State Security, I was a failure, if not an outright liability. What, for example, was I supposed to report from my latest "encounter" with Artemov? That he was happy about someone else's death? Did that make him Korolev's murderer? Filin had been happy about the dead American astronauts, too. And so, to my shame, had I.

I was hoping Uncle Vladimir would release me from service, that he would let me concentrate on being a good engineer for the bureau, and on being a much better boyfriend to Marina.

All he did was invite me to his dacha the next day.

Several of the people who lived in my new building had cars of their own, storing them in sheds in what was supposed to have been park land just down the street. So I was able to beg a ride as far as downtown Moscow that Sunday morning, to the Arbat, where I could catch the train as far as Usovo, the end of the line, where Uncle Vladimir met me himself. Dressed more casually than I've ever seen him, he was driving his own car.

His three-room dacha, gray, weathered, pieced together from available boards and planks, sat in a birch forest near the Iskra River. Through the bare trees I could see other, similar structures—and several that did not look pieced together, but rather designed and constructed. As if Uncle Vladimir was the piggy with house of sticks, while down the lane lived a piggy in a house of bricks.

As a further surprise, there was a woman staying with him. Katya Pershina was her name, and she was, I judged, in her middle thirties, with a quick, easy smile. She was tall—taller than I, and even taller than Uncle Vladimir, with the regal bearing of a Scandinavian film star. Perhaps it was her pale blue eyes, which looked through me with almost complete disinterest. She was clearly no stranger to Uncle Vladimir and his ways. "I'm going down to the village," she said after we had been introduced. "Hope to see you later, Yuri."

Uncle Vladimir said nothing about her, but merely led me outside, where he had been chopping wood.

"Sabotage?" I said, sounding even stupider than I felt.

"It's happened," he said, violently cleaving another log. "When Korolev was alive, we had a suspicious series of accidents. A whole spacecraft getting dropped from an airplane, a self-destruct signal coming out of nowhere."

" 'Those responsible have been punished,' " I said, not thinking.

Uncle Vladimir looked at me. "Yes. As a matter of fact, they were." *Chunk* went another log. "The lucky ones are probably doing the very same thing today that I am, though in a much colder place.

"The more we looked into your bureau and its ministry, and their relationships with the military, the more suspicious it all became. There has been a pattern of failure over the past year, wouldn't you say?"

"It would be hard to find any successes at *all*," I said.

"Yes. And because of the nature of your space business, it's the Korolev organization which cuts across all of it. You're here in Moscow, you're at the factories, you're at the launch center, the tracking sites."

"And Artemov goes to all of them."

"Artemov. Or someone close to him." Finished with his task—actually, he'd done an amazing amount of work for a man his size—he set the ax aside and picked up the last of the firewood himself. "Who's to say it's only Artemov, hmmm?"

I followed him to the door.

"Pasternak lived over there, did you know that?" he said, gesturing with the ax. He smiled. "And now Khrushchev does."

Katya returned not long after that, and we had a pleasant meal in front of a very warm, noisy fire. I could not figure out her relationship with Uncle Vladimir, whether they were lovers or just good friends. I had never seen my uncle with a woman, but, given the few times I had seen him, period, that was not surprising.

My uninformed guess was that Katya worked in State Security, and when she slipped effortlessly into perfect English (singing along with some music Uncle Vladimir was playing—Shirley Bassey?), I felt sure they were colleagues at the very least.

Eventually I had to be taken back to the train. As Katya said good-bye, she happened to add: "I completely forgot to ask. You must know Marina Torchillova. A wonderful girl. Say hello to her from me."

On the drive to the station, while I was thinking that over, Uncle Vladimir gave me my orders: to watch for any sabotage, any sign of "wrecking." He gave me a special phone number to call, an escalating series of codes. "You're between the condition we call Scorpion 2, which is the presence of enemy agents in a closed area." Scorpion 1, I learned, was the mere suspicion of enemy activity.

Enemy activity. Uncle Vladimir also told me that I might not be dealing with mere "anti-socialist" forces, but with our country's main enemy—the CIA itself.

Thus ended my Sunday in the country, which began with my simple hope to give up a career as a snitch and ended with my enrollment as a full-fledged antisaboteur and Cold Warrior.

As the gateway to dacha country, where all the Kremlin bigshots had their places, the Usovo Station had one of the best markets in the entire USSR. Waiting for the train back to the Arbat, I strolled through them, happening upon one selling flowered-silk scarves. Since it was Sunday night and the grandmother running the kiosk was anxious to get home, I was able to buy one for only two rubles. Grandmother even tied the scarf in a ribbon for me.

The purchase encouraged me to change my travel plans. Once back in Moscow, I chose not to continue on to Kaliningrad, but instead took the metro to the Bauman area, heading for Marina's flat. Since I was fortified with a proper gift and charged with a personal mission from Katya Pershina, I felt justified in calling on Marina without warning.

It had been a strange time for the two of us. Between Marina's studies and working trips, and my own six-day-a-week schedule at the bureau, we had barely seen each other, no more than twice a month. Well, we had spent one glorious weekend alone in my new Kaliningrad flat, bare floors and all, in August, where we reached a truce about my "cosmonaut career," which had progressed not one centimeter since spring.

At other times we would go out, see a film or a concert, as if we were second-year students, then find some semiprivate place to make love. She seemed to need it as much as I did; when one night we wrapped ourselves in our coats and made love on the snowy grounds of the Peter and Paul Cathedral, I realized that both of us had completely lost our sense of shyness. Perhaps our decency, too.

As I walked up the steps to Marina's building, I could actually feel my excitement growing, like a hunger.

The key lady this Sunday evening was an older man, a veteran of the Great Patriotic War, judging from the medals he wore on his olive jacket. "Stop right there," he ordered.

I told him I was just going up to see Marina Torchillova.

"She's not in."

"You must keep a pretty good eye on the girls to know that." There were probably two hundred of them living in that building.

He obviously heard something in my voice he didn't like. His eyes narrowed, and I felt like a recruit about to be chewed out by a drill sergeant. "It's my business to know who goes in and out of this place. And you, snot-nose, are *not* going in."

I have a temper, but, thanks to my father's physical corrections at an early age, have learned to control it. Barely. For an instant I considered simply walking up the stairs, making him yell for the militia, or telling him to pick up the phone and call, for example, Uncle Vladimir, who would utter the magic words "State Security."

But it passed. I realized that it was late, that I had an early flight to Baikonur ahead of me in the morning. And, frankly, I was a little afraid of the way Marina might react to a surprise visit. "You're doing a good job," I told the guard. "Would you be kind enough to see that Marina gets this?" I handed him the wrapped scarf, and added a ruble. "Tell her it's from Yuri."

That softened him quite nicely. In fact, he insisted that I share a little "sip" of vodka with him. Which, knowing I faced a cold walk, I accepted.

On the way back to the metro stop, I ran into Lev Tselauri carrying two bags of produce in the same direction. "Lev!" I called.

His head jerked, as if he had heard a gunshot instead of my voice. "What are you doing down here?" he asked.

I told him. "And what are you doing over here?"

He held up his bags. "My turn to shop."

I grabbed one of the bags and walked with him down the street, across the bridge, catching up quickly on the latest adventures of the Omsk Twins, and of the oversized young student from the Caucasus— a big eater, apparently—who had taken my place.

"Have you been in touch with Filin at all?" It had been too early for Lev to join our bureau last spring, or rather, too late, since his thesis was being supervised by an adviser who worked for Chelomei. But he was now at the point I had been, ready to sign up for permanent employment.

"No." He actually looked ashamed of himself.

"He said the door was open for you." No answer. "Things can't be going very well with Chelomei."

He sighed. "It's all military work, and, yes, it's not going very well."

"You heard about the American astronauts?" He nodded. "It's our opening, Lev. We have the chance to catch them, maybe pass them. I'm going to talk to Filin tomorrow. You need to write him a letter. Now's the time!"

We had reached our old building. "You're right. I can't wait." He smiled, finally. "You're a good friend, Yuri. Lucky I ran into you tonight. Let's storm the cosmos."

I walked away, laughing, feeling better than I had in days, weeks. Ready to storm the cosmos.

20

THE RECOVERY TEAM

My newfound elation and enthusiasm for my work—both official and unofficial—lasted through takeoff from Chkalov air base until we were almost halfway to Baikonur.

We were in a noisy old Antonov-12, the various propulsion and guidance specialists from other departments in the bureau, plus our handful of crew equipment specialists from Department 731 under Triyanov. Other planes had been taking off that morning, carrying Filin, Artemov, several of the bureau's cosmonauts, and whole groups of military officers. If things went well, the flight of Soyuz spacecraft Number 3 would be the last unmanned test. In early April we would put crews aboard Numbers 4 and 5 and dock them together in space.

Somewhere in the skies between Samara and Orenburg, Triyanov landed on the bench next to me. "Scouting our landing zones?" he said. "Good."

I hadn't thought of that at all, of course; I'd merely been watching the snowy landscape slide past. It was a clear day, and, like all days spent flying to Baikonur, a shortened one. But I realized that Triyanov was right: Gagarin himself had parachuted out of his Vostok from this altitude and roughly this area.

I also realized that Triyanov had my arm in a death grip. "What did you say to Artemov?"

"I haven't spoken to Artemov at all." This was the truth. I had *seen* him, together with Filin, at the Chkalov base the previous Saturday. But I hadn't said a word to him, nor had he directed any remarks to me.

"Well, he's added your name to his shitlist."

I felt sick, not only thinking about what this meant to my bureau career, but also what it meant to my work for Uncle Vladimir. "I don't know why."

Triyanov shrugged. Clearly this was not an issue for him. "Well, it happens. Maybe your reports on the EVA tests have been too critical." That was certainly a possibility. Triyanov smiled slyly, and lowered his voice. "Maybe one of your colleagues denounced you."

For a moment I couldn't imagine why—I got along well with the various cosmonauts and test engineers, all of whom were senior to me. Then I remembered my "stroke of genius" regarding the last Soyuz failure.

Triyanov read my thoughts. " 'It's the tall weed that gets cut down,' " he quoted. "Well, whoever or whatever, we've got to deal with this. You can't work on the EVA anymore."

"But I'm the only one who never gets sick."

"I didn't say the decision makes any sense, Yuri." He frowned. "The trouble is, I don't have anywhere to put you that will keep you out of Artemov's sight, not with a launch coming up—"

Now I was getting angry. "Should I catch the next plane back to Moscow?"

"There won't be a plane back to Moscow anytime soon. And you didn't let me finish. I don't want to disrupt the other teams before the launch, but there is one area that has no representative from our department, and really needs it: the recovery team."

"I thought that was the responsibility of the Air Force."

"Kamanin and the Air Force are supposed to do search and rescue, yes. And we have bureau people who fly out with them to secure the spacecraft and make it safe for shipping back to Kaliningrad. But we have no one to deal with our crew members and their needs. They will be surrounded by doctors and military people."

I saw the logic in this. "Fine. But we won't have a crew member on this launch."

"Better yet. Go along with Kamanin's people and see how they screw up, and maybe we can fix the problems *before* we actually fly, hmmm?" He handed me a pass. "Find General Kamanin or one of his people. They are airmen, not rocketeers."

"I know the difference."

Baikonur was clutched in winter's death grip when we arrived. The wind blew so much snow around that I was sure we would have to abort our landing and divert to Tashkent, but we bumped down.

I'd never seen so many people around the hotel at Area 17, military and civilians, and civilians from a whole variety of bureaus, including Chelomei's. They were to launch a Proton rocket with an unmanned L-1 two weeks after the Soyuz.

Naturally, the day after we arrived, the Soyuz launch was postponed several days, to February 7. The guidance team was still struggling with fixes to prevent another unplanned firing of the launch escape system.

The delay gave me a chance to begin attending daily briefings at Area 2 on the status of recovery forces, and to make myself known to General Kamanin and his team, one of whom was cosmonaut Ivan Saditsky, who greeted me like an old school classmate. "When are you going to fly Soyuz?" I asked him.

"Not until next year. No one would admit that *Voskhod 3* was really canceled for months, so poor Kostin and I were stuck on that until November, while everyone else got to study Soyuz. Now we're in the group, but not in any of the crews, while we catch up."

He laughed when I told him I was here to work with the search-and-rescue team. "First you have to find *them*! The Air Force hates spaceflight so much that they starve us for money. I think they allow us a dozen helicopters to search the recovery zones, that's it. No wonder Leonov and Belyayev had to sit there fighting off the wolves."

I was startled to hear this, but learned that it was true. The Soviet Air Force had been given the authority to train cosmonauts because they were selected from the ranks of single-seat fighter pilots. But most of the military money and power had gone to the Strategic Rocket Force, which grew out of the regular army and artillery units. The rocketeers controlled the launch sites and tracking stations, and operated the military satellites. Kamanin had to fight his own Air Force leadership to get any kind of support at all. "Come on, meet Kamanin."

Having grown up in a military family, I was amazed at Saditsky's casual manner with his three-star general, a slim, short man in his late fifties. Saditsky actually patted Kamanin on the shoulder to get his attention.

Kamanin seemed not to mind. When we were introduced, he said, "Any relation to General Nikolai Ribko?"

"My father."

"We fought together during the war. The Voronezh and Second Ukrainian Fronts. I used to see him at headquarters. How is your mother?"

My mother was six years dead at this point. Obviously Kamanin didn't know. I chose to lie rather than embarrass him. "Last time I saw her, she was fine." This, of course, wasn't true at all: The last time I saw my mother, she was gray, emaciated, a travesty of herself.

"Say hello for me, please."

Why had I lied? Perhaps, having alienated Artemov, I wanted to avoid adding the head of the Air Force's space program to my list of enemies.

As Kamanin and his hangers-on departed, Saditsky said to me, "You were lucky. You saw his grandpa side. He can also be a Stalinist bastard, so be careful."

I was glad for the warning, and, though I'm ashamed to admit it, glad for my own dishonesty, because I was going to be spending a lot of time around General Kamanin.

The various delays caused the launch of Soyuz Number 3 to take place at 6:20 A.M. on February 7, 1967. The weather had warmed considerably, but the wind was blowing at eight meters a second, a good clip, though not enough to force another postponement.

The launcher rose quickly, brightly, into the gray morning sky, as, not wishing to be trapped behind a third-floor window in case of another accident, we watched from the grounds outside the assembly building. Within minutes Kamanin and the head of the State Commission had arrived from the blockhouse and comandeered their cars. They were all headed for the Crimea.

Not me, however. I was to "stand by" with the primary recovery aircraft at Outskirts Airport. However, since Soyuz Number 3 was not scheduled for reentry until the tenth, three days hence, I was free to remain at Baikonur itself.

Which I did, joining some of the other recovery pilots and engineers at the tracking station at Area 18. I felt conspicuous as one of very few civilians in a group of men in green uniforms, and more than once caught them glancing at me with cautious curiosity.

Upon reaching its planned orbit successfully, Soyuz Number 3 had been given the official name of *Cosmos 140*. There was a worrisome communications failure early on, but it cleared itself up.

All went well until the fifth orbit, about eight hours after launch, when the guidance system (remember the gyroscope problem?) refused to lock onto the sun as planned, to allow the winglike solar panels to provide power. While rolling around, Soyuz proceeded to burn up a lot of fuel unnecessarily.

Once the spacecraft was put in the proper attitude, the main engine on the Soyuz—essential for any rendezvous—was fired. That event, on the twenty-second orbit, was a success. But it was clear that the spacecraft wasn't going to orient itself, so Artemov, Kamanin, Tyulin, and the other commissioners down at the flight control center in the Crimea, reluctantly decided to bring her down early, on orbit 33, when the trajectory would intersect the main recovery zone fifty kilometers northwest of Baikonur itself.

Once that decision had been made, I grabbed my bag and joined the group rushing back to Area 17. Early the next morning I boarded an An-12 transport and waited for a signal from the tracking radars of the Air Defense Force.

A weak signal from *Cosmos 140* was received at 7:49 local time, indicating that the spacecraft had fired its retros and survived reentry into the atmosphere. The weakness of the signal meant that the spacecraft was going to land short of its aiming point.

Nevertheless, we took off into the winter sky and headed west.

For three hours the planes from Baikonur, and others from Air Force fields in Aralsk and Novokazalinsk, crisscrossed the recovery zone, working toward the west in search of the site of the last transmission from the spacecraft.

Finally our plane had to put into Aralsk to be refueled. While we were still on the ground, our pilot learned that the crew of another An-12 had sighted a parachute on the ice of the Aral Sea. They were low on fuel, too, so were heading back to Aralsk.

But this report gave me and the three-man military recovery team time to climb into one of the helicopters waiting there. This little squadron headed southwest, quickly crossing a strip of frozen desert, over Cape Shevchenko, then onto the ice of the Aral.

Dubnin, a young para-rescue officer, asked me if the Soyuz could float. "Haven't you trained for a water rescue?" I asked, amazed at such a basic question.

"Are you kidding? This squad only got assigned to this jump two weeks ago. So help me out." I assured him that the Soyuz was designed to float. "And you're absolutely sure about this?"

"We even train the cosmonauts to egress while they are in the water. Why?"

"Because the report said 'parachute,' not spacecraft."

"Maybe they got separated somehow." Dubnin didn't seem encouraged by this. "Hey, it's on the ice, isn't it?"

He pointed out the window. "How thick do you think it is down there?"

When I looked, I saw patches of open water. Obviously the ice couldn't be very thick at all.

It took our squadron of helicopters less than twenty minutes to reach the site. The parachute was easy to spot, its red stripes standing out clearly against the snow-covered ice. As we got closer, I also saw a smear of soot, like a giant's footprint, spreading out from the spot.

But I couldn't see the spacecraft. As we circled, all we saw was a spacecraft-sized hole in the ice.

"Shit," Dubnin said, seeing the same thing.

As the lead helicopter, we descended first, hovering two meters off the ice close to the parachute canopy, which billowed in the wash from our rotor. Dubnin attached a line to himself and dropped out of the door—safely. "Come out," he signaled. The other two guys on his team, disdaining the safety lines, jumped down. After putting on my gloves, and saying a prayer, I followed them.

The ice seemed solid, but Dubnin signaled the helicopter to stand off. The second helicopter, a Mi-8, designed for heavy lifting, moved in, the heavy cable and tow hook dangling from it.

The three of us approached the spacecraft—rather, the hole in the ice where the spacecraft should have been—cautiously. Dubnin stopped about three meters from the jagged edge and got down on his belly and began to push himself along like a crawling baby. "You, too," he said. "Distribute your weight."

I was soon glad we did: The ice had been shattered by the impact of the spacecraft and the heat of its soft-landing rocket. The edge of the hole showed that the thickness of the ice was five or six centimeters— enough to support the weight of a man, if he were careful. But we could see cracks in the snow beneath us. "Can we land the chopper?"

"No," Dubnin said. "How deep down is it?"

It was hard to see, with chunks of melting ice obscuring the view through the water. But there was the shiny silvery nose hatch of the Soyuz, bobbing ever so slightly. The heavy lines of the parachute rigging ran down to it. "Two meters," I said.

"Shit, shit." Dubnin signaled the transport chopper closer. "We've got to get a line on it now. It's filling with water."

I saw that he was right. The other two rescuers were rolling up the parachute, and literally trying to hold onto it. Not that they were likely to keep a metal ball weighing a ton from sinking while standing on ice!

As the hook came swinging down, I thought of the dead American astronaut Grissom, whose first spaceflight in Mercury had ended with near disaster in the water. The hatch on his spacecraft had blown open prematurely, filling it with water as Grissom swam for his life. His rescue helicopter had already hooked on, but could not lift the weight of a spacecraft filled with ocean, and had had to release it to the depths. Grissom had almost drowned.

Dubin tried to grab the swinging hook, but missed. I snagged it, only to find there was no tension in the line. With the hook in my hand, I fell right into the hole in the ice.

I don't know which hurt more, the shock of the icy water, which felt like a million needles on my face and hands, or hitting the Soyuz with my side. Somehow I managed to hold onto the hook, still slack, as I floated there, my coat and boots filling with water, blinking at the horror of my situation. I am a good swimmer; my father even took me snorkeling during our time in the south. Being underwater was nothing to fear . . . unless you were freezing, and hurt, and wearing several kilograms of heavy winter clothing.

I held onto the ringlike collar of Soyuz, trying not to breathe, then saw what I should do. I jammed the hook of the towline into the joint where the parachute lines attached to the spacecraft. (There was a special hook somewhere on that spacecraft for recovery, but I didn't have time to look for it.) The line went taut, and I pulled myself up, one arm, then another, to be grabbed by Dubnin, who was screaming. "You fucking idiot!"

It was even colder out of the water, as a very slight wind froze me to my bones. I was gasping. Dubnin hauled me back toward our helicopter, which had lowered itself to within a few centimeters of the ice. He pushed me inside and screamed at a crewman, "Get those clothes off him!"

He must have given orders to the pilot, too, because we lifted off, leaving the rescue team on the ice, and started heading back toward Aralsk.

Looking back, my teeth chattering, my whole body shivering as I painfully peeled off my wet, frozen clothing, I saw Soyuz Number 3, also known as *Cosmos 140*, being lifted out of the hole, a stream of water pouring from its bottom, as Dubnin and his men stumbled and fell gathering up the parachute rigging while trying not to repeat my icy dive.

The spacecraft was safely returned to Kaliningrad, where it was discovered that a small plug in the base of Soyuz Number 3—a section made deliberately removable to allow maintenance on a thermal gauge in that location—had burned through during reentry, scorching the interior of the spacecraft and allowing it to fill with water and sink following touchdown on the ice.

Analysis of the flight showed that the guidance system was still unreliable, the power margins were slim, and the reentry trajectory was unpredictable. The heat shielding was so faulty that it would have burned, or drowned, a crew.

Confronted with this string of failures, what did the State Commission do?

It authorized the launch of four cosmonauts on Soyuz vehicles 4 and 5 two months hence, in April 1967.

21 GENERAL RIBKO

After several nights in an astonishingly primitive hospital in Aralsk, I returned to Kaliningrad a quiet hero, as Triyanov described it. "You get credit for saving the spacecraft for analysis," he said. "But remember that the results of the analysis are embarrassing for many people, so they don't want to be reminded of your heroism."

Frankly, I was relieved not to be criticized for my clumsiness. I had not made a heroic leap into the icy deeps—I had stumbled!

There was also a small bonus for my actions—fifty rubles—which when added to my small-but-steady salary made me feel, for the first time in my life, relatively rich. I needed furniture in my apartment, of course, but I could also begin to think about a car of my own. Perhaps in three or four years' time.

My first night back, my father visited my apartment for the first time. I wasn't completely surprised: He had called me from Air Force H.Q. a couple of hours before his arrival. Actually, the call itself was the surprise. (I was still getting used to the idea of having a telephone of my own.) I had seen him only briefly in the last six months, perhaps half a dozen times since our bizarre encounter at the Foros resort, and not at all since the new year: He had been on assignment in Europe.

As he stood there in the open door, wearing his full military uniform, including its bright-red Hero of the Soviet Union star, holding a loaf of bread, a package of salt, and a bottle of brandy in one arm, he looked better than he had in years—certainly vastly improved over the tired, aging man with his arm in a cast I had seen in Foros. To add to the strangeness, before he entered he actually saluted me! "It gives me great pleasure to recognize your quick thinking and courage," he said, like Brezhnev bestowing a medal.

I blushed, and even though I was wearing civilian clothing, snapped my best reserve officer salute in return. "Thank you, Comrade Colonel-General."

Then he did give me a big bear hug. "You can't believe how many generals have been talking to me about my son the past few days. The story came right up the chain in the rescue services to Kutasin himself." My father smiled knowingly. "He was *extremely* relieved to be able to report to the ministers that the spacecraft had been safely recovered, rather than have to explain why it was lost."

"I can't take credit for the recovery," I said, telling my father about my misadventure with the grappling line, having to be fished out of the icy water by Dubnin and his team.

"It's the idiot who sets out to be hero who gets himself and everyone around him killed." He patted his medal. "I won this because I let myself get blinded by the sun and broke off an attack." He was opening the brandy; I handed him my only two glasses. He poured two fingers in each, no more. "We were dropping on a formation of Nazi tanks at Kursk and I lost my bearings, pulled up. I can still hear Frolov screaming at me, calling me a motherfucker right before his plane exploded.

"I was ashamed of myself, but because I had turned away from the attack, I saw this pair of Messerschmidts coming in behind everyone. So I dived on them and got them with my cannon." My father had rarely spoken of his activities in the war, though I knew he had flown almost two hundred combat missions in the Ilyushin-2, a dive-bomber. He had certainly never given me any details on this pivotal event in his career. "So my big heroic act came about because I had screwed up. And even though I shot down those two Nazi bastards, if Frolov had lived I might have been court-martialed instead!" This was a sentiment I could easily share. We clinked glasses.

Then I had to explain how I had wound up on the recovery team, a story that was even more inglorious in the telling. He grunted with approval when I mentioned General Kamanin. "I haven't talked to him in years. He's one of the chief's nephews." The chief in this case being Marshal Vershinin, the commander in chief of the Air Force. "He's very by-the-book. Not a bad man to work for, though. You could do worse."

When I came to my arrival on Artemov's blacklist, my father got angry. "That drunken son of a bitch had better watch himself," he said.

"Do you know Artemov?"

"I know *of* him. I may not see Kamanin, but I see Rudenko, the chief of staff." I had never bothered to clarify my father's position on the high command of the Soviet Air Force, though I knew Vershinin was alone at the top of the pyramid, with a chief of staff directly below him, through which several "deputy commanders" reported. Kamanin was a deputy commander for space, among other things. My father was on the staff, responsible for some activity in the Moscow military district. "Just this morning he was complaining about your bureau and the way it burns up money. There's a huge fight right now about your rescue forces, did you know that?"

"No."

"It's bad enough that we have to spend money to chase down your spaceships every few months, but for this man-on-the-Moon business we're being asked to assign eighteen thousand people and dozens of aircraft because your ships could land anywhere on the planet!

"Vershinin supports Kamanin, wants the Air Force to be in the space business, so he lets Rudenko take this request for a billion-ruble 'air army' to Grechko." Grechko was the minister of defense, an old-line infantry officer from the war. "Remember, now, Grechko's got the Navy coming in at the same time, because they have to start deploying recovery ships in the ocean, so he blows his top! 'We're not going to the Moon!' he says. 'Let the fucking scientists build these rockets out of their own pockets! No, no, no!' "

My father was red-faced laughing at this memory. "Ustinov himself had to intervene, and even he would authorize only half the money Kamanin wanted. And this is for programs we don't control—we have to rely on Artemov to build his rockets and his spaceships and make them work, which they don't."

I couldn't disagree. In fact, I agreed with enthusiasm, a bad habit of mine when alcohol affects me. And it was certainly at work on me that evening.

"Yuri, are you *happy* in this work?"

"It's fascinating," I said, "if I get to do it."

"You can't do anything from the shithouse."

"Eventually someone else will take my place there."

"That just means there will be more people in the shithouse with you. Since he took over your bureau, Artemov has been acting more and more like an emperor." He refilled my glass. Maybe it was my recent exposure to cold, the fact that I hadn't eaten well in the last couple of days, but I was drunk. My father was barely sipping. "We should find you something else to do, some other work."

"But I have to stay where I am."

"No you don't."

"Vladimir *wants* me there." Had I not been alight with drunken camaraderie, I would never have dared mention Uncle Vladimir's name.

My father's eyes narrowed. He set his glass down carefully, as if afraid it would shatter in his hand. "Have you been working for Vladimir?"

"Yes." I could have added that my "spy" work had been a total failure for months, but could see that my father wasn't going to be satisfied with a half-truth.

"Goddamnit." Now his face was red, and not with amusement. "I told you to stay away from that business! No wonder Artemov got rid of you! He probably found out."

I had allowed myself to linger on that possibility, but not for long, choosing instead to believe I had been denounced by one of my fellow engineers. My father's passion made that hesitation seem all the more foolish: In addition to being a murderer, possibly even a saboteur, Artemov had all kinds of powerful connections. It was plain he knew I was a spy.

"What should I do? Where can I go?" They almost certainly wouldn't take me at the Chelomei bureau, assuming I would even want to work there.

"The space units." He meant the Central Space Office, which was still part of the Strategic Rocket Force.

"I'm a civilian."

"You're also a senior lieutenant in the reserve. You could be placed on active duty with a single phone call." A year ago I had tried very hard to avoid military service. Now I was sitting in my own apartment, working for the Korolev bureau, thinking about embracing it.

"I want to think about it."

My father got to his feet. "Don't take too much time. The longer you wait, the more damage Artemov can do to you."

———

The next night Marina called to congratulate me on my safe return, heroics, and so on, and she happily agreed to meet me in the morning, which was Saturday, February 18. Now swollen with rubles like a cartoon capitalist, I offered to take Marina to Uncle Vladimir's restaurant in the Ostankino Tower.

At ten o'clock, after no more than the usual misadventures, including a stop at a book kiosk at the Yaroslavl Station, I arrived at her building. This time I was waved upstairs by the bemedaled porter, and, gift book in hand, knocked on Marina's door.

Alla, her pretty little hard-line roommate, answered. "I don't think Marina can go out today," she said.

"Why not?" I could see past her into the room; everything looked normal, though there was no sign of Marina.

Then I heard a retching. "Oh," I said.

Alla looked rueful. "It started yesterday. She thought she'd be feeling better, but . . ."

"I understand. I'll call tomorrow, to see how she's doing. Here." I handed Alla the book, Hemingway's *Across the River and into the Trees*, which had just come out. Marina had made us read lots of untranslated Hemingway during our English-language classes.

Disappointed, with rubles burning a hole in my pocket, I spent the day lurking in downtown Moscow. I believe I wound up buying a chair and hauling it back to Kaliningrad on the train.

22 MARINA

At the bureau the next week, we received a special shipment of American magazines with information on the Apollo fire. Triyanov was going to send them to the documentation center for translation, but both Yastrebov and I pointed out that we read English, so we were given several pieces each to abstract.

I was horrified to learn that the astronauts had been locked inside their Apollo, high on its launchpad, with their spacecraft pressurized to *more than one atmosphere* at one-hundred-percent oxygen! In that environment a spark immediately explodes into a flame, and materials that should not burn will burn happily. Apparently this was what happened aboard Apollo that night: A stray spark, perhaps from some arcing wire, had blossomed in the rich oxygen, quickly spreading to fabric netting, Velcro, the canvas of the astronauts' couches. Even the air itself became superheated.

This would have been a serious accident rather than a disaster if not for the fact that Apollo's main hatch was a heavy three-piece monstrosity that could not be opened in less than two minutes under the best of conditions. The high pressure inside the spacecraft made it almost impossible to remove the inner hatch, which was partially sealed against the spacecraft wall by that pressure.

Some reports said that the astronauts had succumbed quickly, asphyxiated by toxic gases sucked into their pressure suits when hoses melted through. Other reports said that they were burned to a crisp. Horrible stories.

What fascinated me most was the bitter criticism directed at NASA and at North American, the main contractor for Apollo—the equivalent of the Korolev bureau—for lax workmanship and for disregard of safety in such a hazardous test.

All of the articles agreed on one thing: America's race to the Moon had come to a complete halt. Everyone expected the Soviets to catch and pass them, and soon. Well, at the end of the month we were scheduled to launch our first unmanned L-1—a Soyuz modified for flight around the Moon with better navigational systems, and minus the spherical orbit module on the nose.

The recovery challenges were immense. Even though the goal of the first L-1 was to get aimed somewhere in the general direction of the Moon, we all hoped the spacecraft could be commanded to a return on planet Earth. If we were lucky enough to be faced with that, the possible landing sites were many, ranging from most of the USSR to the world's equatorial oceans and all countries between fifty-one degrees north and south latitude. (It was this possibility that caused Defense Minister Grechko to choke on the cost of creating a recovery force.)

Even assuming unlimited money, the USSR didn't have the vehicles or personnel to create a standby team, so our Ministry of Foreign Affairs stepped up its campaign in favor of treaties regarding the peaceful return of peaceful spacecraft to their country of origin, while we at the bureau concentrated on the mechanics: transponders and trajectories.

It was tedious work, especially coming after the translations, but I was happy for it, because it kept me from wondering why Marina had not contacted me since the Saturday I found her sick with the flu.

I was in touch with her. I spoke to her several times by telephone in the days immediately after our near–dinner date, in which she confessed to a lingering illness that prevented our seeing each other. As any man would, I wondered if she were avoiding me—but on the phone she sounded ill. I even got Alla on the phone by mistake, and she told me, without prompting, that Marina was off at the Bauman clinic that afternoon.

So I burrowed into my work and did not ask questions, and was very surprised to come home one Wednesday night at eight P.M. to find Marina waiting patiently in the lobby of the building. The porter, a pale young man whose name I never managed to get, had made her a cup of tea, as if she were some visiting aunt. To be fair to the porter, Marina looked pale, drawn, and frail. I almost felt as though I had to help her up the stairs.

I knew instantly that her visit was going to be "special"—no one, even in the best of health, would venture out to Kaliningrad on a cold winter night in the middle of the week. But I was so pleased to see her again, so proud to be showing off my apartment, now equipped with *two* chairs and a table in addition to the bed, that it was half an hour before we really began to talk. "Alla said you'd gone to the clinic. What did they tell you?"

Her eyes filled with tears, and I began to get worried. What if she were truly ill? I had seen that look on my mother's face. "I'm pregnant," she said, her voice barely a whisper.

My ears roared. Birth control in the USSR, in those days, was primitive. The pill existed only in the West; we were encouraged to use condoms, assuming you could ever find them in a store. In truth, couples tried to be careful, and when caught, turned to abortion. I'm sure I turned several different colors as my emotions wrenched from fear to relief to an entirely new kind of fear. "What do you want to do?"

"I don't know yet."

I nodded. I didn't know what I wanted yet, either. Nor did I know what to say. "How far along?"

"About eight weeks. Less than three months, they think." I handed her a handkerchief, because tears were spilling down her face without letup.

"Well, then." I took her in my arms. "I have all kinds of information on the State wedding palace . . ." I had made inquiries last year, when our relationship seemed so strong.

"Yuri, I can't marry you."

"Why not? Don't worry about my father. Don't worry about anything. Half the people we know got married because the girl got pregnant."

She blinked furiously now, and wound her open hand as if that gesture would help her speak. "It's not your baby," she said, finally, fatally, her face suddenly defiant.

"What do you mean?" I said, stupidly and helplessly.

"What do you think I mean! There was *someone else*, okay? The baby could not be yours." She blew her nose. "You're the engineer. Do the math."

In fact, by then I had. There had been a period of six, maybe eight weeks from November to the New Year where we had not even seen each other, much less made love.

"Who is it?"

She stood up. "I'm not going to tell you."

"You owe me—" I was angry now.

"I'm not going to tell you!"

I flung my glass at the wall. Fortunately, it didn't break, though it spewed cold tea across the room, then caromed onto the floor with a truly annoying clatter. I was immediately ashamed of my temper. As ashamed as I was disgusted with the sight of Marina right then.

All I could think to do was to slink over to the corner and pick up the glass. I went into my kitchen area to get a towel.

When I returned, Marina had stopped crying and put on her coat. "I'm sorry," she said.

"Where do you think you're going?"

"Home."

"At this time of night? Alone?" Actually, I would have relished kicking her out into the snow, but she was sick—with morning sickness, obviously—and I couldn't be that cruel. "Stay here." She was weak enough to accept the offer.

I slept on the floor, wrapped in my winter coat, and not very well. I woke instantly when Marina rose early the next morning, while it was still dark, and ran directly to the bathroom to throw up.

God help me, I pretended to be asleep as she cleaned herself up, gathered her things, and quietly left.

23 MY MOTHER

My disastrous personal life obviously had an effect on my work in Department 731—rather, on the enthusiasm I brought to it. Remember that I had been pushed off to the side, away from the exciting work of preparing my colleagues Yeliseyev and Kubasov, as well as military cosmonauts Khrunov and Gorbatko, for their upcoming spacewalk. Three other bureau engineers, Grechko, Makarov, and Volkov, had been accepted for cosmonaut training by General Kamanin, and half a dozen others—including Triyanov himself—were running back and forth to Chkalov air base for zero-G flights and parachute jumps, getting in line for future Soyuz crews.

I, on the other hand, occupied my time writing memos on the lack of recovery resources.

My role in the "investigation" of the murder of Sergei Korolev or the "sabotage" of our programs dwindled to nothing. Filin had been cleared; Artemov struck me as a power-hungry thug who was certainly capable of either crime, or both, but he was inaccessible to me now.

The only bright spot was the news that Lev Tselauri had been hired by the bureau and would be joining Department 731. I didn't hear this from Lev himself, but from Filin, whom I saw briefly at one of the endless committee meetings for the upcoming L-1 launch, which took place on March 10, 1967, under the cover name *Cosmos 146*.

Since recovery wasn't part of the *Cosmos 146* flight plan (it was considered a sufficient challenge just to successfully fire Chelomei's fifth

Proton into orbit, then launch L-1 toward the Moon using the new upper stage), I remained at the bureau, working toward a more ambitious test of the second L-1, to follow in early April.

On Sunday, March 12, I took the train and metro across and around Moscow to the Vagankov Cemetery, which, I realized, was not far from IMBP, where I had undergone medical tests last spring.

My mother was buried there, under an expensive monument that still bore her portrait, somewhat faded after six years, much like my memories of her. As usual, I had to bribe the guard to gain access to the cemetery, which was supposedly closed for maintenance, though I suspect the sign was put up by the guards whenever they ran short of cash. Then I was allowed to rent a bucket containing a sponge and some cleaning solvent.

Following a brutal year of decline, my mother Zhanna died on March 12, 1961, one month to the day before Yuri Gagarin's triumphant first spaceflight. At the time, we had returned to Moscow after years of what my mother certainly saw as exile in the Crimea. She was a Moscow girl who met my father at a Party gathering celebrating the Soviet nonaggression pact with Hitler. (They were both understandably coy about telling me this for many years.) My father was then a pilot junior enough to have been spared the purges that destroyed the upper ranks of the Air Force in the late 1930s; he had been stationed in the Leningrad Military District and had flown combat missions against the Finns before winning a transfer to a demonstration unit based at the Central Airfield.

My parents were married in January 1941 and settled down to the constrained but pleasant life of a junior officer in Moscow; my mother was working as an elementary-school teacher when the Nazis attacked that June. Within weeks she had been evacuated, with her whole school, to Kazan, where she discovered she was pregnant.

My father, of course, had gone to the front shortly after the conjugal visit that resulted in my conception. They did not see each other for almost two years; he only saw me for the first time when I was fifteen months old.

Reunited at war's end, we did not return to Moscow, but moved to the Feodosiya in the Crimea, where my father was given command of a fighter squadron; then, after completing a correspondence course at the Red Banner Academy (I can remember him sitting up nights, cursing the papers in front of him), an air regiment. My mother resumed teaching. Her mother, Galina, came to live with us.

It was, I realize, a happy time. I had friends; so did my parents. The Crimea has nicer weather than any other part of the USSR. When I was thirteen, however, my father was transferred to Kazakhstan, to a remote posting at a secret base. Only my mother was allowed to accompany him there: I remained in the Crimea with Grandmother Galina for two years, until we all moved to Moscow in the year of the Sputnik, 1957.

Something had gone wrong with my parents' marriage during those two years in the desert, though the posting had had the opposite effect on my father's career. (He had offended someone in Moscow, or he would have stayed in the capital at war's end.) Even though he was over the age limit, he was enrolled at the academy for general staff officers and, in due time, became a general. My mother never taught after her sojourn in the desert, made no new friends, even though she had grown up in Moscow. She spent her time nursing Galina through her last days. Even before her final year, she herself was frequently hospitalized.

Such was the outline of her life—and I knew little more than that.

I had no flowers to bring; they could not be found in Moscow that March. But I was prepared to clean the monument.

Someone had beaten me to it. The winter grime had already been cleared away, and given the visible streaks on the marble facing, not long ago, either. I looked around. Sure enough, through the trees thirty meters away, standing in front of another monument, was a stocky man in a green Air Force greatcoat carrying a bucket of his own. My father, who as far as I knew, had never entered this cemetery since the day his wife was buried.

I only took time to touch the monument—for luck, I suppose—before hurrying off, calling, "Papa!"

He turned toward me, blinking in surprise, gesturing toward my bucket with his. "You, too?"

"Every year."

If he took that as reproach for his own years of neglect, he didn't show it. "It's hard to believe it's been six years."

"I'm glad to see you here."

Nor did he react to my words. "My driver's over this way." He assumed—rightly—that I would appreciate a ride. "How have you been?"

Giving up the idea of sharing any conversation about my mother, I went ahead and told him about the end of my relationship with Marina, including the pregnancy.

That brought him back to life. "I'm glad you're finished with that little whore."

"Please don't call her that."

He grunted. "When you begin to see her more clearly, Yuri, you won't like it much. She wrecked one marriage already, and the kind of work she does . . ." He stopped, shaking his head at the disgrace of it all. "How is *your* work?"

I couldn't help smiling. "It makes my personal life look like a happy dream."

He stopped and took my arm. "Have you thought about my offer?"

Yes, I had. During my frequent bus rides all over the northeast sector of the Moscow district, I had wondered what it might be like to go on active duty. I had worn a uniform during my reserve training; God knows I was familiar with the military life. "It's interesting," I said, "but I don't want to wind up assigned to Baikonur for five years. Or up north."

"Suppose I promised you you could stay in Moscow?"

Being an active-duty officer in Moscow was far from the worst job in the world. A good number of the people working at the Korolev bureau wore uniforms, and aside from that, their professional lives were identical to those of their civilian colleagues. "That would be different."

"You know, too, that your commitment is only five years. You can transfer back to the reserve and take a job in industry then, after Artemov's sins have caught up with him." I laughed. Five years or fifteen—at that moment all I wanted was a change in my circumstances. Joining the Strategic Rocket Force was as close as I could come to enlisting in the French Foreign Legion. "It will also get you out of Vladimir's clutches."

That made up my mind. "Go ahead, then."

He hugged me. "I'll take care of this in the morning."

We reached his car. Before we climbed in, I took my father's arm. "Where were you stationed when you and Mama went to the desert?"

"Semipalatinsk. The nuclear-test range. It's not actually very far from your Baikonur. I had given up fighters to fly Tupolevs on bomb tests. Why?" He grinned. "Don't worry: I won't let them send you there. In fact, I may have a surprise for you."

"What kind of surprise?"

"Come on, Yuri! Let your father have some fun!" We got in the car. "If I told you, what kind of a surprise would it be?"

24

THE DANGERS OF ROCKET FUEL

On Monday, all of Department 731 was bused over to Star Town for the opening of the new flight simulation building.

I had been to the center once before, when undergoing my test on the centrifuge. Visits by bureau personnel other than our Soyuz cosmonauts were discouraged—not by the military people, but by Triyanov and others in the bureau. "Why should we build simulators here, then have to ship them to the Air Force so they can pretend to control our spaceflights?" he had said more than once.

Nevertheless, a series of "peace treaties" between the Air Force, represented by General Kamanin, and our bureau, notably Artemov and Triyanov, had resulted in the construction of the appropriate simulators.

I had seen the building under construction last spring. It was a three-story structure right across from the centrifuge. We spilled out of the buses, perhaps forty of us, and stomped around in the cold waiting for whoever had the keys to the place. There were several Air Force officers milling around with us—student cosmonauts, I assumed—and one familiar face from the other bus, Lev Tselauri.

He was hanging back in a different group, but I pushed my way through it to greet him cheerfully. "When did you start?"

"Today is my first official day, though I've been running errands for the past few weeks."

"That sounds familiar. Filin apparently likes to test his students as secretaries first."

"Actually, this was for Artemov. Excuse me, Yuri." He hurried away, to catch up with the others, who were now being ushered into the building. The speed with which he ran away was unnecessary; in fact, during the whole of our brief conversation, Lev had seemed nervous and awkward. Of course, it was his first day on the job and first visit to the cosmonaut training center. Since he had spent time doing menial tasks for Artemov, he might also have heard that I was on his boss's shitlist.

These were all good reasons, but they left me feeling more alone than ever.

General Kamanin and several other high-ranking types, including Artemov, were waiting for us inside. Apparently toasts had been drunk, even at this relatively early hour, because some of the guys were red-faced and laughing. Not all: Kamanin stood dourly off to one side, arms crossed like a schoolteacher regarding a rowdy classroom.

"Is everyone here? Good. Welcome to the new facility." The speaker was none other than Colonel Yuri Gagarin himself, dressed, like his fellow seven Soyuz cosmonauts, in a track suit and wearing a white headset around his neck. He had been assigned as the backup commander for the "active" Soyuz, which was to be piloted by Colonel Komarov.

Komarov and the others were clustered around the docking simulator. It fell to the world-famous Gagarin, who also served as deputy director of the training center, to serve as our host. He did his job well, though I wondered then how much damage this administrative work did to his flying skills.

He gave a short speech about the benefits of having so much training equipment "finally under one roof." It seems outrageous in retrospect, but with less than a month to go before their launch, the Soyuz crews had never had a single place in which to do the bulk of their integrated training, where they could sit in spacecraft mockups that actually resembled the flight article, talking on the radio to the same people who would be controlling and assisting their mission, reading data on their control panels that reflected real flight parameters, and seeing outside their windows the sights they would see in orbit. Obviously the zero-G flights had to launch from an airfield, but these poor guys had done their training at our bureau, in chambers at Chkalov, at the spacesuit factory in southeast Moscow, and at Baikonur, too. "We are just in time for the first flights of Soyuz."

There was no open acknowledgment of the irony of Gagarin's statement, except a muttered, "Not a moment too soon," from an officer behind me. It was Saditsky, of course, who made the statement for my ears alone, I think. We shook hands as General Kuznetsov, head of the training center, began to repeat Gagarin's welcome, though not as artfully.

"It's better than Voskhod, isn't it?" I said.

"Anything's better than Voskhod. Soyuz will be a good ship." He glanced around, not wishing to be overheard. "I wish we had more time for training. And I wish you guys had more time to get the bugs out."

"Everybody's in a hurry to beat the Americans."

"The Americans were in a big hurry to beat us, and look what happened." Given Saditsky's candor, I wondered, and not for the first time, how he had ever managed to become a cosmonaut. "So, Ribko, when are you coming to train with us?"

"Not for years," I said. "There are too many people in line ahead of me." This was a polite lie, of course. My brief career as a bureau "cosmonaut" had less to do with my undeniable lack of seniority than with my colossal mistake in going to work for Uncle Vladimir.

"Well, hang in there. We'll be flying a lot this year." He knocked on the side of the simulator for luck. "This *is* wood, isn't it?"

As we spoke, the greetings concluded and people were free to move about. Like two pensioners out for a summer stroll in Gorky Park, we ambled around the primary simulator, a collection of walls, operator consoles, and wiring that had a mockup spacecraft buried somewhere inside it.

Further into the hall, which was a long, open area resembling a narrow basketball court, I found mockups of other spacecraft: One appeared to be a Soyuz. It had the telltale bell-shaped reentry module of that vehicle. But it was on the nose of a long, cylindrical vehicle that had a habitation area behind the bell. Through an opening in the cylinder I could see a hatch cut through what should be the heat shield.

"How'd you like to ride that thing through reentry?" I asked a young captain who happened to be taking the same sort of tour. (I was thinking about the scorched interior of the Soyuz we'd fished out of the Aral Sea. And that spacecraft had a one-piece heat shield, however defective.)

The captain laughed nervously. "I'm sure they'll test it many times."

More than twice, I hoped.

There was another completely different type of vehicle on display here, too: This one looked like a copy of the American Mercury or

Gemini—a cone perhaps three meters across at its base, topped by a smaller cylinder with its own tapering cylindrical nose. This unit was mounted in front of an even larger habitation module—one that had an actual antiaircraft cannon mounted on the exterior.

I walked around to the other side to get a better look at this phenomenon when I happened upon a knot of people that included Artemov and some colonel, who asked our chief, "Now that we've got our Soyuz simulator, Boris, when do we get the L-1?"

Everyone laughed except Artemov, who snapped, "What do you need L-1 for?"

"Well, we might be *flying* it this summer," the colonel said, smiling. More laughter.

"L-1 will be flying, but it's far from certain that *your* people will be aboard."

Sudden silence throughout the hall. I saw a couple of the Soyuz guys—military—shaking their heads, and heard someone behind me, not Saditsky, mutter, "Here we go again. . . ."

"Listen to that drunken bastard," said another.

Artemov persisted. "We design the rockets and the spacecraft, and we can fly them. You guys should stick to airplanes." He pointed back at the upside-down Soyuz and then at the big Mercury-Gemini copy behind him. "Besides, you've got all these fine military vehicles here from Kozlov and Chelomei. Fly them." He turned his finger into a pistol and made shooting noises. "Guns! You Air Force guys never change!"

He walked away, laughing and shaking his head. Realizing I was the only civilian in a group of angry officers, I also made a quiet but steady retreat.

"He's clearly unstable."

So said Uncle Vladimir to me that night when I told him of Artemov's latest display. After returning to the bureau, I had run off to my apartment, using the classic Russian technique of leaving my jacket behind. ("Ribko? Haven't seen him lately, but he must be around somewhere. His jacket's still on the chair.") I had not wanted to test a bogus excuse on Triyanov.

I felt I had to phone Uncle Vladimir not only about Artemov, but also about my potential enrollment in military service, and could not have done so from the bureau. (There are now pay telephones in Moscow, but they were not to be found in Kaliningrad in those days.) He took the call, and suggested I come down to his office near the Belorussia Station as soon as possible.

This left me in an awkward situation: I was absent from the bureau without leave. I had thought I could run home, make the call, and return within the hour. A trip down to the State Security annex would finish the day.

Yet, I felt I had to see Uncle Vladimir.

I make no apologies for my dithering. This was how I lived my life, always trying to be the dutiful son, especially when I was not. Within moments I had remembered the reasons for my call to Uncle Vladimir, and after leaving a message with Triyanov's office saying I would not be back today for personal reasons, grabbed my only other coat and headed for the train.

Eventually I found myself back inside that huge, messy office, feeling just as nervous as I had a year ago. I noted my own red folder on Uncle Vladimir's desk; it was noticeably fatter than I remembered.

"He's certainly drinking," I said of Artemov.

"I think his problems go deeper than that. He strikes me as a man in a crisis." He had been tapping a pencil, which he now dropped, a gesture of considerable frustration by Uncle Vladimir's standards. "I wish I could get you closer to him."

"My friend Lev is working for him now."

"Yes, your Georgian buddy," he said, adding, "We have our eye on him." It was said most casually, but made me wonder: Did he consider Lev to be a potential watcher, or someone to be watched? "As we will have our eye on Artemov during this next launch. The number of accidents and failures is appalling, like the first days of a war." He blinked. "Where will you be?"

"At Baikonur to begin with, then wherever the recovery team goes."

"You're wasted there."

"I think so, too," I said. Seeing an opportunity to make the transition to the next, painful subject, I added, "Which is why I'm leaving the bureau."

Uncle Vladimir listened to this, then smiled in disbelief. "That's interesting, Yuri. Where are you going to be working?"

"In the Strategic Rocket Force. As an officer."

I believe I surprised him. "I see." He pushed back in his chair, looking down at his desk for a moment. "You've been listening to your father again."

"He *is* my father."

"And I would be the last person to ask you to go against your father's wishes. Even in the service of the Party."

"I think I can serve the Party as an officer."

"Yes, yes, yes. But it will be more difficult for you to help me. You see that, Yuri?"

"I can't see that I've been much help to you at all."

"It's not a question of what arrests we make based on what you tell me. Our business is to gather information, and you have been quite good about that. You give me the ability to keep other sources honest, for example. And your career in the bureau has just begun. Who knows where you might wind up in a few months or years?"

"As long as Artemov is in charge, I'll be staying right where I am, in the outhouse."

He waved away the whole idea of Artemov. "Artemov will be lucky if he doesn't wind up in prison." He leaned forward. "All right, how far along have you gotten?"

I told him I was scheduled to take my military medical exams on Thursday. If I passed, and there was little doubt I would, given that I had passed the substantially more rigorous cosmonaut training tests, I would be subject to immediate call-up. "All right, take your exams, but don't take the oath without talking to me. I'm going to see if we can't improve your situation."

That, of course, was the last thing I wanted, given that the original "improvement" in my situation as Filin's assistant had marked me as a spy. But I felt I had to make some concession to Uncle Vladimir. "Okay," I said, "I'll call you first."

We shook hands, and I got out of there as fast as I could.

25 THE CREDENTIALS COMMITTEE

It turned out that Triyanov never knew I was absent that afternoon. He had stayed at Star Town to smooth ruffled eagle feathers. It was especially lucky for me, because two days later I needed a whole morning off. This time, though, I actually managed to formulate an excuse that fit the situation. "I have to take an examination regarding my military reserve status."

"Anytime you want to get out of that, let me know," Triyanov said. "The reserve people are very good at excusing engineers doing important space research."

I thanked him for his offer, but nevertheless presented myself early Thursday at the same Aviation Hospital in Sokolniki, where my father had been hospitalized after his car crash the previous spring. It was slightly irregular, in that my prior military medical examinations had been performed in a clinic at Bauman, but my father had arranged it.

The doctors there were exactly like those at the IMBP, except that they wore uniforms under their white coats. They also had my IMBP tests in front of them, and contented themselves with a few hours of completely routine checks—blood pressure, hearing, eyesight—to confirm the earlier data. I think their primary criterion was whether or not my breath would fog a mirror held up to my nose.

As I was dressing to go, my father arrived carrying a garment bag over his shoulder. "You passed," he said. "Congratulations."

I thanked him, then said, regarding the bag, "A new uniform?"

"Yes. For you." He thrust it at me. "Put it on. You're coming with me."

As a reserve senior lieutenant, I was allowed to wear a uniform, and had a faded one back home in my closet, complete with my rocketeer badge. But this was new! "Shouldn't I take the service oath first?"

"Don't worry about it. There are going to be others just like you where we're going."

"Where are we going?"

"Star Town."

On the drive out of Moscow, I guessed that this maneuver was my father's lure; even if technically a member of the Strategic Rocket Force, I would be assigned to the cosmonaut training center. Somehow he had been able to pull strings with the Air Force officials who controlled the place. Why couldn't he have done that eighteen months ago? It would have saved me two false steps in my career.

The parking lot in front of the main administration building at the training center was jammed with an unusual number of expensive official cars. I had been teetering on the edge of nervousness. At this point I gave in to the emotion. "I can't go in there!"

"Of course you can."

"What if they ask me a military question?"

My father waved the folder in front of me. "They will know your background, Yuri. You aren't the only reserve officer they're considering today. There are people here from missile factories and even from the universities. It's a military credentials committee, so they are looking at you as a potential military officer."

Feeling the pinch of the stiff collar and tie, trying not to slip on the ice in my shiny new shoes, and trying (uselessly) to slick down my non-regulation hair, I followed my father into the building. "It seems like a lot of fuss to hire engineers for the center."

Now my father smiled in triumph. "They don't have committees like this to hire engineers, Yuri. This is for the next enrollment in the cosmonaut team."

In a hallway on the first floor, outside the meeting room, a row of chairs had been set up. I was given the last one.

The chairs were filled with officers and even a pair of sergeants from the Air Force, Air Defense Force and the Strategic Rocket Force, perhaps thirty men in all. The only thing they all had in common was obvious good health. Even the ages ranged from the low twenties to mid-thirties. Each man sat there, hands folded, eyes closed, or in some cases, open and staring, waiting for what would surely be a turning point in his life.

Mine, too, I realized. I had taken several small steps down the road to becoming a member of the bureau's cosmonaut team, but could not have expected to train for a flight for at least two or three years, perhaps longer. Now I was about to jump ahead in line. The USSR had not had a manned flight for over two years, but I expected that sorry situation to change in the next month. And given the number of military vehicles being built, it was possible that soon we could be flying missions to Earth orbit or the Moon every other month.

I rehearsed a statement saying how eager I was to fulfill any missions the Party and nation would ask of me.

Every ten to fifteen minutes the door to the meeting room would open—the interviewee would emerge to disappear back to his military base (never to return?). A colonel named Nikeryasov, a man even bigger, rounder, and more intimidating than Uncle Vladimir, would then summon the next candidate.

If the credentials committee took a lunch break, I never saw it. Fully four hours after my arrival, I was the last to be summoned. "Senior Lieutenant Ribko, Yuri Nikolayevich," Colonel Nikeryasov announced.

I rose and, in my best parade-ground manner, entered the room.

There were twenty generals and colonels waiting for me, and no place to sit. Nikeryasov merely pointed to a place on the floor facing the committee, I saluted and stood at attention.

The chair of the panel was none other than General Kamanin. I also recognized Colonel Belyayev, one of the famous Voskhod cosmonauts. Several of the other officers wore the insignia of the military medical services. The rest were jowly, bored-looking Air Force men.

Kamanin announced my name to his fellows, and gave my personal data, birthdate, place, education, Party (Komsomol) status, finishing with employment: engineer, Department 731, Central Experimental Design Bureau of Machine-Building, Postbox V-2572. (I'm not sure I had ever heard the bureau's official new name at that time.) One of the generals, recognizing the address, grunted and sneered, "One of Artemov's people," as if that were a curse.

Then the questioning began. What did I know about spaceflight? What military training did I have? Did I plan to become a full member of the Communist Party? How was my health?

The only time I gave what was clearly an unsatisfactory answer was when asked if I had undergone parachute training. I had not, while, I'm sure, every pilot who was a candidate, and most of the engineers, had done so.

"Lieutenant Ribko can become qualified as a parachutist," Kamanin said. "We already have evidence of his fearlessness, in the recovery of spacecraft Soyuz." Several panel members turned to that page of my dossier, and were somewhat mollified.

The final question was this: Why did I want to become a cosmonaut? Here I drew on my childhood, citing the imaginary novels by Wells, Verne, and Tsiolkovsky that my mother had urged on me, how I had shaped my education in order to make some of those visions a reality, not only for the romance of discovery and exploration, but for the glory of the socialist state, and its security. I said I wanted the first man to walk on the Moon to be a Communist from the USSR. (And managed to half-believe it even as I said it.)

Finally Kamanin said, "Do you have any questions for us, Lieutenant Ribko?"

"Only this, Comrade General: How many candidates will be enrolled at this time?"

"We will accept as many as twenty," he said, "reporting on May 7." Nobody timed anything for the first week of May in my country. People were too busy celebrating May Day and the days that followed.

Thus dismissed, I thanked the general and the committee, executed a smart salute, turned on my heel, and walked out.

I remember thinking that my chances of selection were good, with twenty possible cosmonauts out of the thirty candidates I had seen. I said as much to my father as we drove away. "Yuri," he said, shaking his head, "this is only the third of four days of meetings. You are also competing with dozens of men who barely missed the cut two years ago."

All right, I thought: twenty out of a possible two hundred. I still felt good about my chances. After all, hadn't General Kamanin himself remembered me?

26

UNIVERSAL ROCKET 500

My fancy new uniform took its place in my closet right beside its more tattered predecessor, and I went back to work at the bureau. Everything there was frantic, since we were preparing the unmanned L-1 for launch on April 7–8, along with the two manned Soyuz craft on April 20–22. I had no contact with my father, except for one telephone call telling me that the credentials committee would not announce its choices until the end of April. That was fine, since I could not possibly leave the bureau before then. More disturbing, however, was his news that the committee was now saying it was likely to select only fifteen candidates, or possibly as few as ten.

I had no more contact with Marina; I saw Lev only at several program reviews, and then only at a distance. He was attached to Artemov like a third arm, and probably as useful. It was two weeks of madness, fifteen hours a day, until we left for Baikonur on Thursday, April 6, 1967.

The Tyuratam hotels were jammed to twice their normal capacity, understandably, given that the vehicles belonged to two entirely different—and, need I say, not remotely friendly—organizations. The rivalry was complicated by the fact that the lunar version of Chelomei's Proton carried our bureau's L-1 spacecraft, which itself would be pushed out of Earth orbit by our Block D upper stage. Block D was part of the even more gigantic Carrier rocket.

There were engineers from different engine-design teams, too, plus officials from two different State Commissions overseeing matters for the Central Committee, not to mention Air and Rocket Force officers. Everybody wanted to be part of the excitement: Here in April 1967, the Soviet Union would reclaim its rightful place as the world's leader in the exploration of space.

It helped, I think, that spring was early here on the steppes of Kazakhstan. While Moscow was still trudging through the end of a long winter, fresh southern breezes were caressing the town and the launch center. The same breezes, of course, would soon become hot, nasty winds. Tulips were beginning to bloom, for a brief time, before being scorched.

Friday, the day before the launch, I had a chance to see my first Proton rocket up close. What a monster! Unlike the Voskhod and Soyuz rockets, which had a quaint, old-church Russian look to them, the Proton was pure socialist realism: a thick white cylinder except for the base, where six slim fuel tanks hugged the central core, and at the top, where the bureau's Block D upper stage and L-1 marred the clean line. Even the names suggested different mentalities: The Voskhod and Soyuz were cousins of the original "Seven" booster. Proton's official name was Universal Rocket #500K. Universal Rocket! It should have been serviced by gleaming silver robots.

"It's like a soldier," a familiar voice said. "A sentry knowing he must storm the cosmos in the morning."

I turned and saw none other than Sergeant Oleg, my escort to the home of space dogs Breezy and Blackie from last February. He looked exactly as he had then, though the beautiful weather better fit his lack of an overcoat. He had a knapsack slung over a shoulder. "You're a poet, Sergeant!"

He grinned, showing missing teeth. "Some reporter said it right over there." He nodded toward another clump of sightseers, one of several crawling all over Area 82 like vermin.

"Well, you're an honest man, at least." Sergeant Oleg had been right about one thing: The support structure for the Proton Universal Rocket was also futuristic. Where the veteran Seven rockets sat enclosed in a cocoon of girders that opened only at liftoff, the Proton's structure slid off to one side, as if to make sure that at the proper moment all eyes were only on the rocket.

I asked Sergeant Oleg what he was up to, realizing that I had never been quite sure of his job. It was not technical; he seemed a bit too grimy to be allowed into the assembly buildings. He could have been a guard, but here again his appearance worked against him; he would never pass an inspection. My guess was that he was a truck driver. "Hunting," he answered, proving me wrong in an instant.

"What is there to hunt around here?"

"Damned little. But the dukes want fresh meat for their table, so . . ." He shrugged. I almost laughed at "dukes," wondered if he meant the Baikonur generals, or the many visiting civilian nobles. Probably both. "I'm off to the east. They've got a license for saigak at Dzhusaly." Saigak were a species of deer native to that area, perhaps fifty kilometers away, the location of the downrange tracking stations.

"Won't you need a rifle?"

"They keep the official rifle locked up there."

"Where's your truck?"

He hefted his knapsack. "They can't spare a truck for me until I've got a kill." And he took off walking, heading in the general direction of China.

Those of us in the recovery team gathered at the new and freshly painted Area 82 assembly building late the next morning for the launch. All the preparations went smoothly; except for the fact that everyone's attention kept drifting to the Universal Rocket on its pad, it might have been any lazy Saturday afternoon in spring—perfect for a subbotnik, helping the farmers plant crops.

A horn sounded somewhere in the distance at the five-minute mark. We all shaded our eyes in the bright sunlight, and at a few seconds after noon we saw bright fire from the base of the Proton. For the longest time, the rocket sat there spewing clouds of steam, building up thrust. Then it slowly began to rise as the sound and vibration reached us: a rapid but violent popping that only hinted at the power needed to send this beast into the sky.

And into the sky it went, faster and faster, until it was just a contrail heading wherever it was Sergeant Oleg went. We found ourselves clapping. "That's the most beautiful thing I've ever seen," a female voice said.

I thought no more about that voice for the moment, since I had to follow the rest of the team back around to the front of the building where the cars and buses were parked. There we waited, until another group emerged from the building itself with the news that the L-1 space-craft and its Block D stage were safely in orbit. The vehicle was to be publicly known as *Cosmos 154*.

Only then did I recognize the face that matched the female voice I had heard. It was Uncle Vladimir's beautiful lady friend from State Security. "Katya?"

Pale blue eyes narrowed, she glanced at me for a moment, obviously having no idea of who I was. "Vladimir Nefedov's nephew—" I started to say, when she brightened. "Yuri! Hello! I wondered if I would see you here!"

With all the high-ranking officials swarming over Tyuratam and Bai-konur with their "secretaries" or girlfriends, the launch center was hardly an all-male environment. But Katya was literally the first woman I had conversed with in all my previous travels, other than the occasional key lady or shopgirl.

It turned out that Katya was staying at the same hotel as I was, having come along with a group from the Academy of Sciences. We arranged to meet later that night, if all went well.

Unfortunately, all did not go well. Returning to the hotel, I learned that the Block D upper stage had exploded when reignited to boost L-1 toward the Moon. This left me with no L-1 to recover, since the damaged spacecraft was now wobbling uncontrollably in the wrong orbit, and would reenter the atmosphere when and where the laws of physics, not the flight-control center, chose.

In spite of the failure—or perhaps because of it—Katya and I met that evening in the lobby of the hotel. I was going out for a walk and she was coming in with her group of scientists. "When will be you be off duty?" I asked, assuming she was serving as State Security control over the scientists.

"I went off duty when the spacecraft blew up," she said. "I'll meet you down here in ten minutes."

True to her promise, she returned shortly, hair brushed and lipstick freshened, looking more like a movie star than ever. She was also carrying a bottle of Georgian wine. "A gift from an admirer?" I asked, wondering if Uncle Vladimir was that admirer.

"How ever did you know?" And she smiled.

"I hope he won't be upset that he'll be missing out."

"If I'm happy, he'll be happy." She linked her arm in mine. "I believe your mission is clear." To make her happy? In what ways? I think I blushed.

Attached to the hotel was a café where I had eaten quick breakfasts, never dinner. But there were few dining options in that part of Tyuratam in those days, so I had no real choice but to take Katya there.

Either we were early, or the various military and civilian officials were busy drowning their sorrows, because the café was half-empty. Nevertheless, we stood in line to get a table, then stood in line to order. Finally we were able to sit and open our wine, knowing it would be a long wait for our actual meal.

"How have your scientists been behaving?" I asked, trying to be as sociable as possible without mentioning State Security.

"They were quite good until news of the failure hit them. Now I suspect they're behaving badly, though God knows where. Go ahead, taste it." She had poured the wine, which was sweet and fruity, typical Georgian stuff I knew from my teens. "I don't work for your uncle, by the way."

I blushed again. "I assumed you did."

"I work at the Space Research Institute on studies of the surface of the Moon. We had a camera aboard your spacecraft that was supposed to take pictures and help us finish our maps."

"How did you meet Vladimir, then?"

"The cameras came from a military satellite, so we had to decide who would have access to the raw photos. Your uncle and I were both on the committee."

I hadn't realized Uncle Vladimir reached into other areas of the space program but then, I really knew almost nothing about his responsibilities. Or powers.

But as we talked, I thought less about my uncle and more about Katya. She had graduated from Bauman and had even studied under some of the same professors. She knew Filin (though not Artemov) because she had done graduate work in the Korolev bureau on the very first Luna probes, which were the first in the world to hit the Moon, then fly around it and take pictures of its "dark" side. She had joined the Space Research Institute when it was founded three years ago, something she openly admitted she regretted: "Science is the poor cousin in the space business. The engineers do whatever they want and only throw the military enough bones to keep them paying the bills. We are only brought out when some idiot Westerners visit Moscow and want to see a 'space center' and the geniuses of our program." She sounded more amused than bitter. Then she raised her glass. "To the *next* L-1."

Maybe it was the wine or the beautiful spring evening or the gypsy music being piped into the café, but I found myself completely entranced with Katya, in spite of the ten-year age difference.

Eventually our food arrived, and we soon found ourselves with empty plates and an equally empty bottle of wine. Since there was still a rosy light in the western sky, I suggested a walk outside.

We could hear voices from the open windows of the ten-story apartment buildings nearby. Occasional bits of music. Shouts and laughter that came from the hotel, along with the sound of at least one smashed glass.

We had only gone a little way down the road when Katya took my hand, and let my arms encircle her. Awkwardly, since she was taller than me even without heels, we kissed standing right by the side of the road, swept by the headlights of at least one passing car, whose occupants cheered us on.

"Come to my room, Yuri," was all she said, and I did.

Long after midnight I crept back to the room I shared with my friend from the bureau, feeling more alive than I had in my life. Katya in bed was—how shall I put this?—very different from Marina.

I lay awake for at least an hour, trying to remember the touch of her beautiful skin, her fragrance, wondering when and where I could see her again, and just how Uncle Vladimir was going to react to *this* news.

27

SOYUZ 1

I had to be off to Area 2 early the next morning and didn't dare stop by Katya's room. The eight Soyuz cosmonauts were entering their final days of training, and one of their tasks this morning was to rehearse emergency egress from their two spacecraft, both of which were still sitting upright on the floor of the assembly building next to their Soyuz launch vehicles. As a member of the team that would recover both crews, I had to take part.

The first set of exercises involved the backup crews, with Gagarin, Kubasov, and Gorbatko showing that they could climb through the nose hatch of Soyuz Number 4, the active docking craft.

Of course, Soyuz Number 4, like Soyuz Number 5, already had its spherical orbital module in place in preparation for launch. (It would be jettisoned prior to reentry.) So the egress of the three men was very time-consuming, and not at all realistic, especially when all three cosmonauts had to be extra careful not to damage any switches or other equipment as they unstrapped and climbed out.

Nikolayev, the backup commander, completed his escape from Number 5 in almost the same amount of time it took for the three in Number 4 to do the same thing. When apprised of this, Nikolayev joked, "Yuri's smaller than anyone," which happened to be true and caused everyone, including the great Gagarin himself, to laugh.

Then we watched as the crewmen who would actually fly the mission went through the same rigmarole. Komarov, Yeliseyev, and Khrunov out of 4, Bykovsky out of 5. Bykovsky, who wasn't much larger than Gagarin, was the clear champion, though the Komarov team showed it could move when needed. I was encouraged to know that they were sufficiently at home in their spacecraft to move about it with some confidence. It would certainly make things easier for them once they'd thumped down out on the steppes.

Saditsky, Kostin, and several other cosmonauts were present, as was General Kamanin, who smiled and nodded at me. Kamanin and Gagarin were called away before the egress training could be completed. "The State Commission just now realized that Gagarin is the backup commander, meaning he could command the next Soyuz mission," Saditsky told me. "They had a shitfit."

"What's the problem?"

"They don't want to risk their big hero."

"What does Gagarin think about this?"

"He fought to get himself assigned to the crew! He says he's too young to be a museum exhibit."

"What do you think?"

Saditsky smiled. "I wish I was the only cosmonaut in the team, so I could be the first man in space *and* the first to walk on the Moon. Failing that . . . Gagarin's a pilot: He's been sitting on his ass for six years and he wants to fly. Let him."

Just as the cosmonauts were packing for their next destination, the big doors at the far end of the building opened and two forklift trucks pulled in, each one dragging a pair of green bundles on a trailer. These were the Soyuz recovery parachutes, a primary and a reserve for each vehicle, packed and fresh from testing in Feodosiya and ready to be installed. Having no interest in this procedure, I was about to leave when a group of my colleagues from the bureau, led by none other than Artemov himself, arrived, with Lev Tselauri tagging along like a puppy.

Feeling a bit resentful at Lev's iciness, or arrogant about my chances with the military cosmonaut team, I approached them. Artemov, who was busy giving unnecessary orders to the installation team, didn't notice, but I saw a look of dread move across Lev's face, like a cloud passing in front of the sun. But only momentarily. "How did the egress go?" he asked.

"The prime crews did a good job. Backups could use more work."

"That's the way it should be."

"How have you been?" I asked.

From the way he slumped, you'd think I had just told him his family had been wiped out by Nazis. "I have something to tell you," he said, his voice a harsh whisper.

Lev took me by the arm and marched me away from the crowd around the spacecraft, all the way into the April afternoon.

"I've been avoiding you."

"I noticed."

"I'm sorry. But you will understand." I hoped so: This was not the cheerful, cynical, brilliant Georgian I had lived with for two years. "You see, I'm getting married."

He seemed anything but happy. "Congratulations."

"To Marina."

For a moment I couldn't see or hear anything. For an even longer moment, I couldn't say anything. Lev waited—did he think I was going to hit him? I suppose that crossed my mind. But all I could do was say, "Oh. I hope you'll be very happy."

"You have a right to be angry."

"Don't tell me about my rights." By then I was walking away, blind with fury. *Marina and Lev!* I remembered the time I had run into him in her neighborhood when I made a surprise visit to her building. I stopped, turned back. "When did it start?"

"Last summer." Having confessed, he now seemed defiant, ready to answer any question, no matter how painful.

But I had no desire to hear any more answers. I felt exhausted and wanted only to return to the hotel.

Which did not happen for two more hours. I spent them sitting alone on the bus, trying not to hate Marina and Lev, torturing myself with the knowledge that my father had been right about her.

I don't remember much about the preparations for the launch of the vehicles that would officially become *Soyuz 1* and *Soyuz 2*. The weather turned bad after a week, bringing cold, almost wintry rain that doused the launch center, the town of Tyuratam, and everyone's spirits. Defense Minister Ustinov flew in for the meeting of the State Commission, and threw everyone into a tizzy by questioning plans for the Soyuz docking. He thought the commander of the active craft—Komarov—should rely more on the automatic docking systems, which had never actually been tested in orbit.

It was impossible to change the procedures this late in the training, of course, but that didn't stop Artemov and his deputies from putting Komarov and Gagarin through a series of pointless exercises.

On April 19, a group of Air Force generals flew into Tyuratam, among them my father. He left me a note at the desk telling me that he had arrived, that he would be with Marshal Rudenko and General Kamanin and the other chiefs, but he hoped we would see each other.

There was also a letter from Katya, mailed from Moscow. It was just a few lines, saying how much she had enjoyed spending time with me, and most importantly, giving me her address and phone number. That simple letter, following the revelation of Marina's treachery, lifted my spirits so much that I looked forward to going back to Moscow, something which, for several days, seemed unappealing, now that I knew of the approaching Lev and Marina wedding, not to mention the birth of their child!

On the evening of the twenty-first, my father asked me to join him and the other generals at a dinner in old-town Tyuratam. "It'll be a great opportunity for you," he said when I balked. "Buy a few rounds and make sure you thank everyone, because these are the guys who signed your appointment to active duty."

It was a horrible evening, since I knew no one but my father. Out of boredom—or was it despair over Marina?—I got drunker than I have in years.

What makes the evening stand out in memory was the sight, at two A.M., as we all staggered out of our cars back at the hotel, of cosmonauts Khrunov and Komarov playing tennis! (The eight cosmonauts, along with their trainers and General Kamanin, were staying at another—the only other—hotel near ours. There were too many of them to spend the night in Korolev's old cottage out at the launch site.) "What the hell are these guys doing out at this hour?" some two-star general grumbled.

"They're sleep-shifted, General. The launches will take place before dawn, which means they have to wake up around midnight. So they've been going to bed and waking up earlier and earlier each night, to change their internal clocks." That, at least, is what I tried to say . . . God only knows what the general heard.

But he nodded in approval, and gave me a bear hug. "It's good to have one of these smart guys along to explain these things," he said, and over the shoulder of my newfound friend, I could see my father nodding in approval, as behind him, the gentle Komarov smoothly returned the vicious serves of my friend Khrunov.

Three-fifteen A.M., the cold morning of Sunday, April 23, 1967, Area 2, Baikonur. I stood with the crowd outside the assembly building that served the Area 2 pad, and the one at Area 31. Bathed in spotlights, Soyuz spacecraft and launchers stood in both places. Here, in front of me, Colonel Vladimir Komarov, the forty-year-old Hero of the Soviet Union, the first Soviet cosmonaut to make a second flight into space, stepped up to a microphone and addressed the dignitaries about the great honor of making the first manned test flight of Soyuz. Wearing a leather flying jacket over a coverall much like a track suit, Komarov looked rested and eager, unlike the rest of us, who were not sleep-shifted, but merely awake indecently early.

The brief ceremonies concluded, Komarov waved and, accompanied by Gagarin, Artemov, Kamanin, and the crew of the second Soyuz, got into the bus that would take him to the gantry three kilometers away.

Some of the onlookers dispersed to various posts in the control center, others went searching for tea. I hung back, watching the proceedings, wondering how I would feel should I be lucky enough to be in Komarov's place someday. I could see the brightly lit, frozen, and steaming rocket rising above me. Then the dark landscape of the cosmodrome falling away as I rode the elevator to the ingress level with *my* backup pilot, with *my* general, and with the chief designer of *my* spacecraft.

There was very little room at the top level of the gantry. Kamanin and Artemov would have to stay at the elevator, leaving Gagarin to hand Komarov himself over to the four technicians who would help him into Soyuz. Two of them guided him through the EVA hatch (still too small!) in the side of the orbital module. Another tech waited inside, braced on wooden blocks so as to avoid touching flight equipment, helping Komarov lower himself to a plastic slide we called the "shoehorn," allowing him to slip feetfirst through the even smaller nose hatch down into the bell-shaped command module. There, the fourth tech, sitting in the empty flight engineer's couch on the right side of the spacecraft, helped steady Komarov as he carefully descended into the commander's couch, then helped him hook up his comm lines and fasten his straps. It would be up to this same technician to squeeze past Komarov back up the nose hatch, removing the blocks and shoehorn as he went. The outer hatch would be dogged shut, and the team of technicians and the backup pilot would withdraw.

Within moments Komarov would be alone on top of the rocket, the only human being within a circle six kilometers across.

I had sat in those couches in a similar Soyuz; you hooked your heels into stirrups at the base of your couch, which forced your knees up toward your chin. Of course, it would be roomier in orbit. But if all went well, Komarov would have to make room for two new companions a day into the mission, too!

At 5:30 the viewing area fell silent as flames appeared at the base of the Soyuz, lighting up the dark sky. Sheets of ice cascaded off the rocket as it built up power, then slowly rose, the gantry opening for its escape, the rumble and roar of the first-stage engines rattling the buildings around us.

Soyuz 1 wasn't even out of sight when I found myself glancing over to the second pad, where *Soyuz 2* waited for its turn, twenty-four hours from now.

Shivering with cold, and convinced we had another day of dismal weather ahead of us, I went inside the assembly building, seeing smiling faces wherever I went, including Lev Tselauri's. *Soyuz 1* had reached orbit as planned, eight minutes after launch, and Komarov had reported that all systems were working well. "The Americans better watch out now," I told Lev.

Grateful for any words from me that weren't reproachful, Lev smiled and nodded.

I went looking for a couch to take a nap, since there was no point in returning to the hotel, forty kilometers away, only to have to come back here later in the day for the second launch. Besides, most members of the State Commission and the dozens of journalists covering the mission were right here, filling the offices on the second floor.

I had barely stretched out under my coat on a bed of tarps when I felt someone shaking my shoulder. "Get up, Ribko." It was Dubnin, my comrade from the Aral Sea rescue. "We're going on standby."

Things had started to go wrong with *Soyuz 1* an hour after reaching orbit. One of the twin solar-power panels, designed to spring out from the side of the equipment module like a wing, had failed to deploy. This was a fairly serious problem, since it limited the amount of power available for necessary spacecraft systems such as life support and navigation. In fact, without the second solar panel, *Soyuz 1* could probably only operate for about twenty hours of flight. Now, this was enough time to perform a docking with *Soyuz 2* and the EVA. My good friend cosmonaut Saditsky, one of several carrying information to and from the commission members on the second floor, said that some bureau engineers were talking about having Khrunov and Yeliseyev physically free the stuck panel during their EVA, an idea that I thought insane. It would be difficult enough for them to perform the simple tasks they had rehearsed: To effect repair work on equipment not designed for it, on a panel that could suddenly spring free and hit them, was dangerously stupid.

The diminished power problem, though serious, was not the biggest threat to the success of the mission. Komarov was unable to orient the spacecraft with any predictability. Engineers here at Baikonur, and with the team of specialists down at the control center in Yevpatoriya, suspected that exhaust gases from steering rockets had fogged over the optical sensor designed to lock onto the sun and certain stars.

Without orientation, there was no way for Komarov to perform the engine burns that would shape his orbit for rendezvous. He was, after all, flying the active craft of the pair.

In early afternoon, on his fifth orbit, Komarov tried to orient *Soyuz* by sighting on Earth's horizon. This, too, failed. Shortly after that, his *Soyuz 1* sailed off into a series of orbits that took him over Africa and America, outside our tracking and communication system. Komarov was supposed to rest during this eight-hour period, but I doubt he slept any more than did the commission members boiling up and down the stairs to the second floor, hurrying into and out of cars that roared off toward Tyuratam. (One of the earlier ones carried Gagarin, off to serve as a voice link to Komarov from Yevpatoriya.) Or any better than his comrades, Bykovsky, Khrunov, and Yeliseyev, who had to go to bed about two P.M. that afternoon, just in case they still had to launch.

By seven P.M., the rescue team had moved to the Outskirts Airfield, and were standing by, which for most of us meant finding food, smoking, or catching naps.

Since I was known to have been a bureau engineer on Soyuz, I was continually asked what I thought. Would we be flying out to recover

Komarov next morning? Or would it be Komarov, Yeliseyev, Khrunov the following day? I wanted to be honest about the unlikelihood of a second launch and docking, but didn't want to encourage the others to relax. So I stuck to the Party line: Komarov was a well-trained pilot and engineer, support teams here at Baikonur, at Yevpatoriya, and in Moscow were working to fulfill the mission, and so on.

"You're full of shit," Dubnin said, finally.

Complicating our preparations was a rainstorm that blew through the area in the afternoon, just enough water to turn every spot of bare earth into a muddy sea. Flight controllers wouldn't want to land Komarov in the middle of this, but then, the prime recovery zone was dozens of kilometers to the north and west. Was it raining there? Nobody seemed to know.

At midnight, contact was reestablished with Komarov. He had slept fitfully; the solar panel was still stuck; and the solar orientation system was still broken. The State Commission canceled the *Soyuz 2* launch, and decided to land Komarov at the beginning of his seventeenth orbit, about 5:30 in the morning.

We were ordered to be ready to take off in three hours.

28   ORSK

An hour before we climbed into the Ilyushin-18 that was to carry us to Aralsk—site of my "hospitalization" following my adventure on the ice—the word came to "stand by."

"What's gone wrong now?" Dubnin asked.

Since I had at least a theoretical chance of understanding what was causing the delay, I got on the telephone to the tower dispatcher who had waved us off, and learned that as Komarov and *Soyuz 1* flew around Earth on their fifteenth orbit, instructions for his reentry burn were radioed up to him. But communications were spotty, and no one on the ground was certain he would be able to execute them with the failed orientation system.

Sure enough, ninety minutes later, as Komarov flew over Africa at the end of his sixteenth orbit, the stations tracking *Soyuz 1* saw no change in its trajectory. Once in voice contact, Komarov confirmed that the ion sensor had lost its fix as the spacecraft moved into darkness, and the Soyuz autopilot had prevented the retro-rockets from firing.

This was a problem, but not a disaster, and not even unprecedented: The *Voskhod 2* cosmonauts, Belyayev and Leonov, had had to postpone a reentry burn. What complicated matters was the lack of power aboard *Soyuz 1*. Komarov couldn't just go round and round Earth waiting for the perfect daylight opportunity. He only had two more chances, the seventeenth and eighteenth orbits. And there was no time to recalculate the complex maneuvers for a manual reentry in time to get them to Komarov for a landing on the seventeenth.

So it was to be the eighteenth orbit, with a projected touchdown time of 8:30 Baikonur time.

This information allowed us to file a new flight plan, because the prime landing zone shifted farther to the west, toward the city of Oren-burg, a two-hour flight.

We couldn't take off as quickly as we wanted; we had to wait for General Kamanin and several of his staff, who came racing up in a single car, right onto the pavement of the runway apron, where one of the local generals met them.

Finally we took off, at 6:45, hours after we should have, knowing that Komarov's Soyuz was probably going to have landed by the time we reached the area. The local Air Defense Force units, not officially part of the recovery team, were put on alert and told to have helicopters ready.

Kamanin brought us the latest information, that Komarov had made a good reentry burn, though he would now follow a ballistic trajectory. The bell-shaped Soyuz, like Gemini and Apollo, had a slightly offset center of gravity, allowing it to generate a small amount of lift in order to adjust its landing point. But the orientation had to be perfect, which was not the case for *Soyuz 1*. Using the ballistic method, the spacecraft would spin slowly about its long axis, negating the lift, making the tra-jectory steeper and increasing the G forces felt by the pilot. Knowing this, however, flight controllers projected Komarov's landing site to be east of the city of Orsk, which was itself almost two hundred kilometers east of Orenburg, shortening our trip by half an hour.

Like most of those on the plane, I dozed as we droned west. Only Kamanin, carefully writing in a small notebook, stayed awake.

At one point, halfway to Orsk, a pale lieutenant colonel with Ka-manin muttered, "He should be down by now."

"Thank God," Kamanin said. "This was too ambitious for a first flight. Two spacecraft, four cosmonauts, docking, spacewalks. What the hell were we thinking?"

He noticed me blinking sleepily across from him. "Getting out of Artemov's organization is a smart move for you, Ribko."

I was so tired it took me fifteen minutes to realize that Kamanin had just told me I was getting a job at the cosmonaut training center. I wasn't so tired, however, that I assumed he meant as a cosmonaut.

Even from the air, Orsk looked like a grim little town, nothing but identical gray apartment buildings wreathed in smoke and dust. The only striking sights on the horizon were several factory smokestacks, clearly the source of the pollution.

As we strapped in for landing a little after ten A.M., Dubnin wound up next to me. "Your cosmonaut should be at the airport by now." I hoped so. Kamanin and the other generals would take charge of him, while Dubnin and I flew off with helicopters to recover the spacecraft.

Taxiing in, however, it was clear that Komarov had not arrived. A faded yellow bus raced toward us, meeting our party as we came down the stairs. It had barely stopped and we had barely managed to drink in the noxious spring air of Orsk when a bald major general popped out of the bus, a gray look on his face. "General Kamanin, I'm General Avtonomov, deputy district commander. *Soyuz 1* landed at 8:24 about sixty-five kilometers east of here." He clearly didn't want to say what came next: "The spacecraft is reported to be on fire and the cosmonaut has not been found."

Kamanin and his colleagues exchanged quick glances. So did Dubnin and I. Fatigued and confused, I could not really react to the awful news. Soyuz on fire? Where would Komarov be? He couldn't *eject*.

Just then a smaller car drove up, disgorging another general, this one wearing two stars, identifying himself as Lieutenant General Tsedrik, Avtonomov's boss. "We just got a telephone call from a Rocket Force unit in Novo-orsk. They say Komarov is in a hospital in a settlement a few kilometers from the landing site."

That was more promising: *Soyuz 1* could have crash-landed, injuring Komarov, who was then taken to a hospital. "Let's get going," Dubnin said, but Tsedrik was going on: "I've reported this information to the Ministry of Defense."

"We're going to the landing site," Kamanin said. "Is the helicopter ready?"

"Minister Ustinov insisted that you call him the moment you arrived," Tsedrik said nervously, obviously not wanting to get into a crossfire between Ustinov and Kamanin.

"Until I've found Komarov and visited the spacecraft, I have nothing to report," Kamanin snapped. He pointed at Tsedrik, at one of his generals, one of his colonels, then at Dubnin and me. "Come along." And we marched toward the Mi-8, whose rotor was already beginning to turn.

Within five minutes we were in the air, and not long after that the navigator of the helicopter handed a message to Kamanin, who glanced at it, and smiled bitterly. "It's from Vershinin himself," he said to his aide, naming the commander in chief of the Soviet Air Force. "He wants me to go back to Orsk and call Ustinov."

"What do I tell the pilot?" the navigator asked.

"Keep flying," Kamanin ordered.

Which we did, for half an hour. Finally Dubnin could stand it no longer. "We should be there by now," he said, then he hauled himself up to the cockpit.

"He's right," Kamanin said, following him.

It was difficult to hear over the flapping of the rotors, but Kamanin and Dubnin got into an argument with the pilot.

Moments later they were back with the rest of us, faces flushed. "Can you believe that?" Dubnin was practically screaming. "They were taking us in the *wrong* fucking direction!"

Kamanin overlooked Dubnin's intemperate outburst, probably because he shared the sentiment. "Remind me to call Kutasin the moment I am back in Orsk," he said to Tsedrik. "I look forward to hearing how a trained rescue crew can get lost in clear weather."

Kutasin was the guy in charge of the recovery aircraft and pilots. From Kamanin's voice, I assumed he wouldn't be in charge much longer.

It was 11:30, three hours after Komarov's landing, that his official welcoming team finally reached the landing site, a grassy prairie unbroken by tree or hill. The wind blew from the west, carrying a heavy, burning-chemical smell.

Our misdirection meant that a second helicopter from Orsk, carrying the rest of Kamanin's staff, beat us. The original rescue helicopter was also still parked here. A small crowd had also gathered—workers from some nearby collective farm, a couple of soldiers in the uniform of the Rocket Force, and for some reason, a group of science students. I guess they had happened to be in the area.

Soyuz 1 itself could not be seen—not as a spacecraft, anyway. It was a smoldering lump of earth at one end of a tangled parachute. "Go to that hospital, now," Kamanin ordered Tsedrik. "See if Komarov is there."

Tsedrik saluted and turned back to our helicopter. Did he realize how pointless his mission was? No one could have survived this crash.

As we walked toward the wreckage, we were briefed by the pilot of the original search-and-rescue helicopter. "The farmers say the vehicle came down like a rock, twisting at the end of the 'chute, which didn't open." Not only one parachute, I saw, but both the primary and reserves; they had somehow deployed together. Komarov never had a chance.

"The vehicle hit, then exploded and began to burn."

"The soft-landing rockets," I said, though no one asked me.

"The farmers threw dirt on it, to kill the flames, but . . ." He shrugged. There was truly nothing more that he could say.

Dubnin grabbed a shovel from one of the onlookers and began jabbing it into the wreckage. "Careful!" I said. "The fumes are toxic."

"I'll hold my breath."

In the mound of dirt and shattered metal, only one piece of the spacecraft was identifiable: the round silvery ring of the forward hatch that connected the command module and orbital module.

I got a shovel myself, and for the next hour Dubnin and I struggled to remove the earth that had been piled on the wreckage. "What did they use, a bulldozer?" Dubnin said at one point. In any other circumstances, I'd have laughed.

Eventually we were able to push the hatch ring to one side. Below it were the remains of the control panel, which had merely shattered into a mass of wires and metal fragments rather than simply burning. This conglomeration was imbedded in a completely scorched set of structures that I recognized as the crew couches. In the middle of this was a twisted, broken microphone attached to a blackened fragment of a white communications headset—and, I soon saw, a blackened lump that was all that remained of Colonel Komarov.

My father's generation saw much of death, women and children blown to pieces by Nazi bombs, soldiers cut in half by machine-gun bullets and vaporized by artillery shells, friends who disappeared into the cellar of the Lubiyanka, and thence to some lime pit.

I had only my mother's slow, painful deterioration to guide me. The sight of poor Komarov in his destroyed Soyuz made me weep. All I could do was point with the shovel. Dubnin signaled to Kamanin and the others—"We need a coffin!"—and I was gently moved aside as the medical team took over.

One of the farmer's wives brought me some tea and I sat on the grass. Kamanin examined the wreckage, then, patting me on the shoulder, hurried back to his helicopter to make his horrifying report to Ustinov and the Central Committee.

After a while Dubnin sat down with me, offering a shot of the worst vodka I have ever tasted. "We have nothing left to do. They want the wreckage to stay as it is."

"Forever?" I said, stupidly.

"Until they've analyzed the site." Only then did I see that a photographer was making a record of the pathetic scene. "Some specialists from Moscow are on their way. They deal with airplane crashes."

Our small recovery team was ignored for the next several hours, as various aircraft and vehicles arrived. Some carried members of the State Commission from Baikonur—General Kerimov, General Tyulin, General Rudenko. A lot of generals. Kamanin returned from Orsk.

Artemov came from Yevpatoriya with a group of bureau types to stand there shaking their heads.

Gagarin arrived with Artemov. He looked like a man who had lost his brother and wanted to take it out on someone. "This was your fault," he said to Artemov.

"We don't know whose fault this was," Artemov replied, lamely.

"Bullshit. You broke your own rules to launch this thing because you wanted to look like a big hero for May Day. How do you like it now? Think you're going to be made a Hero of Socialist Labor for this fuckup?"

Gagarin was a tiny man compared to Artemov but the Ukrainian shrank from him in fear. Kamanin, who wasn't much taller than Gagarin, intervened at this point and steered the first man in space away to cool down. Artemov was left shaking with rage, pointing at Gagarin's back. I don't know exactly what he said, but the words "that little shit" carried to me.

It was getting dark out on the prairie, and the helicopter carrying Komarov's coffin was ready to lift off. Kamanin ordered the official photographer, Dubnin, and me to fly with him back to Orsk. By this time I believe he had been awake for thirty hours straight; he fell asleep the moment we were in the air.

A battalion of cadets from a local military school were lined up on the runway as an honor guard as Kamanin and his aides and Dubnin and I carried the coffin to the same Il-18 that had brought us here from Baikonur about a month ago—or so it seemed that night.

Before we took off, there was another call from Moscow, from Marshal Vershinin, its contents relayed to Kamanin by one of the aides. "The marshal wants to be reassured that Komarov's body isn't too disfigured for an open-casket ceremony."

For the first time all day, Kamanin's temper exploded. He told me to open the coffin and summoned the photographer. I did as told, trying not to look at the slab of coal, perhaps the size of a human thigh, resting on white satin. "Take a picture for the marshal." Then he turned to the aide: "Tell the marshal that the body will be cremated as soon as we reach Moscow. If he wants to view something, let him view an urn."

29 SENIOR ENGINEER-LIEUTENANT RIBKO

Even the flight back to Moscow grew complicated and troublesome: Weather closed Chkalov air base, which was our primary destination, since it was next door to Star Town. Nor could we go to Vnukovo, the big airport that, had things gone better, would have been the site of a May Day greeting for cosmonauts Komarov, Bykovsky, Yeliseyev, and Khrunov.

We wound up at Sheremetyevo, a smaller airport northwest of Moscow, where we waited almost two hours for transportation. While we sat there, we were joined by the other Soyuz crew members, who had flown first from Baikonur to Orsk, then followed us to the Moscow area.

The convoy of official cars brought Komarov's widow in addition to several cosmonauts from the center. I had seen and felt enough sadness for one day, so I got myself away from them.

Among those greeting us was my father. "Don't you have any luggage?" he said.

"It's still in Tyuratam." The only personal item I carried, other than my passport and my clothing, was the letter from Katya.

As we walked to the car, we could hear wailing behind us. Even some of the waiting drivers were wiping away tears. "Christ," my father said, "this is terrible. People haven't cried like this since Stalin died."

I had been so immersed in the sorry business at hand I had completely forgotten about the larger world. Obviously Komarov's death had been announced to the public, which included the Americans. Were they jumping up and down now, realizing that once again the Moon race was even?

Or was it even? The very ambitious and complex goals planned for *Soyuz 1* and *Soyuz 2* had been met by the Americans a year or more ahead of us. They had conducted rendezvous half a dozen times while we had yet to accomplish it once. Their tracking and recovery systems were superb. Their Saturn rockets were now equal or superior to our Proton, and their even more powerful Saturn V-5 was inching closer to a test.

Perhaps it was my fatigue, but that night, as my father's driver took us back to Kaliningrad, I felt that the race was over, that our programs were second- or even third-rate—fine for scoring risky "spectaculars," not so good for a complex challenge like landing a man on the Moon, and returning him safely to Earth.

Imagine my feelings, then, when my father turned to me and said, "Vershinin signed the order yesterday, before he knew about Komarov."

"What order?" I'm sure I sounded irritated.

"The order enrolling you in the cosmonaut team."

The order—? So I had made it after all. Kamanin had known it before we left Baikonur. How did I respond? I laughed out loud. "*That* is perfect timing."

My father frowned. "What do you mean?"

"Our space program just *crashed*, Papa. Could there be a *worse* time to become a cosmonaut?"

"Airplanes crash all the time."

"Airplanes fly by the hundreds. Not once every two years."

"They'll be flying again by November seventh." This was another big anniversary, of the 1917 Revolution. "That's what they're saying at headquarters."

"They can say whatever they want. There aren't going to be any Russian cosmonauts in space for a year, maybe two."

Now he was getting irritated. "You're tired. Get some sleep and maybe in the morning you can appreciate the chance you've got."

"I do appreciate it. Thank you. Thank you for everything you've done." I was sincere, though it took me a moment to realize it. "When am I supposed to report?" I didn't want to show up at Star Town in my uniform the day of Komarov's funeral. I would also need a couple of weeks to get free of the bureau. My God, I had to break this news to Triyanov, to Filin.

And to Uncle Vladimir.

"Monday, May eighth. It's all in the papers."

I nodded. Actually, I had it easy: I already lived in the neighborhood. Some of my new colleagues would be coming from remote air bases, uprooting families.

We pulled up to my building. "Yuri, you'll do fine in the service. Even if you don't fly in space, they'll have work to do. Space engineering, which is what you said you wanted."

"I know."

"You're better off in the military than with Artemov. I didn't like what I saw out at Baikonur, and I wasn't the only one. I don't care who his protector is, bad things are going to happen to that man, and you don't want to get caught in the wash. Get out of that bureau and stay as far away from it as you can."

This was a tone of voice I had rarely heard from my father. It reminded me, in fact, of Uncle Vladimir's, when talking about the "basement." I didn't want to see anyone arrested and shot, but at the moment I had little sympathy for Artemov, or for Lev, or for the many people in the bureau between those two.

I said good-bye, then went up to my flat.

I didn't sleep well that night. On the plane from Orsk to Moscow, I had heard enough details about Komarov's heroism to thoroughly imagine his last moments. How he had performed a manual orientation of Soyuz as it approached the end of the seventeenth orbit, lining up the spacecraft by sighting on the day/night terminator, then restarting the autopilot to steer the vehicle through the darkness. He had had to resume manual control for a brief, frantic moment when *Soyuz 1* emerged into sunlight again, to make sure it was still oriented properly, then let the autopilot command the engine firing. All this while knowing he had at best three more hours of power, that an orientation failure would mean death in the atmosphere, and even the delay of another orbit would force him to try to land in Europe or, more likely, in the Atlantic Ocean.

Komarov was well-trained for each of these events, but had never rehearsed them all in this sequence, and in such demanding circumstances.

Yet, he had done the job brilliantly, performing the guidance checks, observing the retro firing, the jettisoning of the equipment module followed by the orbital module, and plunging into the atmosphere—where the last Soyuz had suffered a heat-shield failure, frying its insides.

He emerged from the radio blackout caused by reentry and reported the burn times to Yevpatoriya. The only other communication from him was a mention of the parachute problem. Then nothing, as *Soyuz 1* plummeted to the prairie at three hundred kilometers an hour.

Hearing all this, is it any wonder I dreamed I was falling, falling, falling?

At a few moments past eight the next morning, after this fitful sleep, I stood in Triyanov's office as he examined the documents from the Ministry of Defense. "I don't believe this!" He was so angry his face flushed and the muscles stood out in his neck. "Have we treated you that badly, Ribko?"

"No, sir," I said, lying only slightly. Triyanov had been fair and supportive. Artemov was another matter. "I felt I could better serve my country—" I started to say.

"Don't give me that shit," he said. "Don't even try to justify it! You're going over to the enemy." He seemed to boil over. "You won't like serving under Kuznetsov: He's from the old school." Kuznetsov was the commander of the cosmonaut training center under Kamanin. I had not heard many good things about him. "You're going to regret this."

I couldn't let that statement go unchallenged. "How can you say that? You spent thirty years in the Air Force."

"I had no other choice! I didn't have a fancy Bauman education and a job like this." He practically threw the papers back at me. "You think you're getting off the ship just before it sinks, don't you?".

I was too slow denying it. Triyanov smiled bitterly. "Well, maybe you'll be right. God knows, we're in for a rough few months." He fumed in silence for a moment. "Well, you might as well leave now. Everything here will be frozen while those responsible for *Soyuz 1* are identified and punished." He stood up then, and to my surprise, rather than punching me, held out his hand. "Good luck, Yuri."

I shook it. Then, surprising me again, Triyanov snapped a salute, which I returned. "Better work on that," he said.

———

By noon I had cleaned out my desk, gathered my Baikonur luggage (which had arrived back at Chkalov early that morning), and signed out at the bureau personnel office. I had one more stop to make—Filin.

Nadiya the bird-woman was guarding the gate, as usual. "He's not here," she said, not even bothering to look up, or hear what I had to say.

"Do you expect him soon?"

Now she raised her head. "He had to leave for Feodosiya this morning." Feodosiya was the test site in the Crimea where parachutes were packed. Yes, there would many trips to Feodosiya in the next few weeks for those investigating the *Soyuz 1* disaster.

I took out a pencil and paper, and scribbled a note. "Would you give this to him?"

Then I walked out the main gate, away from the job I had dreamed about such a short time ago.

There remained the matter of Uncle Vladimir. When I returned to my flat, I telephoned his office, and was put directly through to him. "I already heard," he said. There was no reproach in his voice, only a tiredness, which surprised me. After experiencing Triyanov's rumblings, I expected Uncle Vladimir to explode at me like Vesuvius. But all he said was, "Congratulations."

"Thank you."

Then he surprised me again. "Our association will continue. I will be in touch with you shortly concerning your new tasks."

He hung up then, not waiting for an argument, not that I was in a position to make one. The message was frightening: It was one thing to be a spy inside an organization like the Korolev bureau . . . it was one of the functions of State Security to report on industrial enterprises.

But the military was different. There, political officers represented the Party, serving as a guard against sabotage or subversion. There weren't supposed to be informants like me, especially in elite units like the cosmonaut team.

I had been unable to escape detection in the Korolev bureau, and it had effectively ruined my career. What price could I expect to pay if discovered? It would be a lot worse than exile to the spacecraft recovery team, possibly even prison.

So I had not escaped after all. I was merely going to be Uncle Vladimir's spy inside Star Town.

These were my thoughts as I listened to somber music on the radio, and the announcer describing Komarov's funeral cortege into Red Square.

I glanced at the new uniform hanging in my open closet, and felt more lonely than I had in years, since the day my mother died.

I took the crumpled letter off my table and dialed Katya's number.

INTERLUDE

Spring

I had to leave Russia after my second series of tapings with Yuri Ribko—to his relief, I suspect. It must have been difficult for him to sit there with me, hour by hour, discussing this very painful period in his country's life, not to mention his own personal crises.

But he did it, with generally good grace, and I piled up a dozen cassettes filled with his narrative before returning home to Washington, where the travails of our chief executive were drawing journalists like, to borrow a phrase from Yuri Ribko, shit draws flies.

As the presidential scandal played itself out, another crisis erupted in Russia itself, this one over the collapse of the ruble. As my magazine's Russia "specialist," and the one least eager to pry "scoops" out of the special prosecutor's office, I was shipped back to Moscow for a shorter visit.

Even though only a few months had passed since my winter trip, I could see that people were in a more subdued, resigned mood, almost like wartime. Dennis Gulyayev, my contact at the Russian Space Agency, was actually hostile. "Your bankers did this to us," whatever *this* was.

So I was on my own reaching Yuri Ribko, calling his flat from the Penta Hotel one night, in between charmingly accented messages from various prostitutes offering to drop by.

At Ribko's, a woman answered, in English. "Oh, yes, I'm sure he'd like to talk to you."

Yuri answered, quickly determined where I was, and offered to come down and see me. "You won't have any luck traveling out here."

He hung up before I could ask the name of the woman on the phone. Katya?

Yuri was limping as he entered the lobby of the Penta. He looked thinner, paler. "I tripped on the street, like a drunk," he said, when I expressed concern. "Stone-cold sober, too."

We found a quiet place in the hotel bar, not an impossible task on this weekday night. "Nineteen sixty-seven was a terrible year for everyone," Ribko said suddenly. "You lost your Apollo astronauts in January, and then had all these other accidents." It was true: 1967 was a black year for American astronauts. In addition to Grissom, White, and Chaffee, two other NASA astronauts died in accidents (car and airplane crashes) while one of the Air Force's Manned Orbiting Laboratory astronauts got killed at Edwards. The X-15 had its first fatal crash in 1967, too.

"We lost Komarov, then had two L-1 missions fail miserably. They never even reached orbit." I had my notes on these: L-1 Number 4 failed on September 18, 1967, when only five of the six engines in the first stage of its Universal Rocket lit as planned, a failure that allowed the L-1 to make a successful test of the launch escape system.

L-1 Number 5, launched November 21, 1967, got a little higher before the second stage of its Universal Rocket failed. The launch escape system was tested again, landing the reentry module some 285 kilometers downrange.

"There was one triumph," Ribko said. "We finally got two Soyuz ships docked in orbit, and returned them safely." He was talking about the *Cosmos 186* and *188* missions of late October 1967, which accomplished a tricky automatic docking in space, before separating and reentering separately. "Even then, the damned orientation system on one of the craft failed and it made a ballistic reentry, just like poor Komarov."

"Did it crash?"

"No. We'd solved the parachute problem by then." He went on to tell me how the commissions investigating the Komarov disaster had taken two months to come to the official conclusion that the parachutes had been packed improperly. "The real problem, I found out later," Ribko said, "was that during a thermal test of both spacecraft, some idiot left the covers off the parachute canisters. The heat melted parts of the canisters and prevented the 'chutes from coming out cleanly. Neither ship was safe to fly.

"This means that even if the other problems hadn't happened, if we had gone ahead and launched *Soyuz 2*, we would have had *four* dead cosmonauts, not just one."

As for the Americans, 1967 was a time for regrouping. Only on November 7 of that year, the very day Ustinov and the Central Committee had once hoped to mark with a manned L-1 flight around the Moon, NASA launched the first of its giant Saturn 5 moon rockets, a spectacular success. "Yes, the Saturn V-5," Ribko insisted on calling it, noting its genesis in the design of the Nazi V-2 rocket, and its builder, Wernher von Braun.

"By December 1967, both of us, the USSR and the U.S.A., had picked ourselves up, like runners who had stumbled in a race, and taken one or two tentative steps. . . ."

SCORPION 3

ENEMY AGENTS
IN THE VICINITY

30 THE FOURTH ENROLLMENT

On the cold morning of Monday, December 25, 1967, when all of North and South America and much of Europe were celebrating Christmas Day, I trudged across a snowy field at the Chkalov air base toward an actual An-2 biplane, reciting aloud several lines from a poem by Pushkin.

There were thirteen of us in a ragged line, I and my colleagues from the Fourth Enrollment, as our group of student-cosmonauts was known. All of us wore leather jackets, tall boots, and old-fashioned soft aviators' caps. Oh, yes, on our chests and backs were parachutes. As part of our "operational" education, we were to begin jumping.

The thirteen of us ranged in age from twenty-four (at twenty-five, I was the second-youngest) to thirty-five years old. Our backgrounds were quite different; six of us were pilots (four from fighters, two from transports), three were aircraft navigators, another three were research scientists from the Academy of Air Defense, while I was the lone engineer.

We had been brought together by our orders in early May of that year, those orders having been signed by Marshal Vershinin the day of Komarov's death, which transferred us to Military Unit 26266, the cosmonaut training center, located at the military village known as Star Town.

We were the fourth such group of students to be assigned to Military Unit 26266, the first having been the famous group of twenty pilots chosen with Yuri Gagarin in March 1960. The Second Enrollment was a group of fifteen pilots and engineers chosen in January 1963, while the Third was a collection of twenty-two younger pilots and engineers recruited in October 1965, who were nearing the end of the last phase of their "student" training and, in fact, were commencing their final examinations this very morning. (Think of them as college seniors, while we thirteen were sophomores.)

There had also been a group of five women, chosen in March 1962, but with the exception of Valentina Tereshkova, who in June 1963 had become the first woman to make a spaceflight, they were not considered full-fledged members of the team.

For the first seven months our training had largely consisted of classroom study, learning the basics of aerospace navigation, astronomy, orbital mechanics, aerospace physiology, in addition to courses in Marxism-Leninism.

My education at Bauman, not to mention my year at the Korolev bureau, helped me tremendously in the classroom, and I ranked consistently at the top of the list, ahead of even our very talented military researchers. I found myself tutoring Sergei Shiborin, a young transport pilot. He, in turn, guided me in the ways of the Air Force of the USSR, though not without a bit of hazing: He convinced me to buy expensive presents for each member of the Fourth Enrollment to celebrate my appointment to active duty, and it wasn't until months later that he confessed he had made up the "tradition."

Our other main activity during these first months was mandatory physical training. Six mornings a week we were expected to report to the gym for running and calisthenics, for occasional hockey and—when the weather was warm—basketball games. A special pool was being built, too, since the doctors had decided that high-diving would be good training for weightlessness.

Some mornings I enjoyed it; some mornings I had to drag myself out of bed by any means possible. I was helped in this by the miserable condition of my bed and personal surroundings. Upon being enrolled in the cosmonaut unit, my former colleagues at the Korolev bureau took vengeful and illegal steps to have me evicted from my Kaliningrad flat, claiming falsely that it belonged to employees of that organization. Had I chosen to fight their action, I would have won.

But I had been officially assigned a flat at Star Town, and disliking the early morning commute by bus, which put me back in contact with surly bureau types, I let go of the Kaliningrad place and moved into the "temporary" barracks at Star Town with the rest of the Fourth Enroll-ment, where we waited for our official housing to be built.

As the only unmarried officer, I was given a flat of my own while the others shared larger, but equally decrepit, quarters, which had been built seven years ago as "temporary" housing for those who carved Star Town and the training center out of the woods here.

It hadn't been so bad during the summer months, but when autumn came, what had been a pleasantly cool darkness became freezing damp-ness. I bought a portable heater, which, based on its performance, was as likely to asphyxiate me or burn down the whole building as it was to provide heat.

So I spent as little time in my Star Town flat as possible, rising for breakfast at the canteen, followed by the workouts, then class, lunch, more class. I did my evening studies in our lecture room, or in the library of the Star Town elementary school, newly named for the late Vladimir Komarov.

On this December morning we were to enter the second, opera-tional phase of our training, qualifying as parachutists and aircraft crew members so that we would be something more than useless baggage on future flights of Soyuz, Almaz, Program L, or 7K-VI spacecraft.

I had informal experience with radio protocols, for example, from the bureau, and I believe this put me ahead of my scientific colleagues, who had spent their careers learning how to shoot down American mis-siles. But my experience was nothing compared to the pilots and navi-gators in our group, who rode the bus to Chkalov in high spirits, returning to what was, for them, familiar ground, while the scientists and I—wrenched out of our cozy classrooms—sat lost in thought, won-dering what had possessed us to volunteer for a job that involved being hurled out of a thirty-year-old airplane at three thousand meters.

I tried to remind myself that part of the cosmonaut's job was being blasted to an altitude of 250 kilometers atop a missile, surely more dan-gerous than parachuting. But in my mind I kept picturing the charred wreckage of *Soyuz 1*.

I paid strict attention during two hours of briefings on parachuting basics: "When the static line yanks your 'chute open, look up and make sure it's round, and that there are no holes in it. If it's okay, pull the red cord on your harness. That will disable your emergency 'chute."

"What happens if the canopy is not round, or if it has holes in it?" one of the scientists asked.

Our instructor, an army major with a reported two thousand such jumps to his credit, smiled and pulled a knife out of his boot sheath. "Cut here and here," he said, indicating the place above the right and left shoulders where the parachute shrouds would be attached to the harness. "The lines will be taut and the knife will be sharp. You won't have any trouble."

"But then I'm falling," the scientist said, persisting.

"That's when you pull the blue cord." This was supposed to activate the emergency parachute. "It will come out in front of you, not off your back, so watch your nose." He laughed, and was joined by some of our pilot colleagues as well as our team of instructors from the training center.

There was more information, much more, such as how to hook up the static line, which would automatically deploy our primary 'chute; the proper posture for landing; and the need to collapse the 'chute once on the ground, so you didn't get dragged across the snow.

So far, this was all as expected. Shiborin, a veteran of ten such jumps, confirmed this. But the special needs of cosmonaut training required that we also demonstrate our ability to observe and cope with a new situation.

Each of us was carrying a small notebook and pencil—both attached to our harnesses by string, so they wouldn't get lost—with which we were to record our impressions.

And we had each been ordered to memorize a piece of poetry over the weekend, some few stanzas we would recite on our climb to altitude. Hence my Pushkin, competing with more Pushkin and Mandelstam and, strangely, a bit of Pasternak, chosen by my colleagues.

Just as we reached the An-2, which was to carry us to glory, we were told to wait. The An-2's single propeller, which had roared to life as we approached, strangely sputtered and died.

Shiborin, always fearless in circumstances like this, poked his head in the cockpit and yelled at the pilot, "What the fuck is the problem now?"

I couldn't hear the pilot's response, though it took a few moments. Then Shiborin trudged back over to where I was standing. "Come on," he said. "We've got to see this."

Shiborin was a country boy who had grown up on a collective farm, and in spite of that experience became the most fervent Communist I knew. Compared to him, Leonid Brezhnev was a blood-sucking Wall Street banker and enemy of the people.

Perhaps it was part of his fervent belief that all people were equal that he also delighted in ignoring rank, for seeing the mighty brought low.

It's the only way I can explain why we left our colleagues and instructors and crossed the taxiway to where a MiG-15 trainer was getting ready to take off. "The weather has fallen below minimums for jets," Shiborin shouted to me, raising, then dashing, my hopes for a postponement of our jump in the space of a single sentence. "Gagarin wants to take off and they won't let him." He nodded at the trainer. "He's in that plane."

During the past year, General Kamanin had succeeded in getting the Air Force to create a flight-support unit, the 70th Special Training Squadron, for the cosmonaut training center, a group of pilots and aircraft that were ours to use exclusively. The An-2 was part of the squadron, for example, and so was the Tu-104 transport.

But the heart of the 70th was a collection of MiG-15 two-seat trainers, to be flown by pilot cosmonauts with instructors, or by pilot cosmonauts carrying nonpilots like me. (MiG-15 flights were to become part of our curriculum in the next two months.)

The MiGs became a terrific source of conflict between the cosmonauts of the First and Second Enrollments. Recall that those in the First had been relatively junior pilots when selected, and that between academic studies, training for space missions, and (for the famous ones) endless public appearances for propaganda purposes, they had done almost no flying since becoming cosmonauts.

The pilots selected in 1963, however, were highly experienced Air Force inspectors and squadron commanders. It was they who lobbied Kamanin for creation of the 70th, and once its planes arrived, they happily added to their hours, remaining qualified in all-weather and night flying, zooming around in the sky one or more times a week, while poor souls like Gagarin, Nikolayev, and my friend Saditsky had to fight for one or two cockpit hours every couple of months.

What we saw was Colonel Yuri Gagarin, Hero of the Soviet Union, first man in space, and deputy commander of Military Unit 26266, climbing out of a cockpit and down a ladder, to be replaced by another pilot.

"Who's getting in the plane?" I asked Shiborin.

"Shatalov, I think." Shatalov was one of the more senior, aggressive, and capable members of the Second Enrollment. Gagarin never glanced at him, but instead threw his helmet at another man in a flight suit, who dodged the projectile successfully, but could not get out of the way when Gagarin tackled him. It was almost comical, since Gagarin was the smallest of the cosmonauts, and this tall pilot hit the ground like a tree felled by an ax.

Shiborin clapped his hands together, like a child at the circus. "Boy, he's mad!"

"He should be."

The scuffle lasted only a moment, ending as the MiG taxied off with Shatalov in Gagarin's place, as Gagarin helped the other pilot to his feet. With the roar of the MiG's Tumansky engine diminishing, we could clearly hear Gagarin's protests: "They promised me I could fly today!"

"I know, Colonel, but the weather's bad in the zone—"

"Shatalov is flying into it!"

"Shatalov is qualified—"

"How the hell am I going to *get* qualified if I never get off the ground!"

Red-faced with anger, Gagarin walked right past Shiborin and me as we tried to be invisible.

We succeeded, but only for a moment. "Hey, you two!" It was our parachuting instructor. "Let's go!"

Seated on hard metal benches, feeling the cold through three layers of clothing, we took off a few moments later. Over the clatter of the old engine, I asked Shiborin, my expert in matters aeronautical, why it was acceptable for *us* to fly, but not Gagarin. "The MiGs operate in a different zone, where the weather is below minimums," he said, as if this were not the stupidest question in the world. "We're not dropping in the same place."

Thus soothed, I returned to my labored written record of my emotions—scribbled with frozen fingers—as we climbed higher and higher. (I looked at those notes some time later and saw that the only observation was how our exhaled breath created a mini-cloud layer in the center of the cabin.)

A horn began honking and a red light at the rear of the cabin lit up. We were almost there.

Our jump master got up and opened the door, swinging it inside the cabin and locking it open. A freezing hurricane added to the roar of the An-2's motor. My fellow jumpers began making eager thumbs-up. All I could offer in return was a pathetic smile.

The light changed to yellow. "Left side, stand up, hook up!" the jump master commanded. Shiborin and I were in the middle of that left side. Like robots, we raised our arms, clicking our static lines into place, tugging slightly to take up the slack, as if we had been doing this for years.

"Go!" Just like that, the first jumper went out the door. We all moved up. "Go!" Next jumper. By then I had convinced myself that this was just another step on the road to the Moon—

"Go!" Shiborin vanished through the door. I began to recite my Pushkin poem, hoping I was loud enough for the instructors to hear—

"Go!"

Suddenly, without any deliberate step, I was out, falling into the wind on my back as the static line played out behind me, seeing the An-2 rising away with surprising speed—

Wham! I felt myself yanked forward, as if some giant had grabbed me by the crotch and shoulders and straightened me out.

I was no longer falling, but sinking quickly. (There was a difference in the sensation, believe me.) It took me a few moments to realize that the snowy landing zone was below me, partly hidden by wisps of cloud. That the An-2 was gone from sight and sound. Time to make the routine, or was it perfunctory, check on my canopy. I grabbed the lines extending from my shoulder harness and raised my chin.

Above me there was a nest of strings leading to a white circle. I remembered that I was supposed to disarm my emergency 'chute, and reached for the red lanyard.

Wait. I could see sky through the 'chute! One of the panels was torn.

I took a breath. Looked around me. The ground seemed to be rising slowly, perhaps it was fine—

No! With a missing panel, I would be badly injured. My instructors had been very insistent on this.

Besides, I hadn't disarmed the backup 'chute. Was I too late? Would both 'chutes tangle like Komarov's?

I reached to my right boot and hauled out the knife. Trying not to think, I quickly put it up to the left side of my neck and pushed.

The strap snapped and I began to twist from left to right. It was more difficult to cut the right strap with my right hand, but I was certainly not going to risk dropping the knife by shifting it! I brought the knife into the right strap from the outside, toward my neck, sawing once, twice—

Then I was falling again and the ground suddenly seemed very close. I clawed for the ripcord to the emergency chute and yanked it.

The pack on my chest tore open and a mass of white flew out. A second *wham!* Now I was hanging like a rag doll at the end of a new parachute as trees rose toward me. I saw a field, a road, a grimy truck on the road, and tried to brace myself for impact.

Which I don't remember. One moment I had reached the treetops, the next I was lying on my back, embedded in the snow, the wind knocked out of me. Thankfully there wasn't much breeze, or I'd have been dragged through the snow like a sack of cabbages.

Remembering my instructions, I tried to rise and collapse my parachute. Standing was surprisingly difficult. I couldn't seem to put weight on my left side. So, hobbling on one foot, I began hauling on the lines to my parachute.

I looked around. Not far away in one direction, another student-cosmonaut was coming in for a landing. He, too, had a tough time of it, pitching onto his hands and knees.

"Yuri! Yuri, my God!" I realized someone was calling my name. Shiborin was running toward me, as much as anyone could run in the knee-deep snow.

I had made a complete mess of my first parachute jump. No one was going to trust me with a spacecraft if I couldn't handle this.

I raised a hand in a weak greeting. "I have to sit down," I said.

31   THE PURGE

The whole team was collected and trucked back to Chkalov, a process that took an hour. At the clinic there, a flight surgeon who smelled of booze determined that I had probably broken my leg, a diagnosis I, a medical amateur, had made while sober. Nevertheless, since my leg was now extremely painful, I took the offered shot of vodka. Which did nothing for the pain, but improved my spirits.

"We'll take you over to Shchelkovo," the jump master said cheerfully, perhaps in response to the flight surgeon's condition. There was no real hospital at Star Town, just a clinic, like this one.

All I could do was nod dumbly. I wasn't the only casualty—Alexei Ledovsky had bloodied his nose and Vladimir Agov had wrenched his shoulder—but I was definitely the worst one.

The others, Shiborin and even Ledovsky and Agov, had chattered happily through the post-jump debrief on the truck, like students who have survived a final examination. I could see them glancing at me with pity, figuring, as I did, that the Fourth Enrollment had just lost its first member.

The thirteen of us got along as well as any group of men who are suddenly thrown together in a competitive environment. Our competition was not as fierce as that of the Gagarin group, where twenty men had been chosen knowing only one of them could be first into space.

We competed instead for the attention of our instructors and commanders, and of the senior cosmonauts.

One of those who filled both roles was Colonel Pavel Belyayev, commander of the *Voskhod 2* mission in 1965, now serving as chief of staff of the training center. He had been the one to officially greet us back in May with the words (surprisingly encouraging, given the recent death of his friend Vladimir Komarov) that "General Kamanin had hoped to select twenty new students this time. That is the number we can successfully train.

"He still hopes to add fifty new students over the next few years, until we have several squadrons of pilots and crew members for all these programs. There will be room for *all* of you."

I had since learned of the amazingly ambitious dreams behind Kamanin's personnel targets. First of all, we were planning various flights of the "improved" Soyuz-to-Earth orbit (hopefully this coming April), of the L-1 version to lunar orbit (by the end of 1968), and, ultimately, of the L-3 to the surface of the Moon (in 1970).

What was truly startling were figures from the next Five Year Plan for military programs: Starting in 1969, the Ministry of Defense wanted to launch fifteen Almaz space stations, three per year, each station operating for four months and hosting rotating three-man crews every two weeks. The primary mission of Almaz was surveillance of the territory and forces of the Main Enemy, that is, the United States. By late 1967 the USSR had begun to launch its own fleet of spy satellites based on the Vostok design, but these were unreliable and limited in use. It was hoped that trained military officers—such as Senior Engineer Lieutenant Yuri Nikolayevich Ribko—would provide better target selection while also performing communications interception and missile warning.

Another military manned spacecraft was the 7K-VI, a version of Soyuz (7K). (The letters V and I stood for "military research.") Two cosmonauts would fly this one for shorter missions, though exactly how the 7K-VI would differ from the Almaz was never clear to me. A group of cosmonauts was assigned to this program, including a friend of Shiborin's who had said it was "never going to fly." Still, it remained on the schedule.

There was even a small spaceplane called Spiral in development.

Looked at it this way, Military Unit 26266 was indeed woefully undermanned.

Yet, strangely, as I hobbled carefully around Star Town that last week of 1967, forbidden to continue operational training with my class-mates, I learned that five students from the Third Enrollment were missing. I noticed this when I reported the following Monday morning for physical training. (The fact that I was hobbled did not excuse me from reporting.)

I edged up to Shiborin, who was working out with weights, and asked if he knew the reason for the absences. "They've been dismissed," he said.

"I can't believe *that* many of them failed the exams!" Not after two years of study. Surely the weaker ones would have flunked out before this.

"It wasn't the examinations. A couple of them weren't even allowed to take them." He carefully glanced around, to be sure we were alone. "They're being sent back to their squadrons. Or given other jobs away from Star Town."

This was surprising. In those days an assignment to a facility like Star Town was more or less permanent, especially since it carried the valuable passport allowing you to live in the Moscow District. It was simply unheard of for an officer holding such a passport to be deprived of it, to be returned to some remote base on Kamchatka or Turkmen-istan. "Girl problems?" We had been warned that chasing women had cost a couple of the early cosmonauts their jobs here.

"Political. For some reason, they went back and reviewed everyone's personnel files and found a lot of problems."

This was even more stunning than the idea that the five were being shipped out of Star Town. You couldn't even *apply* to become a cos-monaut without being a Party or Komsomol member, and then your life was examined by the credentials committee! "How could there be problems?" I said.

"Turned out one of them had a relative in the West. Another one's father turned out to have fought on the wrong side down in the Ukraine."

"I can't believe State Security missed things like that!"

"I don't think this was State Security," Shiborin said. "It might have been military intelligence."

I felt sick. If State Security reviewed the backgrounds of the Fourth Enrollment, my association with Uncle Vladimir would probably remain secret. But if military intelligence found out, my career was over.

RED MOON | 223

"Why do you suppose they did it now?" I asked. I certainly had no idea.

"There's some kind of war going on. Your old friend Artemov has been making trouble." I had heard that much, but could see no connection to the purge of the Third Enrollment.

I realized that I needed to talk to Uncle Vladimir. Before I could do that, I needed more information. To get the information, I needed some reason to see my commander.

Within moments I marched out of the gym and headed for the administration building, asking for Colonel Belyayev. None of the student-cosmonauts was in the habit of simply dropping in on Belyayev, though he encouraged us to visit whenever we had questions or problems. He was, after all, the officer who signed our fitness reports. Knowing that, my pathetic plan was to use my accident as an excuse to volunteer for some other work, preferably the kind of duties I performed for Filin in my student days back at the bureau.

But Colonel Belyayev was not in the office today, not expected. I saw my little scheme vanish like a soap bubble, and turned away, only to hear the assistant say, "Colonel Gagarin is in. Would you like to speak to him?"

Why not? "Yes."

On that morning Yuri Gagarin was thirty-three years old, though he seemed much older. He had gotten heavy again, understandably, given a crushing schedule that required him to make dozens of public appearances where drinking was mandatory. He had no time for physical exercise. I already knew he was angry about his inability to log any time in the air. And, of course, given what happened to Komarov, there was no chance our ministers would allow him to fly in space again.

"Ribko! I'd forgotten about your injury," he said when I hobbled into his office. "I was hoping you could drive me into town."

"If your car has an automatic transmission, I can."

"You're sure?"

"There's no physical problem. I'm supposed to be at a geology class at ten A.M.—"

He picked up the telephone and told Belyayev's assistant that Ribko was being excused for the day. Then he grabbed a notebook and his overcoat and hat, and held the door for me. "This way."

Gagarin needed me to drive him because he was frantically trying to finish his degree at Zhukovsky. "I've been writing a thesis since September," he said. "It never seems to get done."

The subject was winged aerospace vehicles. "Like Spiral," I offered.

"Yes. Though my conclusions won't make our Spiral friends very happy." Gagarin had concluded that the only part of an aerospace plane system that the USSR could claim to have demonstrated was the launch system. "We've built several models and mockups, but they're just that . . . models. We need special materials for the wings and body, to keep the plane from burning up when it reenters the atmosphere. We also need better computer guidance systems, since a pilot will never be able to fly such a reentry." He went on for quite a while, obviously rehearsing material from the thesis.

"What it lacks most is a mission," he said, finally. "I can't figure out what a spaceplane will do that a satellite or a Soyuz couldn't do better. The fact that we are devoting millions of rubles to this fantasy is stupid."

By now we had been driving for half an hour, and had reached the Garden Ring Road. I felt brave enough to ask our first man in space, "Why do they make you go to Zhukovsky, when you've got so much other work to do?"

He grinned, and I saw a bit of the young pilot who had become so famous so quickly. "General Kamanin wants the first cosmonauts to be pioneers in the command of new space forces. You can't be a general without an education, and I shouldn't even have been made a colonel." I mentioned my father, who had struggled to get through the Red Banner Academy after years of flying.

"Yes. The system now takes pilots and forces them to be bureaucrats. Kamanin said that his plan was to fly us once or twice, then build a bigger cosmonaut team and a larger training center around us.

"He's also been trying to get control of launch vehicles moved from the Central Space Office to the Air Force. I think he would also like to put the manufacturers back in their place, too."

"You mean the Korolev bureau?"

"*All* of the bureaus. They forget that the military is the customer."

"Because the military doesn't want to go to the Moon."

"Yes. It's not all their fault. The problems are higher up." Then, looking back down at his papers, he added, casually, "We wrote a letter to Brezhnev about that."

"A letter?"

"The cosmonauts, those who have flown. We drafted a letter about the confusion in all our space efforts and sent it to the Central Committee. They have to do something, and soon."

I was stunned to hear this. Heroes of the Soviet Union did not, as a rule, write critical letters to the leadership. Especially not a group of them! "Has there been any response?"

"Well," Gagarin said, his eyes narrowing, "we are all being examined by military intelligence. Five men are being kicked out of the detachment. We may have started a war."

I was glad that we were crawling bumper-to-bumper on Leningrad Road, because the news that it was indeed military intelligence "reviewing" our files nearly caused me to lose control of the vehicle. This was very bad news.

We had reached the entrance to the Zhukovsky Academy. I pulled over and asked Gagarin if he wanted me to wait. "No, I'll ride back with Titov; he's meeting me. Please take the car back to the center. Thank you for being my chauffeur, and remember—things are going to change in our program. I promise you."

With that, the short, increasingly stout first man in space hurried off to school.

I retraced my route, heading back down Leningrad Road toward the Belorussia Station and Uncle Vladimir's office. This was dangerously close to being absent without leave, but I had been excused from classes for the day, and was simply making one stop on the way back to Star Town. Or so I was prepared to testify.

The guard telephoned to Uncle Vladimir's office. To my surprise, he was present and available, though I was instructed to meet him in half an hour, at the gate to Dynamo Stadium, several blocks away.

I used the time to buy a roll from a kiosk, and was sitting on the hood of the car eating when I saw him approach, on foot. He was red-faced with exertion. "This is the longest distance I have walked in ten years," he said by way of greeting.

"I'm sorry."

"It was my choice. It wouldn't be good for either of us for you to be seen wandering the halls there." He seemed to have recovered. "How have you been?" We had not seen each other in months, and had rarely spoken since I had told him that I was going to be enrolled in the military cosmonaut team. "Aside from your poor ankle," he said, noting my cast. "A savage beating by your military rivals?"

I explained about my parachuting mishap.

"And you really thought going into the service was somehow safer than working at the bureau?" He was teasing me, which was a relief. I had been prepared for anything up to and including physical violence. "What brings you crawling back to me?"

I wasn't even going to question his statement, especially since it was more or less correct. "There's a war going on between the clans," I said, and briefly laid out what Gagarin had told me, without naming Gagarin as my source.

Uncle Vladimir listened carefully as I spoke, nodding now and then; then he grabbed me by the shoulder. "It's new, and yet not new at all. I had heard grumblings about the space program coming from much higher up." He made a little circling gesture with a finger, as if indicating an airplane. Perhaps one circling Mount Olympus, observing a war of the gods. "You're in some danger yourself."

"That's what I was afraid of."

"Don't despair. I won't let them drag you off to the basement."

"But can you stop them from shipping me off to the Arctic Circle?"

"We may have to turn to your father for help, if that becomes the question."

"When he finds out I've been working for you, he may not be so eager to save me."

Uncle Vladimir laughed. "That's the spirit! Always think the worst! Then you're never surprised or disappointed." He got serious again. "I can talk to your father, if that becomes necessary. I doubt that it will.

"Go back to work. If there are any further developments concerning Gagarin and the cosmonauts in their revolt against the Central Committee, tell me *immediately*."

32) KATYA

When I returned to my lonely room that night, I found I had a visitor—Katya. This was the first time we had seen each other since my accident. "Oh my God, look at you!" she said, referring to my cast. "They're going to kill you, if you're not careful."

"I'm careful," I said.

She nudged the cast with the toe of her boot. "Not careful enough." Then she kissed me.

Since our meeting at Baikonur, we had struck up a relationship of sorts. My training left me little time for a social life; the relative inaccessibility of Star Town was also an obstacle. Then you had Katya's travel schedule, which often took her to the Central Observatory in the Crimea and no doubt to other scattered institutes of the Academy of Sciences.

It was much like my relationship with Marina—long absences punctuated by brief hours of passion. It wasn't love, of that I was sure. Katya was a decade older than me, with not only a husband but a good number of other lovers before me. And possibly at the same time. I never asked; Katya's regal bearing, the sweep with which she entered a room, or a conversation, made such questions seem almost blasphemous.

"It's bad enough they make you live in a closet. Now they've crippled you so you can't leave."

"I can leave. I was in Moscow today. I even saw Vladimir." This was what passed for dangerous conversation between us, the fact that I had met her through my uncle. I had never told him that we had met again, much less become lovers, leaving that to Katya, who in any case saw Vladimir more often than I.

"Dear Vladimir," she said, sighing. I asked her what she was doing at Star Town. "Instruction in lunar geography and photography," she said.

It was my turn to laugh. "That was the class I missed today!"

"I know. I was handed a very formal excuse by some young officer. Besides, I wasn't the actual lecturer: I was merely along to control the materials, to make sure they didn't fall into the wrong hands."

"Meaning the Air Force of the USSR?"

She smiled. "Exactly." Then she looked around my quarters. "Do you have anything to eat . . . ?"

"Not even a potato," I said. "But there is a café at the station." I meant Tsiolkovsky train station, the stop nearest Star Town.

"You're spending all your money!" Katya was much like my mother in her frugality.

"I'm only using the money I'm saving on furniture." This was pathetic, but true. The flat had come with some of the worst furniture I had ever seen in my life, and I had grown up on military bases. It was heavy, blocky, badly varnished, if at all. The couch was covered with some greasy green fabric that had, I think, formerly been used to protect a truck.

Katya reached for her coat. As she did, there was a knock at the door, which I answered. It was Shiborin, looking flushed and excited, as if he had just run to the residence block from the training center. "There's a lot of excitement," he said, panting.

Then he saw Katya behind me, and froze. With her experience in the world of Security, she said, quietly, "Would you like me to leave? Or do you want to talk out there."

Before I could answer, Shiborin said, "Out here. It will only be a minute."

Door closed, he got excited again. "Did you tell me you worked for Artemov?"

"I was at the bureau when he took it over last year. But I never worked directly for him."

"Good, then you're probably safe."

"Safe from what?"

Shiborin looked down the dark, dingy hallway. "Artemov was taken in for questioning by State Security today."

"How do you know that?"

"I happened to be in the sauna when Belyayev and Saditsky came in. They had been over at the bureau trying to find out why the civilians have a better L-1 simulator than we do, and suddenly this whole meeting was called off. They saw Artemov and a bunch of other people being loaded into cars, and Saditsky recognized them as State Security."

I still didn't believe it. "Even if they got in those cars, it doesn't mean they were being arrested or questioned—"

"Belyayev asked these guys, the men in the black coats, he called them. And they just flashed passports at him—a Hero of the Soviet Union!—and told him to mind his own business!" Shiborin shook his head. "He was still pretty steamed when he got to the sauna." He grinned, to make sure I got his joke.

"Who was taken with him?" I was thinking of poor Filin, who would have to be hospitalized for months to recover from something like this.

"A bunch of second-level people—his little group of pets. Oh yeah, that guy you said you knew—the Georgian." I had pointed out Lev Tselauri to Shiborin and my classmates during one of our pointless, if not openly hostile, meetings with Artemov and his staff. So Lev had been swept up.

He and I had avoided each other since our last meetings at Baikonur, back in April. I had no idea of how he and Marina were doing, whether she had given birth to a boy or a girl. I didn't even know where they were living.

"Who would be powerful enough to haul Artemov around?" I asked. "Who's bigger than Ustinov?"

"The Central Committee and the Politburo," Shiborin said, with satisfaction. "Representing the Party and the people—"

He was in danger of lapsing into boilerplate propaganda, so I interrupted. "I'll see what I can find out." I thanked Shiborin, and went inside my flat.

I told Katya about Artemov and State Security. "Good. It's about time someone disciplined that drunken, incompetent bastard." This was vintage Katya, never leaving anyone in doubt as to her opinion. "I'm starving."

The trains back to Moscow stopped running at ten, so after dinner I packed Katya off. In other circumstances, I would have asked her to spend the night, but knowing how much she hated the flat, feeling somewhat awkward with my cast, and needing badly to speak to my father, I reluctantly let her go.

I wasn't able to reach him until the next morning. "Yes, I know all about Artemov," he said. "He's not being arrested, but questions have been raised about sabotage." I can't remember what my father said immediately thereafter, because I didn't hear him. Maybe it was the word sabotage coming on the heels of mention of Artemov, but it was at that moment that I realized my conversation yesterday with Uncle Vladimir had triggered this. "Yuri?"

My father had noticed my strange silence. "I'm still here."

"I said, someone probably wants to throw a scare into him. He just arbitrarily canceled one of our programs, you know. Refused to support it." I had heard rumors that the 7K-VI program was in trouble; this was additional confirmation. "He's also having big fights on your Moon rocket."

"Do you think they'll replace him?"

"Only if he quits."

"He'll never do that."

"Then we have to hope that they'll throw him in prison." I laughed, which was apparently the wrong response. "There's nothing funny about this, Yuri! There is a war going on at the very highest level! Anyone who's got his head sticking up is going to get it chopped off!"

"What are you trying to tell me, Papa?"

I could picture the exasperation on his face. "Don't go anywhere you aren't ordered to go for a while. That way you won't have to make any explanations."

"That sounds ominous."

"It's meant to. Remember when I warned you about working for Vladimir? This warning is double strength."

"I understand." And I said good-bye.

Understanding my father, of course, did not mean obeying him. He still didn't know—though given his warning, he might have suspected— that I *had* gone to work for his brother-in-law. So I had no choice but to continue my investigations. Actually, given their moribund state, to renew them, to finally get some answers to all these open questions. Why would Uncle Vladimir want to pressure Artemov? Could he have new evidence about the Korolev murder? And what did Gagarin's letter have to do with any of this?

My friends of the Fourth Enrollment were scheduled for another day of parachuting, meaning I had a relatively free day. I reported for exercises, then, still hobbling, caught the train headed for Kaliningrad.

33 LEV AND MARINA

I had no idea of where Lev and Marina lived, though I knew it had to be Kaliningrad. Both would have completed their studies at Bauman in the spring, and Lev's employment in the bureau would have entitled him to a flat nearby.

It occurred to me that one new flat had become available in the summer of 1967—the one I had formerly occupied. Why shouldn't Lev inherit my flat? He had already inherited my girlfriend!

So I went first to my former building, which was already beginning to show signs of deterioration: Bricks had fallen off the facing. In fact, there was netting over the entrance to prevent passersby from being clobbered. When I knocked on my former door, I was greeted by a young woman, a recent mother, to judge from the squalling child in the room.

But it was not Marina. I made a hurried apology and got out of there.

I had thought I was terribly clever—much as I had, early in the investigation of the Korolev murder, believed myself to be a master spy. And with as much success. Now I had no backup plan. I could contact someone in the bureau, Filin's office, perhaps, or even Triyanov, who might tell me where to find Lev. Or I could leave a message for the Omsk Twins, if they were still at Bauman—

Here came Marina, bundled in her fur coat and boots, grocery bags in each hand, walking up to the building. Before I could offer any sort of greeting, she saw me. She stopped, dropped the bags to the sidewalk, and began to weep.

I got her upstairs to her flat, which turned out to be located in the same corner of the building as mine, but one floor higher up. I was busy trying to contain the spilled groceries, since the bags had torn, while trying to comfort Marina, so I didn't ask about the baby. Or maybe I assumed her mother or Lev's mother, if Lev had a mother, was upstairs with it.

But the flat was clearly that of a young childless couple. Silent, empty, free of toys or clothing, or that smell of baby food and other essences.

By now Marina had calmed down. Allowing for a momentary redness around her eyes, she looked heartbreakingly wonderful, prettier than I remembered, and I was about to get angry at Lev all over again. "Where is he? Or she?"

"Who?"

"The baby."

She closed her eyes, and for a moment I thought she would cry. But she just sighed. "There is no baby," she said. "I miscarried at six months."

"I'm sorry. I didn't know."

"I doubt that anyone was eager to tell you." We put the groceries away as if we were back in our respective student flats. "I shouldn't have cried like that."

"It's all right." I desperately wanted to take her in my arms. "How is Lev?"

She turned toward me. "Isn't that why you're here?"

"Yes, I came to check on him—"

"To check on him. Oh, Yuri. I don't believe you." She walked out of the kitchen.

I followed, catching her hand. "What do you mean?"

"You know he was taken in, right?"

"Yes. And I came to see if you needed help—"

"Just like a Bolshevik—"

"Marina, what the hell are you talking about?"

"Denounce a man, then swoop down on his abandoned wife all full of concern—"

"I didn't denounce Lev!" No wonder she had burst into tears when she saw me. "I only *heard* that he was taken in for questioning along with Artemov—"

"And, of course, you had nothing to do with that, either!"

"No!" I was confused and angry. "Marina . . ."

She was looking into my eyes. "You still don't know."

"Obviously not, or I wouldn't be sitting here like an idiot."

Then, strangely, she began to laugh. "Yuri, who do you think I work for? Who sent me to Europe? Who is the head of the Sixth Directorate in State Security?" She only waited long enough for me to indicate that I had no idea. "Vladimir Alexandrovich Nefedov. I believe you know the name."

Uncle Vladimir, head of a directorate in State Security? That was like being a four-star general, perhaps even a marshal of the Soviet Union, a rank greater than my father's. "I know he has a high position in the organization, but—"

"—But! He's been surrounding promising technical students at Bauman with his agents for years! The Sixth Directorate handles industrial and economic espionage, and future managers come from our school. He took a very long view of things."

"It all sounds logical."

"Even when he targets his own nephew?"

I still had never told Marina about my working relationship with Uncle Vladimir. Now did not seem like the right time. "Why should I be any different from other students?"

My poor attempt at a joke failed. "Yuri, you got into my class because your uncle put you on the list. He encouraged me to get to know you. Just as he encouraged me to marry a man so we could carry out surveillance in England."

I sat silently, trying to absorb this terrible news. I guess I had suspected that Marina's first marriage had been arranged—she had said as much in the past. But *our* relationship?

"Tell me," I said, trying hard to be very calm, "did you ever love me? Or did my uncle give you orders to dump me and take up with Lev?"

It was her turn to sit silent, to consider her response. "You must believe me, Yuri. No matter what I've just told you, I am not a whore for State Security. I did their work because it saved my father's life, but my heart was always my own. When I went to England, I was too young to realize that I was caught up in the romance and adventure, that my husband was a cruel, ruthless bastard.

"But I *did* fall in love with you. Or we would never have seen each other outside of class. You must believe me. By telling you these things, I've risked my career."

"What about Lev?"

"You . . . withdrew from our relationship, Yuri. Think back to the time you started full-time at the bureau. You never had time for me anymore. Lev was there." She frowned. "Though lately that fucking bureau has robbed me of *his* attention, too."

That sounded like the Marina I knew and loved, a mixture of righteous indignation and spoiled girlishness.

"I'm sure he'll be back soon, safe and sound." I stood up, clumsily, my foot asleep in its cast. Marina caught me as I wobbled, and we kissed, deeply, warmly, as we used to.

Then I held her in the dark room—neither of us had turned on a light—swaying with her, like lovers on an empty dance floor in some movie about the Great Patriotic War, the pretty girl in her simple skirt and white blouse, the soldier in his uniform. . . .

"I should go." I was confused by my own feelings, and, in truth, we had worn ourselves out emotionally.

There were tears in her eyes again. "Yes."

Soon thereafter I was in an empty train heading out of Podlipki Station, trying to rearrange the puzzle pieces of my existence. Maybe I was still angry about Marina's betrayal, no matter how justified she might have felt. But I was still not ready to tell her the truth of my situation.

Especially since I was completely confused about that situation. What was Uncle Vladimir up to? He had had me targeted for intelligence work long before he had approached me. Had he merely used the Korolev murder as a pretext to "activate" me?

Or was it something worse than that? Uncle Vladimir had been present in the Kremlin Hospital the day Korolev died. No murderer had yet been arrested.

Had Uncle Vladimir killed Korolev? If so, what had he hoped to gain? (Ridiculous . . . he was not even in the same wing of the hospital as Korolev.)

Or, had Uncle Vladimir somehow arranged for Artemov to take

over? But why would he be persecuting him now, if, indeed, he was behind that?

Was there some way to link these events? Or was I feverish, emotionally distraught? Could Katya help me?

Too many questions. I had almost none of the information required for intelligent answers, and I needed to be intelligent, because the penalty for mistakes in this particular game was, indeed, death.

THE AMERICAN
FILM CREW

"They only kept him for a few hours, then let him go," Shiborin said the next morning, as we made our way—he too slowly for comfort, I too fast for my cast—down the icy sidewalk outside our flat.

"Artemov? Everybody?"

"I guess they sweated the junior guys a little more, knowing they would run to Artemov and complain as soon as they got back to the bureau."

"Who tells you these things?"

He smiled. "Heroes of the Soviet Union."

We paused as we came to Building Three, the last of the residential buildings to be finished. A truck was parked here and a young woman I didn't know was holding a baby while trying desperately to keep soldiers from breaking her furniture. "One of the nearly departed," Shiborin said. "Back to the squadron after being a cosmonaut. Can you imagine how terrible that would be?"

"Moving out with a small child in the middle of winter would be bad enough," I said, sensitized to domestic challenges by my meeting with Marina. I realized it was good we were heading for the gym, because otherwise I would have telephoned Marina simply to hear her voice, adding more fuel to the fires of confusion.

When we arrived, one of Belyayev's deputies was waiting with a message for me: "They need you over at the air base this morning," he said.

"Why?"

"Your English. They have some foreign visitors there today."

I was stunned. *Foreign visitors* at Chkalov? "Are they going to Baikonur next?" I said, joking.

Passing by, Shiborin overheard this. "They were here yesterday, while you were gone. It's a film crew from America making some kind of documentary on the Soviet space program, in case we beat Apollo to the Moon." He smiled. "Of course, people like you and I are secret, so they hauled out a couple of doctors and called them 'student-cosmonauts.' "

Even if I hadn't been able to speak some English, I would have wanted to see this, though I wondered who would request my services. Surely there were better English-speakers available to the State Security escorts. "One more thing," the messenger told me: "Civilian clothing."

I hurried back to my flat, and got changed just in time to catch the bus.

As I clomped from the administration building toward the flight line, I saw that Chkalov air base was surprisingly active this gray morning. I quickly realized it was an illusion. Yes, there were more cars parked in view, and perhaps two dozen people standing around. But there were no planes or helicopters taking off, only one MiG-17 out on the taxiway, its engines running.

I looked for the cameras, sound and lighting people, and found them at the center of a crowd at the hangar entrance. As I pushed my way through, I heard a familiar voice call my name: "Yuri, over here!"

It was Katya, her face rosy in the cold. She made no move to kiss me, nor I her: This was not only an official event, it was controlled by State Security. There were undoubtedly more agents present than subjects. In fact, since Katya and I were part-time assets, it was possible that the only people *not* working for State Security were the Americans themselves! "You got my message."

"You asked for me?"

"I thought you might enjoy this. Besides, you understand a lot of the technical terms."

"Glad to be useful."

I had to subtract two from my estimate of State Security agents present in that group, because Gagarin was there, too, along with Colonel Seregin, the commander of the 70th Squadron. Gagarin was wearing a flight helmet and was being filmed getting ready for a training mission. Seregin was filling the role of a briefing officer, complete with clipboard.

They were not on microphone as they walked toward the MiG-17, and a good thing, too, because rather than discussing the particular quirks of the 17, a high-performance jet which, I was quite sure, Gagarin had never flown, Seregin was saying, "How much longer is this shit going to go on?"

"Now you know what my life is like," Gagarin said. "I should be at the academy this morning instead of freezing my ass off here."

Naturally, at that moment Katya and what I assumed to be the American producer asked me what they were discussing. So I made up some plausible nonsense about weather, call signs, and traffic patterns.

The technician who had started up the aircraft engines climbed out, and Gagarin went up the ladder to the cockpit, with Seregin close behind. As the camera crew moved down the runway for some establishing shots (that was the term they used), I edged up to Katya. "What are you going to do? Gagarin can't fly that thing."

"I know." She frowned. "They didn't tell us until we got here. So he's not going to fly it. He's just going to . . . drive it out onto the runway."

"Taxi it."

"Yes. And then they can edit in a shot of the same jet taking off with someone else at the controls."

From what I knew of the accuracy of such documentaries, the footage would show an entirely different aircraft, possibly American, even an old propeller-driven one. But I kept my mouth shut.

Even taxiing an unfamiliar aircraft was a bit of a trick. I could see Seregin going through the procedures step by step with Gagarin. Then, as satisfied as he was going to get, he climbed down and pulled the ladder away himself.

We all backed away to see the first man in space off on his routine training mission. "Here we go," Katya whispered to me, quoting Gagarin's first words at the launch of *Vostok 1*, though not, I believe, deliberately.

It all seemed to go well. Gagarin was a rusty aviator, but he had the basic skills. Slowly, but smoothly, he rolled the MiG down the taxiway, turned around at the far end, then drove back to the hangar. There he halted.

The crew wasn't satisfied yet. They wanted footage from another angle, something about better lighting allowing them to see into the cockpit itself with a long lens. Katya asked me to explain this to Gagarin, so I hobbled over to the plane, its engines idling.

Gagarin opened the canopy. "What now?"

"They want you to make one more pass, down to the end of the taxiway and turn onto the runway," I shouted.

"And then we'll be done?"

No one had said anything, but from the look of frustration on Gagarin's face, I knew this would be the end of his part in the filming. "Yes!"

He waved acknowledgment, then closed the canopy again. He fired up the engines and rolled past the hangar toward the crew, which by now was at the far end, near the turn onto the runway.

I had just reached Katya, Seregin, and the others when I heard Seregin say, insistently, and to no one in particular, "Slow down!"

As we watched, the MiG reached the end of the taxiway going a lot faster than it had the first time. So fast, in fact, that as Gagarin turned it toward the runway, it began to fishtail.

"Oh, shit," Seregin said. He began to run.

"What's going on?" Katya said.

The film crew scattered as the big silver jet slid sideways off the icy concrete into the mountain range of old snow piled where they stood.

The heat from the engines and their exhaust raised an immediate cloud of steam. The engines shut off, whether by Gagarin himself or because they choked on snow being sucked through the inlets. And there, tilted crazily, sat the plane, the right wheel of its landing gear still turning, in front of Colonel Seregin, a dozen State Security agents, and half a dozen Americans, who had gotten the whole pathetic spectacle *on film*.

Poor Gagarin. He was out of the cockpit by the time I reached him, several minutes after the others. He didn't need a ladder, of course, since he was able to crawl out onto the mounds of snow into which he had driven the MiG.

In contrast to the day he had had his flight canceled, throwing his helmet, Gagarin was subdued, shaking his head and showing with his hands where and how he had lost control on the turn. Seregin was talking to him. Everyone else was keeping his or her distance.

"The Americans say they'll give us that footage," Katya told me.

"Nice of them." As if there were even a *possibility* of their escaping from Chkalov with it.

"How were we supposed to know the big hero couldn't *fly*?" she snapped.

"Nobody lets him," I said, though I doubt she heard me.

In truth, it was a minor accident. There would be some damage to the plane, all easily repairable. Gagarin could probably make a case that the runway had not been properly cleared.

As the many State Security watchers conferred with the American film crew, Gagarin and Seregin passed me. "That's it!" Gagarin said. "I'm tired of being everybody's tool. I'm calling Kamanin and Kuznetsov and putting an end to all this bullshit." Off they went, Seregin trying to calm the first man in space even though, I suspect, he agreed with everything Gagarin was saying.

This was exactly the kind of incident that Uncle Vladimir wanted me to tell him about, but I, in my first act of overt rebellion against him, would not.

The problem was, someone else was *sure* to report it.

35 THE MOONSTONE

Six weeks after my accident, on the morning of Monday, January 29, 1968, I returned to the hospital in Shchelkovo to have my cast removed. It had become such an inconvenience that I would gladly have walked the seven kilometers.

My ankle was a sorry sight, shrunken and pale, but losing the added weight of that industrial-strength plaster made me feel like the lead in the Bolshoi.

Clutching the certificates that authorized my return to active training, including parachuting, I raced for the train back to Star Town. At noon General Kamanin was scheduled to meet with the entire cosmonaut team, something that had never occurred in my nine months at the center.

I had had no further contact with Marina and relatively little with Katya since the awful incident with Gagarin at the air base. I was scrupulously following my father's advice to keep my head down while the clans waged war above me.

Not that I had any idea of how that war was going. I would have welcomed insights from my father, but he spent most of January in Czechoslovakia. So I was eagerly looking forward to Kamanin's briefing, hoping it would bring some order to my life.

Eager or not, the train ran late, and I barely reached it in time.

The location was the main classroom in which we student-cosmonauts studied. Ideally suited for a group of thirty, it was stuffed with at least twice that many—fifty cosmonauts and student-cosmonauts, and perhaps ten senior officers, including General Kamanin and his deputies, and General Kuznetsov, head of Military Unit 26266.

Kamanin wasted no time. "Last Monday the United States tested its lunar landing module for the first time." *Apollo 5*, as it was called, had been put into space by the Saturn launcher—the Saturn I-B, much smaller than the Saturn V-5. The payload was the buglike Apollo lunar module, both its descent and ascent stages, flying without a crew onboard. "The test was only a partial success. The engines on both stages worked to perfection, but there were numerous computer problems which will probably require another test flight this summer.

"Nevertheless, the Americans are completing their recovery from the *Apollo 1* fire." I realized that the tragedy had occurred almost exactly a year ago. "They have another Saturn 5 test scheduled for April. By late summer they will put astronauts Schirra, Cunningham, and Eisele into space aboard the redesigned Apollo. We expect them to fly a manned Apollo into lunar orbit by the summer of 1969. If all goes well, they will be able to attempt a lunar landing by the end of that year."

I certainly knew most of this information, since I was able to read the American news magazines that arrived at the Star Town library. To judge from the murmurs around the room, most of my fellow cosmonauts were surprised to hear it laid out so cleanly. Americans on the Moon by the end of 1969!

"That's if all goes well," one of the senior cosmonauts said, to nervous laughter.

"Unfortunately, our schedules depend on things *not* going well for the Americans," Kamanin said. "As for our program, we will launch the sixth L-1 to the Moon the week of March one, followed by two more unmanned Soyuz the last week of March." Someone applauded at this. "The State Commission will require two successful L-1 missions before a manned flight around the Moon can be attempted. Assuming a success with Number 6, Number 7 would fly unmanned in May, with a manned attempt possible in July 1968."

"A year ahead of the Americans," Colonel Belyayev said with great satisfaction.

"Assuming all goes well for us, and not so well for them." That came from Gagarin, prompting more laughter. Fortunately, Kamanin was in an indulgent mood.

"The first manned Soyuz flights are scheduled now for June. Obviously Soyuz will have to fly manned before L-1 can be flown with a crew. We have been trying to get the various State Commissions and Minister Afanasyev to understand this.

"With those launch dates in mind, we are resuming active training." He then began to read off names of crew commanders in the Soyuz group and the L-1 group. Most of them were senior people like Bykovsky and Leonov, who had finally graduated from Zhukovsky, freeing them to be cosmonauts rather than college students. I was pleased to hear my friend Ivan Saditsky named as a Soyuz commander. "Of course, all of these commanders will be joined by engineers from the Korolev bureau." There was some booing at this.

"We also hope to end the neglect our military programs have suffered. Unfortunately, the 7K-VI program has been canceled." This was no surprise to anyone. "I and the other members of the Air Force Military-Technical Council have strongly protested this decision, and it's possible it will be reversed. But for now, those of you involved in the VI program will work on the Almaz station.

"This is an ambitious set of programs. I don't think a rich country like America could operate four separate manned programs at the same time, and we are trying to . . . encourage the Ministries of Defense and General Machine-Building to bring us all together under one organization, preferably the Air Force." For some reason, I found myself glancing at Gagarin, who was sitting to Kamanin's right, just in time to catch him nodding with satisfaction.

"It won't be easy. But it's a fight we must win if we are to beat America to the Moon, and keep the Soviet Union first in the new realm of space." There was genuine applause at this, and with a self-conscious smile, Kamanin waved and walked out. Belyayev, Gagarin, and Nikolayev followed him, leaving the rest of us to disperse as we wished.

I made my way to Saditsky, who was having his shoulder punched by Leonov, and offered my congratulations. "It sounds better than it is," Saditsky said, once Leonov walked off. "Your old boss Artemov has decided that Feoktistov should command the next Soyuz flight, and even Triyanov is getting into the act."

I was surprised. "I can see either one of them as flight engineers, but *commanding*? I thought the commander always had to be an Air Force officer."

"You know that, I know that, the Central Committee knows that . . . but for some reason, Artemov doesn't." He looked at his watch. "Leonov wants me over in Building 44. Come along."

Building 44 was one of the new structures constantly in the process of rising from the birch forests in which the training center was located. It was the size and shape of a warehouse, and could have passed for one, except for the barbed wire and armed guards around it. And this was inside the perimeter of Star Town and the training center!

Once inside with Saditsky, I saw the reason for the extra security: A mock lunar landscape had been laid out using real soil. The sky was black, thanks to curtains, and in the middle of it all sat a white, lopsided vehicle with four legs . . . the L-3 lunar lander.

"God, will you look at this thing," Saditsky said. We stood there at the border of the lunar "surface," like children at the edge of a sandbox. Leonov and several of the other cosmonauts newly assigned to lunar crews were clustered around the L-3 in their white lab coats. Someone— I couldn't tell who—was in a pressure suit complete with helmet, trying to demonstrate a tricky egress out of the side hatch of the L-3, backing down the ladder. The whole process was made more realistic—and vastly more complicated—by rigging that connected the suited cosmonaut to an overhead crane, giving the tester a chance to see what it would be like to move in lunar gravity. The cosmonaut's foot slipped off the ladder with each step, but luckily the tester never fell.

"It's finally real," I heard myself saying. That's certainly what I felt.

"A real monstrosity," Saditsky said. "There's one pilot in the L-3, where the Americans will have two. Every move, like opening the hatch and climbing down the ladder, is a one-man job. That's assuming you survive the landing. They're saying that once you pitch over out of the descent burn, you'll have thirty seconds to locate your landing site. That's not very much time."

I remembered some of the details from my time at the bureau and my classes: During the firing of the engines, which would lower the L-3 from lunar orbit to within a few hundred meters of the surface, the pilot would be on his back, looking up at the sky; rotating the vehicle so he could face down toward the surface wouldn't help the problem, since the pilot would be flying over a sunless landscape until the very end. "So you don't want to fly it?" I said to Saditsky.

"Don't be an idiot. If engineers are crazy enough to build these things, I'm certainly crazy enough to fly them. I only have to find some way to be first!" He grinned and headed toward his comrades.

I wanted to linger there, to walk on this lunar surface. I could easily imagine myself coming down the ladder from the L-3—not on the first flight, obviously, but at some point, five or even ten years from now.

To do that, of course, I had to remain a cosmonaut. And to remain a cosmonaut, I had to learn some answers. Maybe it was my exposure to Saditsky and his take-the-hill attitude, perhaps it was my newly re-gained mobility, but at that moment I knew I had to start fighting back, to be something other than a tool.

I was scheduled to attend a Party meeting that afternoon. I had been so faithful in participating in the regular discussions, condemnations, and so on, that I felt sure I could skip this one without jeopardizing my status.

What was I worrying about? If I actually executed the vague plan then taking shape in my brain, my Party attendance record would not be an issue.

As if to prove to myself that I was independent, I stole a small rock from our fake lunar surface.

An hour later I was on the train to Moscow.

I had telephoned Katya's office before leaving Star Town, to ask if I could visit that evening.

Her flat was on the northwest side just off the Leningrad Highway, roughly between the Institute for Medical-Biological Problems and the Zhukovsky Academy. The Institute for Space Research was located nearby, too, and so was Uncle Vladimir's branch office of State Security. This neighborhood, in fact, was becoming as familiar to me as the one around the Bauman School.

Katya greeted me at her door with a warm hug and kiss, pressing a glass of red wine into my hand before I could even take off my coat or present her with the oranges I had bought at the Star Town commissary. "Sit while I finish cooking," she said, going back to her kitchenette and juggling the oranges as she went.

So I sat, sipping the wine, which I didn't particularly like.

Marina's confession that she had been steered to me by Uncle Vla-dimir had made me wonder about Katya: Was she, too, performing some kind of surveillance on me? It seemed unlikely. If Uncle Vladimir had wanted to replace Marina in my life, he surely would not have introduced me to Katya at his cottage. Nor had Katya ever probed for information, quite the contrary: I had learned more from her than she ever learned from me. I really believed that we were two lost souls who happened to find each other at the right moment, both of us knowing that the relationship was short-lived, like a summer flower.

Yet, when she came out of the kitchen, announcing that dinner was ready, she looked lovely and desirable in a way entirely unlike Marina. She was tall and blonde and graceful, lighting a cigarette like a Western film star, arching an eyebrow at my inability to move. "Like what you see?" she said, in English. Then she laughed, and we sat down to dinner.

Eventually I was able to present her with my second gift: "Have you ever seen a stone from the Moon?"

"Only in pictures, and then from very, very far away."

I took the gray rock out of my pocket. "It's not authentic, of course, but it's as close as you'll get—"

"—Until the Americans land?" she said.

I had always been able to depend on Katya for a conversational challenge. "Kamanin and Gagarin did a big show today. They're convinced we will beat them. In fact, training for the lunar crews started this very afternoon."

"What makes them so optimistic?"

"I think it was Artemov's stumble. It's as if they've been gathering their forces for a big attack, like Zhukov." By this time we were clearing the table. "Gagarin has been active behind the scenes. He's a military man supporting the military, so they listen to him. And he's a national hero, so the politicians and big bosses pay attention to him, too."

"He's come a long way for a little man from Gzhatsk." Katya named the tiny village west of Moscow where Gagarin had grown up.

"He got a lot taller the day they shot him into orbit."

I had delivered my message, putting Katya to the test. Then I made love to her, like that famous secret agent, James Bond.

36

THE OUTLYING REGIONS OF NEAR-EARTH SPACE

On March 2, 1968, the sixth L-1 spacecraft, still unmanned, roared into Earth orbit from Baikonur atop another Universal Rocket. Problems in the L-1 guidance system still hadn't been completely corrected and we wanted the simplest trajectory possible, so the goal of the mission was not a flight around the Moon, but to a point over 330,000 kilometers out in space. For that reason, the L-1 was announced as the fourth in the series of Zond interplanetary space probes, this one designed to explore "the outlying regions of near-Earth space."

The big managers of the ministry and State Commission hoped that a safe return and splashdown of *Zond 4* would mark another space first, something our country had not accomplished since *Luna 9* two years ago.

For two days the mission went beautifully. The troublesome Block D upper stage fired as scheduled early on March 3, sending the spacecraft soaring out into empty space. At the same time, a group of lunar cosmonauts led by Gagarin himself were down at the flight-control center in Yevpatoriya, duplicating the maneuvers in a simulated flight of their own.

Unfortunately, early on March 4, 1968, the same guidance system that had plagued earlier flights, including poor Komarov's, failed to orient *Zond 4* for a correction burn, which had to be canceled. Another attempt a day later also failed, but on March 6, as *Zond 4* reached its apogee and began its slow fall back to Earth, the burn put *Zond 4* on the desired trajectory for a safe reentry into the atmosphere.

As planned, on March 9, *Zond 4* fell closer and closer to earth, diving into the atmosphere to an altitude of less than forty-six kilometers. Had cosmonauts been aboard *Zond 4*, they would have experienced twenty Gs at this time, dangerously high, but still survivable.

Scorched and slowed by the dive, the spacecraft then regained altitude, climbing back to 145 kilometers to begin its final, slower, more controllable descent.

At that point a series of small mistakes paid big penalties. Our knowledge of the upper atmosphere was incomplete; so was our knowledge of the flying characteristics of an L-1 vehicle in this regime. By the time flight controllers realized that *Zond 4* was going to land six thousand kilometers short of its target zone, half a world away from the territory of the USSR, it was too late to make any adjustments. Once Tyulin and Artemov and the other members of the commission learned that *Zond 4* was descending by parachute into the Gulf of Guinea off the west coast of Africa, they commanded it to self-destruct so as to prevent agents of the Main Enemy from recovering it. The flight of *Zond 4* ended thirteen kilometers above the Atlantic Ocean with an explosion.

Publicly, the world was merely told that contact had been lost with "interplanetary space probe *Zond 4*." At the center, where we all took turns dropping into Belyayev's office for updates, we realized we had taken one baby step closer to a round-the-Moon flight.

The weather in the Moscow area all through February and into March was terrible, not surprising, but it prevented me from catching up to my Fourth Enrollment colleagues on parachute jumps. I needed ten to qualify; by mid March, I still had four to go.

Catching up was all the more difficult, because we student-cosmonauts had largely completed classroom training, where I excelled, and even much of the operational training, where I lagged, and were beginning to take on flight-support roles. For example, during the next pair of Soyuz missions, still scheduled for the middle of April (though lack of docking simulators was slowing the training), three of my engineer colleagues would be assigned to control and tracking stations around the USSR. Two others in the group had been told they were to be sent to the Astrakhan region in September to qualify as test pilots for the Spiral spaceplane program, while another pair were going to work on a successor to the canceled 7K-VI program called Zvezda, this one built by Artemov himself—as if his organization didn't have enough to do!

The rest, including Shiborin and me, remained unassigned, which made us both extremely nervous. "You have to eat shit to taste the golden apples," he said, far too often. "Not that being a test pilot is eating shit."

I succeeded in keeping Marina out of my thoughts, and continued to see Katya. The lack of any overt move against Gagarin or other senior cosmonauts convinced me she had not run to Uncle Vladimir.

My father returned from his inspection tour in Czechoslovakia, and came to see me at Star Town early on the gray morning of Wednesday, March 27, 1968.

"We're going to be at war this summer," he announced the moment I made the mistake of asking him how his trip had gone. "That country is going to pieces. The leadership is making the same mistakes the Hungarians made. And the same thing will happen."

I was fourteen when the "brotherly" tanks of the USSR and the Warsaw Pact had been "invited" into Hungary to "restore order." The thought that we could be planning the same sort of bloodbath in Czechoslovakia was a depressing reminder of how little things had really changed. Our leaders wore nicer suits now, but deep down they were still Bolshevik thugs.

"How have you been feeling, Papa?" I said, hoping to change the subject from global power politics.

"Never better," he said, with such strength that I almost believed him. He rotated his arm for me. "No more pain and stiffness here. I could probably pass a physical and go back to the cockpit."

I smiled. I had not heard him say that in years, not since my mother died. "Do you have business at Monino today?" The Red Banner Air Force Academy at Monino was two train stops further out from Star Town.

"Chkalov," he said. I gave him a cup of tea, and noticed that in spite of his claims of robust health, his hand shook.

"Straightening out our flight support?" Nobody at Star Town seemed to be happy with Seregin's 70th Squadron. Pilot cosmonauts complained about the arbitrary scheduling and availability of aircraft while nonpilots like me seemed to be completely frozen out. I had heard that the technical staff of the center was unable to use transport craft when needed.

The problem wasn't necessarily the fault of Colonel Seregin and his team. The 70th had been created upon orders from Marshal Vershinin with no warning and no study of the impact on operations at Chkalov, which was still home to a busy branch of the military's flight-test center. It also served as a private airport for Party officials.

My father grunted. "We can't tell which is more screwed up right now, the squadron or the test center. It's time both operations got cleaned up." He didn't need to add, *when we start fighting in Czechoslovakia*.

"Have you had breakfast?"

"No." As he said this, he glanced around my hovel. "I was going to stop at the commissary at Chkalov." He smiled. "It's the one thing they do right."

"We have a good one here, too."

"I need to be at the base by eight." It was already 7:30.

I offered to walk him to his car and driver, which waited in front of the administration building. The day was miserably cold and drizzly, typical for early spring. The sun appeared for a few seconds, only to be swallowed up in clouds. "I hope you're not flying today," my father said.

"Our group is studying a new spacecraft this week." Endless, tedious lectures on the bureau's new Zvezda, in fact. Today's subject was to be power systems.

"Good."

As we passed House 3, the main residence building, our path intersected with two other officers. "Here comes Gagarin," I whispered to my father.

"I know." He seemed indifferent.

Gagarin and the other pilot, a lieutenant colonel named Dobrovolsky, nodded greetings as they headed into the commissary and up the stairs.

"Here is where I leave you," my father said, and gave me a warm hug and kiss. As he turned away, I saw that there were tears in his eyes. I wanted to stop him, but he hurried away so quickly it was if he were running.

———

The Star Town commissary had a section that served as a decent restaurant comparable to the Stakhanov in Ostankino Tower, but most of the time we used the cafeteria section, loading trays with food and beginning to eat before we even sat down. We were, after all, busy cosmonauts.

Saditsky came up in line behind me. "Still trying to catch up on parachuting?"

"Yes."

He nodded his head toward the tables where the senior cosmonauts were gathered, including Gagarin, Dobrovolsky, and Leonov. "Dobrovolsky isn't going to jump today; he's taking a driver's test. So Leonov has room for one more. . . ."

The idea of jumping under Leonov's direction was intimidating: Not only was he one of the most talented of the first cosmonauts, he had turned himself into a master parachutist with a hundred or more jumps to his credit. But I needed to reach that qualifying number, and if not now, when? "Go ahead," Saditsky said.

I marched over there, set down my tray, saluted, and in my best military voice said, "Senior Lieutenant Ribko requests permission to join Colonel Leonov's squad for the day."

Leonov looked at Saditsky. "Why are you recruiting stragglers for me?" he said, clearly joking. "We leave in fifteen minutes," he said to me. It was already eight A.M.

I grabbed my food off my tray and ran back to my flat to pick up my pass for the air base. (They might let Gagarin or Leonov in without one, but not student-cosmonaut Ribko.) Running was still difficult, and it took me longer than I planned.

Then I had to stop at Belyayev's office to report my change in plans.

It was already after 8:15 when I raced out to the parking lot for the bus. Fortunately, they had waited. "Let's go," Gagarin said.

At Chkalov, Gagarin and a couple of pilots went off to the operations building while I followed Leonov and the rest of his lunar team to get suited up. In the locker room we met a couple of engineers from the bureau who had come over from Kaliningrad—Sevastanov and Rukavishnikov. We exchanged cool greetings; neither had been that active in Triyanov's kindergarten while I was still there, but they obviously knew me as a defector.

By 9:30 A.M., we were on the taxiway. As we passed one of the hangars, I saw my father—alone—standing there with his hands folded behind his back, staring at a pair of MiG-15s. I waved, but there was no chance he could see me. Then we were in the air heading for the drop zone over Kirzhach, sixty kilometers away.

We had moved so quickly that I had no time to be nervous, and by 10:15 was standing in a muddy field near the small airport there, having successfully completed my seventh jump. The lunar group was planning to make at least two today, and I actually looked forward to another.

As our An-2 came in for a landing, Leonov gathered us all together. "I just checked the weather. We've got clouds moving in and we'll be below minimums shortly. So it's back to the base." Thus my eagerness was short-lived.

We were lining up to reboard the An-2 when we heard the roar of a jet somewhere above us in the clouds, but very low. "That's a 15," one of the pilots said.

"They shouldn't be that low in these conditions," Leonov said.

"Maybe they're on their way back," the other pilot said.

I heard a strange sound from the sky—a pop, almost like a misfire. This on top of the noise from the jet's engine. I glanced around to see if anyone else noticed it: unlikely, since they were either already inside the An-2, or wearing hard helmets. (I had a soft leather one.)

Then we all heard a *whump*! in the distance, an explosion that literally sent a jolt through the ground. That brought Leonov and Bykovsky out of the An-2 in a hurry. "What the hell was that?" Bykovsky said.

Leonov told him to be quiet and listen. There was no more jet noise. "Something crashed," he said.

"Who was flying today?"

"Gubarev, Nikolayev, and Shatalov," he said, naming three of the senior pilot cosmonauts. He looked worried. "Let's get back."

37) THE COLUMBUS OF SPACE

When we reached Chkalov, we learned that the missing pilot was not Gubarev, Nikolayev, or Shatalov, nor any of the half-dozen other pilots flying for the 70th or the test center, but Gagarin himself. With him in the two-seat Mig-15 trainer was Colonel Seregin.

Leonov ordered his lunar team back to Star Town and Kaliningrad, then took off for the operations building. Since I was not a member of his team, I received no orders, and decided to find my father, if he was still at the base.

The flight line was busier than I'd ever seen it. A MiG-21 came screaming in for a landing, then two Mi-4 helicopters took off. Another MiG-15 trainer landed, and an Il-14 transport took to the air. I learned later that at eleven A.M., with Gagarin and Seregin's plane missing and now out of fuel, all Chkalov aircraft had been recalled while at the same time, resources were mobilized for a search of the area around Kirzhach.

I wasn't ready to believe Gagarin and Seregin were dead: If they had had a problem with their aircraft, they could have ejected. And in that snowy, tree-filled wilderness northeast of Moscow, they could easily be lost for hours.

When I reached the administration building, I found only a single frantic junior lieutenant manning the guard desk. "I don't know General Ribko and now is not a good time to be asking," he said, as if he had more important things on his mind. Well, the aircraft-operations people did: I'm not sure how this guy was going to be helping to rescue the

Columbus of Spaceflight. Maybe the fact that I was still wearing my leather jacket and flight overalls encouraged him to believe I was either junior to him, or possibly even a lowly civilian.

"Stand at attention when you address me, Lieutenant," I found myself saying. "You will answer me in a civil tone or you will be guarding a radar site in Kamchatka, is that understood?"

The junior lieutenant's face went red, but he got the message, coming to a full brace, eyes forward. I was slightly amazed at the result. Although I had been on the receiving end of military-style reaming, I had never actually delivered one.

"I am looking for Colonel-General Nikolai Ribko, Hero of the Soviet Union, inspector for the Air Force staff. He's the only three-star general at this base today."

Thanks to my threats, the junior lieutenant's memory had magically improved. "I saw a colonel-general on the flight line half an hour ago. I have not seen him since."

I could have had him phone his superior officer, whoever that might be, for more information, but I had also seen my father out by the hangars. The operations building was a more likely place to find him. "Thank you, Lieutenant," I said, offering my best salute, turning on my heel and marching out.

I was reluctant to get too close to the operations building, because everyone there would be busy. But I knew my father; he would probably be right in the middle of things.

As I approached, a familiar face emerged. It wasn't my father, however, but Shiborin, still in his uniform. "Yuri!"

"What are you doing here?" I asked.

"They called over to the center to get extra transport pilots for the search." He was walking toward the locker room, and I hurried to keep pace. "I'm supposed to take one of the Il-14s out. Come along. We could use the extra eyes."

Not seeing my father, and wanting to be useful, I went along.

As Shiborin suited up, he briefed me on the conditions. Actually, he had me hold the clipboard where he had just written his instructions while he said them aloud, to more firmly embed them in his memory, much as I had helped him study orbital mechanics. "We're going to have two planes and four helicopters in the air at all times, working our way through search areas that are ten-by-ten kilometers.

"The helicopters will be down low, at a hundred or even fifty meters, while we'll be at three hundred to six hundred meters."

We headed for the plane, and I asked what had happened to Gagarin and Seregin. "I guess he showed up hoping to make a solo flight in a 17, and found out the weather was below his minimums. So Seregin offered to fly with him in a 15 trainer. They took off at 10:19 toward Kirzhach, leveled off at four thousand meters. Weather was supposed to be acceptable: a cloud layer at a thousand meters and another one at 4,800. Ten kilometers visibility.

"The flight plan called for simple ground loops, nothing too tricky, in Zones 20 and 21." These were the two pie-shaped operating areas. The Kirzhach airfield sat on the extreme northern edge of Zone 20. Because of the congestion of air traffic in the Moscow area, most training flights from Chkalov were vectored into those two small, narrow zones extending about seventy kilometers northeast of the base. "The plane only carried enough fuel for about forty-five minutes in the air. The last transmission from Gagarin was at 10:30, when he requested permission to make the turn back toward Chkalov. Heading 75 degrees and in Zone 21."

I remembered that our parachute jumping team had also been in Kirzhach, at the small airfield there. It was shortly after ten-thirty when we heard a low-flying jet, that strange popping sound, then the explosion of the crash. I told this to Shiborin, who nodded. "Leonov reported that, so our search is going to concentrate on the area south of that airfield."

Then we climbed into the cockpit of the Il-14, which was being refueled from an earlier mission. A copilot waited. I strapped into a jump seat in the main cabin while Shiborin ran confidently through his pre-flight checklist. Within ten minutes we had lumbered into the air.

It took us another fifteen minutes to reach our search zone. I had my nose pressed up against a window as we dropped through the clouds and leveled off, it seemed, just above the treetops.

Spring had come a week ago, but there were no signs of it here in the woods northeast of Moscow. Some bare patches of earth, yes, but the open fields were still white with deep snow. Even the branches of the trees were still fluffy from the last snowfall.

"This is going to be tough," Shiborin said. He had come out of the cockpit to get a better look through the side windows. "Their parachutes are white."

"Do you think they ejected?"

"They should have. Unless they collided with another plane." He clapped me on the shoulder and returned to the cockpit.

I kept thinking about that popping sound—could it have been the ejection seats firing away from the stricken aircraft?

We were actually searching for three objects: two men on foot in addition to the wreckage of the plane. Over the course of our two-hour search, however, we saw nothing but forest, fields, country roads, and tiny villages.

By two-thirty we were back at Chkalov for refueling as another Il-14 took our place. I went with Shiborin into the operations building to grab a bit of food before resuming, and here I saw General Kamanin in heated conversation with two other generals, one of them my father.

Seeing me, my father broke away. He seemed upset, understandable, given the situation. "I thought you were going to be at Star Town all day."

I didn't want to get into a lengthy justification for my presence, so I said, "They called some of us in to help with the search."

He accepted that, then said, "The search is over. They just found the wreckage of Gagarin's plane."

"Where?"

"Three kilometers from some little place called Novoslevo."

I remembered the name from the charts we had used in the search. It was south and east of Kirzhach, roughly the direction of the crashing jet we had heard. "What about the pilots?"

"Nothing so far." Kamanin and the other general brushed past us at that moment, headed for the flight line, where a pair of Mi-4 helicopters waited, rotors revving up to speed. We watched them climb aboard, then take off. Then my father said, "Can I give you a ride back to Star Town?"

"I'm still helping with the search," I said.

He nodded, as if lost in thought, probably, like me, wondering what would happen if it turned out that Gagarin had indeed been killed. "I'm going back to headquarters. They don't need me here."

We shook hands and he walked away, never looking back. I ran to catch up with Shiborin inside the control center. He was already peeling off his flight jacket. "They've stopped the search. It's getting dark and they want to see what they find at the crash site."

I nodded, and followed him to the locker room, where we changed back into our uniforms. Only there did I notice that I had gotten dirt on my hand—dried black grease of some kind, with a peculiar smell. It was probably from the Il-14. I washed it off and thought no more about it.

What General Kamanin found at the crash site, we learned that evening, was a watery hole in the forest where the MiG-15 had plunged almost nose-down, shearing off trees at a 45-degree angle. Wreckage from the explosion had scattered fragments of the plane into the trees and throughout the forest, but the cockpit itself was buried more than five meters deep.

Part of a human jaw was recovered before dark. It held gold and silver crowns and could be identified by one of the Chkalov doctors as belonging to Seregin.

As dark and cold covered the site, there was no sign of Yuri Gagarin, the Columbus of Space.

"... WHILE FULFILLING HIS DUTIES"

The remains of Yuri Gagarin were discovered shortly after dawn on March 28, when Kamanin and the others returned to the crash site. Even the night before, a fragment of a pilot's kneeboard had been found. On it, a torn piece of a flight plan marked in red—the same kind of marker Gagarin was seen using the morning of the twenty-seventh. This evidence didn't prove that Gagarin had not ejected ... but a day of searching had not located him.

Even if he'd been injured, the area of Novoselovo was not uninhabited. In fact, the first to arrive at the crash site was a farmer on his tractor. Surely someone would have noticed a parachuting man in the area.

At around eight in the morning (so we heard later that day at Star Town), Kamanin and some other searcher found a piece of a flight jacket hanging from a tree a dozen meters in the air. In the pocket was a receipt for Gagarin's breakfast at the Star Town commissary.

Kamanin departed immediately, to officially inform the widows Gagarin and Seregin of their loss, while the crash team began the sad business of removing the wreckage from its cold, wet grave.

At Star Town the mood was of complete shock. People stopped and talked, heads shaking. Mothers hushed noisy children. Even Saditsky, never one to show a serious emotion, had red-rimmed eyes when I met him coming back from exercises on Thursday morning. (Only about a dozen cosmonauts showed up, all of them from the Third and Fourth Enrollments.) "This is truly terrible," he said.

"He must have been a good friend."

"Yes, but more than that. They talk about how he proved that you could survive a trip into space, and he certainly did that. But he also survived the return—with all the attention, all the booze, the politics. He could have turned into a complete monster, with a big car and a dacha and all the women in the world, but he didn't. To the very end he was looking out for the rest of us. He was fighting for us." He put his hands to his eyes for a moment. "And they killed him."

I could see that Saditsky was upset, not thinking straight. "By pushing him back into the cockpit so soon?"

"No. They took advantage of him. He'd wanted to fly again for years, but the bigshots wouldn't let him. So when he started fighting them, they had to get rid of him. What better way than a plane crash?"

I remember my father telling me that whenever someone in the military dies under unusual circumstances, it's always reported as a "plane crash." Marshal Nedelin, head of the Rocket Force, had been vaporized along with 150 others in an October 1960 explosion at Baikonur. His official obituary said he had died in a "plane crash while fulfilling his duties."

"I thought the 15 was supposed to be our most reliable aircraft."

"Every aircraft is reliable, until it fails."

That was the last I saw of Saditsky until nine P.M., when all of the sixty-some cosmonauts were bused to a facility in northeast Moscow, where the remains of Gagarin and Seregin were cremated. The urns containing the ashes were to go on public display at the Central Army House at nine the next morning.

Unlike every other bus ride I've taken with my fellow cosmonauts, this one returning us to Star Town was subdued, almost entirely silent. I sat with Shiborin toward the back, where I quite innocently told him what Saditsky had said, that Gagarin had been killed.

To my surprise, Shiborin reacted as if I had just told him he had a nose on his face somewhere below and between his two brown eyes. "No question. He was getting too powerful. Somebody wanted him dead."

I don't know which shocked me more—the automatic confirmation of what seemed, to me, a paranoid fantasy, or the fact that I was hearing it from *Shiborin*, the world's purest Communist. "Who? Brezhnev? The Hammer? Artemov?"

"None of them. But somebody around them, absolutely. Look at our pathetic history and tell me that it would surprise you."

Well, I had long ago accepted the idea that a mysterious someone had probably murdered Sergei Korolev. Accepting the idea that Gagarin could have been killed did not require me to reorder my thinking on a major scale.

However, if you believed that *both* had been murdered, you had to start wondering if the killings were linked. Who would want to cut the heart out of the Soviet space program?

I pondered this over the next two days, as the normal work of Star Town ceased and we gave ourselves over to public mourning. All of the cosmonauts of Military Unit 26266 took turns standing honor guard at the Central Army House, where the line of mourners was so long we were forced to open the viewing early, and keep it open almost to midnight.

I returned home to find an invitation slipped under my door: "The family and friends of Yu. A. Gagarin and V. S. Seregin invite you to honor the memory of Yuri Alexeyevich and Vladimir Sergeyevich on the day of their funeral, March 30, 1968, at 1600 in the Central House of the Soviet Army (Commune Square, Building 2)."

So, on that Saturday afternoon, with the first hints of spring in the air, with all of the cosmonauts, both military and civilian, in attendance, not to mention Brezhnev, Kosygin, Ustinov, Afanasyev, and a multitude of marshals and generals (among them, Colonel-General Nikolai Ribko), the urns carrying the ashes of Yuri Gagarin and Vladimir Seregin were carried from the Central Army House to nearby Commune Square, then down Neglinny Street toward the House of Unions. The streets were lined with mourners, Muscovites of all ages weeping openly.

At the House of Unions the urns were placed on motorized gun carriages as the procession proceeded into Red Square, where the urns were placed in the Kremlin Wall next to Marshal Malinovsky, not far from both Vladimir Komarov and Sergei Korolev. The whole pathetic ceremony was over by three P.M.

At four-thirty, however, we were back at the Central Army House for the memorial speeches. Exhausted, emotionally drained, most of us departed by eight.

I believe some of those speeches are still going on.

As in any military unit, especially one devoted to flight, you mourn the loss of your comrades, you wear the black armband for the appropriate time, then you move on.

That was the air around Star Town as March became April. Of course, all I saw was my own little part of it, that involving the Fourth Enrollment. What was being said by senior cosmonauts such as Leonov and Belyayev, friends of Gagarin, I did not know.

I tried to find some way to link the murder of Korolev with the possible murder of Gagarin, and found nothing. No single person or group that would have benefited from both. I still wasn't clear who benefited from the death of Korolev, unless it was the Americans. Who, by the way, conducted the second flight of their giant Saturn V-5 rocket on April 4. (I am always able to remember this date, because the great African-American leader Martin Luther King was murdered the same day.)

Unlike the first test, this second Saturn V-5 came close to disaster. During the flight of the first stage, a vicious pogo effect started, in which the spacecraft began to vibrate up and down as many as five or six times a second, with the force of up to ten Gs.

The first stage separated as planned, however, but the more fragile second stage paid the price, losing one of its five engines four minutes into its burn, followed by a second engine moments later. The whole vehicle was in danger of going out of control and having to be destroyed.

The NASA flight controllers showed patience and courage, however, simply waiting to see what might happen. Luckily, the two failed engines were opposite each other, so the overall thrust of that stage remained symmetrical.

Of course, with thrust reduced by forty percent, the three remaining engines were forced to keep burning longer than planned and to a higher altitude. When the second stage shut down and the single third-stage engine took over, the third-stage guidance reacted with alarm to its unusual altitude, so it actually tried to point itself *down toward the center of the Earth* in order to get back on the proper path!

After a minute or so of that, the third-stage guidance realized it was now too low, so it pitched up, so far that it actually went into orbit *backward*.

In retrospect, it was almost a comical performance, one that was beyond the capability of any Soviet rocket, which would have destroyed itself with the initial violent pogo effect.

But it showed that America still hadn't mastered the equipment it needed to land on the Moon. We still had a chance.

Most of these details I learned later, of course. What occupied me most beginning at the end of that first week in April was an order to report to Colonel Belyayev on the morning of Saturday, April 6.

It was a brief meeting—Belyayev still seemed to be exhausted by the events of the past ten days. His health was not good, I had heard. "The State Commission investigating the crash of Gagarin and Seregin has set up four subcommissions. Each subcommission will include representatives from the cosmonaut team. Because of your training as an aircraft engineer, by special request you are to work with the subcommission reconstructing the last hours of Gagarin and Seregin and of their MiG-15."

I accepted the assignment at once, then found the strength to ask: "Comrade Colonel, you mentioned a special request . . . ?"

"One of the other agencies represented on the subcommission asked for you by name." He shuffled through the papers on his desk, looking for the order. "A Vladimir Nefedov."

Uncle Vladimir of State Security. The same Uncle Vladimir who was present at the Kremlin Hospital the day Korolev died, who complained about Gagarin's ambitions.

Was *this* the link I was looking for?

39   SUBCOMMISION NUMBER 1

I had no time to act on my suspicions, since I went directly from Belyayev's office to Chkalov, where I joined a team flown by helicopter back to the crash site near Novoselovo. There my valuable aeronautical training was put to use searching for fragments of Gagarin and Seregin's MiG-15.

My immediate supervisor was an engineer named Davydov from the Ministry of Aviation Production, which oversaw the development and manufacture of aircraft, and was thus responsible for the MiG-15. Davydov was in his thirties, short, dark-haired, thick, and, as I soon learned, strict to the point of idiocy. He had that annoying habit of speaking to you as if reading from a manual: "You are to proceed along the ground only in the direction indicated. At the first sign of an anomaly, you are to stop and signal a supervisor."

Well and good. Ten of us, "specialists" all, lined up an arm's length apart in the woods to the north of the crash site itself, which I now saw for the first time: a jagged crater surrounded by stumps of trees destroyed in the explosion. There was also an ominous trail of shattered branches leading back toward Kirzhach. It was here that we searched.

During the initial briefing at Chkalov, and on the flight over, I learned that the demolished mass of the cockpit, including what was left of Gagarin and Seregin, had already been dug out of the crater and hauled off to the base for examination. The larger wing and tail sections had also been removed, but the impact of the crash had been so violent that the MiG had smashed like a jar dropped on cement. There were hundreds—thousands—of metal fragments yet to be recovered, each one a potential witness in the investigation.

So far, the various subcommissions had established that the plane was not damaged prior to the crash (ruling out a collision with another aircraft), that the engine was still operating at the time of impact, and that the pilots did not eject. Maintenance records of this particular MiG-15, officially UTI MiG-15 #612739, call sign "625," were up to date and in order. There was no obvious cause for the crash.

Further, a bit of a mystery was taking shape. The last transmission from 625 to the control tower at Chkalov was at 10:32 A.M., when Gagarin requested permission to turn to a heading of 75 degrees, which the tower acknowledged. At that time, 625 was thirty kilometers from the runway at Chkalov and heading toward it.

But the crash site was sixty-four kilometers away.

There was no further transmission after 10:32, but the air-traffic radar at Chkalov had 625 on its screen until 10:44.

What happened in those twelve minutes to turn 625 around, send it thirty-some kilometers in the other direction, then knock it out of the sky? It seemed that the answer lay in the damp, matted needles of this forest floor, still dotted with clumps of snow.

I had taken perhaps eight steps when one of the other searchers, to my left, said, "I have something!"

"Nobody move!" Davydov ordered, scuttling down the line behind us and falling to his knees with a camera to record the exact position of the fragment. Only then did he reach down with a pair of tongs and raise it, placing it in a plastic bag.

He stood and made a notation on a chart. "Continue!" he said, and so we did.

During the course of that afternoon, we discovered almost fifty pieces of metal or debris, some as large as a hand. I myself found two items, one a shard of steel later determined to be from the skin of the tail section, and a rusted washer, which might have fallen from a Novoselovo tractor.

I spent the next week tromping through the woods under Davydov's lash as life at Star Town resumed its former rhythms—if anything, the tempo increased as we looked forward to the launching of another pair of unmanned Soyuz vehicles. During the week another unmanned Luna probe, Number 14, was sent to the Moon. This one was to photograph the lunar surface from orbit, providing information about future landing sites.

Coming in late on the evening of Thursday, April 11, the night before the seventh anniversary of Gagarin's pioneering flight, I found Shiborin staggering up the sidewalk.

He was more of a drinker than I, but not a steady or committed one. This day he had found himself forced to keep up in a highly emotional contest to prove his love for the late Gagarin on his anniversary. This, at least, was my reconstruction of events, once I had, at Shiborin's request, steered him into my flat. "Don't let Anna see me like this."

For a while it was unlikely anyone would see Shiborin at all, as he collapsed onto my couch and passed out. I busied myself with other matters for the next hour, occasionally checking to be sure he was still all right.

Around midnight he stirred, hauled himself to the bathroom, then back, where I started handing him cups of tea, juice, anything. He was understandably subdued, first telling me the news that our training center was going to be named for Gagarin, as was the Red Banner Air Force Academy down the road in Monino, as well as Gagarin's birthplace, the village of Gzhatsk. Seregin's name would henceforth honor his 70th Training Squadron.

I thought that was the end of his report, but then he leaned forward for a moment, finally raising his eyes. "The war's still going on."

"What war?"

"Between the Air Force and everyone else. Gagarin was leading the charge, but even in death he's valuable. Maybe more so: Kamanin apparently went to Ustinov yesterday with a whole bunch of proposals, one of them to take manned vehicles completely away from the Central Space Office."

"What difference would that make?"

"It would mean that the Hammer and his son-of-a-bitch Artemov worked for *us*. We wouldn't have to beg them to live up to their agreements anymore; we could order them to comply, or give the work to Chelomei or somebody else." I could certainly see the benefits in this, from the Air Force's point of view. "We know they're fighting back." He stood, wobbling, hand flailing as he reached for the door. "Now they're saying Gagarin was drunk when he took off."

"Not on the commission, they're not." Bits of tissue had been saved for an analysis of blood alcohol, and none had been found in either pilot. Nor had we found any witnesses—other pilots or support personnel—who had seen Gagarin or Seregin downing a shot before climbing in the cockpit.

"Facts have nothing to do with it. It's only to discredit Gagarin's judgment so that his proposals can be ignored."

"What is going to happen, then?" I asked. Maybe it was the fatigue, or a delayed reaction to the events of the past week, the past eighteen months, but I felt myself getting angrier. I was tired of being shuffled around by everyone from Uncle Vladimir to Engineer Davydov. I was going to be twenty-six years old in two days. It was time I began to make my own decisions, take my own actions.

I wasn't even sure that the positions pushed by Gagarin or Kamanin—or my father, for that matter—were the right ones. But at that moment I wanted to see them win. Perhaps I was just more supportive of people I knew as opposed to those I didn't. Or more sympathetic to the feelings of those who flew the aircraft and spacecraft than of those who bought and sold them, the ministers, the bureau chiefs, the State Commissioners, and especially the State Security apparatus, which fed on all of us.

"We'll fight to get control of our fate," Shiborin said, laboring over the words. "And because we are pilots and not politicians, we'll lose." He smiled. "It will be a great tragedy."

Then he left, walking slowly down the hall.

I spent Friday, April 12, the day before my birthday, working with the subcommission. During the morning hours we worked the crash site, turning up more and more fragments; then, when it began to rain, we returned to Chkalov, where I became a recording secretary for a general meeting of the commission chiefs, learning, for example, that UTI MiG-15 Number 612739 had actually been built in Czechoslovakia in 1956, with a design lifetime of 2,100 flying hours. That on the day of the crash, it had logged 1,113 of those hours, only slightly more than half-way through its operational life. That its jet engine, RD-45-FA Number 84445a, had been manufactured at State Aviation Factory 478 in December 1954, with a design life of one hundred flying hours before maintenance. On March 27, 1968, it had been sixty-seven hours since its last major overhaul. It, too, was well within its useful service life.

Further, that the accident rate for the MiG-15 was the lowest in the entire Soviet Air Force, with one accident every 18,440 hours flown. (The Su-11, apparently a death trap of an aircraft, suffered a major accident every 2,100 flying hours!)

It was all facts and figures, the substance of what was, I was sure, going to be thirty thick volumes of data. Yet no one had so far discovered a good reason why two healthy, talented pilots simply dived out of the sky and into the forest.

Katya had made plans to celebrate my birthday on Saturday, and I managed to get out of Star Town early that morning, before any other innovative duty could find me. When we spoke by telephone on Friday, the morning after my emboldening encounter with the drunk Shiborin, I had asked Katya if Uncle Vladimir would be present. "I was only planning a lunch for the two of us," she said, sounding mystified.

"Just get a message to him that I have information for him. Maybe he can meet us after lunch."

"I'll do my best," she said, mystification turning to irritation. I had felt bad about that, but only briefly. I had enjoyed my time with Katya, but clearly it was coming to an end.

Besides, if I actually managed to carry out the plans taking shape in my head, she would be better off rid of me.

I reached the base of Ostankino Tower before Katya did, and had the pleasure of seeing her strolling toward me from the metro station. For a moment—or several moments—I was about to abort my new mission, to surrender to whatever Katya, Uncle Vladimir, my father, and the heads of Military Unit 26266 planned for me.

It was even worse when we kissed, and she gave me my present, a novel in English called *Marooned* by an American journalist named Caidin, whose earlier works I had read and admired. "One of our people at the embassy in New York bought several copies for the institute."

I thanked her, and then we went up the tower to lunch. The service staff did not bow and scrape as they had when Uncle Vladimir and I first dined there, but Katya's connections through the Space Research Institute hadn't hurt.

Almost at the stroke of one P.M., as we were having some pastry for dessert, the elevator door opened, ejecting the bulk of Vladimir Nefedov.

He waved off the waiter who flew toward him like a bird of prey, and came directly to our table. He seemed relaxed, even amused, as he kissed Katya and me. "I've been wondering when you would chose to reveal this illicit friendship," he said, lowering himself to a chair that had magically appeared for him.

Katya closed her eyes and glanced out the window. This was awkward for her. "Is it illicit?" I asked.

"Of course not," Uncle Vladimir said, expansively. "Though you *acted* as though it was."

Katya rose. "Excuse me," she said, and patting Uncle Vladimir on the shoulder, as if to reassure him that she was not upset at his presence, went off to, I assume, the ladies' room.

Uncle Vladimir watched her go with what could only have been appreciation. Then he turned to me. "I was actually a bit upset when I first learned that you two were seeing each other."

"Because you and Katya had a relationship?"

This was unusually blunt for me to say to him, perhaps for anyone. I think it shocked him. "A relationship," he said, as if he had never used the word before. "Katya and I have . . . many relationships."

"Yes. That's one of the things I wanted to talk to you about." I had his full attention by now. "How long have you had me under surveillance?"

"Me personally, or State Security as an institution?"

"Either one."

He looked down at his chubby hands, anxious, I think, for something to put in them. A pencil, perhaps. "You've been under *some* kind of surveillance all your life, Yuri."

"Because my father was on the staff?"

"Because your mother, my sister, worked for State Security." Before I could question this, he continued: "She was not really an active agent past the time you were born—but she reported from time to time on the personal activities of your father and his fellow pilots, and their wives and children. Surely this can't be a surprise to you." He actually laughed. "Our whole society would cease to function without such reports. Look at the work you've been doing for me!"

"That's my next question," I said, still stunned by the revelation about my mother. "I don't want to be your spy anymore."

"It's difficult work. May I ask why not?"

"Because I believe you killed Korolev. Possibly Gagarin, too."

Katya chose that moment to reappear. A gesture from Uncle Vladimir, one so subtle I'm not sure I saw it, froze her . . . made her stumble . . . turned her around and sent her back the way she had come!

Uncle Vladimir spoke calmly. "The price we pay for doing surveillance is that we forget who to trust. Enemies are everywhere. No one is what he seems." He looked directly into my eyes. "I did not kill either Korolev or Gagarin."

At that moment I believed him; he had not touched Korolev. "But you know who did."

Now he sighed and showed frustration. "How can I take you into my confidence, Yuri, when you no longer work for me?"

Laboriously, he rose from the chair. He picked up Katya's half-empty glass of wine. "Did you have some cake?" He touched his glass to mine, but did not drink. "Happy birthday."

Then he walked away.

40   THE WEATHER BALLOON

The rest of that birthday was even less successful than the lunch. Katya returned, was furious with me, said not a word as we rode down the elevator. As she walked, she kept a proper distance from me, too, like some Victorian maiden out with a questionable suitor.

Finally I said, "Katya—"

She glanced at me, eyes blazing. "You're being an idiot."

I stopped, keeping distance between us. I felt ashamed, foolish, but told myself it had to be done. I had to sever my links with Uncle Vladimir, and that included Katya. Yes, as a good Party member would say, for her own good. "I *had* to tell him."

"You had to do no such thing! It's not even a question of being rude to your own uncle, and to me, on your birthday—it's stupid! He's a very powerful man, and in case you haven't noticed, he ranks the Party above family."

"So he'll have me killed?"

Katya merely closed her eyes, a sign she was exasperated almost beyond belief. "I know you must have some intelligence, Yuri. You graduated from Bauman. You made it into the cosmonaut team. Maybe it's because I'm older, but sometimes you make no sense to me. You have no knowledge, no vision, only a response to whatever happened to you last.

"In fact, you have a lot of growing up to do. Maybe you should call me when you're older. Ten years older."

She turned and walked away. I chose not to follow her. I'm not sure I could have moved, in any case.

On Sunday, April 14, 1968, Soyuz spacecraft Number 8, configured as the active craft for a planned docking sequence, was launched success-fully from Baikonur, and given the name *Cosmos 212*. The next day, April 15, Soyuz Number 7 reached orbit as *Cosmos 213*, the new target ship starting out four kilometers ahead of its pursuer, which closed in almost immediately for a successful docking that we were able to watch on television in the Star Town auditorium. (Those members of the Fourth Enrollment not assigned to remote tracking stations, such as Senior Lieutenants Ribko and Shiborin, were excused from other duties for this event, like students on a field trip to a museum.)

Within four hours, *Cosmos 212* and *213* separated and went on to test improvements in the guidance systems. *Cosmos 212* returned safely to Earth on Wednesday, April 17, making a controlled reentry (using the bell of the Soyuz to create lift and steering) for the first time. The only anomaly was that high winds in the landing zone caught the re-covery parachutes after touchdown, dragging *Cosmos 212* five kilometers across the steppe, beating the hell out of its skin and heat shield.

Cosmos 213, returning the next day, suffered almost the same fate, performing a controlled reentry only to be dragged across the ground by winds. This time the high winds kicked up a dust storm that kept the spacecraft from being recovered for hours.

Had cosmonauts been aboard, of course, the parachutes could have been manually separated, sparing the spacecraft their bumpy rides.

The twin docking, the second such success in a row, encouraged the Soyuz crews to hope that the next flights would be manned. This in spite of Defense Minister Ustinov's order that there would be more unmanned tests no matter how well the *Cosmos 212–213* mission went. Nobody could tell them for sure, so their feelings about the week's events were mixed.

And early on the morning of April 23, 1968, the seventh unmanned L-1 was launched for a planned loop around the Moon and return to Earth. Unfortunately, six minutes and twenty seconds into the flight, the second-stage engines of the Universal Rocket 500K abruptly stopped and the launch escape system fired, pulling the L-1 away. It was quickly learned that a component failure had mistakenly ordered the shutdown, causing the loss of the mission.

For every two steps we took forward, there was another giant step back.

In the middle of the next week, the Moscow area suffered one of its spring freezes, and with eighty percent of Gagarin and Seregin's MiG-15 now recovered, the commission suspended additional searches.

So far, the study of the wreckage had produced no clue to the cause of the crash, except this: There was no Plexiglas from the canopy.

There could have been several mundane explanations for that. If Gagarin or Seregin had taken the first step toward firing their ejection seats just before impact, the canopy would have been fired away first. The problem with that explanation was that no one had yet found the canopy, and it should have been within one or two hundred yards of the crash site.

The other possible reason? The impact of the crash was so violent that it shattered the Plexiglas into shards too small to be found. Several investigators clung to this; others, such as Davydov, with the experience of a dozen such accidents, scoffed at it.

Something, then, had shattered the canopy before the crash. But what?

Perhaps two days after this mystery appeared, so did an explanation. Some other search team—State Security's, perhaps?—had found wreckage of a weather balloon suspiciously close to the ground track of the Gagarin-Seregin aircraft between Kirzhach and the crash site. The balloon had been shattered by some sort of impact.

Now, the words "weather balloon" suggest something filmy, lighter than air, like a soap bubble, but in fact, the vehicle is a thin metallic ball under pressure, giving it considerable rigidity and resistance. An aircraft hitting such an object could easily be damaged, possibly shattering a canopy and incapacitating the pilots.

Possibly. I found it suspicious that this weather-balloon wreckage magically appeared after the subcommission realized that the MiG-15's canopy was missing. No agency had yet come forward to claim the weather balloon, either. Was it from the Air Force, who had three airfields in the vicinity, and routinely launched weather balloons? Or from the State Meteorological Service? Did they have a launching site or station nearby? Well, no one seemed quite sure of that, at least not in the last week of April, 1968.

Nevertheless, as I heard in the few meetings I was allowed to attend, the weather balloon was seized upon as the "cause" of the crash that killed Yuri Gagarin and Vladimir Seregin.

The only dissenters to this conclusion were the lower ranks, like me, and even Davydov, who scoffed openly at the idea. "What were these pilots supposedly doing? Flying with their eyes closed? The sky was clear in Zone 20 at the time of the crash. They would have seen that balloon five kilometers away."

The cosmonaut team also protested, even writing a letter to Ustinov himself complaining about the conclusions of the overall commission. They never received a reply or even an acknowledgment.

So as the spring of 1968 turned into summer, as my father's world prepared for war, as I saw lines of battle sketched in ink between the Cosmonaut Training Center named for Yuri Gagarin and Artemov's bureau and its allies, as my personal life shrank to nonexistence, as I weighed the truth of the revelation that my mother had been a spy for State Security, as my country and America kept racing for the Moon, I waited nervously for Uncle Vladimir's next move.

INTERLUDE

Summer

"I always heard the story that Gagarin and Seregin got distracted because they were hunting," I said to Yuri Ribko. It had been months since our last meetings at my hotel. We were back at the Rendezvous in Korolev early on a cold winter night. I had managed to free myself from coverage of a Presidential impeachment to accompany a group of NASA astronauts doing winter survival training at the Gagarin Center. Some months prior to this, the first two elements of the International Space Station, the Russian Zarya and the American Unity, had been docked together by the crew of STS-88. The astronauts now shivering inside some Soyuz descent module on a field northeast of Moscow hoped to someday live in those modules. Assuming the missing pieces got delivered, which was still an open question, one which, thankfully, Yuri Ribko and I did not have to answer.

"Hunting?" he said.

"The story I heard," and I had heard it from one of the first cosmonauts, "was that Gagarin or Seregin spotted some elk from the jet as they were on their way back, and decided to strafe the beasts to have some nice fresh meat."

Ribko laughed. "Well, it's certainly true that fresh meat was always welcome. We were having it flown in from other parts of Russia, right into Chkalov, in those days. But it's fiction," he said. "Their MiG-15 was a trainer: no guns. Even if it had had guns, they wouldn't have had bullets in them. Good God, there were enough disgruntled pilots taking off from that base that one of them was sure to strafe the commander's office!"

"Well, it was just a story."

"Typical. Colorful, with perhaps a tiny sliver of truth."

"Unlike the stories that your Uncle Vladimir somehow killed Korolev and Gagarin."

Saying that so bluntly was a risk—Yuri could have exploded at me and walked out, never to be seen again, and my hours of interviewing would have gotten me three-fourths of a book that would never be finished. But I had to let him know that I had doubts. Because others would, too.

I was worried about Yuri, in any case. He looked even thinner than the last time I had seen him. "Slimfast," he said, joking. "I want to look like an American movie star when I do my book tour."

(But did Slimfast also make your hair fall out?)

"I realize it all sounds quite fantastic. What's the term? Science fiction?"

"Fantasy is what they'll call it. That your Uncle Vladimir Nefedov, whose name appears nowhere in any history of the Soviet space program, somehow murdered Sergei Korolev and Yuri Gagarin, and thus cost Russia a chance to be first to the Moon."

He put his hand on my wrist; in my experience, when a source does that, he's preparing to tell me something important. And true. It's a better indicator than a lie-detector test. "I'm sorry, Misha. Did I give you the impression that the murder mystery ended with Uncle Vladimir?"

"Well, actually, yes."

He shook his head and smiled. "You owe it to yourself to hear the rest of my story. Then you can decide what you believe."

SCORPION 4

ENEMY AGENTS ON SITE

41

THE FRATERNITY OF EAGLES

On Monday, May 6, 1968, almost a year to the day of my arrival at Star Town, I was called into Colonel Belyayev's office along with Shiborin after we had showered following exercise.

Belyayev looked tired and unhappy; Shiborin, thanks to his friends in the fraternity of eagles (as the pilots called themselves), had told me earlier that the training center doctors were trying to ground Belyayev. "They say he's got some problem with his heart, like Slayton, the American astronaut. But who can believe those sons of bitches after what happened in January?"

January, of course, was when the cosmonaut team had suffered a purge in which five students had been dismissed. Every one of the dismissals eventually was laid to "medical disqualification," thanks to the willingness of the medical staff to cooperate with General Kamanin— who, through no coincidence, supervised the Aviation Hospital in addition to the manned space program—in finding a face-saving way of getting rid of those he wanted to get rid of. It was ludicrous to believe that five healthy young officers, having already passed the rigorous medical exams to get into the cosmonaut team, would in two years' time become so unfit they had to be dismissed!

"I thought hero-cosmonauts didn't have to worry about the doctors."

"As long as Kamanin and Kuznetsov are on their side. But both of them are angry with Belyayev." Well, he had let discipline slide: A couple of weeks ago a couple of inspectors from Kamanin's staff had made a surprise visit to the morning exercises, which, luckily enough, both Shiborin and I were attending, and found less than a third of the cosmonauts present. Belyayev was also being blamed because some of the boys got drunk during the trips to Baikonur and Yevpatoriya supporting the last L-1 failure, though I don't know what Kamanin and the others expected; you ship these guys off to fairly remote locations to do a job, then punish them when they find some way to amuse themselves when the job vanishes. "They're going to put Nikolayev in Gagarin's post, and that leaves Belyayev right where he is."

Gagarin had been the deputy director of the training center when he died, and it was clear Kamanin was grooming him to eventually take over from Kuznetsov. Being director of the center was a very desirable job: interesting work, tremendous power, and the ability—if one chose to exploit it—to live like the ruler of a small country.

"So they won't let him fly, but they won't let him move up the chain of command." A very frustrating situation, even if you weren't an eagle.

"He'll probably chew us out just to make himself feel better."

Nothing like that happened, of course. Belyayev merely acknowledged our salutes, and told us to sit down. "You've both performed well in your initial training so far, and with the search-and-rescue teams for the crash.

"We are assigning you both to support the lunar programs L-1 and L-3. These will be part-time positions; you will still continue your student training under my supervision, including the mandatory exercise program." Belyayev was looking at paperwork on his desk when he added this, missing the smug look Shiborin fired at me. "Your primary job will be to serve as flight-crew representatives to the factories making the rocket and the spacecraft. It's not flying, but it's very important work. We need our own eyes and ears in these places."

Just like that, my cosmonaut career took a major turn. I was going to be spared the tedium of working on the military Soyuz program, or in the Almaz space-station team—both vehicles were years away from test flights and had yet to appear at the center in the form of actual hardware rather than wooden mockups.

The lunar programs were the reason I had wanted to become a cosmonaut. I was still thrilled with the idea of planting my country's flag on that dark, rocky soil, a crescent earth above me. I knew, of course, that I could never be first: One of our cosmonauts, or some American, would beat me. But to get there at all would be a dream, and to work on the hardware was one giant step toward fulfilling that dream.

My only regret, hearing the news of the assignment (and the further orders that Shiborin and I were to fly to Baikonur tomorrow morning), was that I would have no chance to pursue my private investigation of the deaths of Korolev and Gagarin. Given the resources available to me at that time—which is to say, none—perhaps this was for the best.

Shiborin, ever the eagle, managed to talk his way into the cockpit of the Tu-104 heading east the next morning. I rode on the hard metal benches with a group of engineers from, I soon learned, the Kuznetsov bureau, builders of jet engines who had moved into the rocket field in the past couple of years. Not too happily, to judge from their comments.

As the green of the Moscow District gave way to steppe and desert, I began to think of my mother, now revealed to me as a spy for State Security. Or so Uncle Vladimir had said; again, I had no confirmation. She had been exiled to a wasteland populated only by dangerous weapons and those who worked on them, and never seemed the same. What had happened to her out here?

What would happen to *me*?

Gagarin's death did nothing to appease the demons dragging down our space program—demons who worked for Uncle Vladimir, I was now convinced. Ustinov insisted on additional unmanned test flights of the Soyuz; fine, in principle, but there were only two more vehicles that could be ready for launch within the next few months. The canny minds in the Ministry of General Machine-Building had not been able to find enough money to build more Soyuz spacecraft when they were needed. If two more were wasted on yet another set of tests, there would be no manned launch until the fall of the year.

These same ministers were insisting we send two cosmonauts around the Moon in a relatively untested L-1! The eighth L-1 wasn't even completely built, though we expected it to be shipped to Baikonur in time for a launch attempt in July. Two successful unmanned tests of the L-1 were required before Soviet cosmonauts could follow.

What was waiting for Shiborin and me and the boys from the Kuznetsov organization at Baikonur was the first of the Carrier rockets, the giant white shells (at least that's what the Carrier looked like to me: an artillery round) that were to lift the L-3 lander and yet another version of the Soyuz into Earth orbit, then fire them toward the Moon.

The weather at Tyuratam was beautifully springlike. We were quartered in a new hotel, the Cosmonaut, just opened in spite of the fact that it was not completely finished: The floors in my room were still bare wood. But with the warm nights and warmer days, it was tolerable.

That afternoon Shiborin and I were bused to the launch site along with the Kuznetsov workers. I had not visited Baikonur since joining the military cosmonaut team, and was stunned by the amount of construction that had been finished in little more than a year: The assembly building at Area 1 that had formerly dominated the landscape was now dwarfed by a longer, taller structure to the north. Beyond that was a pair of launchpads, massive concrete pits, each one flanked by a lightning tower 180 meters tall and a launch-support structure, an open collection of platforms, pipes, and girders 145 meters high, that, I was informed by one of my fellow travelers, actually *moved to one side* prior to ignition of the Carrier rocket itself.

This new assembly complex was called Area 110; the pads were 100-Right and 100-Left. And heading for 100-Right was a Carrier, flat on its side, giant conical tail first.

Even Shiborin was impressed. "Too bad the Americans can't take a look at this. They'd quit."

"Their Saturn is bigger," I said. "And, believe me, they're watching this right now. We could stand out on a field and wave, and in a few days our pictures would be at the CIA." I think my statement surprised him. The fact that the USSR flew picture-taking spy satellites for years was well-known; it was what most, if not all, of our many Cosmos spacecraft were. Shiborin was probably not aware that America's spy-satellite program was even more extensive, and had been active longer, or so my father had once told me.

"Maybe I should drop my pants and show them my ass." Shiborin hated any suggestion that the U.S. was superior to the Worker's Paradise.

We entered the cavernous assembly building, where pieces of yet another Carrier were stacked. I got my first good look at the first stage of the monster, and counted thirty engines in it! It was as appalling as it was daring. Even the American rocket program, blessed with the cream of Nazi designers and their years of experience, had shied away from the Nova rocket because its first stage required eight engines. I could have stood looking at this beast all afternoon, but at that moment I saw something equally, or even more, interesting—my old friend Lev Tselauri.

He was, as we all were by now, wearing a white coat. Unlike Shiborin and me, who were gaping at the unassembled Carrier like peasants inspecting a new tractor, he was busily putting our Kuznetsov bureau companions to work. I debated how to approach him. If I should.

Then he solved the problem for me, excusing himself from the clutch of white coats and walking toward me. Shiborin noted this. "Friend of yours?" he said.

"I don't exactly know."

Lev's arms opened and he embraced me. "It's good to see you," he said. "Marina told me how you came to check on her."

Remembering the exact events of that social call—I tortured myself by thinking about our kiss at every opportunity—only made me feel more guilty. But it was clear that Lev was once again my friend. Or, at least, my ally. I felt this when I introduced him to Shiborin, when Lev asked if we could speak privately.

"I feel responsible for what happened to you," I told Lev. "Your interrogation."

"Why? Did you denounce me?"

"No. But I talked you into leaving the Chelomei bureau."

He laughed. "I wouldn't have missed the last year for anything! It's been most educational. Artemov, Filin, Feoktistov, all of them—they are fascinating men. Brilliant engineers, each in his own way." He pointed up at the Carrier's first stage. "Of course, my old boss, Chelomei, has a monster Moon rocket of his own on the drawing board. Much better than this."

"Is he going to build it?"

"If he had the money, he would. But our country is committed now to this one."

"It looks impressive."

"Yes, it does. If it flies, it will be even more impressive."

"You sound doubtful."

Lev shook his head and looked at the concrete floor. Though new, it was already showing cracks, perhaps due to the strain of bearing the monstrous weight of the Carrier. "It's a collection of compromises. Too many engines. My God, thirty in the first stage. The Saturn 5 has only five. So did the second stage of that vehicle, though they were smaller, and two of them failed on the launch last month."

"Well, with thirty engines, surely we can withstand a failure or two."

"If one engine fails, you automatically lose a second." Now he pointed at the tail section, where two dozen engines were arrayed around the rim, like points on a twenty-four-hour clock, with six clustered in the center. "Each engine has a twin on the opposite side. If, say, number 3 fails, number 17 automatically shuts down, to keep the thrust symmetrical."

"Then the remaining engines have to burn slightly longer."

"Correct. I see that you've retained your keen Bauman training." He smiled as he took out a cigarette and lit it. "It's a plumbing nightmare, though."

"How did such brilliant engineers like Artemov and Filin let this happen?"

"The failures of this design, according to Artemov, are Korolev's fault. For one thing, he wouldn't use the fuels Glushko wanted." Glushko was the master builder of Soviet rocket engines. "They had such a *huge* disagreement that Glushko refused to work on the project. Which is why we've got Kuznetsov's designs, which aren't as powerful or reliable—"

"Which is why you've got thirty engines as opposed to twelve or—"

"—or five, like the Saturn or Chelomei's 700 rocket. It's going to be very difficult to teach the Carrier to fly. The one on the pad right now never will."

That was news to me. "I thought the first launch was going to take place as soon as the fit checks were complete."

"Theoretically, it could." He gestured with his cigarette toward the area just above the thirty clustered engines. "But we found stress cracks in the first one before we even raised it to vertical. Someone badly blundered in calculating the strength of materials, especially once subjected to extreme cold." The fuel tanks in the Carrier used only kerosene, as Korolev had insisted, but the oxidizer was liquid oxygen, cooled to minus 150 degrees.

" 'Those responsible will be punished.' " I assumed Triyanov and the rest of the kindergarten still had reason to say this.

"If not punished, then interrogated at length."

"That must have been awful."

"Surprisingly." He took one last drag from his cigarette, then stubbed it out against the skin of the Carrier tail section. No one seemed to notice. "At first we all thought it was some kind of joke. But they actually drove some black vans up to the bureau and started taking us away."

"Where to?"

"The Lubiyanka itself. Not to the basement, just to the interrogation rooms. They started grilling us about sabotage. The L-1 failures, the parachutes on Soyuz, the fucking guidance system. Of course, you know and I know that most of the failures are subsystems: The bureau doesn't build the parachutes, we subcontract them to Tkachev's bureau. Guidance, too. We do the overall design and assembly, but we depend on the subcontractors to deliver parts to spec.

"They didn't give a shit about the facts. I mean, they started complaining about Proton failures. Well, first-stage problems were Chelomei's business. The upper stage was the only thing you could fairly blame us for.

"As far as I know, every one of those failures can be explained by sloppy workmanship, poor design, obsolete electronics, or just bad luck. But they claimed to have evidence that unauthorized people had access to the vehicles in the assembly buildings here in Baikonur." He lit up another cigarette. "I guess some mystery saboteur was able to throw a wrench into one engine or pull a wire somewhere else. Who knows?"

"Who was doing the questioning?"

"State Security. One guy in particular was really beating up on me, some fat bastard in a fancy suit. Artemov said later his name was Nefedov."

He was called away at that point, and I was left there with pieces of the Carrier rocket, knowing I finally had some proof that my dear Uncle Vladimir was truly at the heart of a conspiracy to destroy our Moon program.

42 / CARRIER

Lev's prediction regarding the Carrier turned out to be true. As soon as the vehicle was raised into position for launch, cracks were "discovered" by inspectors working for the State Commission. The planned launch, still several weeks off, was canceled and the first vehicle written off as a "model" for "fit checks" of the new launch structure. This was a valuable use for it, though we'd have learned the same from a vehicle capable of flight. (In fact, a number of flaws were discovered in the gantry itself, some of them serious enough to have forced the first Carrier to be rolled back to the assembly building while repairs were made.)

All of this took days to decide, days in which Shiborin and I acted as test crewmen for the mockup of the L-3 lander and yet another version of the Soyuz/L-1 command module, this one known as the LOK, for lunar orbit cabin. The L-3 and LOK were scheduled to be fired into orbit aboard the second Carrier. Our work involved climbing into the seats of the LOK, Shiborin as commander, me as flight engineer, and carrying out many tedious commands from the staff a few meters away.

It was slightly more fun to take turns climbing into the L-3 landing vehicle, though it was not complete. We took turns because the L-3 would only descend to the surface of the Moon carrying a single crew member, the military commander, while the flight engineer remained in orbit aboard the LOK. You could peer out the forward window and imagine yourself seeing the craters of the Sea of Serenity from the height of a few thousand meters. This work was also more tiring, since the L-3 lander didn't have a seat; restrained by a series of straps, the pilot simply stood up to fly it. Shiborin solved this problem by liberating a small wooden ladder from the construction team and sticking that inside the cabin. It wasn't comfortable, but it did allow us to sit down without having to be extracted from the cabin during the long periods of time when the test team was engaged in argument.

No sooner had we completed this series of tests than the first Carrier was rolled back into the assembly building to be taken apart, and we repeated the tests with *its* LOK and L-3. This made little sense because both spacecraft would have to be reintegrated with a new launch vehicle at some point in the future, and any tests made now repeated. But much of what we did in those days made little sense.

Once we had completed that work, the L-1 vehicle Number 8 was declared ready for mating with its Universal Rocket, so Shiborin and I, and our test team, which included Lev Tselauri, shifted to the Proton assembly building at Area 92, several kilometers to the east.

We had left Star Town on May 7 thinking we would be absent for a week, no more. We were still living at the Hotel Cosmonaut when June turned into July. It was difficult enough for me, having packed for a shorter trip, but there was no one to miss me back home. Shiborin, on the other hand, was married, and frequently bitter about the separation. On a couple of weekends he managed to get himself assigned as a copilot on one of the transports commuting between Tyuratam and Chkalov, and go home for a few days.

These trips allowed him to catch up on the news. The commission investigating the Gagarin-Seregin accident had still not found the cause, the weather balloon having been discredited. Pilot error was now the leading theory, which rightly infuriated the community of eagles. There had been a formal ceremony naming the training center after Gagarin. Nikolayev had been appointed deputy in Gagarin's place, and Belyayev, as expected, had been passed over. Colonel Bykovsky, to the surprise of many, had been jumped over Leonov as commander of the first squad within the cosmonaut team—the one for civilian programs, including Soyuz and the lunar missions. Bykovsky had been the commander of the spacecraft intended to dock with Komarov's doomed Soyuz and I had worked with him, though not much. He was quiet and competent and his appointment was a good move.

The war over the next Soyuz missions was still raging, with Star Town and the Korolev bureau arguing about the composition of the crews, while above them, Ustinov insisted that the next pair of spacecraft be flown without crews at all.

And, meanwhile, a completely redesigned Apollo spacecraft was delivered to Cape Kennedy for a return to manned flight in September.

Even though the weather at Tyuratam had grown hot, dusty, and dry, even though I was spending a growing amount of time searching for my own food, taking care of my own laundry, and trying not to become romantically entangled with a certain dark-eyed waitress at the commissary in Hotel Cosmonaut (I had heard she was in the business of collecting cosmonauts, and I would have been in her second ten, I believe), I decided I was better off in Baikonur for the moment.

One night in late June, as I was leaving the Area 92 building hoping to catch a ride back to Tyuratam, I found a familiar figure rummaging through the trash piled high beside the building. It was Sergeant Oleg Pokrovsky, the scrounger and hunter I had met on my first visit here.

If possible, he seemed even more raggedy than when I last saw him, though that had been at the beginning of a winter hunt. I said hello, and, I was pleased to see, he recognized me. "The young man who was interested in Blackie and Breezy."

"The same."

"Not the same." He gestured at my uniform. "I see I am to salute you." He straightened up and executed a perfect one, a bizarre sight, this aged scarecrow in a shabby uniform standing at attention next to a heap of garbage.

In return, I gave him the most half-assed salute possible, adding, "You have heroically fulfilled the tasks of the Motherland," one of the many automatic phrases used in the military. "I regret that I don't have a drink to offer you tonight."

He grinned. "I am Oleg Pokrovsky, and I *always* have something to drink." It wasn't vodka, but a bottle of beer, already open.

Even though I never much cared for beer, I took a swig and was surprised at how good it tasted. Perhaps my exile to Baikonur was changing me.

"The last time I saw you, you were heading off to kill zaigak."

"Last week?"

"A year ago. When Komarov was killed."

Oleg shook his head. "I killed my first zaigak a few days ago."

Among my bad habits is insisting on my point of view beyond the point where it would be polite to stop. "Maybe you only got one then, but last April you were heading off to one of the tracking sites to do the same thing. They kept the 'official rifle' there, you said."

"Yes," he said. "And that's what I used."

It was as though we were speaking two different languages. Either that, or Sergeant Oleg lived in a time zone entirely his own, where a year could be confused with a week, like a character in a science fiction story. "Well," I said, enjoying the private fantasy, but not wishing to prolong the debate, "I hope you got a good dinner out of it."

"Look what they paid me." He opened the flap of his own bag, and pulled out a pistol, its gray metal gleaming in the light of the street lamp overhead. I had fired a pistol several times in my reserve training, now five years in the past, but that had been a heavy Borodin, not this sleek thing.

"What do they call it?"

"The officer who gave it to me said it was a PB-8. The Special Forces use it." Special Forces were the elite commando units of the Soviet Army. "He said he had won it in a bet, and it made him nervous to have it around."

"How does it make you feel?"

He hefted it, then twirled it on his finger like a character from an American cowboy movie. Until, that is, he dropped the pistol on the pavement. We bumped heads trying to recover it. All right, perhaps we had kept swigging from the beer—with Sergeant Oleg several swigs, if not whole bottles, ahead of me. Finally he recovered the weapon. "Careful," I said. "It might be loaded." Like the two of us.

"Oh, it's loaded," he announced with glee. He even ejected the clip and showed it to me. "Eight rounds!"

"You could get into a lot of trouble with eight rounds."

I was thinking of the damage one could do to an enemy, but Oleg misunderstood. "Do you think so? I know we're not issued weapons, but . . ."

I would have explained, but sweeping headlights told me a car was coming, and I still needed a ride. I said good-bye to Sergeant Oleg, promising to see him again, and ran toward the car, waving frantically to get it to stop.

The next morning, when I went downstairs to rendezvous with Shiborin, I found a message from my father. He had arrived with some inspection team yesterday afternoon, and was staying at the old hotel.

I had not seen my father in a couple of months, not since the death of Gagarin, though we had talked briefly on the telephone during one of his trips to Eastern Europe. His sudden presence here at Baikonur filled me with dread, because I knew I needed, finally, to be open and honest with him, and that it would be difficult.

Thanks to Shiborin, I made an early exit from the day's work and met my father at his hotel. It was still light, still hot and dusty, but he insisted on walking through the streets of old-town Tyuratam. Imagine an Arab bazaar taking place in a canyon lined with Khrushchev-era concrete buildings.

He bought nothing, so I got food for both of us from a vendor. When I asked him why we bothered to leave the relative comforts of the hotel, he said, "Watchers."

I found this humorous. "Who would be watching Colonel-General Ribko?"

"You'd be surprised," he said. "With this stupid business in Czechoslovakia, not to mention all the problems in the space program, all security forces are on alert." He grunted, disgusted. "Most of them wind up watching each other."

I realized this was my best opportunity. "I've been one of them," I said. "One of Uncle Vladimir's watchers."

For a moment I thought he hadn't heard, since he kept walking as usual. Then his left hand shot out and grabbed my right arm above the elbow, painfully. He drew me close. "After I told you not to?" he said. The look of betrayal on his face made me ashamed.

"It was already too late," I said, lamely.

"And you kept it secret from me all this time? You went into the cosmonaut team working for that man?" Each sentence was like a slap, as my father's sense of betrayal gave way to disbelief, then anger. "Do you have *any idea* of the risks you've taken?"

"I think I do. Now."

He rubbed his hand on his face, as if wiping away a stain. "You should have told me."

Now, driven by embarrassment, I got angry myself. "You should have told me about Mama."

"What do you mean?"

"She worked for State Security, too. So I've joined the Air Force *and* become a spy; so what? It's in my blood!"

Had I been younger, he would have hit me. Or maybe it was the very public location of our argument that restrained him. "He told you that, did he? Vladimir?"

"Who else?"

"Is that what he used to get you to work for him?"

"He offered to get me a job in the Korolev bureau," I said. "Something you refused to do."

"Don't be childish!" Now he was almost pleading. "I wanted you to live your own life! Be an engineer, whatever. Not a snitch." He flicked his hand at my uniform shirt. "Not a soldier."

"Well, I'm not a snitch anymore. I told Vladimir I wouldn't make reports to him."

He thought about that for a moment, then laughed. "Good. Good for you, standing up for yourself. He'll destroy you, but at least you've repossessed your soul."

"Why would he destroy me? He wasn't happy, but I'm certainly no threat to him."

"What were you investigating, Yuri?"

"Korolev's murder. If it was murder. I don't know anything anymore."

"Oh, Korolev was murdered. And he was not the only one. Yuri, there is a war going on, not just for the space program or who gets to the Moon, but for the whole country. On one side you have the Party and State Security, on the other—well, other forces."

"Clans," I said, remembering Triyanov's warnings to me when I worked at the bureau.

"Exactly! And unless you are in one of the clans, you'll never understand anything. The only way to remain safe is to stay completely out of it!"

"Well, I've gotten out of it."

"You think so. You worked for State Security, yet you wear an Air Force uniform. No one knows which side you're on, and that's the most dangerous position of all." Somehow we had gotten turned around and were headed back to the hotels, just a father and son, senior and junior military officers out for a pleasant stroll in one of the socialist republics.

If ever I needed a father's advice, now was the time. "Tell me, then, what do I do?"

"Nothing. Nothing but your cosmonaut work. That should keep you busy enough." He spoke slowly, as if formulating some plan in the part of his brain not engaged in speaking to me.

"And what will you do?" I hoped he would share his plan with me.

"I'll take care of everything." He grabbed my arm again; this time it actually hurt. "But you have to promise me: no more intelligence work. No more reports to *anyone*."

What else could I do? I had failed horribly as a spy, anyway. "I promise."

Even as I gave my word, I knew I was certain to break it. I had questions that needed answers—answers I knew I would never hear from my father.

43 ⟩ THE DEVIL'S VENOM

I managed to stay out of my father's way for the next several days, a task made easier by the flood of new State Commission members arriving for the launch of the eighth unmanned L-1, now scheduled for no earlier than July 16.

Shiborin and I knew that we would stay at Baikonur through the launch, returning to Star Town via Yevpatoriya with Bykovsky and Leonov and their flight engineers, who came for the launch with the bigshots.

On the morning of the thirteenth, a new Universal Rocket 500 was rolled out to its pad at Area 92. Shiborin and I were prepared to walk with it, into the hot, dusty wind, when Lev showed up wearing a makeshift burnoose and holding two others, which he handed to Shiborin and me. "When it gets like this, you've got to be a Bedouin," he said.

Much amused, we arranged ourselves, marching out behind the giant rocket and the puffing train engines. As we got closer to the concrete launchpad and the towering support structure, Shiborin departed, and Lev and I were alone.

"Who would have believed this?" he said, looking up at the tower, at the Universal Rocket slowly being lifted to vertical. "Two years ago we were students!"

" 'The Party makes use of talent,' " I said, quoting some inane Komsomol slogan.

Lev laughed. Then, surprising me, he said, "You never ask about Marina."

This was true. I had deliberately avoided the entire subject. I wasn't ready to have a serious discussion. "Marina?" I said, as if it were the most natural question in the world, one friend to another on the streets of Moscow. "How *is* she?"

He laughed again. "She's fine. She asks about you whenever we talk." Then he frowned, and seemed to hesitate, which was unusual for him. "Come and see us. Come and see *her*."

I realized I couldn't avoid the subject any longer. "The burnoose was a good idea, Lev. Having me come to see you and Marina is a bad one. We'll all be uncomfortable."

"More uncomfortable than we are now? You and I used to live together. We work in the same business. We've been together every day for the past eight weeks!"

"You should have thought of that when you started seeing Marina behind my back."

"I was wrong. She was wrong. Maybe you were wrong, too." He was red-faced now, whether from embarrassment or anger, I couldn't tell. Perhaps both. "It wasn't as though I pursued her. She felt neglected." He held up a hand to silence my protest: "Nevertheless, the fault is mine. I'm ashamed of myself. But I want us to be friends again."

Even in my anger, I knew I was hardly blameless—not just for neglecting Marina, for lying to her, but in kissing her during our last meeting. "All right," I said, worn down. "I will come and see both of you as soon as we get back." And so I made a second promise I was unlikely to keep.

Lev kissed me. "We have to stick together, Yuri. Being questioned by State Security was frightening. Imagine what they will do if there's another 'accident.'"

"But there will be accidents. These are very complex machines."

"You and I know that because we're professionals. But State Security doesn't, and nor do most of the politicians they serve. Besides . . ." He actually looked over his shoulder, as if expecting to see a black van lurking there on the launchpad. "There *have* been a number of mysterious accidents."

"What are you talking about?"

"I mean, systems that worked perfectly during final checkout—the same kind of work you and I have been doing the past few weeks—

suddenly fail the day of launch, as if somebody walked in at the last minute and pulled a wire or jabbed a screwdriver into a tank. Some mindless bit of vandalism that would be enough to cause a short or a leak."

"Nobody gets into the assembly buildings without clearance."

He practically snorted. "In theory," he said. "The same theory that makes all Soviet citizens equal. Yes, all the military and bureau people have passes, but people from the commissions walk through all the time. Who checks them?"

"Who *needs* to check them? They're bigshots."

"Any one of them could do the damage, just the same."

"So could a disgruntled member of the checkout team."

He was patting at his shirt for a cigarette. "Yes, yes, yes. If there's another suspicious accident, the finger will point to one of us." He found his cigarette.

"Don't light up here."

He ignored me. "Don't worry. They don't start fueling for hours yet."

Shortly before ten o'clock that evening, as the upper stages of the Universal Rocket were being pumped full of liquid nitrogen and hydrazine—what Sergei Korolev had called the "devil's venom"—a weld failed. Poisonous hydrazine spewed out of its tank like water from a hose. Fortunately the hydrazine did not come into contact with its oxidizer; they were hypergolic fuels, meaning they would have ignited all by themselves, causing a conflagration that would have undoubtedly destroyed the Universal Rocket and its L-1 payload, and possibly the Area 92 pad, too.

However, three members of the crew were overcome by fumes; in fact, their lungs liquefied on contact with the hydrazine.

Shiborin and I learned this horrible news at breakfast at the Hotel Cosmonaut. The next L-1 launch would be delayed, of course, since the Universal Rocket had to be returned to the assembly building. "Shit," Shiborin said. "We could be stuck here all summer."

Fortunately not. We ran into Lev Tselauri on the bus to Area 92, and he told us that there would be no testing for a month, possibly longer, while this latest accident was investigated. He did not add anything in front of Shiborin, but the look on his face was clear enough: investigated by State Security, he meant.

All that Shiborin and I could do that morning was collect our personal belongings and express condolences to the surviving members of the launch team.

Well, I did do one other thing. As soon as I heard about the latest disaster, I sought out Sergeant Oleg Pokrovsky and purchased his PB-8 Special Forces pistol for a fistful of rubles and the most expensive bottle of vodka I was able to buy at the Hotel Cosmonaut.

Maybe I overpaid, but I thought that I would need protection in the days to come.

The Tu-104 returning to Chkalov that afternoon was packed with people from the Korolev bureau, including my former bosses Filin and Triyanov, sitting together and looking exhausted. I would have said hello immediately, but was stuck several seats away, wedged into a window by a sleeping Shiborin—who had somehow failed to get himself assigned as copilot on this flight. I watched Filin and saw clearly the telltale signs of stress . . . glasses off, fingers to the bridge of his nose, then opening to rub his temples. He would, I judged, require immediate hospitalization upon returning to the Moscow District.

Triyanov was, in spite of tired eyes, more relaxed, frequently shrugging, offering nothing.

Somewhere over the Urals, Shiborin awoke and decided to visit the cockpit. Shortly thereafter Triyanov took a walk down the aisle and spotted me. "Senior Lieutenant Ribko!" he announced, cheerfully tossing me a casual salute. "How does the uniform fit?"

"Quite well."

He dropped into Shiborin's seat. "I hear you are in Bykovsky's group."

"Since early May."

"It's not the best place for a military engineer, you know. All the lunar crews will have civilians in that second seat. Your seat."

"*Is* there a good place for a military engineer?"

Triyanov laughed. "From what I hear, maybe not." He and I both knew that the Chelomei military projects were stalled, not likely to require crews for two years or more. "You've managed to keep your sense of humor. Given what your center has endured this year, that should qualify for a Hero of Socialist Labor at the very least."

"I'll be sure to invite you to the ceremony."

He slapped my knee. "You should never have left the bureau, young man. In time, people would have forgotten your . . . tainted origins." He lowered his voice. "You certainly weren't the only one serving two masters."

This was a dangerous subject for a public conversation. "Did you know Colonel Seregin?" I asked, hoping to change the subject completely.

"Very well. He and I worked on a program together at Akhtubinsk six or seven years ago. He was a good pilot. So was Gagarin, for that matter. Not a lot of recent stick time, but he had the natural skills."

"They're saying the crash was pilot error."

"That's bullshit." He shifted in his seat, perhaps to better aim his index finger between my eyes. "I had a situation once in a 15 that could have ended the same way. I was making a low pass—two hundred meters off the ground—when a bulb on the display exploded this far from my face." He held his hand a few centimeters from his nose. "I was completely blinded, face bloody, all I could do was react by instinct and pull up.

"It worked, thank God, but I was *seconds* away from death, and no investigators would have known why. The only damage was to me— cuts on my face, blood in my eyes. One tiny missing bulb on the control panel. All that evidence would have been obliterated if I'd punched a hole in the ground." He sat back, still indignant on behalf of Gagarin and Seregin. "They'd have said 'pilot error,' and they'd have been just as wrong."

"They haven't been able to find the canopy."

"No. Because something happened to those guys. Some oxygen canister or hydraulic cylinder could have gone blooey, blown out the canopy and knocked Gagarin and Seregin out long enough for them to hit the ground." He was silent for a moment, picturing the horror. "It doesn't take much."

Shiborin had returned, looking to claim his seat. Triyanov rose and threw him a salute, too, which Shiborin returned. As Triyanov departed, Shiborin looked after him. "Who the hell was that?"

I kept forgetting about the giant walls between the bureau and the Gagarin Center. Tired, and growing more nervous about the pistol in my baggage—suppose State Security was waiting at Chkalov to search us? I could be sent to prison for possession of a firearm—I simply told Shiborin that Triyanov was an old friend from my time in the bureau, which had the virtue of being partly true.

My father may have ordered me to give up spying, but no one, it seemed, could stop me from lying to my friends.

44 SEMIPALATINSK-20

The day after my return from Baikonur, I learned—along with the rest of the Fourth Enrollment—that we would shortly be sent to Feodosiya on the Black Sea, a place I knew slightly from my teenage years in the Crimea. For two weeks we would be either in the woods, simulating off-course Soyuz landings on Mother Russia, or bobbing in the water practicing landings at sea. The primary Soyuz crews were off on a long holiday because there were no manned vehicles for them to fly; the lunar teams, including support personnel Ribko and Shiborin, were not needed for at least a month due to the recent accident at Baikonur.

This news was profoundly depressing to Shiborin, who had just returned from two months away from home. I found it helpful, since it forced me to examine my situation and make a plan. I had good evidence that Uncle Vladimir was involved in Korolev's death—confirmed, in a way, by my own father—and in the sabotage of the lunar program, thanks to Lev's information.

But I could no more confront Uncle Vladimir than I could march into the Kremlin and punch Brezhnev in the nose. Nor was there any law-enforcement agency I could trust. Yes, my father said he would "take care" of things. But my impending departure for Feodosiya, sure to be followed by another stay at Baikonur, made me impatient.

I wanted answers about Uncle Vladimir, about what he had told me about my mother. Who would know?

I had had no contact with Katya since my awful birthday party at Ostankino Tower. She had told me not to call her, but even foolish and naive as I was in those days, I knew this would not absolve me of blame. Nor would my forced absence in the gardens of Kazakhstan. Before I could learn anything useful—assuming Katya had information she would share—I needed to get back in her good graces.

And as much as I wanted her to help me combat Uncle Vladimir, I truly did want to repair our relationship.

I have not gone into great details concerning that relationship. It was intensely physical and, I can see now, more emotional on her side than it was on mine. I loved her, in a way, but never dreamed of spending my life with her as I did with Marina.

I don't claim that Katya wanted to marry me. At thirty-six, she had already arranged her life to her satisfaction, I think. But she seemed to enjoy my company, especially our lovemaking. I did, too, though I was first confused and even frightened by her aggressiveness: I thought I was supposed to be the initiator, as I had largely been with Marina. Not so. In fact, Katya initiated most of our activities, social as well as sexual.

I couldn't just appear at her front door with an armful of flowers, though this was the only idea I had. I needed romantic advice, but my two closest friends were Shiborin—married since the age of nineteen— and Lev, an unlikely source of information for a variety of reasons.

At physical training one morning I found myself running through the woods with Ivan Saditsky. Well, *I* was running; he was walking ahead of me, huffing and puffing like a pensioner, when I caught up to him. He looked so ill, pale and bent over, that I stopped and asked how he was.

"Trying not to vomit," he said, waving his hand dismissively.

"I'll call Novikov." He was our instructor that morning.

"No, you won't. You'll leave me to die here in peace, thank you." He straightened out; color began to reappear in his face. "What idiot thinks that running through the forest is any kind of preparation for going to the Moon?"

"Well, they claim we're in a race," I said, joking.

Saditsky grunted. "Given the way our rockets have been working, we'll probably *have* to walk." He blinked. "Do you have a cigarette?" I reminded him that I didn't smoke. "Remind me to denounce you at the next Party meeting." That was typical Saditsky: While I was a grudging but regular attendee, I had never actually caught him at a meeting. And he was a full Party member.

I knew better than to ask him how Soyuz was going: The program was stalled while the factories struggled to build spacecraft. But here it occurred to me that he might be of assistance with my problem. "Ivan," I said, "do you remember Katya?"

"I never forget a nice ass," he said. "When are you going to bring her around again?"

"That's the problem: We had a big fight a while back, and she's not speaking to me."

He grinned slyly. "Maybe I shouldn't help you. I bet I can find her myself."

It was stupid for me to worry about Saditsky taking Katya away from me; she wasn't in any sense *with* me. But I felt some jealousy, anyway, which he must have noticed. "I'm joking. I am a married officer in the Soviet Air Force, after all." Saditsky's marriage was widely known to be troubled, though not so troubled that his wife Anya complained to Belyayev or others—which could have ruined his career. Apparently she was willing to look the other way regarding the womanizing as long as Saditsky's cosmonaut career brought them both rewards. What would happen after Saditsky flew Soyuz and became a Hero of the Soviet Union was another matter.

"There are two possible approaches, Yuri. The honest one where you go crawling back to Katya on your hands and knees, begging her to take you back."

"That was my first thought."

"It's a terrible idea. It gives her all the advantage, and, forgive me, from what I've seen of this Katya, she's got enough advantages."

"What's the other approach?"

"Plan very carefully to meet her by accident. Run into her at a market or at some subbotnik project, like picking potatoes out in Dmitrov." It was the Party that came up with subbotniks, those Saturday work projects that took us all to the fields in summer to engage in proletarian labor. During spring and autumn, we often helped on construction. This not only reminded effete city dwellers and bureaucrats of the price others had to pay for university educations, electric lights, and so forth, it also provided much-needed field hands. "Make sure she sees you, then get all embarrassed and flustered and try to get away. If she comes after you, *you've* got the advantage." He grinned again. "I know you, Ribko. You can handle the flustered business like an ace."

"Then what?"

Now he laughed out loud. "If you can't figure out what to do when the gorgeous Katya throws herself back at you, you don't deserve her!"

Then, wheezing, he staggered off to complete his run.

At this time of year there was always a subbotnik going on, especially at places like Katya's institute, which was still in the process of being built. So I shamelessly followed Saditsky's cynical orders and went directly to the center's political officer, Colonel Nikeryasov, asking to be put on a subbotnik at the Institute for Space Research. Two days later—on Friday morning—I was told to report to the institute in question at seven on Saturday morning, to help with pouring concrete.

I knew less about pouring concrete than I did about female psychology, but subbotniks did not require expertise, only enthusiasm. In civilian clothes, I took the train into the city.

I believe it was General Borodin, hero of the war against Napoleon, who said, "No battle plan survives contact with the enemy." My clever plan died a painful death before I even reached the institute.

For one thing, the weather was terrible, a cold rain more suited to Moscow in April than in July. This alone meant that pouring concrete was going to be difficult, if attempted at all. The foul weather also affected the guards at the institute, who looked at my military pass and lack of military garb, and decided to detain me.

So I sat in the cramped entryway, waiting for the guards' supervisor to wrench himself away from his cozy office, while unhappy people tracked in mud from Khoroshev Street. The supervisor arrived prepared to berate or possibly arrest me. But on inspection, my passport turned out to be sufficiently important-looking that he began to grumble to the guards first. "You idiots. Can't you make a fucking decision without disturbing me?" Then he asked me why I was at the institute today.

"I'm helping with your subbotnik."

The supervisor was prepared for any answer but that. To think some engineer-lieutenant in the Air Force would voluntarily visit a civilian institute to "help" with a communal work project! Now he had to make a telephone call.

Before he could get to it, however, Katya entered.

She saw me instantly, and I her, as if we had planned this rendezvous. Given the location, and the presence of the guards, it was impossible for me to think about making a sudden run for it. For one thing, the supervisor still held my passport. For another, the guards would have pulled out their guns. So I stood there, empty-handed, a foolish look on my face that wavered between happiness and sheer surprise.

Katya's face betrayed a quick change of emotion, too, from confusion to annoyance to what seemed like resignation. "Is this supposed to be flattering?" she said by way of greeting.

"You know this officer?" the guard supervisor asked her.

"He's strangely familiar to me." Resignation had been replaced by her usual sense of amusement.

"You can vouch for the fact that he's not a spy?"

A look passed between Katya and me. "He's no danger to the institute," she said, her hesitation noticed only by me. "He is, however, a very naughty boy."

Now the supervisor and the guards got the idea. There was some elbowing, some winking, and within moments I had retrieved my passport and been waved into the institute.

With Katya.

"Why today of all days?" she said, as we walked into the rainy central courtyard. She had yet to say hello.

"I just got back from two months in Baikonur."

"There are several weeks between your birthday and your departure still unaccounted for."

"I was hurt and angry." It was true enough.

"No, Yuri, I was hurt and angry. I was the one who waited for a call or a letter or any kind of apology."

"I'm apologizing now, in person."

"Can you even remember why?"

"For embarrassing you in front of Uncle Vladimir."

That apparently was close enough to soothe her. At least it took the edge off her anger. "Are you really here for the subbotnik?"

"Yes. I arranged it so I could see you."

She smiled. "Well, you've seen me and you've stumbled your way through the beginnings of an apology. Now that you've accomplished your mission, why don't you run back to Star Town before they actually make use of you."

I could thank the Ribko bullheadedness for my answer. "I came to work. I hope I can see you later." And I marched off with no idea of where I was going, only that I was putting meters between Katya and me.

The weather made it impossible to pour concrete or do any work outside, but those of us on the Party detail found other tasks. Mine was to paint the hallways of a new laboratory building, which I did happily, if sloppily, for the rest of the day. They fed us a hot stew, which was a nice surprise, and at four o'clock I felt more virtuous—a good little Komsomol member—than I had in months. Perhaps in two years.

I left the institute the same way I entered, passing the same guards, who this time shared a friendly wave. I headed for the street wondering what I would do with the rest of my Saturday, when Katya appeared from my left, taking my arm.

"All right. Eight hours of hard labor is sentence enough. I forgive you. But be very careful."

She was tugging me toward the bus stop. "Where are we going?"

"To my flat. Where else?"

"Your parents were stationed at Semipalatinsk-20. It's in Kazakhstan, east of Baikonur."

This was hours later, after ten that evening. We had gone directly from the institute to Katya's flat, where we made angry, almost savage love without discarding much of our clothing. Or so it seemed. I do remember taking off my shoes.

We went out to find food for dinner, then returned, and made love again, just as desperately as before. Then lay in each other's arms, talking as if no time had passed, as if there had been no awful scene in front of Uncle Vladimir.

"I haven't seen him more than once or twice since then," she said. "He's been busy with his schemes."

"He seems to have a lot of them."

"You have no idea." I was beginning to get some idea, of course, but didn't want to spoil the moment by pressing. "I'm surprised you know so little about your own family. I got the impression your mother and your uncle were extremely close." And that is how we came to the subject of where my mother and father lived when I was a teenager. Semipalatinsk-20, one of our many defense "mailbox" cities.

"Never heard of it," I said.

"It's where most of our atomic bombs are exploded."

"I can't imagine what they were doing there."

"Your father was flying aircraft that dropped bombs."

"You know for sure?"

She sighed. "Vladimir told me once that Zhanna died because of that place. Because of your father's work. Yes."

I sat up in bed. "How could my father's work have killed my mother?"

Katya lay back, running her hands through her blond hair, which had grown tangled and matted by the violence of our lovemaking. The sheet covering her slid down as she did, exposing her breasts. The sight alone was enough to cause my heart to pound. I would have reached for her again, had I been doing anything but hearing my family's secrets.

"Your mother hadn't wanted to go to Semipalatinsk. She wanted to stay with you." Katya brushed the hair back from her face, adjusted her covering sheet. "You must have been adorable at that age."

"Absolutely," I said, "and I've deteriorated since then. Why did my mother go?" I had always wanted to ask her, but never had.

"Your father insisted. Maybe he didn't want to be alone out there." Maybe, I thought, he knew that if Zhanna were exiled with her husband, Vladimir would have to find some way to get them *both* back to Moscow. "They used to drop atomic bombs from airplanes. I did some studies on the radiation patterns when I was in college. We were horribly care-less . . . marching divisions of soldiers through ground zero a few hours after an explosion.

"There was one test that really went wrong. A-2, September 1956, it was. A bomber was supposed to drop a device in a certain zone, but the pilot misread his chart."

"Maybe the chart was wrong." I'd seen enough mistakes like that in the space program.

"Very likely. But the bomb went off too close to one of the viewing sites. Everyone there got a severe dose of radiation. I think there were twenty or so, and most of them were dead within five or six years."

"Including my mother."

"Yes."

I had always sensed that the relationship between my mother and father grew colder during those three years in the desert. When I was younger and we all lived in the Crimea, they had been affectionate with each other, touching, laughing. And with me.

When we were finally reunited in Moscow when I was sixteen, that had all changed. They were cordial with each other, but distant, somehow. At the time I thought it was because we had all grown so much older, and because my father was beginning his travels all over the USSR and Europe, which kept him away from home.

Suppose it was due to this terrible accident? It was as if my mother had died in a car crash where my father was driving . . . but had lingered like a ghost, haunting him, for years.

It was impossible for me to imagine the horror my mother faced—killed by her husband, seeing herself slowly and steadily withering. Even people sentenced to the Gulag, or the basement of the Lubiyanka, had hope. Not my mother.

"I'm surprised my father ever got promoted after something like that."

"I think they found someone else to blame. The navigator of the plane, maybe. And, really, Yuri, this is why I was so angry with you on your birthday."

"Why?"

"Your uncle made sure the reports emphasized Colonel Ribko's heroism under difficult circumstances, all of that. Vladimir *saved* your father."

45 THE SECOND COSMIC VELOCITY

The Monday after my reunion with Katya, I departed for the Crimea, returning to Star Town after two weeks only to enter a period of intense medical testing in which all members of the Fourth Enrollment were subjected to a series of centrifuge rides. Actually, we had been offered the chance to volunteer. To no one's surprise, all thirteen of us did so, though I believe one of my colleagues, Captain Sasha Korchugin, an Air Force navigator, surely wished he hadn't. His heart stopped during one of the tests. Fortunately, he was revived, but he was immediately packed off to the Aviation Hospital to convalesce, and we all knew that our group had suffered its first real casualty.

I didn't see Katya during that month, though I sent her a letter from Feodosiya, and spoke to her by telephone when I got back to Star Town. Our relationship seemed to have been rebuilt.

I had no contact at all with my father. He might well have been taking care of things, as he had promised. Certainly I saw no signs that I was under surveillance. (That is, no more than any of us were.) I believe he was also distracted from my problems by the "rescue" of Communism in Czechoslovakia by the armies of "brother" nations, which began in mid-August.

The first week of September found Shiborin and me back on the plane to Baikonur. At the Hotel Cosmonaut, we crossed paths with our colleagues in the Soyuz branch of the cosmonaut team, including Beregovoy, Shatalov, and Saditsky. They had just supported the successful unmanned launch of spacecraft Number 9 on August 28 under the cover name of *Cosmos 238*. Number 9 operated flawlessly for three days, then thumped down safely in the prime landing zone. "A gigantic waste of resources," Saditsky told me. "They were nervous about the parachute system, fine. But you don't need to launch the vehicle into space to test that: You can kick it out the door of an airplane." He shook his head. "And we're going to waste yet another Soyuz next month because everyone's afraid." According to the very conservative plan ordered by Minister Ustinov, even with the success of *Cosmos 238*, the next phase of the program would allow a single-manned Soyuz to dock with another unmanned one. The ambitious EVA originally planned for Komarov's flight sixteen months in the past was seen to be too risky.

My attention turned to the L-1 lunar orbit program. A new spacecraft, Number 9 (not to be confused with the newest Soyuz) was in the assembly building being mated to a new Universal Rocket 500. The welds in the upper stages of the rocket had been examined and no leaks were expected. Nevertheless, I wasn't overly confident. I heard from Lev, who also flew in with the Korolev bureau team, that the investigation of the stage that had failed so disastrously in July had not turned up any flaws in *its* welds, either.

In spite of my misgivings, early on the morning of September 15, 1968, the latest Universal Rocket 500 rose from the Area 81 pad, lighting up the summer night as it carried the lunar space probe that would be announced to the world as *Zond 5*. We watched the launch from the range tracking site at Area 97, several kilometers to the south, under a half-Moon, with summer breezes gently stirring the trees.

Over the next few hours, the upper stages, including the bureau's troubled Block D, performed flawlessly, sending *Zond 5* on its climb to that half-Moon.

At midday Shiborin and I boarded an An-24 with Colonel Bykovsky and his lunar cosmonauts, and flew directly off to Yevpatoriya, to take part in the mission from the primary control center. When we arrived, we learned that *Zond 5* had suffered its first failure, the all-too-familiar inability of the star-tracking system to orient itself. This time, however, a backup system that sighted on Earth and the Moon managed to keep the spacecraft on course, though it lacked precision and meant that the hoped-for reentry into Earth's atmosphere would be uncontrolled.

I did note a lack of the usual generals and ministers at Yevaptoriya. Only Artemov and his bureau deputies, including Filin, and the Hammer's deputy, Tyulin, were there. Not even General Kamanin came. At first I assumed it was for protective reasons: No one wanted to face another inexplicable failure. Then I learned that a very important meeting was being held back at Baikonur to get the Carrier rocket program back on track. The first test launch was rescheduled for November, with a second to follow in February 1969. These dates were important, because we had also learned that the Americans were considering a "surprise" flight around the Moon themselves in January 1969, though they had yet to fly a manned Apollo at all!

It finally seemed as though my country's lunar program was beginning to move, like an army advancing on three fronts.

Zond 5 carried a "crew": a number of turtles, worms, and flies, in addition to some scientific instruments and cameras. On September 18, the spacecraft made its closest approach to the Moon, coming to within 1,950 kilometers of those gray craters and plains as it swung around the far side. Then it headed back toward Earth, speeding up to what *Pravda* called the "second cosmic velocity"—that is, the speed at which a spacecraft reentered the atmosphere, as opposed to the first cosmic velocity, which was required to leave Earth's gravity—aiming toward a window in space no more than thirteen kilometers across.

There was incredible tension among the team in the control center. The failure of the star tracker and the reliance on the relatively crude Earth-Moon orientation system meant that *Zond 5* could not be steered onto a precise trajectory. It was going through that window more or less by luck and momentum, and where it would wind up, nobody could say.

The rescue-and-recovery forces, having learned their lesson, were set up for ocean recovery this time. There would be no self-destruct if *Zond 5* managed to survive reentry.

Zond 5 reached the second cosmic velocity of eleven kilometers a second as it dived into the atmosphere on September 21, the external heat on the skin of the spacecraft reaching thirteen thousand degrees centigrade. The deceleration subjected the worms, turtles, and flies to as much as sixteen Gs—more than twice the desirable load. (And after having been spun up to eight Gs twice within the past month, I could not imagine a crew functioning for long at sixteen. Or at all.)

We expected to wait half an hour or longer to learn the fate of our lunar craft, but within five minutes of the projected landing time, the rescue service reported that *Zond 5* had survived its passage back to Earth, splashing down in the Indian Ocean one hundred and five kilometers from the tracking ship *Borovichy*. The turtles and their companions were alive.

The crew of the *Borovichy* turned the blackened bell of *Zond 5* over to an oceanographic ship, the *Golovnin*, which carried it to Bombay for flight back to the USSR.

On the morning of September 22, 1968, there was not a drop of alcohol to be found within fifty kilometers of the Yevpatoriya Station. I am ashamed to say I consumed my share, and perhaps more. The last thing I remember is a very drunken Saditsky telling me, "Now we've screwed ourselves. If we'd flown Soyuz with a crew last month, we would be ready to launch a manned L-1. We could have beaten the Americans around the Moon."

I didn't believe Saditsky. The Americans hadn't flown Apollo at all.

By the end of September, autumn was already half over, with the trees around Star Town shedding their leaves. I could recall only a few days of summer—no surprise, given that I had spent almost three full months away from home.

Even back at Star Town, I had little free time. Our group training continued with more intensity, though without Sasha Korchugin, who had lost flight status for good and was given a position on the Gagarin Center staff. Part of the syllabus was a series of rides in the back seats of MiG-15 trainers for the nonpilots in the group. Pilots like Shiborin were allowed to fly in the front seats, though always with an instructor from the 70th Seregin Squadron.

Given that my greatest exposure to a MiG-15 was in picking up its shattered pieces, I approached these flights with dread, but found myself enjoying them—half-hour hops out to Kirzhach, then back. On a couple of occasions the instructors let me take the controls, and I got some small sense of how exciting it must be to totally master a fighter jet. No wonder the pilots I knew—Shiborin, Saditsky, Triyanov, even my father—were such arrogant shits most of the time. They had proven themselves in a whole different world.

On October 11, the Americans launched their first manned Apollo, nineteen months behind their original schedule. The eleven-day flight by astronauts Schirra, Eisele, and Cunningham went flawlessly from a technical standpoint, though the crew often quarreled publicly with flight controllers. Hearing this, Shiborin shook his head in amazement. "What kind of training do these Americans have? If a Soviet crew acted that way, they'd get court-martialed!"

This was Shiborin at his most naive. Even as he was watching the antics of Captain Schirra with astonishment, Colonel Beregovoy, the veteran test pilot and cosmonaut assigned to the first manned Soyuz, was failing his final examinations on docking procedures while his backup pilot, Shatalov, was acing them.

Did this make any difference to Beregovoy's assignment? Not a bit. He had friends in high places, even higher than General Kamanin, and extra tutoring was arranged. On October 26, 1968, he was launched into orbit aboard spacecraft Number 10, officially named *Soyuz 3* and designed to be the active partner in a docking. (Spacecraft Number 11, his target, was launched the day before, though not announced and named as *Soyuz 2* until Beregovoy was safely in space.)

Beregovoy's Soyuz was supposed to approach its target on autopilot during the first orbit. At a distance of 180 meters, he took over manual control, and then the fun began. Beregovoy closed in on *Soyuz 2*, only to turn away before docking. He radioed that his orientation system had failed. He was allowed to maneuver *Soyuz 3* away and get some rest before another attempt on the second day.

This one went no better. Beregovoy got to within fifty meters this time, then somehow went sailing past. Again, he blamed the guidance system.

By this time there was no fuel in either Soyuz for additional attempts. At Yevpatoriya there were concerns about Beregovoy's physical state; sensors detected some impurities in the atmosphere aboard Soyuz, which might have affected him.

Soyuz 2 thumped down safely on October 28 and Beregovoy himself followed two days later. He faced some harsh questioning from members of the State Commission, including Artemov and Kamanin, and like any good pilot, stuck to his story that the docking guidance system had failed him. Privately the cosmonauts said it was Beregovoy's error, but since he was the only one aboard, who was going to contradict him?

And to be fair, a postflight investigation showed a whole series of problems that contributed to the failure, beginning with our desire to risk only a single pilot when Soyuz was designed to operate with a pilot *and* flight engineer. Many of Beregovoy's difficult maneuvers had to be carried out in zones where he had no contact with Yevpatoriya or remote tracking stations, and often in literal darkness. Beregovoy did admit, later, that he had been ill the first day of the flight, which surely hadn't helped him. And the Soyuz controls did not match those in the simulator he had trained on so doggedly.

Nevertheless, a cosmonaut had survived a Soyuz flight. Plans were made for an ambitious follow-up—a docking between two manned Soyuz in January, with an EVA by two cosmonauts. This was, of course, the same mission originally intended to be flown in April 1967. Saditsky was assigned as commander of one of the four crews.

In our lunar branch, my bosses Colonel Bykovsky and Colonel Leonov were told that one of them would command a two-man L-1 crew on a flight around the Moon as soon as we demonstrated a controlled reentry. They complained that one more unmanned test would give America the first triumph. (Though NASA had not officially announced it, everyone knew that *Apollo 8* would make such an attempt in late December.) Both cosmonauts claimed they could manually pilot a controlled landing, and failing that, were willing to risk a 16-G ballistic reentry.

But the State Commission, the Hammer, Ustinov, and even Kamanin, who usually sided with the pilots in matters like this, weren't listening. There had been too many failures. No one wanted to kill two more cosmonauts on a risky flight around the Moon when there was no guarantee that *Apollo 8*, which would also be the first manned test of the giant Saturn V-5, would succeed.

It was exciting—almost frantic. It was also the time when my father finally returned to Moscow.

46 ZOND 6

I managed to see Katya again on Saturday, November 1, on my last free weekend before returning to Baikonur for checkout on the tenth L-1, the one that would finally pave our path to and from the Moon.

There were no further explosive revelations regarding my parents' lives, or mine, or Katya's, just another shallow sexual evening that left me feeling drained yet energized, guilty and yet strangely happy. Strangely because weeks, now months, had passed, and I was no closer to proving that Uncle Vladimir had somehow killed Korolev, not one bit more knowledgeable about his plans and powers. And still, when I had the time to think of such things, wondering where and how he would take action against me.

Knowing that snow would soon cover the ground around Star Town, I dressed in a track suit and went for a run early the morning of Sunday, November 2. I didn't particularly enjoy running—almost none of the cosmonauts did—but I had found that it made me feel more energetic, especially with a trip coming up that would require me to sit on my ass in a cramped, cold spacecraft for endless hours.

The building that was intended to be permanent housing for the Fourth Enrollment, among others, had been ninety percent complete in July. It was, I now judged, ninety-one percent complete. After my run, I returned to my lonely flat on its first floor to find my father sitting on a chair in a puddle of sunlight, wearing a civilian overcoat.

Getting over my initial shock and surprise, I greeted him. He seemed genuinely pleased to see me, though, as usual, he had to offer some criticism: "You should lock your door."

"There's nobody in this area but cosmonauts and their families," I said. "Not on a Sunday morning."

"I got in."

"You're an Air Force general."

He flicked at the lapel of his coat, which opened to show that he was wearing civilian clothes. "Not today."

"I don't have anything worth stealing." This was, more or less, true. I had splurged to buy a small television set, which I had used perhaps three times in the past six months. My possessions at that time were limited to military uniforms, athletic gear, my handwritten notes from training classes (there were no workbooks), and a few books. My furniture looked as though it had been salvaged or stolen in the first place.

"I'm not speaking about thieves. It's your personal security."

"Uncle Vladimir's assassins?"

A look of genuine fright passed across my father's face. Then, strangely, he forced himself to laugh. "You've been reading too many spy novels," he said, holding up an index finger in the universal Russian symbol that says: We are under surveillance.

I thought the idea was ridiculous, but elected to play along. "Let me buy you breakfast," I said.

Once we were outdoors, my father said, "I've already eaten."

"Me, too. I just wanted the listeners to know we had a reason to leave."

"This is not a joke, Yuri."

"Sorry." One of my many failings is that I sound as though I'm joking when I'm not. "How was Czechoslovakia?"

"Not as bloody as Hungary, from what they tell me. We didn't have to hang traitors from the streetlights. But we managed to anger everyone in the international community, and most of our allies, too. They know that if the tanks can roll into Prague, they can roll into Warsaw or Bucharest, too. They'll never allow this again."

"Things change."

"Some things." He looked almost wistful. "Now, have you done what I said? Have you stayed away from Vladimir?"

"I haven't spoken to him for months."

"Have you been pressured in any way? Followed?"

"Not that I can tell. You would know better," I said. "You insisted we come outside to talk."

"Just a precaution." He looked around at Star Town, the tall, gray apartment buildings among the birch and pine trees, the central commissary and market building in front of us, the cold-looking lake to our right, the half-finished structures by it. We were the only ones out on this dreary morning. "This place keeps getting bigger and bigger."

"Kamanin is trying to make it bigger yet," I said. "He wants the training center to become a scientific-research institute with twice the staff."

"Yes, yes, and he wants the Air Force to become the Central Space Office, too. I know all about it. Everyone on the high command is sick to death of it."

"They must be pleased by *Zond 5*."

He grunted. "They think it's a giant waste of money, Yuri. The Americans are going to beat us to the Moon. That's been obvious since—"

"—since Korolev died?"

For an instant my father seemed to sag, but he quickly recovered, smiling. "It was obvious that day in 1961 when the Americans announced they were going to go to the Moon. They have too many resources. We never had a real program until 1964, and it *still* wasn't on track when Korolev died. But that doesn't concern us."

"It may not concern *you*, but it sure concerns me! This is my life!"

"Beating the Americans to the Moon? You've never said a thing about that to me."

"Well, there are many things I haven't said to you. Or you to me, such as the truth about Mother's death." I don't know why I chose that moment to raise that subject; the instant the words were said, I wanted to erase them.

My father turned and looked at me as though I were a stranger. "What are you talking about?"

"Your bomb test at Semipalatinsk in September 1956. It was called the A-2, wasn't it? You dropped it from your plane?"

His face reddened, and I knew he was angry. "You lied to me. You said you hadn't spoken to Vladimir."

"I haven't."

Now he was confused. Among the many other things I had never mentioned to him was my relationship with Katya, so who could possibly have told me this terrible secret if not Vladimir? "I've made many mistakes in my life, Yuri. Some were my fault. Some were . . . bad luck. Following the wrong orders," he said, obviously trying to control his voice. "But that day, with that plane, and what it did to your mother and those other people . . . that is the one I live with."

"You never talked about it."

"What should I have said?" he snapped. " 'Oh, by the way, Yuri, when your mother and I were in the desert, I managed to poison her'? It was bad enough watching her die, knowing it was my fault." He started walking back toward my flat. "I need a drink."

I hurried to catch up with him, struggling with my emotions and at the same time wondering if I had anything for him to drink.

He stopped at the front door, blocking it so I couldn't open it. "What are you going to do?"

"About what?"

"Your . . . information."

"What can I do? I'm going to try to be a good cosmonaut and a Communist. I've proven to myself that those are the only things I'm good at." That seemed to satisfy him; he let me open the door.

In my flat I dug through my bags for tomorrow's flight to Baikonur—already packed—and found an unopened bottle of vodka; I had gotten into the habit of buying one before each of my trips, for barter, if nothing else. I handed it to my father, then turned to find some glasses. "Don't bother," he said, drinking directly out of the bottle.

He handed it to me, and I took a drink, too. It tasted quite good after several minutes in the chill and cold. "Yuri, if you will accept one last piece of advice from your father, be patient. These troubles—with Vladimir, with me—they will end."

"Yes. With my exile to the Arctic Circle."

He laughed and raised the bottle in a mock toast. "You have Zhanna's sense of humor. She never lost it, not even at the end."

"That will comfort me as I watch the snow fall in prison."

He capped the bottle and stuck it under his arm. "If you're careful, if you follow your orders, you might survive. But I warn you, any deviation could be dangerous."

Maybe the jolt of that vodka made me feel like an American cowboy. I reached back into my bag and pulled out the PB-8 pistol I had bought from Sergeant Oleg. "I'm ready."

"Put that fucking thing away!"

I suddenly felt stupid and childish. So I did as he said, putting it back in the travel bag. "Yuri, don't travel with that thing. Not now. If it's found in your luggage, you *will* go to jail and I won't be able to save you."

So, like a good son, I did as my father told me, hiding the pistol behind some books on my shelf.

He hugged me and wouldn't let me walk him to the main gate.

November 7 was Revolution Day, and the excuse for celebrations. Even if orbital mechanics had not dictated that the launch of the next L-1 could not take place until November 10, the holiday would have ensured it. In the city of Leninsk, an outpost of Russians surrounded by a sea of indifferent Kazakhs, there were two days of parties that interrupted all work.

On the tenth, however, another white Universal Rocket 500 thundered into the sky carrying an L-1, Number 12 in the series, with improved navigation systems, and a crew of turtles and other small test creatures. The evening launch went well, as did the trans-lunar burns of the Block D engine, sending the spacecraft, now known as *Zond 6*, on its way to the Moon.

As the team flew off to Yevpatoriya in the morning, we learned that an antenna on *Zond 6* had failed to deploy as planned, making communications difficult. But the improved navigation system was working, meaning that the trajectory to and from the Moon could be precise enough to allow a controlled reentry.

On the twelfth, *Zond 6* carried out a major midcourse correction burn, which raised our hopes. Two days later it slipped around the limb of the Moon, dipping to within 2,400 kilometers of the surface, then headed back to Earth.

During this time, Shiborin and I worked with the L-1 cosmonauts, teams of Bykovsky-Rukavishnikov, Leonov-Makarov, Popovich-Sevastyanov, three commanders from the military team, three flight engineers from Department 731 of the bureau, all of them hoping to be aboard the next L-1 as it visited the Moon. The crews took turns inside a bare-bones mockup of an L-1—the same size as the descent module of the Soyuz—performing simulated engine burns and commands.

At one point, when *Zond 6* was out of communication range, Shiborin and I climbed into the mockup, he in the commander's seat, me as flight engineer. Neither of us were big men, but our knees almost touched the control panel above us. "Can you imagine spending seven days in something this small?" Shiborin asked in amazement.

"You can see the whole universe outside the window."

"That might help for the first day. This is really suited only for creatures the size of turtles."

"You'll be weightless. They say that makes the place feel bigger." Shiborin only grunted. "The Gemini astronauts survived eight days, then fourteen days, and they didn't have any more room than this." Now he failed to reply at all. I couldn't blame him. The L-1 cabin seemed even more cramped than the Voskhod in which I had performed my first tasks as a bureau "flight test" engineer.

I suspected that Shiborin was growing tired of the endless classes and weeks away from home. He wanted to fly, and thought he was ready. Well, we were. Any of us in the Fourth Enrollment could have been assigned to a Soyuz or an L-1 crew and been ready for launch in four months. Unfortunately, we had fifty other cosmonauts in line ahead of us.

Zond 6 made midcourse corrections on the sixteenth and the seventeenth, as it fell faster and faster back to Earth. Artemov and his flight controllers began to really feel that a controlled reentry was going to take place. On the evening of the seventeenth, as planned, the L-1 separated from its cylindrical service-and-propulsion module and dived through the narrow target corridor in the sky over Antarctica, nine thousand kilometers from its planned landing point in Kazakhstan.

The first dive slowed Zond 6 from a speed of eleven kilometers per second to little more than seven—still very fast. Then, rolling right and left to generate lift from its bell shape, Zond 6 climbed back out of the atmosphere for several minutes before making a second dive. This one was steeper, slowing the vehicle to less than two hundred meters a second. At no point during the reentry did the G load exceed seven and then only briefly. A cosmonaut crew would have found this ride much less stressful.

The recovery teams in the primary zone received signals showing that Zond 6 was going to land about 150 kilometers south of Baikonur itself. Then nothing.

This silence was not unusual: Our recovery forces were stretched thin, even in the primary zone. Contact could be lost by simply having a helicopter or search aircraft turn in the wrong direction. Further, we knew that one of the antennas on *Zond 6* had failed before the spacecraft left Earth orbit. Perhaps that was the reason for the silence. Analysis of telemetry from one of the remote sites showed that *Zond 6* had deployed its parachute. "The next L-1 will carry two cosmonauts," Artemov announced to the Yevpatoriya team.

In high spirits, we flew back to Moscow the morning of the eighteenth, where there was still no news. I went back to my flat to unpack, and was finishing a bowl of soup when Shiborin came to my door. "I just saw Leonov," he said. "They found the Zond."

I knew it was bad news from the look on his face. "What happened?"

"A seal ruptured during reentry. The inside of the spacecraft burned and the parachute came out early. The whole thing smashed into the desert. The only thing they salvaged was some film from one of the cameras."

I could only imagine what Bykovsky or Leonov, or any of the lunar cosmonauts, were thinking. What else could possibly go wrong? It was as if American agents were playing a game with us—tantalizing us with near success, only to snatch it away at the last second.

Even if *Zond 6* hadn't crashed, we knew it would take a delay of a month or two in the *Apollo 8* launch to give us a chance to beat America around the Moon. Now we would need a miracle—to have the Saturn or Apollo suffer some kind of accident.

Thoughts like that made me ill. The next morning I felt even worse when I saw the newspapers reporting the "triumph" of our country's last attack on the cosmos, proudly publishing a photo of Earth taken from deep space—a photo that had been salvaged from the crushed pieces of *Zond 6*.

47 PYROTECHNICS

In the following week, winter descended on Star Town with short days and blowing snow, and morale sank so low it was as if the beloved Yuri Gagarin had died the day before, not back in March. I resumed my routine of exercise followed by classes. There was one postmortem meeting concerning *Zond 6* that I attended, where I heard the same thing Shiborin had told me, but at much greater length.

However, I was finally able to keep my promise to Lev about visiting him and Marina.

The lunar cosmonauts and their support team—Shiborin and I— were scheduled to spent Saturday, November 30, visiting the rocket test site at Zagorsk, a town a hundred and fifty kilometers northeast of Moscow, directly out the Yaroslavl Highway from Kaliningrad, for our first sight of L-3 lunar-lander hardware in action.

Given the nature of the tests, I knew Lev, not to mention Filin himself, would be present, and so I telephoned Department 731 a day ahead to arrange a return to Kaliningrad with my former colleagues. This (I thought) simple request created a surprising amount of fuss, resulting in a call from Triyanov to Colonel Belyayev. The result was formal approval for me to switch buses in Zagorsk, and a merciless amount of teasing from Leonov, Popovich, Shiborin, and the others for most of the three-hour ride to the site.

Driving through Zagorsk proper, I noted an ancient, tumbledown monastery not far from the road. I had never considered myself particularly religious—not surprising, I suppose, given the official atheism of the Soviet State. But I had also grown up hearing the phrases "thank God" or "God be praised" uttered by even the most ardent Communists, including Uncle Vladimir. I suddenly wanted to see the monastery more than I wanted to see the lunar lander, a desire that was as impractical as it was politically dangerous.

Ten kilometers past the monastery we found a collection of relatively new housing much like Star Town, and on the outskirts of that, the test facility. From my studies and chat in the bus, I knew it had half a dozen stands built into hillsides, where rocket engines of any size could be bolted into place, then fired, their actual thrust measured against the specified amount (never quite the same in practice) and the type of vibration (sometimes enough to destroy the engine).

These tests required the stands to be relatively far apart—if one of the big engines blew up, you didn't want it destroying the stand next door—and immense amounts of piping, tankage, and refrigeration, much like the launchpads at Baikonur.

Today we were going to observe a different kind of test, however. A model of the L-3 lander was hanging from a crane twenty meters up. You couldn't call it a mockup, since it looked nothing like the actual spacecraft: It was merely a cone-shaped mass sitting on a platform containing four legs and the L-3 landing motor. Below this was a patch of bare earth that had been sculpted into a fake lunar landscape, like the one in the building at the Gagarin Center.

As could be expected, preparations for the test were running late when we arrived, leaving us with free time to stand around stomping our feet in the cold. I found Lev as he finished a conversation with one of the bureau's film cameramen. "How long is this going to last?" I asked.

"Don't blink or you'll miss it." He nodded toward the camera operator. "He'll be running film at superhigh speeds, though, so in a couple of days we'll be able to watch everything in slow motion." He clapped his gloved hands together. "You're coming home with me?"

"Yes." I spared him a recitation of the bureaucratic crisis I had caused by making such an outrageous request.

A siren sounded, signaling us to take our places. I rejoined Shiborin and the other military cosmonauts, all of us in our olive-colored greatcoats.

There was no countdown, no obvious warning of any kind. Suddenly we heard a hissing that quickly turned into a high-pitched roar. Bluish flame shot out of the engine at the base of the L-3 mockup, which was then released from the crane.

Still tethered, but no longer supported, it hovered briefly, then dropped straight down to its "lunar" landing site. At the moment its feet touched, we heard and felt a thud. Four little gouts of flame shot up from smaller rockets mounted above each of the four legs. The lander sat there for several seconds, then emitted several smaller pops as coverings flew off the cone.

"Is it quite finished?" one of the cosmonauts behind me said, earning a laugh.

Closer to me, Shiborin muttered, "That would rattle your teeth right out of your head."

I glanced at him. He was frowning and shaking his head. "Maybe they figure you'd prefer one big jolt to several." The smaller rockets that fired upward were designed to keep the L-3 on the ground once it touched down. Our limited data from the Luna probes suggested that a fully loaded L-3, with its high center of gravity (in lunar terms) could easily bounce off the surface and possibly topple over, dooming its pilot.

"And maybe our lander is just too damn tall."

The sound the coverings made as they flew off was familiar to me, though I couldn't remember why. When the lander had been "safed" enough for us to approach it, I found Lev and asked him what they were. "Small pyrotechnics," he said. "Little bombs that blow off covers for sensors and antennas. We had problems with our space pyros on *Zond 6*, so we decided to test some standard military charges. They seem to have done a good job."

The drive back to Kaliningrad took twice as long as the drive out, because snow started to fall and traffic on the highway slowed. To make matters worse, the bureau bus quit at one point, and we all had to get out and push.

It was after seven when we reached Lev and Marina's flat. The bus driver kindly offered to drop us near their building, after I tipped him five rubles.

Marina looked happier and more relaxed than the last time I had seen her, now six months in the past. She was doing her hair differently, and she wore a dark blue dress that hugged her slim hips like silk. I'm not sure it wasn't made of silk.

She had a truly wonderful feast waiting, real beef with potatoes and carrots, a bottle of some French champagne, and for dessert, strawberries with sugar. I thought it would be impolite to ask where Marina had gotten a treasure like strawberries in November, but she offered it unbidden: "My most recent assignment was in Washington," she said.

I wanted to ask about Washington, but Lev abruptly stood up and excused himself, grabbing his coat. "If you're going out, may I have the rest of your dessert?" I said, joking.

"Help yourself," he said. "I've got to run over to the bureau for an hour."

Marina said nothing, so I made the protest on her behalf. "What can be so important that it can't wait a few hours?"

"I've got a presentation to make tomorrow, and I left the notes on my desk." And just like that, he put his coat on and left.

"I suppose he thought we'd stop there before coming here," I said. We began clearing the dishes.

Marina tilted her head to one side, a gesture that meant yes and no. "It's just an excuse," she said. "He wants us to have some time alone."

I was confused. As usual, my only response was a joke. "That's a terrible idea! Suppose I can't keep my hands off you."

Marina set down the dishes and put her arms around my neck, her mouth on mine tasting of strawberries and champagne. After several delicious moments, we broke, and she rested her head on my shoulder. I held her close, drinking in her sweet perfume, my hand roaming up and down her back, as I had so many times before. "Tell me what's going on here," I said.

"Lev and I—our relationship has ended."

Now I was even more confused. "But he's still living with you!"

She shrugged. "We're together only because of the flat. With his travel and mine, we barely cross paths." She took my hands and looked into my eyes. "I didn't know any other way to tell you. Neither did he. So he . . . planned to bring us back together."

"That's what I call a good friend." She smiled. Only then did I realize that she had said "back" together. And only then did I think of Katya.

"Lev is a good man, Yuri. A good friend. He feels terrible about what happened."

At that moment I wanted to stay with Marina forever. I also wanted to flee into the November night. "I don't know what to say," I blurted, helplessly.

She laughed. "Say you still love me."

"I still love you." It was true.

"Then we can be friends again."

"More than friends." I was saying things without any conscious thought, only a vague concern about what they might mean.

"I'm in Moscow through the New Year," she said.

"I'll call you tomorrow." We kissed again. And shortly thereafter I said good night, not wanting to be present when Lev returned.

I don't remember walking to the Podlipki Station, don't remember feeling the cold. That's how wrought up I was.

It was only on the train home to Star Town that I had time to set aside my terror about this possible new future with Marina, about my ill-fated relationship with Katya, and think again about the popping sound and the smell of the pyros.

I had heard the same sound the day Gagarin died, as his plane flew over our group of parachutists on the runway at Kirzhach. Had some small military pyro been used to sabotage Gagarin's plane?

Now if I could only remember where I had encountered that smell.

48 DAVYDOV

The next morning was Sunday, technically a free day. Nevertheless, I showed up at the gym after a light breakfast, hoping to use exercise as a way of straightening out my thoughts.

For an hour I ran and lifted weights. The only sounds I heard were my feet slapping against the floor, the weights creaking, my own panting. The workout felt good, physically. As for my mental state, I did not achieve clarity, only a kind of numbness.

Shortly after nine, as I was about to quit, Shiborin and several others showed up. "Did you hear the news?" Shiborin said.

"No." I was immediately apprehensive. News was usually bad.

"Belyayev met us when we got home last night. They want us to do our winter survival training starting Monday."

"We weren't supposed to do that until January."

"It's already especially cold in Vorkuta," he said, grinning. "Actually, he said they expected us all to be busy in January, with the next Soyuz mission plus the first Carrier launches."

"And yet another L-1."

"Yes. We're rolling rockets out of the factory like sausages." I was surprised to hear this allusion to the famous quote by our former leader, Khrushchev, whose name had disappeared from the newspapers four years ago. Shiborin was growing more openly cynical. Was it my influence? Or that of his fellow eagles, like Saditsky? Or just an inevitable result of exposure to life in Star Town? In a way, it made me sad, like seeing a beautiful young girl starting to smoke cigarettes and wear makeup.

Knowing I would be gone again for at least a week helped focus my thoughts. Not on the Marina or Katya matter, which I knew even then was not solvable without anger and pain, but the nagging business of that popping sound and the pyros.

I needed to talk to Davydov, the air-crash investigator. But where would I find him on a Sunday? There was no telephone directory for the Moscow area; I didn't even know where his institute was located.

But, thinking of Davydov's dogged and relentless work habits, I suspected I could probably find him at Chkalov.

"Did you hear about Kamanin?" Davydov said, as he labored to push open the door to the hangar where the wreckage of Gagarin's plane was laid out.

"No."

"The Central Committee hit him with a formal reprimand."

"Why?"

"For losing Gagarin. And Seregin. 'Failure to exercise proper authority' was the phrase they used."

"Do you think it's fair?"

"It's only fair if they blame everyone else who was responsible. All they really want to do is write 'the end' to the whole story. Careful where you step." I was following him into the darkness. "Don't move."

I froze in place while Davydov moved off like a shadow to turn on a light, which was so dim it was as if the inside of the hangar were bathed in moonlight.

All around me, in a grotesque parody of an aircraft shape, was arrayed the wreckage of Gagarin's MiG-15. Most of the pieces were the size of a hand—mere fragments—though there was a large, intact piece of the tail, and an even bigger chunk that used to be the engine.

I was standing near the nose when Davydov returned to my side. "Now, what's all this about a bomb in the cockpit?"

I told him about the sound I had heard the day of the crash and how I had learned it was a common pyro charge used by our military, adding Triyanov's story about the damage even a small explosion in the cockpit could do. "When I was part of the search team, we couldn't find most of the canopy."

"More than sixty percent of it is still missing."

"So it's plausible that a small pyro could have exploded, shattering the canopy and possibly knocking the pilots unconscious long enough for them to crash."

"Very plausible, given the lack of an obvious mechanical failure." He stooped over to examine some bit of the smashed nose section. When he straightened, his voice was lower. "Most of us think someone wanted Gagarin dead. A small pyro with a pressure trigger, or a small timer. You could place it behind the control panel or between the front and back seats in a few minutes. Step back, watch them take off, and wait. Boom. The charge destroys itself and the timer. Two dead pilots, no evidence."

I could see it all. A hand reaching in, pulling back. A person retreating into the shadows as Gagarin and Seregin approached. "It couldn't be just anyone, of course. Chkalov is a military base and their security is pretty good. It would have to be someone on the ground crew—"

"—or someone with special access."

"Fine. Who?"

"I don't know," I said, feeling sick.

Because I did know. I had remembered where I encountered that distinctive smell of a pyro, not more than an hour after Gagarin and Seregin crashed.

"Yuri?"

Bleary-eyed, my father stared at me from his open door. He was wearing a peasant blouse and old trousers, suspenders hanging down, as if he had just pulled them on. I pushed past him into the flat. "It's midnight!"

"I know what time it is. Close the door."

He was about to make more complaints, but my manner and the look on my face alerted him that this was not a friendly visit.

"You killed Gagarin," I said.

He weighed several responses as he stepped away—out of reach?— and pulled up his suspenders. "You've been spying again."

"Not by choice. Pieces of the puzzle just keep finding me."

He sat down, motioning me to do the same. But I remained standing. I told him about the pyros, the missing canopy, the bogus conclusion of the accident board. About the smell on my hands.

"I thought it was Vladimir, though I was never sure, because I couldn't connect the Gagarin murder to Korolev's. *You* were the only person in both places.

"You were also at Baikonur, the bigshot Air Force inspector. You could have sabotaged those rockets and spacecraft, too."

He stared past me, his eyes clouded. He shook his head, as if trying to deny my charges, but only said, "I tried to protect you."

"It's all true."

"It was necessary."

For the second time in two days, my heart was pounding and I was short of breath, though the circumstances could not have been more different. I had wandered for hours after my meeting with Davydov, eventually returning to my flat and taking out the PB-8 pistol. I had planned to confront my father with the evidence and, I suppose, arrest him.

But as I worked through the things I had seen—the day at the Kremlin Hospital when Korolev died, the times I had seen my father at Baikonur, the encounter at Chkalov—I felt sure I was misinterpreting everything, that I had become as paranoid and suspicious as the State Security spies I hated.

So I left the pistol in the flat and took the train into town to speak to my father, hoping he could dissuade me and place the blame where it belonged: on Uncle Vladimir, or on someone else entirely.

"That's what we've always said in this country, isn't it, Papa? No matter what we do . . . burn the farmers, arrest the dissidents, shoot the Trotskyites, make deals with Nazis . . . it's *necessary*." This was making me sick to my stomach. "Did you kill Mother, too? Was that necessary?"

He tried to hit me, but I blocked it. He was strong, for his age, but after all my months of exercise, so was I. I shoved him back into his chair and held him there.

"I should report you."

"To whom? You *think* you know everything that happened, but you don't."

That was certainly true. It wasn't as though I could turn my father over to the militia; those drunken fools could barely arrest a traffic violator. A three-star general would immediately be turned over to his service, or State Security, where it was very likely that he had allies.

And this was my own father! I wanted him to offer a magic explanation, to clear himself in my eyes.

Nothing was said. For moments the only sound was our breathing. Then the clock struck one A.M. I had to be up in four hours.

"I'm going out of town," I said, finally. "I'll be home at the end of the week. Try not to kill anyone else in the meantime."

I walked out without a backward glance.

49 | VORKUTA

I didn't sleep at all until boarding the An-12 at Chkalov the next morning, when I promptly began to doze, waking as Shiborin shook me two hours later on approach to Vorkuta.

"You didn't miss a thing," he said, nodding out at the landscape, a frozen tundra that was almost treeless. What could be seen of it through the low clouds, that is. "It's been overcast all the way."

The weather matched my mood—cold, colorless, unforgiving. I badly wanted to punish my father for his lies, for his crimes. Next on that list was the Party itself, which allowed all of it to happen.

I felt I should include myself on the list of criminals. I had spied and lied, too.

But in this grim outpost on the Arctic Circle, there was no opportunity for vengeance. Survival was the issue, and not my survival in a simulated "off course" spacecraft landing; surviving in Vorkuta itself as winter approached.

I had heard whispers all my life that Vorkuta was also the center of our country's Gulag, the system of prison work camps, where political prisoners and criminals were sentenced to exile, or to hard labor in the mines. Of course, I saw nothing of these, just blocks of drab, sooty apartment flats, occasional public buildings and factories, and unplowed roads leading off toward the horizon. There was no other reason for the town to be here: no missile center or Air Force base, for example. One look at the primitive airport was enough to convince me of that. Only a small, frozen river running through the middle of the town hinted at any possible commerce. I could imagine boats putting in during the summer months to pick up loads of ore, which would travel a few kilometers north to the sea, then west to Murmansk.

It was already getting dark when the ten of us—four cosmonauts, a doctor, and no fewer than five instructors—reached a military barracks on the north side of the city. One of our instructors from the Gagarin Center, Captain Voronin, took us around to a shed and showed us our Soyuz/L-1 descent capsule. Fitted with two seats, an ancient Air Force radio, and a wooden control panel on which some humorous test subject—possibly Saditsky—had inscribed obscene commands ("Begin penis insertion!"), it was no more than a shell. "You'll each be issued a standard recovery kit," Voronin assured us. "It will be identical to those included in each flight vehicle."

"Will we have a gun to shoot wolves?" Shiborin was friends with Leonov, whose *Voskhod 2* flight had first alerted us to the need for such weaponry.

Voronin looked uncomfortable. "We don't have authorization for firearms, yet. We're too far north for bears here, anyway."

I didn't know whether to believe that or not, but I wished I had packed my illicit PB-8 along, if only to see the look on Shiborin's face when I pulled it out.

"We heat the shell to thirty-five degrees before taking it off the truck," Voronin informed us, returning to his prepared script. "So it will have the same residual heat as a spacecraft that has just reentered."

"They've thought of everything," Shiborin said.

Shiborin and I were the first "crew," wakened at six A.M. in darkness, given a cursory medical examination, then breakfast. "Leonov told me to eat heartily," Shiborin said. I had noticed he was taking double helpings. I wasn't so sure: A full belly would mean less reliance on "emergency" rations, but it would also require more sanitary exercises, as our instructors called them. And there was no toilet in the Soyuz/L-1 descent capsule. I ate lightly.

Then, dressed in flight suits over which we were allowed to wear our officer's coats, we were off to the trucks. It was cold, not bitterly so, but enough so that I had no trouble believing it was a few days before winter, and that I was on the Arctic Circle.

Shiborin teased Voronin: "Do you also warm *us* up before we get dropped in the snow?"

The goal of the test was for the two of us, commander Shiborin and flight engineer Ribko, to survive for forty-eight hours. We had gone through hours of survival lessons back at the center, of course, and had been given pointers and handbooks by our support team last night.

Their advice was simple: Establish communication, stay in the spacecraft as much as possible, and wait for the "rescue" teams to arrive. (Our instructors would be standing by with their radios a kilometer off. I suspected they would also sneak up and check on us from time to time.)

We arrived a few moments after our Soyuz had "landed." The problem was, the spacecraft was tipped onto its *side*. We weren't going to be lowered through the nose hatch like real cosmonauts, we were going to have to crawl on our hands and knees like dogs slipping under a fence. When Shiborin saw the arrangement, he called Voronin "bastard."

Voronin, who was no older than us, seemed unhappy. "Most of the spacecraft have tipped over on landing," he said.

"The ones that haven't crashed or gone through the ice," I said, unable to stop myself.

The metal of the hatchway was, as promised, still warm. Snow had melted underneath the spacecraft, in fact. I crawled in first, and immediately discovered another challenge: The seats were to one side and on top. (Even seeing the spacecraft on its side, I had hoped that they might be on the bottom.)

I curled up in one corner, my side against the control panel, as Shiborin entered and saw the layout. "This isn't training," he said, "this is torture."

The hatch was closed behind us, as it would be on landing, and with a final radio check, the test officially began. It was like hide-and-seek, with Shiborin and me counting off fifteen minutes until we could open the hatch from the inside (necessary, because the air quickly began to get stifling) while our instructors ran and hid.

At the stroke of fifteen minutes, I used the radio to call them, was given permission to crack open the hatch. As soon as I did so, Shiborin said, "Let me out of here. I don't feel so good."

The rules allowed him to exit the craft at any point. Better yet, his "sanitary exercise" was also allowed. Even if it were forbidden, were Voronin and his team going to search the area for frozen piles of shit?

Then we settled down to an extremely dull morning. I broke out the rations and water—we had very strict rules about how much water to consume—and amused myself by speculating on how quickly the spacecraft was cooling down, while Shiborin dozed.

When I tired of that, I went back to considering my situation. Maybe it was due to my agitated mental state, but sitting in a cramped, cold Soyuz mockup on the tundra seemed not that far removed from an L-3 parked on the lunar Sea of Serenity. If anything, the L-3 would be more comfortable! And I would have the added pleasure of seeing the surface of the Moon outside my window.

On the Moon there would be no Uncle Vladimir, no General Nikolai Ribko, no Ustinov or the Hammer or their clans. There might be Americans, but there would be no Communist Party.

No matter what, I had to find some way to save my cosmonaut career. I wanted that visit to the Moon.

After our midday reports, and a meal of dry, sublimated curds and nuts, I dozed off, waking in pain and confusion less than an hour later. "What the hell is going on?" Shiborin snapped.

Someone was rapping on the cold metal of the spacecraft! We feigned joy at our "rescue," and opened the hatch all the way.

Voronin was standing there. The others were climbing off the truck with a line to attach to the spacecraft. "The test is canceled," he announced.

"What did we do?" Shiborin said, fearful that his early visit to the toilet might have derailed his cosmonaut career.

"Nothing. You will complete the training another time." Voronin turned to me. "Lieutenant Ribko needs to return to Moscow immediately on personal business."

After a stop at the barracks to collect my belongings, I was driven down to the airport and put on another An-12 heading south.

I had to leave Shiborin and the others behind. Poor Shiborin was told he and Voronin would be teamed for another survival "flight" the next day.

No one had any idea of the nature of my "personal business," which, of course, allowed me several hours to fret. Was I being arrested? Possibly, though surely someone would have arrested me in Vorkuta so I could be returned to Moscow in custody.

I was alarmed that Colonel Belyayev and Ivan Saditsky were at Chkalov to meet me when I arrived. But Belyayev looked elsewhere as Saditsky put his arm around me. "I'm sorry to tell you this, Yuri, but your father is dead."

50 VAGANKOV CEMETERY

These were the facts: At six o'clock that morning, about the time, allowing for the different zones, that Shiborin and I were eating our breakfast in Vorkuta, a militiaman taking the train back to Moscow from his post in Monino happened to get off at the Tsiolkovsky Station, the one closest to Star Town, to buy a newspaper, he said. (One of his fellow officers conceded that it was to buy vodka, which was always in stock at that station.)

He noticed a man's body at the end of the platform, under a dusting of snow, a man in a full military uniform, dead from a gunshot wound to the left temple. No weapon was found in the area, ruling out suicide. This was the official information, of course, which meant nothing to me.

My father, Colonel-General Nikolai Tikhonovich Ribko, Hero of the Soviet Union, Pilot First Class, graduate of the Red Banner Air Force Academy, and holder of the Order of the Red Star.

That was how he was described in a column in *Red Star*, the newspaper of the Soviet armed forces, two days later. He died, of course, "while fulfilling his duties." I could have written a more interesting obituary: shameless tool of the Communist Party, poisoner of hundreds or thousands of Soviet citizens, murderer of at least two, or shall we count my mother as three?

Add coward.

That word could also have been applied to me during the tortured days that followed my return from Vorkuta. I was taken to see the body in the morgue at the Central Aviation Hospital, and gave my permission for its cremation. My father's stars and medals entitled him to burial in the cemetery at Novodevichy Convent, the final resting place of many heroes of Soviet aviation and industry, but I insisted that his ashes should rest in Vagankov, next to those of my mother.

Since there were no other survivors, I inherited the contents of the flat in Frunze Embankment—though not the flat itself, of course. One of my father's adjutants, a Lieutenant Colonel Kozlov, explained that it would be assigned to another member of the Air Force high command, though not for several weeks, at least. They would give me time to dispose of my father's possessions, a process I was not eager to begin.

Katya joined me in a brief visit to the flat, however, the day before the funeral service. I expected to find some explanation, some note, but found nothing unusual, though Katya pointed out that everything was clean and in its place, as if the owner had planned to take a long trip. . . .

The funeral took place on Saturday, December 6, 1968, a cold, bright day—the day when Bykovsky or Leonov could have commanded a manned L-1 launch, had things gone differently.

Had my father not interfered.

There was a good crowd: Shiborin and his wife. Lev and Marina, together but not, I judged, truly together. Filin and Triyanov. Saditsky and several other cosmonauts, plus my father's immediate associates, and General Kamanin himself. (How many of them would have come if they'd known how much more difficult the late General Ribko had made their lives?)

And, of course, Katya and Uncle Vladimir.

I had received a genuinely warm call of condolences from Uncle Vladimir the day I returned from Vorkuta, which was especially painful, given my long suspicions of him. His manner at the funeral was completely proper, and caused me to doubt my own feelings.

But then, doubt was my most dominant emotion that week, and for several that followed.

Katya, who had rushed to Star Town the moment she heard the news of my father's death, had won my gratitude (if not my heart) for all time for the way she stayed by my side, helping me deal with the awful postmortem rituals and necessities, ultimately organizing and serving as hostess for a reception following the funeral that we held at the flat. Here I accepted condolences for what seemed like the tenth time, and drank far too heavily toasting the memory of General Ribko—whose official portrait, now bordered in black, dominated the living room.

"This has been a terrible year," General Kamanin said. "So many losses. It feels like the war." For him, it was true: Gagarin, Seregin, Ribko. And he could hardly have forgotten about poor Komarov. Of course, one of his friends had murdered the others. But things like that happened in war.

Eventually the mourners began to leave. I sent Katya home and accepted a ride back to Star Town with the Shiborins. I walked into my flat more alone in the world than I had ever been. I was now an orphan.

Through all of my mourning I had stayed dry-eyed, but here, now, I wept. I wept for myself, like a child. I wept for my country and my friends. I had lost my father, after all. Long before his actual death.

Colonel Belyayev had encouraged me to take some time off, but I presented myself at morning exercise the Monday after the funeral. I had already lost a week due to the cancellation of my winter survival training; I didn't feel I could afford to miss anything else.

I needn't have bothered. Most of my group's training time was devoted to gossiping about the American program—it appeared as though *Apollo 8* was truly going to be launched soon—or discussing Kamanin's plans to reorganize the Gagarin Center, raising its status from that of a military unit to an actual scientific-research institute, doubling the size. Even the cosmonaut team itself, already divided into various branches, was to be split up.

There were also final examinations for the eight cosmonauts training for the next pair of Soyuz missions, including Saditsky. This time there was no political maneuvering; everyone scored well, and the crews got ready to leave for Baikonur confident we would finally accomplish a manned docking and spacewalk, almost two years after we first tried it.

These distractions were a blessing, because while I was present in body, I could not concentrate. Had I been graded on exercises or even my favorite academic subjects, I would have flunked. Belyayev had been right, and I should have taken a holiday.

After two weeks I began to emerge from my daze, becoming more active. I felt the urge to sweep everything bad out of my life, to start over for the New Year.

One of my first targets was the PB-8 pistol stashed behind my books. But on the morning when I went to find it, it was gone.

In its place was a note—a single piece of paper, written in my father's neat hand. *"Yuri, I will pay the penalty. Remember our good times and your mother, and forgive me. Papa."*

It had never occurred to me to *ask* what gun he had used to kill himself. He had come here and taken mine! No wonder he had been found so close by, at Tsiolkovsky Station.

(Had the weapon been found? If so, by whom?)

On that same day, Saturday, December 21, the American *Apollo 8* roared off its launchpad at the Kennedy Space Center in Florida. Astronauts Borman, Lovell, and Anders were the crew. Within hours they had fired the upper stage of their Saturn V-5 and sent themselves soaring toward the Moon.

Three days later they burned the engine of the Apollo service module, putting themselves into lunar orbit, where they stayed for twenty hours. On December 25—Christmas Day in the West—they began their journey home, splashing safely down in the Pacific on December 28, winning the first heat of the race to the Moon.

51

THE WORLD'S FIRST EXPERIMENTAL SPACE STATION

Our national response to *Apollo 8*, as reported to the cosmonaut team by General Kamanin, was to press the battle on all fronts. An unmanned L-1 would be launched January 20; if it succeeded, a manned L-1 would follow in April.

The Soyuz docking, rendezvous, and EVA test of our prototype Hawk lunar spacesuit was to be launched in mid-January. There would be a second twin docking flight in summer, and two additional docking missions testing the lunar Soyuz/L-3 capture system (which was different from the Soyuz/Soyuz model) in the fall and winter.

The first Carrier launch vehicle would fly in February, a second in May.

The L-3 lander would begin its unmanned orbital trials by late in the year.

Finally, in summer we would send a new type of unmanned probe called the E-8 to the Moon: It would land, as the E-6 had, but dig up some samples, which would then be shot back to Earth and recovered! We hoped this sample-return mission would steal some of Apollo's thunder, and might very well show that the creative Soviet approach to lunar exploration was just as timely and efficient as the American plan.

As we walked out of the meeting, I asked Saditsky what he thought of the staggering number and variety of launchers and spacecraft. "It's like the Zhukov method of clearing a minefield," he said, mentioning our honored commander of the Great Patriotic War. "If you don't have well-trained sappers with useful tools, you simply line up vast numbers of soldiers and march them through it. Many soldiers will die, but the minefield will be cleared."

Shortly thereafter, on Monday, January 13, 1969, Shiborin and I flew back to Baikonur for checkout on L-1 Number 13.

As a Bauman graduate, an engineer, and an atheistic Communist, I was not generally superstitious, but even I noticed the many instances of that unlucky number. Beyond the date of our flight and the serial number of the L-1, one of the two Soyuz was *also* serial number 13. And Lieutenant Colonel Shatalov, who would be launched as the pilot of Soyuz Number 12, was the thirteenth pilot-cosmonaut of the USSR in a line beginnning with Gagarin. (This public honor came complete with medals and special automobile license plates bearing that number!) Shatalov claimed to be unconcerned, but I heard there were discussions among the more superstitious members of the State Commission about the subject. (To this day you can find buildings in Moscow without a thirteenth floor—they call it "12-A." And let's not forget that the original surveyors of the Baikonur Cosmodrome made sure that "Area 13" would become the cemetery!)

In fact, the original launch date for our thirteenth pilot-cosmonaut *was* to have been January 13, but Shiborin and I knew it had been postponed even before we left Chkalov. Technical problems? No one seemed quite sure about the reason.

Nevertheless, on cold and snowy January 14, Vladimir Shatalov became Cosmonaut 13 when his Soyuz reached orbit safely and was announced as *Soyuz 4*. A day later, spacecraft Number 13 with a crew of Volynov, Yeliseyev, and Khrunov was also launched successfully, becoming *Soyuz 5*.

Having learned from the fiasco of Beregovoy's failed docking, our flight directors allowed Shatalov—piloting the active craft in the scenario—two full days to adapt to weightlessness. Even the three cosmonauts aboard *Soyuz 5* were required only to make some small engine burns during the first day, placing their craft in the proper target orbit.

Shortly after noon (Baikonur time) on the sixteenth, *Soyuz 4* approached to within one hundred meters of *Soyuz 5* using the automatic guidance system. Then Shatalov took over manual control and eased into a perfect docking. Watching the events live on state television, we also heard a comment from the crew of *Soyuz 5* as the probe of the active craft entered the drogue of the passive docking unit: "Help, we've been raped!"

I thought of the comments scrawled on the control panel of the Soyuz mockup used for winter survival training as those of us listening in the command post at Area 18 burst into laughter.

As State television's censors no doubt began fielding irate phone calls from members of the Central Committee, our commentators trumpeted the establishment of "the world's first experimental space station," massing over thirteen thousand kilograms and consisting of four different habitable modules. Well, yes and no—to get from one pair of modules to the other, you had to go *outside* the space station, like swimming across a river to reach the other room of your house. Stupid.

Then it was time for the years-delayed EVA. Khrunov and Yeliseyev moved into the orbital module of *Soyuz 5* and donned their white Hawk suits, the same model we had used in zero-G aircraft flights—the suits that had the life-support pack attached to the legs. Volynov remained sealed inside the *Soyuz 5* command module, prepared to film as much of the activity as he could through the small windows.

Shatalov, meanwhile, was sealed inside the command module of *Soyuz 4*, with the outer hatch of his orbital module unlocked.

We saw fuzzy black-and-white pictures of a ghostlike Khrunov emerging from *Soyuz 5* and moving slowly toward us along the handrails built onto the exterior of both orbital modules for this purpose. He stopped to inspect the docking mechanism, taking a series of photographs, then continued on to *Soyuz 4*. Only when he had reached the hatch of the other vehicle did Yeliseyev emerge and follow Khrunov onto the rails.

It took an hour from the time the hatch on *Soyuz 5* opened until Khrunov and Yeliseyev were safely buttoned up inside *Soyuz 4*. From all indications, the Hawk spacesuit worked very well. The two spacecraft separated as planned after four and a half hours together.

Khrunov, Yeliseyev, and Shatalov made a safe landing in the primary zone a day later, on the seventeenth. Volynov, flying *Soyuz 5* alone, had a much more difficult time of it.

Trouble began for him when the cylindrical equipment module failed to separate from the command module after making the all-important retro burn. *Soyuz 5* began its descent into the atmosphere with its heat shield covered. Of course, the spacecraft's center of gravity and basic flight dynamics were totally fouled, too. The spacecraft swung around so that it was reentering nose-first. Temperature inside the spacecraft began to rise. Volynov expected to burn up. He ripped pages out of his journal and stuffed them inside his flight suit, next to his chest, hoping they might survive the flames.

Then, magically, the equipment module separated on its own. Volynov was able to swing the freed command module back to the right attitude and go ahead with a ballistic reentry, which subjected him to nine Gs. He had to have worried about the parachute system, though, which had been subject to excessive heat when *Soyuz 5* was flying nose-forward.

The 'chutes did open as planned, though Volynov's landing was hard enough to knock out several of his teeth. Far from the primary zone, he had to wrap himself in winter survival gear and crawl out of *Soyuz 5* unaided.

(All this we learned later, of course, though I can imagine the horror at the flight-control center in Yevpatoriya. Not again!)

For all of Volynov's troubles, *Soyuz 4* and *Soyuz 5* were two steps forward, back into the race.

On the nineteenth, the latest Universal Rocket 500 thundered off its pad carrying L-1 Number 13 on the flight we hoped would pave the way for a manned L-1 in April or May. I was optimistic: While I didn't believe that all of our failures were my father's work (our own lack of quality-control in the manufacture of rocket engines and electronics would have doomed some of those flights, anyway), he had created bizarre last-minute failures on launch vehicles that had passed stringent checkout.

He was gone now. I myself had sat through the checkout and State Commission reports on the status of the UR-500 and the L-1.

So I was stunned when the new mission ended within five minutes as the second stage of the launcher failed, the escape rocket pulling the L-1 safely away before the self-destruct charges blew, parachuting to a landing downrange.

Then I began to have horrifying doubts: Suppose I had accused my father unfairly? Suppose someone else was tampering with our spacecraft?

No, no, no. I had his letter. I had the other evidence. If I had been wrong, he wouldn't have admitted his guilt.

He wouldn't have killed himself with my pistol.

In any case, these were the things I told myself as I flew back to Moscow with Shiborin and Leonov and the other disappointed lunar cosmonauts.

The day after our return—January 22—there was a parade in honor of the four new Soyuz cosmonauts. Even the student-cosmonauts of the Fourth Enrollment were given the morning off to be bused to Red Square to take part, standing in the crowd in Borovitsky Plaza on the southwest corner of the Kremlin complex.

Our publicly known cosmonauts, such as Nikolayev and Beregovoy, were part of the motorcade. Others, even such long-serving veterans as Ivan Saditsky, who would command one of the next Soyuz flights, stood with the spectators. As we waited, I asked Saditsky when he hoped to fly. "My crew will be ready by July," he said, "but we won't have a vehicle until September. The factories can't keep up with the demand." I could see why: We were trying to test four different models of the Soyuz— the orbital version just flown by Shatalov and his comrades, the L-1 that had just failed, yet another version of the L-1 configured for the first Carrier launch next month, plus the L-3. All were built by the same plant in Kaliningrad. "Meanwhile, the Americans are getting their lunar module ready. They could be on the Moon this summer."

I admired the American successes, but I found that hard to believe. "They say they need to test the lunar module three or four times before they try that."

"They often say one thing and do another. They already announced a lunar landing crew for a flight in July. Armstrong is the commander." I hadn't heard that news, but then, I had been busy with my father's affairs.

"Do you think they'll succeed?"

He stared out over the crowd, many of them stamping their feet on this cold day, others sipping openly from flasks. "Yes." He must have seen the shock on my face. Saditsky was honest, even brutally so, but he was also competitive. "Something went wrong. I don't know when . . . maybe it was when Korolev died." That had been the very day we met, Saditsky, my father, and Gagarin, almost three years ago to the day. And two of those men were now dead. "Maybe it was when Yuri crashed."

At that moment I realized he was right—but far too conservative. Something had indeed gone wrong, but it hadn't started the day Gagarin died, or Korolev, but much earlier. It started when the Glorious Revolution of the Russian people, a genuine attempt to create a new way of life, had become just another case of rule by force. When a small group of men with guns found they could steal without fear, that they could murder those who disagreed with them. What allowed them to survive was their ability to buy silence, with apartments and food and cars, and the promise of a good education, which would make access to apartments, food, and cars that much easier. All they required in return was mute complicity.

My father was a part of it. So was Uncle Vladimir. So was Saditsky, for that matter.

And so was I.

Just then, a line of cars slowed to make the final turn into the Kremlin, and we all heard several sharp sounds. "What was that?" I asked, stupidly.

"Gunfire!" Saditsky snapped. "Look!"

We pushed through the crowd, which had suddenly come alive, in time to see a young officer being flattened by burly security men in dark coats. He waved a gun like a wild man. There was blood on the snow. Shards of shattered glass.

The windows had been shot out of the lead car, the one carrying Nikolayev and Beregovoy. They were crumpled in the back seat, their condition impossible to tell. Shot in the face, their driver lay with his head against the steering wheel.

That was as close as I got. Uniform or no, I was pushed back into the crowd by the growing number of guards who cleared a path for the other cars in the procession to escape.

I lost track of Saditsky and Shiborin as I was moved along with the crowd, down Znamenka Street. Once we were a block from the shooting site, we were able to disperse, and I circled south to where the Star Town bus was parked, on Lenivka.

There I found most of my fellow cosmonauts and their wives, some of them quite shaken by what they had seen and heard.

We waited for the better part of an hour until Saditsky and Artyukhin, another senior cosmonaut, returned. "Everyone is fine," Artyukhin announced. "Nikolayev, Leonov, Tereshkova were completely unhurt. Beregovoy had some cuts from flying glass."

"What about the driver?" I asked. He had *clearly* been hurt.

"The driver is dead." Someone else asked who the assassin had been shooting at. "Brezhnev," Saditsky said. "They think the gunman mistook Beregovoy for Brezhnev." The two did resemble each other.

The bus started up and Saditsky sat down next to me. I could smell the vodka on his breath. "Too bad he missed," he said, so quietly I almost didn't hear him.

"Brezhnev, or Beregovoy?"

"Either one. They're both bastards."

52

RED MOON

The next afternoon I went to see Katya, our first visit since the day of my father's burial. It was a workday, but given my long stay at Baikonur and my various personal crises, Colonel Belyayev was happy to let me leave Star Town early.

I was determined to be honest with Katya, to tell her about my resumed relationship with Marina (though I'd had no contact with her since the funeral, either!), to make as clean a break as possible. I didn't expect it to be easy, or painless.

I had not alerted her to my arrival. For one thing, simply getting in touch with her at the Space Research Institute was a tedious, often fruitless process. For another, I hoped to deliver my message quickly, without giving her a chance to build up some tidal wave of emotion that might drown both of us.

I succeeded in exactly one of my goals: surprising Katya. "Well, since you're here, come in," she said. She immediately headed toward the kitchen. "I just got home. Have you eaten?"

"I had something on the train."

She returned with a bottle and two glasses. "You will have a drink, though."

That was one thing I was finding easier to accept. "Yes."

We touched glasses and drank. Well, I did. She sipped and put hers down. "I need to make a phone call. Sit down."

I did, and she went off to the other room for a moment, door closed.

Was she calling another man, perhaps? Had I disrupted Katya's plans? I suspected so when she returned, a flush on her cheeks.

"Were you at Borovitsky?" she said.

"I saw most of it, yes." I described the events, leaving out Saditsky's comments, and my own thoughts.

"It's a terrible thing. Shooting at Brezhnev won't solve whatever problems this man had." The would-be assassin turned out to be a young army officer with a history of grievances, or as they would now be called, mental problems. "It will only give State Security an excuse to crack down."

"Since when have they ever needed an excuse?"

"Since they started paying attention to what the rest of the world thinks. They'll still smash you in the face, but they want everyone to believe it was for your own good."

This was unusual talk coming from Katya. "Are you afraid of something?"

She wouldn't look at me. "No. No, it's winter." Here she smiled. "I'm a year older. My waist refuses to shrink no matter how much I starve myself, and the sleep lines have become permanent."

I took her hands in mine, kissing them. "Katya, you're beautiful."

"If that were true, you wouldn't be here to break up with me."

She gave my hands a squeeze, then sat back, challenging me to deny it. "Why do you think that?"

"Because you've never gotten over your little dark-haired spy. Marina. No, let me finish." I had started to protest. "You've been distant. You've been on trips for days and weeks and never sent a letter. I've become a convenience to you. And now you don't need me."

"That's not true."

"Which part?" She was challenging me now. Here came that emotional tidal wave.

"You were never a convenience."

I think I surprised her, enough so that her manner became more gentle. "But you *are* here to tell me we won't be seeing each other anymore."

I found I could barely speak, that I had tears in my eyes. "Yes."

She sighed. She also had tears in her eyes—sadness or anger, I couldn't tell. "Then you should probably leave."

I put down the glass and stood up.

So did Katya, reaching for me. Our arms went around each other. I wanted to put her head on my shoulder, to console her, but she was so tall the idea was ludicrous. We merely touched foreheads for a moment. "I'm sorry," I said. "I didn't mean to hurt you." I was failing in my search for magic words.

"I know. I hope you believe the same of me." I opened the door. "One last bit of advice, from someone who was fonder of you than she should have been: When they order you to the hospital, watch out."

This was alarming, not just for what she said, but for the abrupt change of subject.

"Why? Will they try to kill me?"

She smiled and shook her head. "They can kill you *now*, silly. No. When they send you to the hospital, they're getting ready to kick you out of the cosmonaut team."

"How am I supposed to stop them?"

"That's up to you. I just thought you should be warned."

Then I did kiss her, fiercely, passionately, finally.

It was dark, of course, when I left Katya's building and headed for the Belorussia Station. There were few people on the streets and no kiosks open; curious, because it was a typical winter night when people would shop.

I saw that a black Zil was rolling down the street a little behind me. Even more curious. I glanced around, wondering who was being followed.

Me. The car slowed, and I began to run down a cross street.

Another car, this one a Volga, suddenly flashed its lights in front of me. I was trapped. This car had militia plates—local police. So while there was nowhere to run, I had no reason to run. After all, I was a military officer in uniform!

But these militia officers weren't in uniform, which was unusual. One of them, gray-haired, hawk-nosed, said, "Passport."

I handed it over without a word—

—as one of the others hit me from behind, a sharp blow to my back that forced me to my knees. Outraged, wincing, I turned to look at my assailant, who was a heavyset young thug.

And behind him . . . Uncle Vladimir.

He stepped forward and gently helped me to my feet, saying, "That's how it used to be done, Yuri. We would distract you, then hit you from behind." He tapped a finger on the back of my head. "With a bullet."

I was still panting from the pain in my back. It was difficult to talk. "Why are you doing this?"

"You needed a stronger lesson. You're a bright young man with a great future, but you're also bullheaded, like your father. I've learned that I can't be subtle with you." He leaned close. "Let it go."

"Let what go?"

The other thugs had moved off, out of earshot. "Korolev. Gagarin. Sabotage."

"I did."

"If you *had*, your father would still be alive."

He didn't need to say anything else: At that moment I knew for certain what I had already suspected. "He was working for you. You wanted those men killed."

"Your father, Yuri, was a marvelous weapon. Technically trained, able to go anywhere, cold-blooded and ruthless when it was necessary. When he died, I wept genuine tears."

It took all my willpower not to smash him in the face. "He hated you."

"He feared me. Your father, Yuri, was a serf. He came from a family of serfs who had lived in their own shit for a thousand years. Your mother's side of the family—my side, a family you share, Yuri—we're lords. Aristocrats."

"I thought we were all Communists."

Uncle Vladimir laughed so hard I thought he would choke. Hoped he would. "*Someday.* Until that happy day, we use whatever tools we have. A worker is just a tool."

"I don't believe it. My father wasn't an ignorant peasant—"

"True. He was a clever man, as peasants go. Not clever enough to keep himself out of trouble, of course. I had saved him, protected him. He had to do what I wanted."

There was still a dull ache in my back, but I felt as though I could run. If I found the chance, which didn't seem likely. "Why was it necessary?"

"What?"

"The death of Korolev, the sabotage, all of it?"

The look on Uncle Vladimir's face was one I had never seen before—not on his face, at least. It reminded me of Filin, of Lev, even of myself. "Why did you go to Bauman, Yuri?"

"My mother—"

"*My sister* wanted you there. Because I had gone there." He raised his head. "I was one of those dreamers once, Yuri. I even met Tsiolkovsky. But the Revolution turned me into . . . well, into what I am now."

"I still don't understand—"

"They were ruining our program, Yuri! Korolev was completely overextended, failing in health, yet no one would refuse him! He had to leave the scene." It was very clear to me now: Uncle Vladimir was like an earnest college student trying to make a point to a skeptical professor. Old habits took over: God help me, I joined in!

"And Gagarin was a threat from the military."

"Exactly. They would have made things more efficient, yes, but only for weapons and spy satellites. Russia deserves a Red Moon, Yuri. Mars will be ours, too. The Red Planet, right?"

"But, what about the sabotage, Artemov's arrest—"

"Artemov needed to know he was no Korolev." It was true; thanks to the failures, Artemov had only a fraction of Korolev's power. "And you need to know that you are not your father."

I stared stupidly as Uncle Vladimir motioned to one of his thugs, who stepped forward with an object wrapped in a cloth.

My pistol. It was dusty, as if someone had dropped it in flour.

"Did you know that this was the weapon that killed your father?" I had been afraid of that; I nodded. "And that it contains your fingerprints as well as his?"

"Yes."

"Any further . . . disruptions will force me, as an officer of State Security, to reopen the matter of your father's suicide. As a murder." The thug quickly wrapped up the pistol and tucked it away. "The fact that you are a member of the cosmonaut team won't save you. The only thing that saves you now, Yuri, is that you are my only link to my sister." He rubbed his shoulders. "It's getting colder, don't you think?"

"Fuck you."

All he did was smile at me, then turn to his team. "Let's go."

Within moments, I was alone on that dark street.

———

I told no one about the encounter, of course. No one would have believed it.

But my back hampered me, and my physical-training instructor reported it to Colonel Belyayev the next morning, and I was summoned to his office. I told him I had slipped on the ice last night.

"Drinking?"

"No, sir." I don't know whether he believed me nor not.

"Well, a few days in the hospital should shape you up."

Remembering Katya's warning, I almost begged him not to send me to the hospital. "It's only a bruise," I said. "It will heal."

Belyayev hated the military doctors at Star Town, so he was sympathetic. Still: "I have a report here. I've got to take some action."

"Can't I be put on limited duty for a few days?" Here my lack of military experience showed.

"It would have to be for at least two weeks."

"I should be fine after two weeks, sir."

"All right." He signed the papers.

Which, unfortunately, prevented me from going to Baikonur for the launch of the first Carrier rocket on February 20. So I was not present for the heartbreaking moment when that giant failed a minute after liftoff and had to be destroyed.

53 VEHICLE 5L

In early March 1969, the American *Apollo 9* crew commanded by McDivitt made a completely successful test of the lunar landing craft. We thought they would press ahead with a lunar landing attempt on *Apollo 10*, but they stuck to their test program and made plans to send *Apollo 10* to test the lunar module in orbit around the Moon. The LM was too heavy to accomplish a landing, anyway, and there were still many problems, such as communications, to be worked out before a landing could be attempted.

At that same time, Military Unit 26266 was reorganized, with Shiborin and me now assigned to its Fourth Directorate for lunar programs, though there was now one less of these: The manned L-1 mission was canceled. The Council of Ministers and the Central Committee—or was this all Uncle Vladimir's doing?—had realized that a single loop of the Moon by a pair of Soviet cosmonauts would be insufficiently impressive.

All our resources were to be devoted to the E-8 unmanned sample-return mission, and to the L-3 lunar landing program. Even the Soyuz missions were starved for resources to feed L-3; poor Ivan Saditsky's flight, another rendezvous and docking, this time with the passive craft in orbit first, was postponed to October.

I did as I was told, by Colonel Belyayev, now head of the center's First Department, and by Colonel Bykovsky, head of the Fourth Directorate under Belyayev. As a member of the Fourth Enrollment, I made up my winter survival training in March as well as my parachute jumping, then entered the last phase of training, spending several weeks learning the basic systems of the Soyuz, the L-3, and the Almaz military space station as not just a test engineer, but a crew member. I was facing final technical and political examinations to take place in July. They would determine my future as a cosmonaut.

I floated through these days and weeks powerless, dazed, even overwhelmed, much as I had been during my first weeks at Bauman, almost nine years in the past. Katya was out of my life—especially when I realized it must have been her phone call that alerted Uncle Vladimir to my presence the night of our last encounter.

And Marina? For most of this time, March, April, and May of 1969, she was out of Moscow on another assignment, courtesy, I assumed, of Uncle Vladimir. I told myself it was all for the best; an association with me could only harm her.

Which is why I was surprised, one night in late May, just after the safe return of America's *Apollo 10* mission, in which astronauts Stafford and Cernan swooped to within twenty-five kilometers of the lunar surface (were they tempted to simply press on, to make the first landing, knowing they would not be able to return home?) to find Shiborin at my door with a note in his hand.

He waved me outside, into a beautiful spring evening. "Are they changing the schedule again?" I asked. We were both about to depart for Baikonur, for checkout on the payload of the second Carrier rocket.

"No. We got a telephone call for you a couple of hours ago." He handed me the note—Marina wanted me to meet her at Tsiolkovsky Station tonight. "I didn't know your phone was broken."

"It's not," I said, folding the note.

Shiborin looked at me. "That explains why she wanted me to tell you outside." He raised an eyebrow. "Are you under surveillance, Yuri?" The idea seemed to shock him.

I wiggled the note. "Marina seems to think so."

He absorbed this unsettling news, then said something I never forgot: "I don't care what kind of trouble you're in, Yuri. If you need anything—*anything*—tell me."

At that moment, I could have kissed him.

I practically ran for the station, which was half a kilometer from the front gate of Star Town, at the end of a pathway through the woods.

The latest train from Moscow had come and gone, but Marina was waiting at the end of the platform, under the only working light. We had not seen each other in months, and for the first few moments of this reunion we clung to each other like lost souls.

"I don't have much time," she said. In fact, we could see the train returning to Moscow approaching from the southeast.

"Stay the night."

"They're sending me away again tomorrow!" Her voice was shrill; she calmed down. "It's Lev," she said.

"What about him?"

"He's been arrested."

"He was arrested before—"

"That time he was only *questioned*, Yuri! Now he's been charged with sabotage of some rocket! He's in Lefortovo!" That was the prison in downtown Moscow.

"He hadn't moved out?" I was surprised that the idea of the two of them still living together, even as brother and sister, upset me.

"Well, he has *now*." Such venom was unlike Marina, and convinced me that she was upset.

"I'm sorry."

She sighed. "The neighbors told me when I got home."

"What can I do?"

"Talk to your uncle. Talk to Vladimir. He's the only one who can save him."

I would rather have simply traded places with Lev. "I'll try," I said. And I meant it.

The atmosphere around Baikonur during the last days of June 1969 was poisonous, with people shouting for no reason, loudly blaming each other for the smallest of mistakes. The reason, of course, was fear. The assembly building and the offices and the hotel were filled with new faces—including Uncle Vladimir—all there to apply pressure, to make sure this Carrier launch went perfectly. Lev, I learned, was not the only engineer under suspicion, though he was the only one who had actually been arrested and charged.

Since the payload for this Carrier—serial number 5L—included a mockup of an L-3 lunar lander, our checkout team was headed by none other than my old boss, Filin. He was the one who quietly confirmed

Lev's arrest. "Things have gotten very bad in the bureau, Yuri. Everything has been taken out of our hands. I used to think you were crazy to go over to the military, but it can't be any worse there."

The work was monotonous; the weather dry, hot, irritating. I took up smoking simply to give myself more reasons to get out of the gigantic Carrier assembly building during the long days preceding its rollout. (The building was supposed to be air-conditioned, and it was cooler, but some flaw in the system also made it feel damp and swamplike.)

It was while smoking that I managed to reconnect with Sergeant Oleg Pokrovsky, who was now shaven and fitted with a uniform that might not have been clean, but resembled a military garment. He was leading a construction team building a special viewing site here at Area 100. "What's this for?" I asked.

"The big bananas from Moscow," he said. "The blockhouse is too far away to get a good view of the launch." That was true: The twin pads at Area 110 were so distant from the control center that they were over the horizon. The assembly building itself was closer—still a safe couple of kilometers away.

When I asked Sergeant Oleg how he had been, he shook his head. "These are terrible times." I could only shrug in agreement.

There was no opportunity for me to keep my promise to Marina concerning Lev—not that I had much hope that a word from me would have any positive effect on his situation. I saw Uncle Vladimir during those two weeks of preparation only from a distance, only in a crowd of fellow "big bananas" and security people.

He was like royalty; in fact, exactly as he had said.

On the night of July 2, with our checkout work completed and Carrier Number 5L sitting on its pad at Area 110, Filin led a team of us—bureau and military—out to a restaurant in old-town Tyuratam. It served Asian food of some kind, with a rice wine that quickly went to our heads. We sang. We talked about Carrier-powered trips to the Moon beginning next year. "Shiborin and Ribko, colonists at Tycho!" We toasted America's *Apollo 11* crew, Armstrong, Collins, and Aldrin, even now working at their Florida launch site and preparing for an attempted lunar landing.

Before long, Filin was weeping. I could have joined him.

As we staggered out into the summer night, a fleet of automobiles was delivering another party. Uncle Vladimir's.

I had drunk just enough wine to lose my fears of him, and pushed forward, shouting his name. Several bodyguards or lesser royals surrounded me, but Uncle Vladimir said, "He's my nephew. I'm happy to see him." He grabbed me and kissed me, something he had never done. "Be smart, Yuri. Smart and short." His voice was low as he steered me away from the others.

"I want you to let Lev Tselauri go. He's no saboteur, and you know it."

"Of course I know it. He's merely my 'switchman,' the one I can blame. His arrest throws the fear of God into everyone else. *This* Carrier will fly."

"Fine. Everyone is terrified into submission. Lev sits in jail. Why not release him?"

Uncle Vladimir stared at me with what I took to be amusement. "What do you have to offer me?"

"What do you mean?"

"You are asking me for a favor. You offer me something in return."

I could not give him anything, but I could give *up* something. A sacrifice to a lord. "I'll resign from the cosmonaut team. I'll refuse to join the Party and they'll dismiss me."

He stared at me, judging my determination. Then he extended his hand toward his party—still waiting—summoning one of his associates. They conferred briefly; Uncle Vladimir even scribbled a note, which the associate took away. "It's done," he said. "Your friend will be freed tomorrow morning."

"I'll submit my resignation when I return to Star Town." It was a formality: In spirit and in action, I had already delivered my resignation.

The next day—Thursday, July 3, 1969—Filin reported that Lev had indeed been cleared of charges and released. "It was ridiculous to begin with," he said. "They picked him because he was Georgian and didn't have powerful relatives in the business."

I registered this news with no real emotion. I was playing Uncle Vladimir's game now, by his rules.

The 5L launch was scheduled to take place after dark, at ten P.M. The time was dictated by conditions at the Moon, three days hence, when our unmanned L-1 and L-3 mockup should be in orbit over a potential landing site.

At eight P.M., Shiborin and I—who had no blockhouse responsibilities—met at the new viewing site. Bathed in floodlights, Carrier 5L shone against the night sky like the spire of a cathedral.

The two of us were on foot. The actual seats in the stand were reserved for Uncle Vladimir and his fellow members of the State Commission, and a team of photographers who would be standing by to capture their triumphant reactions to the magnificent Carrier launch.

The countdown proceeded smoothly. As the loudspeaker told us there was one minute to go, I saw Uncle Vladimir and his friends smiling at each other like children at a birthday party.

I made sure I was in reach of Shiborin, who was looking at the not-so-distant Carrier coolly, appraising it. "I bet that's a rough ride," he said. "Thirty engines in the first stage. Can you imagine?"

I could; I had seen reports of how the first Carrier launch failed because the savage vibrations had shattered fuel lines. These had now been insulated and rerouted, so they were expected to withstand the stress very nicely.

Thirty seconds.

Nearby, in the open door of the assembly building, Sergeant Oleg stood smoking. I waved at him and he blew smoke toward me.

Fifteen seconds. Even at this distance, I could hear the whirr and whine of motors coming to life on 5L.

Zero. White light appeared at the base of the beast. It would have been blinding in daylight; our night-adjusted eyes saw nothing for several seconds, though we began to hear—and feel—the rattling roar of those thirty engines.

Slowly 5L began to rise, the roar becoming a wall of sound and fury—I could feel it pushing me back toward the building—the light growing even more intense. Then . . .

Then a ball of flame appeared at the base, blossoming like a flower from hell. We felt a dull thud as 5L began to falter. . . .

It actually stopped in midair, a few hundred meters off the ground—

And began to topple!

I grabbed Shiborin, who was standing there, open-mouthed with horror. "Inside!" I shouted.

We plunged toward the door Sergeant Oleg held open, Shiborin ahead of me. I couldn't resist one last look, and saw the escape rocket lifting the L-1 away from the crumbling Carrier just as the spire became a fireball, exploding like an atomic bomb.

The heavy door slammed behind us just as a spray of debris rained against it.

We hurried through the giant building, emerging on the front side, away from the launchpad, gingerly opening the door to be sure it was safe.

"I think everything's fallen down," Sergeant Oleg said.

Shiborin was more skeptical. "Don't be too sure. That thing could have launched pieces ten kilometers high."

So we lingered there, in the doorway, for a few extra minutes. Then, motivated by simple human decency, we worked our way around to the reviewing stand.

It had been shredded, then cooked. All of the royal observers were dead, including my uncle, Vladimir Nefedov of State Security.

EPILOGUE

The Next Summer

Yuri Ribko and I had essentially completed our work when yet more delays on the International Space Station—or was it the war in Serbia? Perhaps both—brought me back to Moscow.

This time he offered to pick me up at my hotel near the Russian Space Agency, and drive me to his flat. When he arrived, however, I didn't recognize him. He was thirty pounds thinner and his hair was gone. I had noted some change in his appearance, but this was shocking.

He saw my reaction. "Yes, I look terrible." He smiled. "But I look great for a man in my physical condition." He admitted that he had been diagnosed with liver cancer months before—after we had started our work. And he would not live to see his story published.

I didn't know what to tell him. I couldn't lie—couldn't promise him that somehow I'd kick the machinery of the American publishing industry into a higher gear.

He shrugged. "I've told my story. If anyone but you hears it, that will be good. But I told it once." He thumped his chest. "It was important for me."

I hugged him. He patted my back. "No more talk of this! Into the car."

Once we were on the road, I asked where we were going. "Let me surprise you," he said.

We headed off into Moscow's murderous traffic. I told Yuri I had finished transcribing his story, right up to that terrible accident in July 1969.

"It was no accident," he said. I had suspected as much. I had been marshaling strength to ask Yuri if he had sabotaged the Carrier. "During the final checkout, I simply jammed a piece of pipe into one of the first-stage engines, into its combustion chamber."

"No one caught you?"

"I was a military officer whom everyone knew. I had worked at the bureau. I was a cosmonaut. The guards were watching other people.

"Besides . . . Vladimir thought I was neutralized. We shared the same dream. Why would I jeopardize it?"

"Why *did* you?"

He drove silently for a minute or more. "I lost faith."

"In the Party?"

"That was long gone. No, I think I lost faith in my people. And in myself. In that moment I was prepared to die, and prepared to kill everyone." Another silence. "I became as big a monster as Vladimir."

I realized we were out in the country. "We aren't going to Korolev?" I said. "I thought you lived there."

Now he grinned. "You'll see where I live."

Ten minutes later we were at the back gate to Star Town.

"My country's rules," he said, as we locked the car into a portable garage only slightly bigger than the vehicle itself. "I was assigned here in 1967, and here I stayed. The same ground-floor flat, by the way."

"Even though you left the cosmonaut team."

"Yes. 'For reasons of health.' "

We followed a sidewalk toward the residential buildings. Some were new; some actually housed American astronauts and their families. In the square I could see the statue of Yuri Gagarin.

"Did anyone suspect your uncle's role in all this? Or yours?"

"No. There was a huge investigation of the 5L accident, of course, and it showed exactly what I had done . . . but there was no one to link me to it. We didn't launch another Carrier for two years." He interrupted himself to say hello to a middle-aged officer wearing the stars of a lieutenant-general. "Shiborin," he said. "He eventually got two space-flights. Now he's head of faculty at the academy."

"Where you work."

"Yes."

"Will he talk to me?"

Ribko smiled. "Are you thinking you need witnesses? Second sources? Corroboration for my fantastic story?"

"Even if I don't, my editors will."

"Shiborin will talk. Others, too. Come."

We turned down a sidewalk that wasn't lit at all, and had to go slowly until entering a building that would have been called a slum in any American city. Yuri led me to a door on the ground floor.

Inside, the place was crowded, but comfortable-looking. Books lined the walls. A relatively new television sat in the corner. There were several framed photos on the wall—a three-star general I took to be Nikolai Ribko, a beautiful woman who must have been Zhanna, and a group portrait of the Fourth Enrollment.

Yuri brought me a beer and we sat.

"It seems that you were in a unique position."

"Absolutely," he said. "Had I stayed in the bureau, I never would have seen the military side. And what I learned at the bureau helped me make sense of what I saw at the training center and the air base. It was only because I had friendships and relationships that crossed lines, that were outside the little boxes, that I was able to learn the truth."

"And take action."

A long silence. "Yes. To take action."

"Suppose the Soviet Union had reached the Moon first—"

"It would have meant a lot of parades in our country, and a lot of weeping and gnashing of teeth in yours. We would have then spent millions or billions more rubles, and then abandoned the whole business. Perhaps Americans would still be going to the Moon today. Or you would have gone to Mars first. Beat the Reds to the Red Planet, hmmm?" He smiled. "We can't change the past. We can barely change the future!"

At that moment, I put aside all my doubts, all my questions, and allowed myself to believe in Yuri Ribko. He had changed the world, and changed it for the better. How many of us ever can or will know that?

The door opened, and a pretty, dark-haired, gray-eyed woman in her fifties entered carrying a shopping bag. "Marina," Yuri said, leaping up to greet her. "Meet my friend!"

ACKNOWLEDGMENTS

Red Moon is a work of fiction, but is inspired by the remarkable series of steps and missteps that caused the Soviet Union to lose the Moon race to the United States. Yuri Ribko, his family and friends and their activities are my inventions.

I was able to re-create some events, notably the horrifying end of *Soyuz 1* and the later crash of Yuri Gagarin, thanks to the diaries of General Nikolai P. Kamanin, three volumes of which have been published in Russian under the title *Skriti Kosmos (Secret Space)*. Kamanin's astonishingly frank, inside account of the Soviet manned space program deserves a wide readership and I hope *Red Moon* will inspire some enterprising organization to translate and publish the entire work.

I am also greatly indebted to *Raketi i Ludi (Missiles and People)*, a four-volume memoir by Boris Chertok, one of the late Sergei Korolev's deputies, about his fifty-year career in the Energiya organization. This book is as frank and open as Kamanin's diaries, and also deserves wider distribution.

Roads to Space (New York: McGraw Hill/Aviation Week Group, 1995, John Rhea, editor), a collection of shorter memoirs from various Soviet space and missile engineers, provided several anecdotes and bits of local color.

A number of individuals deserve my public appreciation, beginning with Charles P. Vick, for years one of the world's foremost authorities on Soviet space programs, especially Program L-1/L-3. Charles generously provided me with facts, figures, drawings, and other materials while patiently answering endless questions. Thank you, Charles.

I personally interviewed a number of cosmonauts from the Korolev design bureau and from Star Town who shared their insights. Bert Vis also provided many more anecdotes from his extensive series of cosmonaut interviews. Bart Hendrickx provided key translations. Rex Hall offered his support.

G. Harry Stine and James Oberg inspired my original interest in the Soviet space program. Jennifer Green and the Friends and Partners in Space Workshop of 1997 allowed me to visit the Russian locations of this long-planned story in the excellent company of historians such as David Woods, Dennis Newkirk, and Glen Swanson, in addition to several named above.

Finally, special thanks to my agent, Richard Curtis, and to my editor, Beth Meacham.

M. C.
Los Angeles, August 1999